"Captain, are you aware of what we have to offer your people?"

Gold held out his hands, palms up.

"To use your frame of reference, Captain, this is approximately one kilogram of our dilithium," Liankataka said, placing the rock in Gold's hands. The weight certainly felt right for a kilo. "From what your scientists tell me, the nugget you hold could help power a *Galaxy*-class starship for well over one of your years at warp nine, with very little waste."

Well, Gold thought, *that wasn't in the official file*. Suddenly, the urgency of securing Drema IV made more sense. He fleetingly wondered what else he hadn't been told.

Until the thunderous boom of an explosion sounded a little too close for comfort—at which point Gold dropped the dilithium to the ground and simply began running toward the noise.

STAR TREK®
CORPS OF ENGINEERS

WHAT'S PAST

Terri Osborne, Steve Mollmann & Michael Schuster,
Richard C. White, Dayton Ward & Kevin Dilmore,
Heather Jarman, and Keith R.A. DeCandido

Based upon STAR TREK
and STAR TREK: THE NEXT GENERATION®
created by Gene Roddenberry
and STAR TREK: DEEP SPACE NINE®
created by Rick Berman & Michael Piller

G

GALLERY BOOKS
New York   London   Toronto   Sydney

G Gallery Books
A Division of Simon & Schuster, Inc.
1230 Avenue of the Americas
New York, NY 10020

First Gallery Books trade paperback edition August 2010

GALLERY BOOKS and colophon are trademarks of Simon & Schuster, Inc.

For information about special discounts for bulk purchases,
please contact Simon & Schuster Special Sales at 1-866-506-1949
or business@simonandschuster.com.

The Simon & Schuster Speakers Bureau can bring authors
to your live event. For more information or to book an event,
contact the Simon & Schuster Speakers Bureau at 1-866-248-3049
or visit our website at www.simonspeakers.com.

Manufactured in the United States of America

10 9 8 7 6 5 4 3 2 1

ISBN 978-1-4391-9486-7

CONTENTS

PROGRESS

Terri Osborne

This story is dedicated to the people of Springhill, Nova Scotia,
and Sago, West Virginia.
May all those lost souls rest in peace.

ACKNOWLEDGMENTS

The ships of the S.C.E. are traditionally named after scientists and engineers who've helped change our view of the world as we know it. The *U.S.S. Trosper* is no different. It's named for Jennifer Trosper, who, as this is being written, has been tapped by the United States to begin work on the Moon/Mars initiative after her work as mission manager for the Spirit rover on the Mars Exploration Rover mission is completed.

The *U.S.S. Landry* is named in honor of Bridget Landry, Deputy Uplink Systems Engineer, Mars Pathfinder.

The shuttlecraft *Reeves* is named in honor of Glenn Reeves, flight software architect for MER, whose foresight helped save *Spirit* from the brink.

These are folks who may not have made the front pages of your local newspaper like their superiors, but their contributions to the pursuit of knowledge are no less worthy of note. To acknowledge their contributions here is the least I can do. Thank you all for helping us learn a little more about the planet next door.

My gratitude for the consultation on Jewish culture goes to Michael and Nomi Burstein, Lesley McBain, and Todd Kogutt. My thanks to Siona for the memory jog on tricorders. And thanks to Carolyn Clowes, who gave us the Belandrid species in her novel *The Pandora Principle*, and to Hannah Louise Shearer and Melinda M. Snodgrass, who wrote "Pen Pals," the episode that gave us Drema IV and Sarjenka.

Thanks, as always, to my excellent writer's group for all of their assistance in bringing this story to you.

Since the e-book publication of this story, the world has lost the man for whom Captain Walsh was named. He was a good friend and a good man. Rest in peace, my friend.

Prologue

May 2377
U.S.S. da Vinci

The comm unit in Captain David Gold's ready room chirped. *"Sir,"* Ensign Susan Haznedl began, *"there's a message coming in for you. It's from Starfleet Command. Marked private."*

The curious tone in Haznedl's voice piqued Gold's interest. The *U.S.S. da Vinci* and her S.C.E. contingent were between missions, and Gold found he was actually beginning to enjoy the nice respite of general peace and quiet. His mind worked through every possible candidate without a solution. Raising one gray eyebrow, he said, "I'll take it in here."

Before he could turn to face the small viewscreen on his desk, it had already shifted to a display of the Federation logo. The logo disappeared, and was replaced by a small text message:

Friend David Gold,
I would like to invite you and your wife to join us in celebrating the occasion of the first of the Dreman people to graduate from your Starfleet Medical Academy. Details will follow if you are so inclined to join us. This would not have been possible without your gracious assistance.

Your friend,
Liankataka

Gold stared at the screen, blinking in surprise. Had it been eight years since Drema IV already?

The memory of a ready room long behind him, one filled with more than pictures in frames, flashed into his mind. Thank-you gifts from starbase commanders, pictures his then-young grandchildren had drawn, dreadful statues that his children had made in their art classes to give as heartfelt Father's Day and Grandfather's Day presents, had all been out on display. After he'd lost so many of those things over the years—mostly thanks to the *da Vinci*'s near destruction at Galvan VI—he'd thought better of having such treasures with him. Boxing up quite a few of the items that had survived, he'd sent them back to Rachel for safe keeping. He'd only kept a few things around after that to remind him of what had come before the *da Vinci*.

The ready room he now occupied seemed far more spartan than the one on the *U.S.S. Progress*. Oddly, he had never really paid that much attention to how this room had smelled before. It was the sterile, austere, almost hospital smell of a room that had known life, but hadn't truly been *lived* in. It served its purpose, and that was all he needed. He missed the old, dusty smell of the aging clay statues mixed with the intense aromas of the dried dill from his wife's herb garden and the mustiness of the books that had unfortunately become more decorative than practical as the years passed. Yet, they were all smells that he hated having grown accustomed to not having around. Still, when push came to shove, they were all just things.

Tsotchkes *are replaceable; people aren't*.

That was the moment the idea occurred to him. Those eight years might have just given him the answer to what he should do about his recalcitrant chief medical officer and her incessant denial over her need for an assistant. Flipping the comm switch on his desk, he said, "Gold to Gomez. I think I've got a solution to our little problem."

CHAPTER

1

Late 2369
Beneath Latik Kerjna, Drema IV
Day 1

Somewhere in the near darkness of the mine level, an all too familiar voice was cursing. Sinterka's head perked at the sound. Not once in five years—including fighting a war—had he ever heard that kind of vulgarity leave anyone's mouth, let alone that of his old friend.

When Sinterka thought that his boss had finished taking the names of every Exile ancestor in vain and calling down the gods upon them back to the dawn of time, he ventured closer. The occasional lamp-covered head bobbed up to see what was going on as he passed, only to return its attention within a few seconds to the greenish-orange stone it was mining. The sharp smell of sweat soaked the air as Sinterka made his way over to where his old friend and shift supervisor, Eliatriel, a normally staid and reserved man, had his hands over something that had been buried deep within the dilithium. On his face was a look of panic unlike anything Sinterka had seen since the Uprisings. "El," Sinterka began, his voice a rasp from the dust in the air, "what did you find?"

His boss raised a long-fingered hand to silence him. "Don't start a riot, Sin. I need your help. We need to clear this shaft as quickly as possible."

Covering something with both hands . . . needing to clear the shaft . . . cursing the Exiles. Slowly, the pieces came together, and Sinterka realized what his boss was hiding. "A *xurta?*"

Eliatriel nodded, brushing a lock of garnet hair out of his eyes. "A *xurta*. And if there's one, there are more."

Sinterka's stomach chose that point to begin making him regret the sandwich he'd had on his meal break. *"More?"*

Eliatriel practically kicked him in the behind. "Yes, now go. Get people up to the surface. I'm going to see if I can get this thing out of here without killing us all."

"Out of the *dilithium*? El, have you lost your mind? What if it goes off?"

Shaking his head, the supervisor said, "What do you want me to do? We need one of these things intact. When was the last time you saw a functioning Exile transporter?" When Sinterka could offer no answer, Eliatriel continued, "We never did figure out how to disarm these bombs during the Uprisings. If we can get this one out, maybe we'll finally be able to find a way to get rid of these things so we can keep mining."

Sinterka gaped at his friend. Finally recovering his wits, he said, "And get yourself killed in the process. El, what about Sarjenka and Rakan? What do I tell them? If that goes off, what will it do to the dilithium? We don't need the tremors to start again."

"You don't think I know that? Sinterka, stop talking to me and get up the shaft. That's an order. I need to concentrate."

Against his better judgment, Sinterka slowly walked back toward the shaft. "Shift's over, guys!" he yelled into the lamplit, oily green darkness. "We need to get to the surface! Nice and steady." To the occasional shouts wondering what was wrong, he said, "Nothing to worry about! Early day today, that's all. A gift from the supervisors for a job well done."

Deep in the back of his mind, however, Sinterka tried not to worry about what he would tell Eliatriel's family if everything went wrong. Of course, there was always the possibility that all the bombs would explode. Then there was the possibility that the dilithium would focus those energies back into the planet, causing it to begin tearing itself apart once again. If that happened—provided he even survived—Sinterka was fairly certain telling Eliatriel's family how he had died would be the least of his concerns.

Please, old friend, take care. Traiaka *keep him safe.* Traiaka *keep us all safe.*

For his part, Eliatriel tried his best to be as safe as possible. The small, cylindrical device had surfaced as he'd been clearing out the beginnings of a new dilithium vein. *Thank the deities for whatever stopped the tremors,* he thought. *If this had been* talrod, *I would not be here.*

He scanned the edges of the device, running his long fingertips over the exposed face once he realized there were no obvious triggers, almost as though he could sense what might set it off. *If we only had one of the Exile transporters remaining.*

After brushing a drop of perspiration off his brow, he reached down and grabbed the smallest pick in his tool kit. Eliatriel adjusted his headlamp, making sure it illuminated his workspace at just the right angle so as to avoid any heat buildup on either the dilithium or the bomb. When he had it where he wanted it, Eliatriel measured out a hand's width from the edge of the cylinder and began to slowly carve around the device. Some of the *xurtas* he'd seen over the course of the Uprising had been connected to heat-sensitive detonators, others to pressure-sensitive ones. He could see no way to determine which of the two was in use in this case. If it was as long as the others he'd seen during the resistance movement, it would be about half the length of his forearm, and pressure-sensitive detonators could have been placed anywhere in that length.

He gently worked at the stone with the tiny pickax for what

felt like an eternity, slowly scraping bits out and allowing them to drop to the level's stone floor. If he only stopped once for food, he figured there was a good chance of getting the thing unearthed before the end of his shift.

And if he were truly fortunate, it wouldn't explode as he brought it to the surface.

CHAPTER

2

FEDERATION COUNCIL
Report on application of fourth planet in the Selcundi
Drema System for Federation Protectorate status.

Commander Jan Siok, filing
Stardate 45998.3

On Stardate 45624.2, a low-band audio-only transmission was received by the U.S.S. Landry, Admiral Jameson Tucker commanding, from the Selcundi Drema system. Enhanced audio on the transmission indicated that it was a specific request intended for the United Federation of Planets. The transmission was determined to have originated from the fourth planet in the system. Admiral Tucker notified Starfleet Command, and it was determined that—in consideration of the past observation by the U.S.S. Enterprise, Captain Jean-Luc Picard commanding [Mission report, Jean-Luc Picard, Captain, U.S.S. Enterprise, NCC-1701-D, Stardate 42865.6, linked here]—Prime Directive protection was no longer to be afforded the Dremans, and the initiation of official first contact protocols should begin.

Federation Ambassador Lanara Diol was dispatched to the system to begin talks. Her report on the first meetings indicates that the people of Drema IV had already been in contact with outsiders, people they referred to as the Exiles. According to Ambassador Diol, the Exiles descended upon Latik Kerjna [Drema IV's capital city] en masse and, using superior technology and weaponry, were able to force the otherwise passive Dremans into servitude. The first dilithium mines had been excavated less than a decade prior, and the Exiles forced the natives to work in the mines to provide dilithium for Exile ships. After approximately ten months, the Dreman people worked up the courage to rebel, and with superior numbers, were able to deal the Exiles a solid defeat. According to the current Guardian of the Dreman people, no Exile survived what they refer to as the Uprising. [Report of Guardian Shalkara, filed with Federation Council on Stardate 45954.4, linked here.]

It was at this point in the planet's history that excavation of a new dilithium mine uncovered remnants of probes carrying the insignia of Starfleet and the Federation. The Dremans chose to attempt to contact the Federation. Their technology is not at the stage where they are able to protect themselves from invasion before the incoming force lands on the surface. They fear Exile reprisals.

Their culture remained prewarp, but Ambassador Diol likened their situation to the planet Bajor after the Cardassian withdrawal, an opinion with which the Federation Council agrees.

The Dremans have offered their considerable resources of dilithium in exchange for consideration of protectorate status. They desire nothing more than protection from another outside invasion, protection which they are not capable of mounting themselves at this time.

A sample of Dreman dilithium was returned to Starfleet Headquarters for examination, where it was discovered that the focal energies produced by one four centimeter by four centimeter crystal were roughly three times the energies produced by a standard dilithium crystal of the same size, with a recrystalization rate twice the norm. It has been determined that the addition of Dreman dilithium to the Federation supply line would increase the lifespan of Federation dilithium at least twofold, possibly more. Dr. Leah Brahms, speaking for the Theoretical Propulsion

Group at Utopia Planitia, stated that the group believes that adjustments to standard warp drive technology will be required to allow for optimal use of the new resource.

Ambassador Diol, speaking before the Council, argued that while the offer of the dilithium is quite generous—and she cannot deny that we should consider such resources and their potential contribution to the Federation in making our decision—she cautioned the Council against greed. The Dreman people have already shaken off one oppressive regime. They do not need to trade the Exiles for another oppressor. The Federation should take cautious steps toward the use of the dilithium resources of Drema IV, and we should consider enlisting the assistance of the native workers in that endeavor. Such a move would help benefit the Dreman economy, and it is Ambassador Diol's position that they should benefit from the presence of such a resource, not work themselves to death because of it.

Application is currently being considered with a favorable status.

Record Update—Stardate 46147.9

By a vote of 122 to 29, the Federation Council has approved Drema IV for protectorate status. In a good-faith show of support, the Council has also commissioned the construction of a starbase to orbit just outside the asteroid belt that is believed to be the remains of the fifth planet in the system.

It is the Council's considered opinion that Federation presence should be felt, but not be oppressive. A starbase constructed in the system, but not in orbit around Drema IV itself, should provide the recommended level of presence.

CHAPTER
3

Late 2369
Latik Kerjna, Drema IV
Capital Square
Day 1

For a planet that was chock full of dilithium—and volcanic on top of that—David Gold couldn't get over how Earth-like Drema IV was. He'd seen the reports about what it had been like during the tremors five years before. The idea that, within his lifetime, a place that had free-flowing liquid magma covering half its surface now held lush, verdant greenery, reminding him of his last trip to the Hawaiian Islands, was nothing short of amazing.

Just as she'd done on that vacation, Gold could hear his wife citing it as proof that perhaps humans weren't ready to know everything about their universe. Rachel had always taken a tremendous amount of comfort in the idea that no matter how much the sciences tried to explain things, there were still subjects that eluded even the most brilliant of intellects. "Sometimes," she would say, "the answer for the scientists is simply 'not yet'."

Dragging himself back to reality, Gold briefly wished he'd brought Pulaski down to the surface with him, instead of leaving her on the *Progress* to finish packing. For reasons unknown to him, his chief medical officer had leapt at the chance to take over these same duties on the new space station built as a result of the protectorate treaty.

Still, in the years he'd known Dr. Katherine Pulaski, she had never been one to stand on ceremony. It wasn't her job to play the diplomat. Taking care of patients was her responsibility; figuring out whether the Federation and Dreman governments would play well together was someone else's. Leaving her to her work had been the best option that Gold could see.

That left him stuck there, on the dais in the middle of the small park—it was more like a vacant clearing, but if the Dremans wanted to refer to it as a park, Gold wasn't about to correct them—in the forest outside the capital that the government had decided to use for this little gathering. They'd managed to set up a small dais, and a few lanterns lined the stonework path, but it was hardly the ceremonial grounds at the Palais de la Concorde on Earth.

What do you expect from a race that just fought off an oppressor? He could hear Rachel's voice in his head. *They've grown to appreciate the simple things, David. Bear with them.*

A quick survey of the crowd that had formed suggested that "little" was a gross understatement. He estimated that there were at least two or three hundred people amassed in the park, their numbers extending back beyond the tree line and into areas where he simply could not see to accurately gauge their numbers.

Gold wasn't keen on the idea of representing the Federation at what was, essentially, Admiral Tucker's shindig, but they'd been planning this event for weeks. The admiral had originally been chosen to fill the political role, as he would also be taking over command of Drema Station when it came online, but an ion storm had delayed the *U.S.S. Landry* from bringing him on time. This had left Gold the ranking officer in the area and stuck with the job when the Dreman government declined to delay the proceedings.

"We would like to formally welcome the Federation to our

planet," the leader of the Dreman government said, extending his arms out as though he were trying to encompass the entire crowd, "both as our friend and our protector. May the Lights of *Traiaka* shine upon us all."

The captain watched the procession of Dreman government representatives as each one walked along the lantern-lined path—though each lantern was now lit to a point of ridiculous brightness—over to him and held out their long-fingered, cinnamon-red hands palms-down and over his shoulders. According to the file on their species, this hand motion was considered a gesture of friendship, but the fact that their palms never touched him as they then each ran their hands down over his arms was more than a little off-putting.

When the head of the Dreman government, a tall man with far more gold than garnet in his hair—something Pulaski had informed him was a sign of age in their species—and an enlarged forehead that was only getting larger from the receding hairline, finally walked over to him with a congenial smile; Gold returned it. "Guardian Liankataka," he said, hoping he'd pronounced it correctly. About three-quarters of the people he'd met to that point had names that were so full of J's, K's, and L's that he was beginning to feel as though he were back in his Hebrew classes. When the man didn't seem offended by Gold's use of his name, the captain continued: "Thank you. It's a pleasure to help bring your people to their rightful place in the galaxy."

A quick glance to Commander Gom suggested that he'd said precisely what he was supposed to have said. The Bolian may have been one of the more laid-back members of his crew, but Gold knew him well enough to be confident that Gom wouldn't give bad direction when it came to matters of protocol. Gom was an aficionado of governmental etiquette, far more than he thought would ever have been encompassed by his normal responsibilities as first officer.

Liankataka nodded. "And without Federation assistance, we may never have known peace again," he said. "The Exiles made certain of that."

Gold had briefed himself on Liankataka before beaming down for the ceremony. "It must have been difficult," Gold said. "The reports filed with the Federation indicated—"

"With respect, Captain, your reports can't possibly reflect what happened here," Liankataka said, his expression obviously haunted by the pain of memory. "We lost many good people. People whose only crime was being in the way."

Why do people who've been attacked always seem to think nobody else could understand their pain? Shaking off the idle thought, he said, "I'm sure the Federation would appreciate any corrections to our record you might be able to offer."

Liankataka shook his head. "Living in the past gains us nothing, Captain. We are a small, close-knit people. If someone wasn't touched by death during the Occupation or the Uprising, they have lost someone working the mines. However, we must take the lessons learned and move forward if we are to succeed in our new role."

Gold's brow furrowed. "But, you said . . ."

The elder Dreman's cheeks turned a dark crimson. "I apologize, Captain. I am aware that my people must move forward, but our scars run deep. My eldest son has only been in his grave for a year. My resolve may not always be as consistent as I might like. It is difficult to push that memory to the back of the mind, but I would be willing to look at your records and correct them as necessary."

He tried to imagine losing his own eldest son, Nathan: having only the memories of his first steps, his first bicycle ride, his first trip to the Statue of Liberty, the publication of his first book. There had been so many moments over the years, and there were still so many more for Nathan in the future.

The guardian saved him more thoughts on the subject by walking over to a small pile of greenish-brown rocks in one corner of the dais. He picked up one that was about the size of a clenched human fist and brought it back over. "Captain, are you aware of what we have to offer your people?"

Gold held out his hands, palms up.

"To use your frame of reference, Captain, this is approximately one kilogram of our dilithium," Liankataka said, placing the rock in Gold's hands. The weight certainly felt right for a kilo. "From what your scientists tell me, the nugget you hold could help power a *Galaxy*-class starship for well over one of your years at warp nine, with very little waste."

Well, Gold thought, *that wasn't in the official file.* Suddenly, the urgency of securing Drema IV made more sense. He fleetingly wondered what else he hadn't been told.

Until the thunderous boom of an explosion sounded a little too close for comfort—at which point Gold dropped the dilithium to the ground and simply began running toward the noise.

CHAPTER
4

Latik Kerjna, Drema IV
Day 1

Sarjenka wadded up the piece of drafting paper and threw it at the overstuffed waste bin, wanting nothing more at that moment than to do the same with the entire concept when the chime at her sleep chamber's entrafield sounded.

"Mealtime."

Sarjenka absently tugged at a strand of shoulder-length, reddish-gold hair. There were times when she would have sworn that her father had programmed the entrafield's acoustic dampener specifically to allow her mother's shrill voice to penetrate.

Pulling herself out of the straight-back chair, she slowly walked the few steps across the small, sparsely decorated bedroom, placed one long-fingered red palm against the entrafield, and triggered it. No sooner did it wink open than the smell of fresh-baked *keena* bread hit her nose, and Sarjenka's stomach reminded her of how long it had been since she'd last eaten.

Her mother looked down on her with a concerned expression in her golden eyes. "How is your project for med-design class coming?" she asked, her voice an attempt at consolation that didn't quite succeed.

Sparing a glance at the overflowing waste bin, she replied, "I don't know. I see these devices, and I know they aren't real, but

I have no idea what it would take to make them. None of the master healers can help."

Her mother gently laughed, but this time Sarjenka noticed a very slight edge of sadness about it. "There are times when you are so much like your father. Remember, young one. You are their apprentice, not their teacher. Come. Perhaps your father can help you figure out the solution when he returns from his shift."

Almost on cue, she heard the mewling of her pet *reeka* work its way up the stairs. "Jenkara! You will eat when we do! Do not bother him!" It was the one behavior of the *reeka*'s that had always driven her mother to distraction, and nothing they could do would train the creature to stop. The animal had a horrible habit of playfully attacking Sarjenka's father at the entrafield, when his clothes were still caked with dilithium dust and he still had the greenish-red tinge to his face that all of the miners she had ever known in her short life seemed to share. Fortunately for all of them, Jenkara was far too small to do anything beyond being playful. The long, thin, well-scaled tail of a full-grown *reeka* could have easily broken bones in one swat. Jenkara, thanks to an injury when he was very young, would never grow to full size.

No sooner did the mewling stop than the field winked open and a booming voice sounded. "Rakan? Rakan? Where are you?"

Sarjenka and her mother shared a look. That wasn't her father. It sounded more like one of his friends from the mine.

Her mother hurried down the stairs. "Sinterka? What is it?"

Sarjenka followed her mother down the stairs, stopping and sitting two steps from the bottom. Sinterka was coated in the greenish dust from the mines, his normally orange coveralls a color Sarjenka had tried several times over the last five years to figure out a way to describe, but failed with each attempt. He smelled as the miners always did—of perspiration, stale vitu-water, and dilithium dust.

Of course, everything had smelled of dilithium dust in the

time since the Exiles had arrived. Not even the Dreman's alliance with the people who called themselves the Federation could change that.

However, Sarjenka had only ever heard that tone of voice from Sinterka once, when her father had been trapped after a newly excavated section of the primary mine had collapsed. A flutter in the back of her mind suggested that whatever disturbed him now was related. "What happened?"

Sinterka held a slender, comforting hand over her mother's shoulder. "El found a *xurta* in the mine today. It was buried inside one of the walls of the first level."

That got Sarjenka's interest. "Father? Is he safe?"

Sinterka's eyes found hers, and she saw a fear in them she'd never seen before. "That's the problem, young one. I don't know."

Ignoring the rumbling that was still emanating from her stomach, Sarjenka stood and took the final two steps of the staircase in one stride. Reaching for her overcoat, she said, "Then I should inform the master healers. If there is a chance that our assistance will be required—"

"No," Sinterka said. His arms fell to his side, and a man Sarjenka had always considered larger than life, despite his slender build, suddenly seemed as small as Jenkara. "Your father was still working on digging the bomb out when he ordered us to leave. The mine was shut down until the area could be secured, and they could determine if there are any more bombs. I was able to get out to tell you only now."

Before he could say another word, something exploded in the distance.

Sinterka's eyes made the journey from surprise to shock to tears in a matter of seconds.

Almost as fast as Rakan's and—Sarjenka was sure—her own.

Wordlessly grabbing her pack, Sarjenka ran out the front entrafield and toward the mine.

CHAPTER
5

Latik Kerjna, Drema IV
Pithead, Dilithium Mine Alpha
Day 1

The first thing David Gold saw when he arrived at the battered, broken structures that surrounded the pithead was the burnt-out shape of something that looked as though it could have been a wagon in its recently ended life. One other Dreman remained, trying desperately to put out the fire that had begun in the ramshackle, old shed that covered the top of the mine, the hiss of the water mixing in a disturbing harmony with the flickering of the flames. The dark gray smoke was getting thicker and more acrid by the second.

Beside the wagon was the burnt, crumpled figure of a man in what looked to have once been orange coveralls. He was flat on his back on a white drop cloth. His right arm was to his side, but there was no sign of a left arm to be found. *Whoever this poor* schlemiel *was, that was one hell of a way to die.*

That was when he saw the right arm move. He'd seen the last twitches of death in muscles far too often before, the last gasp before letting go. The sight of conscious motion in that arm was all he needed.

Pulling the neckline of his uniform tunic up over his mouth

to act as a filter against the smoke, Gold ran toward the motion. Liankataka was on his heels. The burned man's skin ranged from a sickly burgundy-black to patches of a more normal terracotta red, and the smell of the charred flesh brought back more than a few memories of the Cardassian War. He'd seen people die from far less injury back then. How was this man still alive?

Quickly slapping the combadge on his chest, Gold hoped the modified long-range circuits would get his voice where it needed to go. "Gold to *Progress*."

There was no answer.

"Gold to *Progress*. Come in. Gold to Drema Station."

Again, there was no answer. He looked to Liankataka and shook his head. "Damn it! I can't reach my people. The explosion must be interfering somehow."

The Dreman leader already had a small communications unit in his own hand. "Emergency services are on the way. I've asked them to use the tie-line to the station to get through to your ship, Captain."

Gold wiped a hand across his brow. His eyes felt as though a thousand tiny grains of sand had found his corneas at once. "Tell them to get Pulaski down here. She's got the best knowledge of how to help your people of anyone we've got. If there are any more people down there, you'll need her."

Liankataka nodded, dialing his communications unit once again. Giving the requested instruction, he finished the call just in time for the first battery of gawkers to arrive. "By *Traiaka*, what happened?" came from several voices in the crowd.

A rasp sounded from the man at Gold's feet. Kneeling down, he got as close as he comfortably could. All he could hear from the man was something that sounded like, "Shurtah."

"Rest," Gold said. "Help is coming."

"What did he say?" Liankataka asked in a voice filled with disbelief.

Raising his eyes to the guardian, Gold said, "It sounded like 'shurtah.'"

The Dreman's skin flushed to near-pink. "No." Liankataka turned and walked away from the scene. He ran one long-fingered hand over his face. "We thought we had found every *xurta* left behind."

Gold began to put the pieces together. "I take it that's a bomb?"

Liankataka nodded. "The Exiles used to bury them around any installation they considered important. They can be wired to be pressure-sensitive or even heat-sensitive."

"And they obviously must have considered the mine important."

"Yes," the guardian said. "I am sorry, Captain, but this may change our ability to fulfill our bargain with your government. It may take us years to get the bombs out of the mine. There may not even be a mine left."

"With all due respect, Guardian, we need to prove there are more in there first. Have your people developed a way to scan for them?"

A strand of garnet hair slipped out of place as he shook his head. "Not without setting them off."

A short, robustly built Dreman in a white tunic and pants ran over to where they stood, a long, brown box that looked to Gold almost like a toolkit in his hands. "What happened?" he asked.

"*Xurta*," Liankataka simply replied. Judging by the shock on the younger Dreman's features, it was enough.

Fighting the urge to cough that the thickening smoke from the fire triggered in his throat, Gold backed away and allowed the young doctor to kneel by his patient.

Pulling a black and silver stethoscope out of his bag, the doctor quickly stuck the ends in his ears and pressed the plate to one of the less-burned places on the poor man's chest. "His breathing is shallow, but steady. I don't see any active bleeders. It looks like the heat from the explosion cauterized the arteries. Eliatriel, can you hear me?"

Gold took a good look at the man's bloodied and burned features and quickly wished that he hadn't. The Dreman was lucky to be alive. The idea that the young doctor could have recognized who had once been behind the burned skin, missing nose, and forcibly closed eyes was, to Gold, a mystery. Then again, when he considered the average population of the city, not to mention the recent battles, the overall friendliness of the people he'd encountered thus far, and the general close-knit feeling of community that he'd gotten from the moment he'd beamed to the surface, perhaps it wasn't that much of a mystery after all.

Another rasp sounded from Eliatriel's mouth. This one was completely unintelligible from where Gold stood.

"Good. I know it hurts," the doctor said, still checking over the man's injuries and unwrapping what looked like clean white cheesecloth to cover the more severe burns. He checked over the hole that had once been Eliatriel's nose and then draped another cloth bandage over it as well, making sure not to cover the man's mouth or eyes. "I don't think cold water's going to help you here, my friend. We're going to get you to the hospital very soon, okay? I'll let the burn healers know you're coming. They'll take good care of you, I promise."

The roar of fire bellowed from the mineshaft opening. The two Dremans who'd been working on putting out the fire backed away, allowing the flames to lick at the remainder of the shed like a child with an ice cream cone. The fire wasn't going to die until it had consumed it all. Gold jerked his head toward the sight. "Come on," he said to Liankataka, "they need help."

The Dreman female stood with her eyes as wide as saucers as she watched the fire blaze. Admittedly, Gold didn't understand precisely how the dilithium worked, but he knew one thing: dilithium focused energy. Fires gave off energy. If the dilithium did its job, there was no telling what would happen, but he had the distinct feeling it wouldn't be good. Visions of free-flowing lava picked that moment to take up residence in his mind. They needed to get that fire out sooner rather than later.

His boots began to make a disturbing squelching sound in the mud as he approached. Far more water was staying where they stood than making it to the fire. Gold grabbed the empty bucket from the woman's hand, trying to usher her attention to the nearby feeding hose. "Fill this up and then give me the hose," he said. "Let me help."

He could see the panic in her eyes as she turned from the fire to him and back several times before it finally registered that he was there to help. She finally grabbed the hose and filled the bucket, handing the hose to him when she was done. It wasn't an optimal fire hose, but Gold tried his best to make do with it. In between filling the water buckets, he trained the spray on the closest support beam.

The fire was burning white-hot, and Gold thought he felt his eyebrows singe on a couple of occasions, but he kept at it. The spray from the hose was barely powerful enough to reach the fire from where he stood, but he didn't dare inch forward.

"Is there another bucket?"

"What?" Liankataka was on the left side of the support beam infrastructure, bucket in hand, and the fire roaring between them was loud enough to drown out any creature who wasn't screaming.

"Another bucket!" Gold yelled. He managed to suppress a cough as the smoke tried to fill his lungs. "This hose isn't going to last much longer. We need something with more force!"

Almost on cue, a siren sounded in the distance.

"What's that?" Gold asked, once again raising his voice over the sound of the flames.

"Something with more force!" A panicky, but also somehow prideful smile filled Liankataka's face.

The ground shifted slightly under Gold's feet. Forcing the momentary urge to back away from the conflagration into a corner of his mind, he managed to overcome the strong need to be somewhere else and continued trying to fight the fire.

The fire truck—or what passed for it, for when Gold spared a glance at it, he realized he'd seen more advanced firefighting transports in the museums back on Earth—pulled into the small clearing near the pithead and somehow worked around the Dreman doctor who, from what Gold could see, was still trying to stabilize his patient.

Three men disembarked from the transport, all wearing heavier coveralls. Two wore a bright, easily recognizable orange, while the third wore red. The writing across the backs of each man's uniform suggested their names, but Gold hadn't had the chance to study the written Dreman language, so he couldn't be certain. However, he assumed the writing was there for reasons similar to human firefighters back on Earth—identification in the event of catastrophe.

It only took a few seconds for the three men to get the truck set and unroll the water hoses. The man in the red coveralls appeared to be the one in charge. Gold briefly took his eyes off the fire to see where they were, but it was long enough to see him instructing the other two. "Kleera! Take left. Laraka, take right. We need to approach this from both sides, or it's going to take the mine down."

Take the mine down? I don't like the sound of that. Still, he kept to the improvised bucket brigade in an attempt to help the firemen put the fire out. Within seconds, two of the firemen had the hoses pumping water at full-bore against the mine opening. It was helping, but the supports were still being stubborn.

The ground rumbled beneath his feet.

Gold tried desperately to ignore it, but the fire insisted upon keeping him close to the mine entrance. Every now and again, he got a face full of hot spray bouncing back from the streams that the fire hoses were projecting.

Suddenly, the rumbling that he'd been trying to ignore

turned into a roar. Gold tried to back away, keeping his hose trained on the fire, but he could only go so far and still be any help.

In the middle of it all, he heard a woman scream and another woman yelling something about a collapse.

Then the ground beneath his feet ceased to exist, and everything turned very, very black.

CHAPTER

6

U.S.S. Progress—Drema Station
Day 1

Katherine Pulaski checked the records download one last time before disconnecting the portable drive from the *Progress*'s systems. She'd taken her general library over to the station in the massive data dump from the ship's systems, but these were her private, personal files. The first records ever in Federation hands involving Dreman physiology were in there. She'd documented her method of erasing memories from those files—a technique that she'd heard Picard had put to use a second time after she transferred off the *Enterprise*—but beyond that, she hadn't allowed anyone access, not in five years.

Looking around the now-empty office that had been her base of operations these last three years, she wondered what the rest of the crew would do for new assignments. Stocking Drema Station was the last extra-system mission for the *Progress*. The lightly-armed *Mediterranean*-class ship was scheduled to be reassigned to supply runs between Earth and Io, something that hardly required a full crew complement. The last she'd spoken to Captain Gold about the reassignments, he'd mentioned that he hadn't decided yet between the several opportunities for a new captaincy he'd been offered.

Her decision had been, she thought, rather obvious. Where Gold had everything from an admittedly tempting consultant's position at Utopia Planitia to the center seat of that new *Intrepid*-class ship that was supposed to be testing those new bioneural gel packs appearing on *his* list of opportunities, Pulaski had considered and rejected every opportunity on her list, twice. All generic positions, nothing truly as tempting as her brief tenure on the *U.S.S. Enterprise*. Chief medical officer was a difficult posting to come by these days, and she really didn't want to take a step backward in her career.

Still, there had been that teaching job at Starfleet Medical. She'd been seriously considering that option when the search for a CMO for Drema Station had gotten her in its sights.

Drema IV. There was a planet that brought back some difficult memories. She still felt as though, overall, they had done the right thing by interfering. An entire planet, an entire species, had been on the verge of extinction before it really had a chance to blossom into a starfaring civilization. It had gone against everything she had ever believed as a doctor to allow the people to die when they had been in a position to help, no matter how much some Starfleet officers had wanted to hide behind the Prime Directive. She could still remember how hard she'd fought Captain Picard to make the point. She'd always thought the Prime Directive was something that was far too easy to use to shirk humanitarian responsibilities in times of natural disaster. The idea of *not* helping the Dremans had been nothing short of anathema.

In retrospect, she'd admired Lieutenant Commander Data's strategy of isolating the frequency his little friend Sarjenka had been using for her messages before they'd left that meeting in Picard's quarters. No matter how stridently Pulaski may have argued her case, it had been the fear and desperation in that little girl's voice that had finally moved Picard to action.

Jean-Luc Picard may have had a reputation for not

tolerating the presence of children very well, but he was hardly a heartless bastard. She fleetingly wondered if that was why he hadn't made admiral yet.

A part of her was occasionally curious about what might have happened to the Dremans if Sarjenka hadn't made that radio communication. *The curiosity of one child saves an entire world, Pulaski thought. I wonder how she's doing. She should be old enough for a university now, provided the procedure didn't take away too many of her memories.*

She could still remember Captain Picard ordering her to do *that* as well, after Data had, in a fit of cybernetic overprotectiveness bordering on human, brought the child on board the *Enterprise*. The captain had ordered her to erase the child's short-term memory, effectively removing any knowledge she had of the *Enterprise,* her communications with Data, or the fact that she'd seen things she was never, ever meant to see. She would be returned to her family to grow up as she'd been meant to.

The procedure Pulaski had used was experimental at the time, but—fortunately for the little girl—that experiment had been a success. She didn't want to consider what might have happened if the girl had remembered anything. For all they knew at that time, the Dremans were the type of culture who'd believe it when a child said they'd done something utterly fantastical like walk in a spaceship. Then again, for all they knew at the time, the Dreman culture could have held a large green glob of silicone as a supreme deity and worshipped it with offerings of bodily fluids.

She'd seen stranger things over the years.

Pulaski reached for a padd to make a note to check up on Sarjenka when she got to the station. Perhaps a quick visit to the surface would be in order, get to know the government officials, make a more in-depth evaluation of their level of medical technology, and see how she may be able to work with them to get them ready to eventually join the Federation. There might even be a way—provided she could find the child, of course—to make some kind of amends to Sarjenka for what they had to do to her so many years before.

Finding one child on a planet of millions? Talk about your needle in a haystack.

Her combadge chirped, and the relentlessly cheerful voice of the ship's second officer, Lieutenant Commander Crisp, filled the air. *"Bridge to Dr. Pulaski. We've got another ship coming in, headed for Drema IV—the* Trosper. *It's an S.C.E. ship—they say they're responding to a distress call from the station about bombs found in the mine?"*

Pulaski raised one gray eyebrow. To the best of her knowledge, she was the first of the permanent personnel to arrive, which was the only reason she could think of to explain how the message had been routed to her. Still, how'd a distress call get through the station and trigger a ship responding so quickly?

"Can you put it through here, Commander? And send down Lieutenant Klesaris. I need help getting these trauma kits together for transfer to the station."

"Aye, ma'am."

Pulaski slid into her chair just in time for the viewscreen on her desk to flicker to life, showing the Federation logo before switching over to the image of an older man, perhaps her own age, with short, graying hair; a slightly receding hairline; and a round, generally jovial face. She got the impression that this man normally smiled a lot, even though the expression that greeted her from the viewscreen held a wary look. *"You don't look like Admiral Tucker,"* the man's rough voice said.

"No, sir. Katherine Pulaski, chief medical officer. Admiral Tucker's ship has been delayed. Captain . . . ?"

"Don Walsh, Doctor. U.S.S. Trosper. *I assume you received the signal from Drema IV as well?"*

Pulaski tried not to look as lost as she felt. "Nothing that would indicate the need for another ship to come in."

The man on the screen's brow furrowed. *"Lolo was right. It must have routed through the starbase automatically to subspace. It doesn't matter. The distress call was about some possible sabotage to the main dilithium mine on the planet."*

"Sabotage?" Pulaski asked, leaning forward in her seat.

Walsh's lips pursed. *"All we know right now is that one of the shift supervisors for the largest dilithium mine on the planet found a bomb embedded in one of the mine shafts. He was working on trying to get it out without it detonating, but according to the guardian's office, the people who left it are virtually assured to have left more."*

"The people they called the Exiles?" Pulaski asked. She'd tried to keep up with the Dreman people since they'd made contact with the Federation. The reports were sketchy, but suggested that about two years before, a small band of aliens referring to themselves only as Exiles had landed in the planet's capital, and they'd come itching for battle. How a small band of aliens had managed to take over an entire planet, she wasn't entirely certain, but when she considered how calm and quiet Sarjenka had been during her time on the *Enterprise,* she figured the Dremans exhibited a certain level of pacifism that probably had something to do with it. If there were no urge toward violence, how could there be an urge to resist? The Exiles couldn't have been more wrong.

"Yes," Walsh replied. *"From what I can tell, their arrival didn't exactly do these folks any good. I get the feeling if they hadn't come looking for us, we'd still be waiting to make official first contact."*

Pulaski reluctantly had to agree. "Captain Walsh, how's your medical staff? I can arrange to have triage units on-hand if you want. I was chief medical officer on the *Enterprise* when it first came to Drema IV, and I've studied their physiology. I'm drafting notes for the members of my staff who are coming over to Drema Station."

Walsh gave a curt nod. *"Thank you, Doctor; we'd appreciate a copy of those notes, if you don't mind. Right now, though, nobody's been reported injured, and we don't know if there's a legitimate threat. With the differences in focal energies of Dreman dilithium, my people are still running the simulations on what any explosion in the mines might do. If it's what I suspect, there may not be anyone left for your people to treat."*

"I'll have my staff on standby in case you need us, Captain. We're close enough that it would take less than an hour to get to you."

"Hopefully, they're wrong, and we won't need you. I'll keep you apprised. Trosper *out."*

No sooner had the Federation logo cleared from her viewscreen than the comm chirped for her attention once again. *"Bridge to Dr. Pulaski,"* Crisp's voice sounded. *"There's a message coming in for you from the planet, ma'am. Audio only. It's Second Guardian Karjella. She says she's relaying a priority message from Captain Gold."*

Pulaski briefly wondered why the captain hadn't been able to contact the ship directly, but said, "Route it in here, please, Commander."

A hiss over her office's speaker system later, the message began playing, *"This is Second Guardian Karjella to Drema Station or* U.S.S. Progress. *Priority message to Dr. Katherine Pulaski from Captain David Gold. There has been an explosion at the dilithium mining facility on the surface. At least one known casualty at this time. Please send teams for immediate assistance."* Another hiss of static, and the message ended.

Pulaski slowly lowered her head into her hands. Explosions and dilithium were usually a messy combination, one best left to the engineers to figure out how to control. The real problem was going to be doing triage near an area where the energies of that explosion were still being focused and amplified through the ground beneath her feet. She'd already seen this planet try to tear itself apart once. The last thing any of them needed was for it to start trying again while she was in the middle of a delicate treatment.

Grabbing a padd from the desk as she stood, she began to put together a basic triage unit. The ship could spare a couple of nurses, and they'd just resupplied the medical stores in addition to the stockpile for Drema Station, so burn treatments, dermal regenerators and bone knitters were at peak capacity. Grabbing an empty medkit, she began filling it with hypospray canisters of sterilite and asinolyathin. On a whim, she even threw in some canisters of dylovene. She had a feeling they were going to need those just as much as the bone knitters.

And where the hell was Klesaris?

CHAPTER

7

Latik Kerjna, Drema IV
Somewhere in Dilithium Mine Alpha
Day 1

David Gold was falling head-over-heels down a very steep incline. He wasn't sure where or when it was going to end, but he knew that it had to end eventually.

If nothing else, the mine shaft had to have a bottom.

No sooner did that thought enter his mind than he landed—thankfully, feet-first—in an enormous pit of what he assumed was water from the firefighting effort up above. When he finally was able to get his bearings, he realized that the fluid was, in fact, only about one meter deep and had the clean, crisp smell that he'd long grown to associate with cold water. He took a deep breath, only to discover that there was enough dust still floating in the air from the collapse to make breathing unpleasant. He pulled the neck of his tunic back over his mouth. Above him, a blinking pinpoint of light was the only indication he could find of the surface. How far had he fallen?

And why did the air feel so stuffy and cold?

Pulling himself up to his full height, he tried to squint into the darkness to take inventory of his situation. Physically, his ankles hurt like hell from the landing, and he half-expected one—if not both—to be swelling up as he stood there. His arms were a dissonant mass of over-tensed and pulled muscles from involuntarily bracing himself for the impact as he'd fallen. He felt as though he were covered in bruises, and he wondered if the water weren't covering up some bleeding in his lower extremities.

The portion of his body that wasn't submerged in water was chilled to the bone, but that was when he noticed that the portion of him that was in the water was beginning to warm. As far as he was aware, he was the only living thing in the small pond, so it couldn't have been body heat or any other fluids, unless he was bleeding a far cry more than he felt he could have been. So, what was it? *Thermal energy from the dilithium? If that's the case, I do not want to be down in this water for long. The last thing I need is to test the old story about slowly boiling alive.*

A frightened whimper told him there was a person nearby, but the envelope of pitch black that had sealed him up so tightly made him wonder if he hadn't lost his eyesight in the fall. "Hello?"

"You're alive?"

Even though he couldn't see it, he involuntarily looked down at his waterlogged uniform and tried not to laugh about the whole thing. "Either that or Rachel has really been lying to me about the afterlife."

That elicited what sounded like a nervous chuckle out of the woman. He immediately began worrying about her mental state because nothing he said should have made sense to her. The poor woman was probably in shock.

"Good, keep laughing. It'll help me find you."

It amazed him how utterly black the cavern was. He held out a hand, thinking it felt as though it was in front of his face, but he had no visual data to prove it to himself. Gold got two more steps toward her when another rumble preceded the sound of another scream in the distance. This one was distinctly male. Gold scrambled to get out of the pit before whoever was about to join them arrived.

He got out of the way just in time. One enormous splash later, a spluttering Liankataka surfaced. He was quiet for a moment, but then began shouting.

"Guardian, what's wrong?" the woman asked, sounding a little less frightened now that another of her kind was involved.

"My leg," he said. Gold could hear the repressed pain in his voice. "It won't bear weight."

"Do you know how to swim?" Gold asked.

"What?"

"Floating?"

"I'm sorry, Captain. I don't know."

The increasing level of pain he heard in the guardian's voice worried him. It wasn't as though he hadn't dealt with broken bones before. His son Daniel's first adventures in skiing had taught him a lot about that. However, they'd been near a med station there. A bone knitter had been less than an hour away. If the others were still fighting the fire on the surface, there was no way of knowing how long it would be before they were rescued.

"All right," Gold began, stretching his arms out before him and slowly beginning to work his way back toward what he thought was the center of the small pond. "Can you follow the sound of my voice?"

A series of stumbling splashes in the darkness ensued, while Gold tried to direct him with his voice. The slight echo to the splashes gave Gold more than a few moments of confusion as he tried to localize the guardian. Finally, Liankataka's arms flailed against him. It took some convincing, but Gold was able to get the Dreman to hold still and allow the captain to take his floating body in tow.

"Miss?" Gold asked into the darkness.

"Yes?" was the weak reply.

"Please, keep talking. I need to find you. Are you out of the water?"

A moment's pause and then, "Yes."

"Feel the area around you. Do you think it's safe? Does it feel like there's enough room for the three of us?"

The sound of something fleshy patting something wet made it to his ears. After a few seconds, she said, "Yes."

Gold reached down to his waist for his tricorder, thinking perhaps it would have something that might be of use to them. It wasn't a medical tricorder, so trying to use it to diagnose their injuries wouldn't get them very far. Dreman circuitry operated on different frequencies from Starfleet, making it of little more use in connecting them to the surface than his combadge in the mine's depths. Still, it might have some worth beyond its designed intent. Flipping the tricorder open with his free hand, he was comforted as the faint light from the display gave the cavern a slight glow.

It was certainly better than flailing around in the dark.

He forced thoughts of using the frequency modulation to try to contact the surface into the same corner of his mind where the pain resided. Right now, he needed the light more than anything.

Just on the edge of the field of light, he could see a thin, white-sleeved arm reaching toward him. A face leaned into the light, concern on her features.

"What's your name?" he asked.

"Kajana."

Gold was thankful for the faint light from the tricorder, as he'd have had a bear of a time finding her in the dark. "Can you take this?" he asked, holding the tricorder out in front of him. "I can't carry it and the guardian at the same time."

Kajana nodded. He assumed she found a way to brace herself, as the extent to which she reached out over the water wasn't one he would have considered safe. Gold extended the hand with the tricorder as far as he could, even scooting the tricorder across his palm to a point where he was only holding on with his fingertips. That bracing she had found was short-lived, however. Just as her fingers reached the tricorder, she lost her balance, reflexively putting her hand down, but finding only water instead. Her flailing arm hit the tricorder, knocking it out of Gold's grasp.

The light flickered as it tumbled into the water, darkening as it finally came to rest at the bottom with its display facing down. "I'm sorry," Kajana said, her voice not much more than a whisper. "I'm sorry."

Gold tried to secure his own balance, even though he felt as though his calves had become malformed sheaths for the swords that had replaced his feet. "Keep talking. Please try to stay calm. As soon as the guardian is on the ledge with you, I'll get the tricorder."

He was fairly sure he knew how to get Liankataka over to the ledge, but without the light, having her voice to guide him would help the process.

"All right," she said. "I'm not sure how I'm supposed to stay calm, though."

Closing his eyes, Gold focused on the sound, willing himself to sort through the bouncing waves and localize the source, wishing for the dilithium to have had more anechoic properties.

"We're stuck down here for *Traiaka* knows how long."

Tugging Liankataka behind him, Gold gingerly took a step in the direction where he remembered Kajana was waiting, then another. His back shivered as he tried to restrain his reaction to the pain.

"The fire is only going to radiate heat down here."

Kajana left a gap of about a second in between her sentences to allow the sound of her voice to dissipate. It was just enough to keep Gold focused on where he was walking.

Out of nowhere, his left foot slammed into an outcrop. Uncrossing his eyes, he leaned forward to discover that there was a stone ledge about five centimeters above the water line. Keeping his right arm around Liankataka, he reached forward with his left hand and was greeted by what felt like a clothed leg. The limb was still warm, and it was accompanied by a decidedly feminine gasp. "Kajana?" he asked.

"Who else would it be?"

Gold allowed himself a long exhale. Finally, he reached back and got a good grip on Liankataka. "I'm going to need your help. I can't get him onto the ledge alone."

A hand came out of the darkness and fell onto his arm. "Where is he?"

Gold grabbed her hand and guided it to Liankataka's shoulder. Part of him wanted to get on the ledge with her and drag the guardian onto the stone floor from there, but Gold knew that would be harder on any back injury the Dreman might have sustained. Forcing himself to ignore the pain for a few moments more, he placed a hand on Liankataka's arm, using it to guide him as he took careful steps out to where the guardian's feet floated.

With a gentle push, Gold allowed Kajana to guide their patient toward where she was holed up. When she said that she had him, Gold moved alongside the guardian, running his hands up the man's spine to see if there was any obvious sign of damage. *Damn it, Pulaski, why didn't I let you brief me before I came down to the surface?*

"Because it hadn't seemed important at the time," he bitterly answered himself.

"What, Captain?" the guardian asked.

Gold shook his head and then remembered that the Dreman couldn't see him. "Nothing. Just wishing that I'd sat through one more briefing before coming down, that's all. How does your back feel?"

A moment's pause, and then Liankataka said, "Stiff, but no pain."

"Is that normal?"

"For me?" the guardian asked, backing it with a chuckle. "Yes and no. You might say it comes and goes."

While Gold's knowledge of Dreman physiology was virtually nonexistent, one thing he knew very well was that a stiff back wasn't always a sign of spinal damage. Sometimes, it just meant that the muscles had been overtaxed. As Gold didn't feel any obvious signs of damage in the vertebrae, he hoped that was what it meant. Nice, uncomplicated injuries meant that they'd all be able to help themselves out of this predicament.

The way he saw it, this gave him a choice. He could trust that the stiffness meant there really was no significant damage to Liankataka's spine, and with Kajana's assistance he could slide the guardian onto the ledge she occupied, or he could take every precaution imaginable to protect the Dreman's anatomy, but possibly at the cost of his own mobility.

"Captain, you're seriously injured. You are our guest. It is we who should be helping you. Come. Float beside me."

Gold had to admit that did sound nice, but it didn't change his options. Finally, he decided that Pulaski may be able to repair any significant damage to both of them, and they needed to get out of the pool of water. Slowly, he and Kajana managed to get Liankataka to the ledge.

When that was complete, he allowed himself to float on the water's surface, trying to spot the tricorder's faint glow in the water. It took a few moments, but he finally found and recovered the unit. That accomplished, he then slid up alongside Kajana and Liankataka and collapsed in a heap. The pain felt as though it were trying to take over his body. A deep aching scattered through his arms suggested bone-deep bruising that was still forming. His neck was even stiff. There wasn't a part of his body that didn't hurt. Gold leaned his head back against something that had the cold, worked-flat feel of a stone outcrop, but he was too tired and too achy to really care. There was no way he could see to prop up his ankles to avoid swelling. Perhaps if he kept his boots on for as long as he could tolerate them, it might mitigate the damage.

With the immediate danger past, Gold reached a hand toward where he usually wore his combadge. It was gone.

Probably fell off in the fall. The realization was a blow to the hope he'd been trying to foment. If they tried to locate him by the combadge signal, it could have been anywhere in the pile of dirt closing the tunnel shaft to the bottom of the pool of water he'd landed in. And that was provided they could even find the signal through however much dilithium and dirt was above his head.

Sighing, he flipped the tricorder closed to save power. They all needed to rest for a few moments. The tricorder would be there to help them cope with the darkness, and maybe it would even help them contact the surface.

Until the power supply ran out.

Gold had no idea how long that would be and tried not to consider that they'd be down there long enough for it to happen.

CHAPTER

8

Pithead, Dilithium Mine Alpha
Day 1

Sarjenka ran up to the entrance of the pithead just as a small medical transport was pulling away, sirens wailing. What she saw beyond that, however, felt as though someone had pummeled her in the abdomen and refused to stop. The shed that had covered the top of the mine was on fire, a thick gray smoke billowing into the air. Three firefighters were doing their best to put the thing out. The assistant staffing coordinator, a woman Sarjenka had only met once a year or so before and whose name she could not remember to save her life, was standing there gaping at the flames. An older human male in a red and black Starfleet uniform—she assumed it was Admiral Tucker, but she'd never seen a picture of the man to be certain—stood holding a small hose aimed at the shed. The stream of water was barely reaching the flames, but the fact that he was willing to trade his personal safety for the safety of her world was an interesting revelation.

For the moment, the fire looked on the verge of being under control, but she didn't want to think about what was resonating through the dilithium and what it was doing to her father.

The smoke tickled the back of her throat, just enough to

make her think that getting the growing crowd of gawkers to back away may be beneficial to everyone's health.

"Sarjenka!"

She turned toward the voice and found Eklian, Sinterka's mate, standing a few feet away. His arms were wrapped tightly around his midsection, his face had flushed pink, and she couldn't help but note that he looked both nauseated and terrified. A sheen of moisture had formed on his slightly undersized brow, reinforcing the sharp smell of sweat that hit her nostrils. How long had the fire been going?

"Are you okay?" she asked.

Eklian nodded, but his expression never changed. When he briefly released his grip on his midsection, Sarjenka noticed that his sleeves were soaked. It looked almost as though he'd been sticking his hands up to the elbows in water. Had he been trying to fight the fire?

"Sinterka came to warn us," she said, trying to calm him. "He's not down there. He said my father found the bomb." Frantically looking around, she added, "He ran over from the house with us."

At that, Eklian's eyes widened. "You mean—"

"He's here somewhere. Have you seen my father?" she asked. A knot of fear began tightening in her stomach as his face ran a gamut of emotions from frightened to a horrified realization to abject sympathy. "Eklian," she began, "is he—?"

His eyes darted back to the fire. "Sarjenka . . ."

"Please. Where is he?" She grabbed Eklian's upper arm a little more tightly than she had intended, but it got her point across.

"He was on the transport that just left for the hospital. I couldn't get a good look at him, but what I saw was burned. Badly."

The knot in her stomach turned into a tightening noose. Turning her back on the firefighting effort, she began to work her way through the expanding crowd at the pithead, trying to get out to the hospital. The nearest burn healers were only a kilometer away, but it felt as though they might as well have been on another planet.

She was five steps into the crowd when a booming, reverberant roar sounded from behind her. A woman's scream grabbed Sarjenka and brought her away from thoughts of her father. When she turned back around, the top of the mine shaft had partially collapsed, and the staffing assistant had vanished—presumably down into the mine shaft, but Sarjenka couldn't be sure.

The woman may have survived, provided she remembered to curl up and allow herself to roll down the shaft. A straight drop would have killed any of them automatically, but the angle of the shaft was just enough to allow a quick descent for the miners and somehow still kept the roof from caving in.

Normally.

Then again, her father had always commented that if they really thought about how the thing had been constructed, nobody in their proper mind would have gone down there.

Sarjenka's eyes darted back through the mass of people. Eklian had disappeared back into whatever crevasse in the crowd had given rise to him in the first place. She saw familiar face after familiar face, but not one of them was a healer. If the healers were following the procedures from the last drill, she figured them to be at the hospitals awaiting casualties. She had railed against the idea of not setting up first aid as part of the emergency protocols, but thanks to her youth, no one had listened.

Whatever happened, they were going to need a healer on the site.

You're only an apprentice, she told herself. What can you do? Go to the hospital. Be with Father.

But what could she do there beyond console her mother? Could she, *should* she, bring her to the hospital? Would seeing how badly he was injured really help?

Wringing her hands before her, she frantically tried to call upon all of her training to help decide where she could do the most good.

The planet made the decision for her. A rumble began rising from somewhere under her feet. "Everyone back away!" Raising her hands over her head, she began frantically gesturing away from the pithead. Sarjenka briefly regretted not inheriting her father's booming voice. Forcing all of the volume she could muster behind her voice in an effort to be heard over the growing rumble, she yelled, "Move away from the mine! It's collapsing!"

A man screamed from somewhere behind her, then another, but the ground was still growling like a hungry beast. Afraid to turn around, she looked down, thankful to see the blue-green blades of grass beneath her, even though she'd fully expected an expanding chasm.

The crowd that had formed around the fire finally began backing off, much to her surprise. She'd always thought her people to be sane, rational creatures, but apparently that was not the case when true morbid curiosity was added to the mixture.

Sarjenka finally turned around. The shed that had been at the top of the mine for the last four years was gone. An area of ground ringing the mineshaft for about a *kilopar* in each direction had gone with it. She could smell the embers of the burning supports, but they were down there at the bottom of the hole somewhere. Sarjenka edged closer to the hole, not sure where the danger zone for further collapse actually ended.

There were people down there, in what condition, only they knew. If Admiral Tucker was dead, she didn't want to think of what the Federation would do.

She tried not to think of that as she looked around for *jakerga* men to go down and pull them out. These men had numbered fewer than fifty during the last collapse, but they were strong, familiar with the mines, and willing to don a gas mask to protect them from the toxic fumes that occasionally accompanied collapses. It had been the *jakerga* who'd saved her own father's life back during the small cave-in years ago, and she hoped it would be the *jakerga* who saved those people now.

No matter what condition they were in, it would take some time before anyone would be brought back to the surface. Father said that even the best time on the emergency drills had been almost a day.

Sarjenka slowly edged her way through the crowd and began walking toward home. First, to her mother, then to the hospital. Before she allowed herself to become a useless lump of worrying flesh over her father, she might as well check on the one person she may still be able to help.

CHAPTER
9

Katherine Pulaski made a mental note to have the inertial dampeners triple-checked if Lieutenant Xavier was ever scheduled to fly a shuttlecraft for her again.

As Xavier banked the shuttlecraft *Reeves* into a turn fast enough for her stomach to threaten a response, she tried to keep in mind that they were not unlike an ambulance rushing to the scene of an accident. Fast was good. Fast and safe was better. The last thing they needed was for the doctors to be included among the injured.

A fiery red glow began forming around the shuttlecraft's nose as they entered Drema IV's atmosphere. She knew that somewhere behind them, the *Trosper* was finding a parking orbit and would send down crew of her own when it could.

She also knew that it would have been much easier for her to travel to the planet on the *Trosper* with Klesaris and beam down to the surface with the away team full of S.C.E. tech-heads that Captain Walsh was assembling, but to say she didn't care for the transporter would be an understatement.

Of course, she could have always learned about the inertial dampeners herself, learned about flying shuttles, and made her own way through her transporter phobia, but that wasn't her job. She'd *thought* about taking the training courses, but her medical duties won the day. It wasn't her responsibility to make sure the inorganic systems worked properly.

What was her responsibility, however, was to make sure the triage units were set up and ready for incoming wounded. Contrary to earlier reports, as of the last word from the second guardian, six people were missing, including Captain Gold and Guardian Liankataka.

Five injured Dremans, probably seriously, stood to tax their knowledge base. Pulaski planned to get the local doctors involved as quickly as possible, if for no other reason than to have able-bodied, trained medics handy. *The more, the merrier.*

The deep whoosh of the air rushing past the shuttle's nacelles as they entered the atmosphere slowly began to subside, and Pulaski looked out the forward window to see a wide, lush forest coming up ahead of them. She'd heard that the floes of liquid magma that had surfaced during her first visit to the planet had resulted in a rich, verdant plant life, but she hadn't expected such dense greenery. *All of this in five years? I know a few botanists who would love to get their hands on plants that take over so quickly. What we couldn't do with those on a damaged world.*

They didn't run across many planets that were as damaged as Drema IV had been—at least not any that had survived. The odds of that being in the future of any Federation world, well, she didn't want to think about that at that moment.

The shuttle took an abrupt bounce, nearly knocking Pulaski out of her seat.

"Sorry, Doc," Xavier said, quickly turning and giving her an appraising glance. There was a near panic in the young lieutenant's hazel eyes. "The thermals around here are severe, but small. By the time the computer picks them up, I have to take evasive maneuvers."

Pulaski gave him a curt nod. She wanted to tell him it was okay and that she understood, but another thermal chose that moment to make its presence known. She was thrown hard against the restraint on the shuttle's seat. Wincing, she leaned back against the backrest. *Maybe I should reconsider the transporters,* she thought.

Before another thought could form, Xavier said, "Hold on to your stomach, Doc. I'm going to try something."

That was when it felt as though the floor cut out beneath her. Suddenly, she lurched forward. She was quite thankful for the restraint, though she could already feel the bruise forming. Clouds flew past the viewport in just the direction they shouldn't, namely, moving straight up. Whether he had cut the shuttle's engines or intentionally put them into a dive, her inner ear had stopped trying to determine, but she knew they were moving far more quickly in a downward direction than she liked. "Lieutenant," she began, trying not to sound as though she were questioning his sanity too much.

That was as far as she got, however, as Xavier picked that point to bring them out of it. When Pulaski finally got her stomach back in order from the descent, she made the mistake of looking out the viewport again. The treetops were disconcertingly close. "Lieutenant," she said, "please don't ever do that again. One more second . . ."

Xavier audibly exhaled. "Yeah. Sorry, Doc. The sensors misread the bottom edge of that thermal."

Before she could voice a word in protest, the shuttle banked to the right and set down with more stillness than she'd seen the entire ride. *I definitely need to ask the admiral to order regular inertial dampener checks.*

As she and Xavier were the only passengers on the shuttlecraft, it only took a few seconds for her to gather herself and disembark. When she did, she discovered that they'd landed in the middle of a small field, one that looked as though it had very recently been in use for some gathering. However, it also looked as though it had been quickly abandoned, presumably when the explosion occurred. The clearing was edged by trees with lush, blue-green leaves, and there was an overwhelming smell of food mixed in with something that reminded her far too much of her last trip to the arboretum on the *Enterprise*. There were so many different floral aromas floating around, she almost wanted to send a message describing them to the last botanist she'd known—wherever Keiko Ishikawa was these days—and see what she thought.

But that was for later. Now, there were patients for her to treat. Pulaski was just wondering when the team on the *Trosper* would beam down when the familiar high-pitched whine of a transporter beam beginning its work sounded. Three men, two women, and one tiny Belandrid appeared in the first transport wave. As Klesaris's team numbered over a dozen, Pulaski knew there would be more people coming.

The cherubic smile of the *Trosper*'s captain was precisely as she'd expected. That robust, friendly nature appeared to be reflective of the rest of him, as well. While Captain Walsh could easily have been one of the more physically fit members of his crew as he'd risen through the ranks, the mildly expanding midsection under that red-and-black uniform indicated to her that the center seat had apparently agreed with him about as well as replicated Guinness cake.

That did not, however, change the fact that the man immediately extended a hand toward her as soon as the transporter beam finished its work. "Dr. Pulaski," he said. "Nice to meet you in person. Where do you want us to set up?"

Pulaski scanned the field. Outside of the shuttlecraft and the dais, the place was still empty. "First we need to find out how close to the mine we are. Xavier," she said, gesturing toward the dark-skinned pilot, "take the shuttlecraft up and scout around. Make sure we're close enough to be effective here. The last thing we need is to have it take so long to get here that the survivors die en route."

"Yes, ma'am."

"Something tells me you won't have a problem finding the mine by sight, young man," Walsh said. "But our sensors said it was about a half-kilometer north of here. Start there. Look for the crowd of people. I've seen a few of these mining communities before. When the mine's in trouble, everyone shows up thinking they can help, and they end up just standing around waiting."

Xavier nodded curtly. "Yes, sir." Within seconds, he and the shuttlecraft were once again airborne.

Klesaris chose that moment to step forward. Gesturing toward her right, she said, "With your permission, if the site checks out, I'll have the trauma units set up over near the dais."

"Do it," Pulaski said.

Klesaris turned around so quickly her long ponytail almost whipped her in the face. Tapping her combadge, she began speaking to the *Trosper*'s transporter chief about beam-in locations for the equipment.

While the young redhead would probably make some captain an excellent CMO one of these days, Pulaski was still a little concerned over how often she still seemed so . . . young. "And, Mary?"

Klesaris raised her head, "Yes?"

"We're on emergency protocols here. You've got the trauma units. While we're here, that's your department—*your* decisions."

The younger doctor gave a quick nod of understanding, and went back to her conversation.

The tiny Belandrid wandered over to Dr. Pulaski with what appeared to be a tool kit in his seven-fingered right hand. Even though he was standing at his full height, the humanoid little creature barely came up to her waist. Reports from the Federation contact team who had been sent to the ocean planet of Belandros roughly a century before had said that all Belandrid looked alike, yet not even Starfleet's best geneticists had been able to determine how they managed it without cloning technology. Pulaski only knew of three of the species in Starfleet, and they had been allowed to apply after one of their kind had helped save Earth from a biological attack by the Romulans approximately ninety years before. Still, what they might not have had in physical strength, they more than made up for in resilience to injury.

He saluted his captain, and his tiny, circular mouth made a sound not unlike bubbling water before he spoke. "Dddoctor Pulaski?"

"Yes," she said, quickly glancing down at the creature's uniform collar, "what can I do for you, Lieutenant?" She couldn't help but notice that on the creature's translucent blue skin, the yellow and black uniform of a Starfleet engineer looked a little, well, odd.

"Lllolo, please."

She recognized the name from Walsh's mention during their first conversation. "Of course, what is it, Lolo?"

The Belandrid's vertical eyelids opened wide, his neon-yellow eyes centering on her. He shifted his booted right foot on the ground in what Pulaski would, in a human, have considered a gesture of nervousness. Pulaski couldn't help but note that the boots weren't standard-issue, presumably to account for the creature's webbed, yet still seven-toed feet. "Cccaptain Walsh asked me tto mmmaintttain equipment."

"Work with Lieutenant Klesaris. She'll have the most use for your skills."

"Yes, mmma'am. Nnno problem."

With that, Lolo walked off toward Pulaski's assistant. She thought briefly about a quiet comm with Klesaris to make sure she knew about the Belandrid's rather waterlogged manner of speaking—truth be told, he sounded like what Pulaski would have expected to hear if an old-fashioned water cooler had suddenly developed sentience—but realized that, from the meager bits she knew of how the Corps of Engineers worked, Lolo and Klesaris had probably been thrown together on the *Trosper* during the hour they'd had to get the equipment together. If half of what she'd heard about their latent engineering ability was true, she had no doubt of his qualifications when it came to keeping an eye on that equipment.

Pulaski's combadge chirped. *"Xavier to Pulaski."*

The young man's voice came through loud and clear. Tapping her own badge, she said, "Yes what is it, Lieutenant?"

"We should be good, ma'am. The mine is about a half-kilometer due north. Sensors read about seventy-five people at the head of the mine right now. No open area to set up there, so we're as close as we're going to get."

Pulaski gave a curt nod, even though she knew Xavier couldn't see her. "Understood. Get back here as soon as you can."

"Yes, ma'am. Xavier out."

Before she could give a thought to where to begin, one of the *Trosper*'s engineers walked over, padd in hand. "Lieutenant Commander Barreto, ma'am," he said, backing it with a friendly smile. "We're working on a way to get a transporter lock through the interference. It's playing merry hell with the explorer drone. We can't send it down. I've got an idea or two that I think will work."

"Any luck improving the scanning accuracy through the interference?" Walsh asked.

Barreto raised a dark brown eyebrow, running a hand over his close-cropped brown hair. "Not much, sir, but we're still working on it. Ensign Borosh from the *Progress* even had a couple of ideas that we thought might help, but we've been trying to recalibrate the ship's sensors six ways till Sunday and can't get it to improve. We can tell that the area may not be one-hundred percent stable, but as for finding anyone specifically? No. There's something about the dilithium that's keeping us from being able to get a signal through it."

Walsh shook his head. "We do this the old-fashioned way, then. I'm sure the Dremans must have procedures in place for what to do when the mine collapses."

"You mean outside of praying for the souls of the dead?" Pulaski asked, only semi-rhetorically.

Walsh's arms dropped from where they'd been folded over his chest. "I'll go see if I can't find Second Guardian Karjella and get the digging going."

CHAPTER
10

Latik Kerjna, Drema IV
Bottom of Dilithium Mine Alpha
Day 2

Gold fiddled with the tricorder's settings for the fiftieth time.

Thus far, all he'd been able to do was take a basic set of sensor readings on himself, Liankataka, and Kajana. He tried adjusting every setting he could think of, even briefly considering a multiphase pulse in an attempt to let those on the surface know they were still alive, but he didn't want to risk inadvertently doing any more damage.

When he finally decided to stop and admit that the tricorder was going to serve them best as a light source—that was when he heard it.

"Hello?"

They weren't alone.

At first Gold thought he was hallucinating, that he'd banged his head in the fall and the damage was just now surfacing, but when he got a look at Liankataka and Kajana in the faint light from the tricorder's display, their reactions suggested that he wasn't imagining things.

"Hello?" Gold called into the darkness. "Who else is down here?"

For a moment, the blanket of darkness that rested just

outside the tiny glow from the tricorder display seemed to grow a little more oppressive. A rock fell somewhere in the distance.

Or was it right beside him? Not even the Doppler Effect seemed to be working properly. It was either that or his ears had blown out in the fall. In his mind, one was just as likely as the other.

A faint voice called out from the darkness. "Guardian?"

Liankataka tried to prop himself up with his arms. "Yes? Who's there?"

There was a faint rustle that sounded almost like paper, and then, "Name's Eijeth, sir."

"Eijeth?" the Guardian replied, recognition in his voice. "Didn't you get the evacuation signal?'

A pause, and then, "We did sir, but Kajkob here, he fell going up the shaft. Hurt his ankle something awful. It was slow going, so Jakara and I stopped to let him rest, but something exploded up top."

"It was a bomb, Eijeth," Liankataka said, putting on the most consoling—no, Gold realized, it was actually placating—tone possible. "The last gasp of the Exiles."

"*Exiles?*" That seemed to panic the voice more than calm it. "Guardian, they've come back?"

"No, Eijeth," Liankataka said, still trying to comfort the man with his voice. "No, they haven't come back. They merely left a few things behind."

"Scorched earth," Gold absently said.

"What, Captain?"

Gold shook his head, not quite sure he wanted to believe how universal some concepts truly were. "It's an old battle tactic that was also used on Earth centuries ago. Destroy anything useful to an invading enemy while you're retreating from them: food, buildings, arable land. The idea was to keep the invading force from being able to set up shop comfortably. If they can't even grow food, how can they enjoy the spoils of conquest?"

Something that sounded like a snort of derision came from the Guardian's direction. "It's the behavior of children, Captain. 'If I can't have it, they can't either.' Very juvenile. Not at all surprising. The Exiles were a very childlike people in many ways."

"Aren't we all, Guardian?" Gold asked. Turning his attentions to the world outside their tiny sanctuary of light, he said, "Eijeth, do the three of you have food? If we're down here for any length of time, we need to ration every bit of food we have."

He heard muttering from above, then, "Not much. Jakara hasn't eaten his lunch, but Kajkob and I did. We've got about four chunks of *keena* bread, some vituwater, and some dried *teekir* meat."

"Sounds like a feast," Liankataka said. "All that for one day?"

A deeper voice—Gold figured it was Jakara—said, "I work hard, sir. And my wife treats me well."

"Sounds like you found a good woman," the Guardian said. "You'll be okay, Jakara. We'll all be okay."

Gold wished he could be so optimistic.

"Would you please be so kind as to share some of that food with us, Jakara?"

He heard a creaking like metallic hinges opening and closing, some rustling, and then, "Of course, Guardian. Do you need me to bring it down?"

Gold and Liankataka shared a glance, then they both looked toward Kajana, the only uninjured person in their small group. She was huddled in the corner, leaning against the wall with her legs folded up to her chest. When she briefly raised her eyes to them, Gold noticed that the panic was still there. She rapidly shook her head and then huddled back over her legs. There was a good chance that she wouldn't be able to help even herself, let alone them.

"Yes, please," Gold said. "But only if you're able. The Guardian and I are injured, and Kajana isn't able to move."

Someone scuffled their way down the mineshaft, the sound ending in a series of splashes and the entrance of a very large, very muscle-bound Dreman into the circle of light. Suddenly, Liankataka's use of the word 'feast' made much more sense. It would have taken a lot of food to keep a man like this going. What little Gold could see of the man beyond his size showed a face covered in dilithium dust. The whites of his eyes shone in the faint light. "Guardian?" the man asked.

"Jakara?"

The man smiled, "Yes, sir." He held out a small packet toward Liankataka. "The food. I split what I had in half. You want some water?" Jakara glanced back at the pool of water he'd stumbled through and said, "Maybe not. Looks like enough for all of us here."

Liankataka thanked Jakara profusely and then began divvying up the packet's contents. He reached around and handed Gold a hunk about the size of his closed fist of what looked like a kind of whole wheat bread and two strips of dried meat the length of his hand.

Gold's stomach chose that moment to remind him that, in addition to the pain, he'd managed to ignore how hungry he'd become. He was grateful that he was sitting because a mild wave of dizziness came over him at the sight of the food.

"Has anyone tried to get out yet?" Gold asked—his attempt to keep the dizziness at bay mentally complicated by the fact that doing so only made it more difficult to block out the pain.

Jakara shook his head. "No, sir. We were waiting until we were sure the mine was through collapsing before we tried."

Gold couldn't fault him that logic. Trying to dig them out with the tunnel collapsing around them was something of a self-defeating process. He checked the chronometer on the tricorder, just to see how long they'd been down there. Five hours.

Five hours that felt more like five days.

"Jakara," Liankataka began, "we need your help. We need to begin working our way out of here, but Captain Gold and I are both injured. Kajana isn't capable of helping right now. We're going to have to rely on you and Eijeth."

Jakara nodded. "I understand, Guardian. We'll get us out of here."

CHAPTER
11

Latik Kerjna, Drema IV
Day 2

Sarjenka sat back in the overstuffed chair in the front room of her home and waited.

The hospital had threatened to sedate Rakan if she didn't leave, so Sarjenka took her mother home. There was nothing they could do for Eliatriel in either location, but at least at home, Rakan could go through the motions of life.

They'd been through this worry route once before, back when her father had been involved in a minor shift in the structure of the secondary mine. One level had collapsed, trapping a dozen miners for several hours until the rescuers could dig them out. Her father had sustained injuries that they were sure he would not survive, but he had.

As she was neither strong enough in build to be a rescuer nor far enough along with her studies as a healer to offer anything more than first aid for wounded who hadn't shown up yet, there was nothing she could do but wait. She pulled her small music stone from her pocket, holding it tightly in her right hand as it gave off the same lilting melody it had for all the years she'd had it.

She had no idea where the stone had come from. All she knew was that on the morning after the tremors had stopped, she'd awoken with it in her hand. A part of her felt there had to have been something special about it, as nobody she'd shown it to had ever seen a stone that gave off music before; yet no matter how many times she was interrogated on the subject, she had no recollection of how it had come to be in her possession.

The stone's melody had always been a source of comfort to her, though, reminding her that there were things in the universe that she didn't understand—yet. Perhaps her father's fate was one of those things. *If the news were bad,* she reminded herself, *we'd have heard already*.

Her mother, however, wasn't quite as patient. "This is a nightmare. They'll tell us if something happens?" she asked, an edge of hysteria in her voice.

Sarjenka knew the look on Rakan's face far too well. That tone of voice, the panicked look in her eyes, the otherwise placid expression, the wringing of the hands in the lap added up to one thing. Her mother was obsessing over every possible scenario that Eliatriel's life could have taken in the explosion, and the preeminent vision was, Sarjenka was relatively certain, the same one that had been appearing in her mother's mind far too often: Eliatriel's body, skin charred as though it had been a *teekir* steak cooking over an open flame for too long, bones broken from the impact of the explosion, pain like she could not imagine, suffering in ways that no living creature had ever been intended to suffer.

Traiaka, *if it is your choosing, please make your embrace quick. Please don't allow father to suffer anymore.*

"I don't know, Mother. I don't know." While Sarjenka could think of dozens of possible ways her father could still unavoidably die, even sitting in his hospital bed, and think of them in ways even a fully-trained healer couldn't treat, she didn't dare speak of them aloud. Her mother was distraught enough as it was without adding something like that to it. If there were only a way to talk the hospital into allowing her mother to sit with her father, but the burns were so severe they had to place him in a special isolation ward for treatment. Even the slightest risk of infection was more than they were willing to take.

Rakan grabbed a small square of fabric from her skirt pocket and proceeded to wipe her eyes. "What are we to do if he dies?"

"The same thing the other families will do if they lose someone, Mother," Sarjenka replied, her voice far more calm than she actually felt. "We will thank *Traiaka* for his life, and then we will move on."

Rakan sobbed inexorably, her tiny wails the only thing breaking the silence between mother and daughter. Sarjenka considered getting up from the chair and trying to console her mother, but it was becoming increasingly obvious to her that something needed to be done. For one thing, the condition of the house had gone downhill in a drastic manner. It had only been a day, but it felt like a week. Clutter was beginning to form in various locations. The morning news journal sat unread on her father's favorite chair, almost as though it was waiting on his return, too. The full basket sitting by the stairs indicated that her mother hadn't even bothered to put away the clean laundry from the previous morning.

If Rakan intended to be the one to break down, then the responsibility for remaining calm and rational would have to be Sarjenka's.

Pulling herself out of the chair, Sarjenka walked over to the front entrafield. "I can't sit here doing nothing, Mother. I'm going to the hospital."

CHAPTER
12

Latik Kerjna, Drema IV
Central Hospital
Day 2

Sarjenka arrived at the hospital more grateful to be away from her home than anything else.

However, that gratitude was short-lived when she saw Healer Drankla walking toward her. His iridescent white robes were covered in dark blood, and she thought she saw flecks of black on him as he drew closer. His face, which held more than a few well-earned lines of age, seemed suddenly so much older.

"Sarjenka," he said. "I was going to contact your mother."

Drankla had been master to her apprentice for the last two years. She'd grown to know that tone of voice in him far more than she'd have ever cared to admit. Between that and the single raised golden eyebrow, she knew he was trying to figure out how to break some bad news.

To her.

"My father?" she asked, feeling a tinge of guilt that she hoped it was someone else.

Drankla's hands fell to his sides briefly, but he then lifted them to sit just above her shoulders. His face, which she had begun to think would never age, seemed to take on ten years before her eyes. When he lifted his red eyes to her, she could see the exhaustion in them. "He took a turn for the worse after you left last night," he said. "The infection in his right arm began to spread. We were able to slow it down, but the medications are lowering his blood cell counts."

Sarjenka felt as though she'd been kicked in the stomach. While she'd been too young to actually study *xurta* wounds, she'd read enough to know what her next question was going to be. She wasn't sure she wanted to know the answer to it, however. "The infection, is it dilithium poisoning? Did it get into his blood?"

The master healer shook his head, pulling the glimmering white cloth that covered his head and kept his golden hair in check during delicate operations. "Sarjenka. You know the kind of injuries a *xurta* inflicts. Healer Nekara said there was a tremendous amount of dust in the air when he arrived. The best he could do was patch up the damage and get him here. However, I'm not certain how much more we can do. We are not *Traiaka*. We don't have the power to reverse this kind of damage."

Her eyes lowered to the floor between them. If anyone would know what she had and hadn't learned, it would be the master who'd instructed her. In the time since the Uprising, there had been sporadic *xurta* incidents—enough for them to itemize the kind of damage the bomb was capable of inflicting, but not nearly enough to figure out precisely how to disarm them. Nobody could figure out whether they should be thankful for that fact. It was far easier to set the things off than it was to do anything else with them.

That was when a hope took hold in her mind, one she wasn't sure she wanted to cling to, but did, anyway. "What about the Federation? They had the knowledge to stop the tremors before. What about them? Could they help? Maybe they could—I don't know—make another arm for him?"

Drankla shook his head, confusion in his gold eyes. "I don't know. We don't know how much their healers know about us,

Sarjenka. Right now, we need to concentrate on what we can do right here."

She wasn't settling for that. "But there's a possibility they could do more?"

"There are always possibilities."

Sarjenka smiled for the first time since the explosion, turned around, and sprinted out the door.

CHAPTER

13

"The *latkes* were delicious," Gold said as he pushed himself away from the dining room table. Rachel's *latkes* were one of his favorite foods on the face of the earth. He'd even attempted to program the replicators on the *Progress* with the recipe. However, as was the norm with anything Rachel had ever cooked, it seemed, it didn't quite taste the same. This batch, however, had felt as though the recipe were just a little different. "Did you use—"

"A little more scallion than usual," Rachel replied, her delicate hand reaching for the empty plate. His sense of smell had noted the difference almost immediately, but after some of the things he'd been through recently, he wasn't always sure that his senses still worked properly.

His wife smiled that knowing smile of hers. "If they still worked properly, David," she said, "you'd be back on that starship of yours and not stuck in a hole."

Gold's brow furrowed. *Now, where did that come from?*

Rachel walked the few steps from the dining room to the house's state-of-the-art kitchen. The matte-finished metal of the appliances stood out against the dark wood of the cabinets,

almost like stars in the night with the wood-burning stove acting almost like their sun. Of course, that had been one of the
things she'd insisted upon when they remodeled the kitchen.
While she might have had her rabbinical work to help refine
her soul, his wife needed a proper place to practice her art.

He leaned forward, fetching another empty ceramic serving
plate from the table. This one was chartreuse, heavy, and cold.
It looked almost like a flattened crystal of Dreman dilithium.
"Rachel, where did we get this platter?"

All he heard from his wife was a small laugh, followed by
the sound of running water.

No sooner did he stand from his chair than the entire universe around him shifted, and he was standing at attention in
the captain's ready room on the *U.S.S. Boudicca.*

Captain Nechayev leaned back in her chair, sizing him up
with a look. Her blond hair was pulled up into a tight bun, and
the red of her uniform only served to make her usually austere expression hold more than a touch of anger. "Commander
Gold," she said, her voice turning arch. "You do realize the
problem we have here, don't you?"

"No, ma'am," he said, his back remaining stiff as a board.
"I'm sorry, ma'am."

Nechayev let out a long-suffering sigh. Gold had been her
first officer for only a few months, but it had been long enough
to know that whatever Alynna Nechayev wanted, she usually
got, and woe be to the person who stood between her and her
goal.

She'd make a great admiral one of these days.

"Relax, David," she said, putting particular emphasis on the
first word. "You're not going to get out of this if you overana-
lyze and outthink yourself. You want to command a ship of
your own eventually, correct?"

Gold wanted to say that he already had a perfectly good ship
and crew in the *Progress,* but something stopped him. Before
he could formulate a proper reply, the scene shifted again.

This time, it was to the dais where he'd stood just a few

minutes—or was it hours?—before. Only this time, he was alone. The sun was warm and bright in the sky. The air smelled of green, lush, dense, peaty life, with a little of the cool crispness of fresh water mixed in for good measure. He half expected to look past the trees and see a bright, sapphire-blue ocean beyond. A bird chirped in the distance. He couldn't recall the last time he'd known such peace when he hadn't been in space.

Probably the last time I was home. But New York City is never this peaceful. This would be a wonderful place to retire.

That was when Gold realized what was going on. He opened his eyes—at least, he thought he opened them, as the black of the mine tunnels was just as all-encompassing as the darkness behind his closed eyes. *Dreaming,* he thought, chastising himself. Gold felt around the flat stone outcrop that served as their resting place until he found the closed tricorder. He flipped it open, allowing its faint glow to illuminate their small chamber. He was almost grateful for the damage to his ankles, as he doubted that he would have been able to stand in the tiny space. Kajana had said the level had only recently been dug, so it wasn't quite at full capacity yet. *Not quite at full expanse, either.*

Testing his ankles, Gold discovered that taking off his boots shortly before falling asleep had apparently resulted in his ankles being able to do the swelling they'd been trying to do since he'd first come tumbling down the mineshaft. It wasn't the smartest move from a first-aid perspective, but it was either take off the boots and cope with the aftermath or deal with feeling as though his circulation were being cut off. While the boots had hurt like hell to have on thanks to the compression of the swelling, the mere thought of movement now sent tremors of anticipatory pain up the sides of his legs.

Ignoring the pain, Gold followed the sound of snoring and slowly worked his way across the mine floor to where Liankataka lay. The lights from the three miners on the level above them had given out hours before, so Gold was stuck once again with using the faint glow of the tricorder's display as illumination. "Guardian," he whispered. "Are you awake?"

The Dreman continued to make a sound that was somewhere between a dull roar and a clogged, four-hundred-year-old sewage drain.

That would be, "No."

As Liankataka inhaled rather audibly, Gold made a mental note to see if Pulaski had discovered a cure for snoring among the Dremans five years before. If anything, the guardian's mate would probably be grateful.

It was at that point that his throat chose to remind him of its occasional need for such things as water. The merest thought of raising his voice above a whisper only brought on the urge to cough. The pain he could resist. The coughing, however. . . .

A coughing fit racked his body, only serving to leave his throat rawer than it had been before. Sounds of sleepers awakening reached his ears. He tried to apologize, but before he could get the words out, another cough hit. *Damn the pain. I need a drink.*

His entire body shuddered as he slowly moved onto his hands and knees and crawled the few inches to the pool of water. Cupping his hands, he dipped them into the lukewarm pool and lifted them to his lips. It was almost like drinking liquid sandpaper, the dust was so thick, but it was fluid, and that was all that mattered.

Handful after handful of water began to sate his thirst, but it reminded him that he still hadn't allowed himself to indulge in any of the food that Jakara had so graciously split with them. His stomach growled as he dragged himself back to where he'd been laying.

"Captain, are you all right?" Liankataka asked. The Dreman had propped himself up on his elbows, and Gold could see the concern in his features, even in the low light.

"Just thirsty," Gold said, cringing at how scratchy his voice must have sounded. "I'm sorry I woke you." Gold hesitated, then asked, "How can you remain so calm, Guardian?" Gold asked. "Does this happen that often here?"

The guardian smiled. "I have faith in my people, Captain. We run emergency response drills twice a year so we can be prepared for anything our mines wish to do. I trust that my people are prepared."

Finding his ration of food, Gold tore a small piece off of the bread, and a two fingers' width piece from the dried meat. *It's probably not kosher, but I'll talk to Rachel when I get back about the* kashrut *laws in a situation like this.* The bread was dry, but had a honey flavor to it. Mixed in with the honey was a surprising mild nutty flavor. It reminded him of some of the honey-wheat breads that Rachel made. The meat, on the other hand, was both salty and spicy at the same time. It tasted almost like turkey marinated in garlic. In any other instance, he would have found the taste quite welcome, but as soon as he swallowed the last morsel of meat he would allow himself for the time being, he was crawling back over to the water.

Gold checked the chronometer once again. Eighteen excruciating hours had passed since the collapse.

He glanced over at Kajana. The woman's arms were still wrapped tightly around her legs, but she looked as though she'd fallen asleep in that position. "Kajana?" he asked. "Kajana, can you hear me?"

Liankataka reached around and put a hand on her arm. That was enough to cause her to flinch.

She raised her head to them, and there was wildness in her eyes that Gold didn't like. "Be careful. She doesn't look herself."

Liankataka backed his hand away, apparently noticing the same thing. "Kajana," he whispered. "Kajana, I know you're frightened."

"I've seen this before," Gold said. "Kajana, are you afraid of closed spaces?"

The light from the tricorder hit her tear-stained face. She looked at him, but somehow seemed to be looking *through* him. The strained expression she'd worn since they first discovered the trapped miners' existence lessened just a bit. "Yes," she whispered.

"It's okay. So am I," Gold said. He'd seen panic attacks like this before during the Cardassian War. There were times when being able to identify with someone helped. "Have you eaten anything yet?"

She shook her head.

"Where is your ration?"

Kajana retrieved the small packet of food from under her bent knees. She raised her eyes back to him, and Gold could see the pleading in that gaze. She was frightened beyond her capacity to cope and wanted help getting through it.

"Don't be afraid," he said. "Let me help."

As he dragged himself back to his hands and knees, Gold was surprised to discover that the pain in his ankles wasn't quite as severe as it had been just a few minutes ago. It was probably a bad sign, but he was grateful for the temporary respite from the eye-crossing agony. *Don't look a gift horse in the mouth, David.*

He slid into a sitting position beside Kajana, holding out a hand toward the bread. "Trust me."

With a trembling hand, she handed him the small chunk of bread. Gold broke off a small piece and handed it back to her. "Eat this," he said. As she slowly put it into her mouth and began chewing, he reached over and took a slice of meat. He tore off a small portion and handed it to her. "Now this. Eat it slowly."

Kajana was beginning to remind him of Eden when she'd gone through a bout of progressively nasty nightmares shortly before her thirteenth birthday. While Kajana chewed, Gold reached his arm around her shoulders and held her as she ate.

"Guardian?" Eijeth called out from the level above. "Are you all right?"

"Yes," Liankataka replied. "Our lovely companion is a bit frightened, however. Captain Gold is tending to her. How are our diggers?"

"Getting back to work, sir," Jakara said.

While he had yet to actually meet the man behind Eijeth's voice, Gold found that he liked Jakara. There was something old-fashioned about the man. From the way he'd been openly willing to share his only remaining food with them and the way he'd dove into the digging work, Gold didn't think there was a selfish bone in Jakara's rather sizeable body.

As the sound of pebbles falling into the water once again filled the cavern, something occurred to him. "Where is the air coming from?"

"What?" Liankataka asked.

"The air. We've been down here almost a day, and the air hasn't gotten stale yet. Somehow, we're getting air down here."

"The tube," Kajana whispered.

"What?"

Kajana raised her head from Gold's shoulder, nervously licking her lips. "The tube. It runs down the mineshaft in a corner on the floor."

Gold gently patted the side of Kajana's head, urging her to place her head back on his shoulder. He made a mental note to ask Jakara to see if he could find the pipe when the burly Dreman took a break.

At least he had an answer to that question. The eight million more that were going through his head, however. . . .

CHAPTER
14

Latik Kerjna, Drema IV
Capital Square
Day 2

Sarjenka was still running when she reached Federation's triage site. Three small temporary shelters were set up in front of a raised platform. Off to her left, she could see another small structure with what looked to be a transport ship beside it. She'd never actually seen one in person before, but she thought she'd caught sight of something similar flying over the area the afternoon before.

She stepped closer, wondering if anyone was actually there. There was sufficient evidence that someone had been there at one point, but that was meaningless to her right then. She needed someone there *now*.

That was when she caught the aroma of something that smelled absolutely heavenly floating on the breeze. It was a little like *jeeka* sausage, but a little more sweet-smelling, and it was accompanied by an aroma not unlike toasted *keena* bread.

"Hello?" she asked, raising her voice in an attempt to be heard over the few meters between where she stood and the source of that magnificent aroma.

A quick, building whine greeted her, and before she knew it, she was staring at the business end of some kind of weapon.

It was held in the hands of a large—very large—human wearing a uniform that was a wonderful shade of gold, with black sleeves and pants. She didn't know much about human physiology, but from what little she'd discovered, this one looked to be male. She'd never seen skin as dark as this human's on anyone before. For that matter, everything about him was dark, including his eyes, which had yet to waver from where she stood. "I-I-I am a friend." Holding up both hands to show she did not carry a weapon, she stared into that suspicious glare and said, "I'm looking for a healer."

The weapon lowered slightly. "Healer? I thought your people had doctors?"

"Yes," Sarjenka said, giving a quick nod. "But my people don't know how to treat injuries like this."

The suspicious look slowly faded from the human's face. "And you thought we would."

"Yes. Please." She hoped she didn't sound too desparate as she said, "It's my father."

Moving the weapon to his right hand, he retrained it on her as his left hand touched a piece of jewelry on his uniform. "Xavier to Pulaski. I've got a native out here who's asking for a doctor. Says her father's injured."

"Tell them my father found the bomb."

That got a raised eyebrow out of Xavier. "Did you hear that, Doc?"

"I'll be right there."

"Got it. Xavier out."

No sooner did the words leave his mouth than a human woman stepped out from behind the shelter. She, too, wore the uniform of the Federation, but where Xavier's was gold, and Tucker's had been red, hers was blue. She had short, curly, gray hair; pale skin; and a friendly expression. Something tingled in the back of Sarjenka's mind. She knew the feeling too well. The woman—Pulaski, she assumed from the conversation—was familiar, but she couldn't place where or when they'd ever met.

"Yes?"

Under normal conditions, she would have greeted the human healer with the usual *leevka* fingertip greeting, but having a weapon pointed at her hardly made these normal conditions. Sarjenka decided propriety would have to wait. As she could see no sign of recognition from the woman, she tried to push the feeling of familiarity from her mind. Right now, she had more important things to deal with. "Please. We require your assistance. My father is seriously injured. Our healers don't know how to help."

"You said he found the bomb?"

Sarjenka nodded. "When it exploded, it amputated the hand and most of the arm he held it in. He has lost more blood than our healers can handle. The best we can do is patch up his wounds and hope for the best. Can you help him?"

So much for that needle in the haystack.

Katherine Pulaski stared down at the young woman, trying desperately to keep the sense of recognition from seeping into her expression. The features had lengthened slightly as she'd gotten older, and the girl had grown about a half-meter in the last five years, but Pulaski was certain it was Sarjenka. It was an odd sensation, the thought of the child whose memories she'd taken now coming to her for help. But she needed help. Her father needed help. And that was what they were there to offer.

Still, the idea of treating a severely injured bomb victim without a full sickbay to work in wasn't something that filled her with hope. From what Klesaris had told her of the *Trosper,* the sickbay of the *Oberth*-class ship might be sufficient for what she needed, but it would be a borderline scenario at best. Even the most up-to-date upgrades she'd seen on a ship of that class had been ten years out-of-date. *If we could just get him to the station . . .*

"I can't be sure," Pulaski said, knowing full well how evasive she sounded. "Nobody found his arm?"

Sarjenka shook her head, the girl's shoulder-length, red hair showing only the slightest flecks of gold.

"How severe are the burns?"

Sarjenka's expression sank. "Bad. Very bad. I'm only an apprentice healer, but I can tell they're beyond our capacity to treat to recovery. It's up to him. He'll bear the scars for whatever time remains to him."

Pulaski frowned. She hadn't thought about trying to attach a synthetic limb to a Dreman yet, especially not one that had also endured severe burns. She wasn't even sure it was possible, as their vascular system was just different enough from a human's to make it difficult to be sure the connections would work properly.

The dermal regenerators would get a workout, but it might be worth the risk, if she could just examine the patient. "Where's your father?"

Sarjenka smiled more broadly than Pulaski would have thought the girl capable. However, she'd seen smiles like that before. It was the look of someone grabbing onto hope for dear life, but not sure whether that lifeline was covered in thorns.

Pulaski also clung to a hope: the hope that she would be able to fulfill the girl's wish.

CHAPTER
15

Latik Kerjna, Drema IV
Central Hospital
Day 2

"These burns are bad, but if it's any consolation, I've seen worse," Katherine said as she gently peeled back a burn gauze from Sarjenka's heavily-sedated father's remaining arm and looked at the damage with a distasteful expression.

The woman reached into a small pouch she'd referred to as a medkit and pulled out a gadget. Sarjenka stared as she adjusted a few settings, then began running it over the surviving arm.

"You're a healer?" the woman asked, sounding genuinely curious.

Sarjenka wanted to ask what that had to do with her father's condition, but somehow managed to restrain her tongue. Instead, she said, "I'm studying to be one, yes. . . ." Her voice trailed off as she tried to remember what the dark-skinned human had called the woman. It hadn't been Healer. It had been something else. After a few seconds of fighting with her memory, it came back. "Yes, Doctor."

The human woman smiled, kind and benevolent. "You may call me Katherine."

"I'm Sarjenka."

An odd sense of relief appeared in Katherine's eyes. "It's a pleasure to meet you, Sarjenka."

Katherine delicately removed one of the burn gauzes from Eliatriel's remaining forearm. The skin was still heavily blistered, but it appeared that Healer Drankla had been successful in removing all of the bomb fragments from his skin. *What if there are more under the surface?*

Almost as if she had been reading Sarjenka's mind, Katherine pulled out a small unit that had a visual display, extracted something from it, and began running the object over her father's arm. "It appears that your surgeons got all of the shrapnel. I'm not sensing any inorganic objects under the skin."

Sarjenka stared at the small unit Katherine held, trying to figure out why there was something so *familiar* about it.

Katherine moved from her father's arm to the rest of his body. "Did you know there was a small fracture in his fifth cervical vertebra?"

Sarjenka shook her head. "No. What is that you're holding?"

The woman opened her palm to reveal a small, cylindrical unit that barely fit in her hand. "This? It's a medical scanner. It's designed to run several kinds of medical tests and give diagnostic readings of almost any body process. I can have all the important test results I need in a matter of seconds."

A seed of hope began to plant itself in Sarjenka's heart. She hadn't questioned the decision to find a Federation healer when Drankla hadn't been able to handle the level of damage, and now she was seeing proof that she'd been right. The corners of her lips turned up in a small smile. "Thank you."

"For what?" Katherine asked.

"Helping. I feel he will be safe in your hands."

At that, Katherine's expression turned serious. "I may need to take him back to the space station, Sarjenka. I can do the preliminary treatments here, but major dermal regeneration is something this field team just isn't equipped to handle."

She wasn't sure she liked the idea of her father going away to recover, but it was better than the alternative. "Do whatever you need to do, Doctor."

Before she could get another word of gratitude out, the door to Eliatriel's room opened. Sinterka leaned in, his expression somber. "Sarj? Do you have a minute?"

She didn't like the look on his face, not one bit. "What happened?"

"They need you at the pithead."

CHAPTER
16

When Sarjenka arrived at the pithead, she was surprised to see that several healers had come, including Drankla. The senior healer's gold hair was matted with perspiration, his white robes soiled with the green dust of the mines. Healer Nekara looked the same, as did the others.

Federation officers were also milling about the scene, although she wasn't sure precisely what they were doing. A tall female with a blue uniform, long red hair pulled up on the back of her head, and a friendly face seemed to be telling them what to do. Still, Sarjenka was curious about every box, crate, and gadget she saw.

But she couldn't shake that nagging familiarity about some of the equipment.

"Sarjenka!"

Sinterka's voice brought her back to reality. She walked over to where he stood near the pithead itself, with Drankla and Nekara between him and the enormous funnel-shaped hole that had formed around the collapse.

"Tell her," Sinterka said, his voice insistent. "Tell her why we need her."

Drankla and Nekara exchanged a look, almost as though they were trying to figure out who would start. They pulled her from her father's bedside for this?

"Would one of you please tell me?" she asked, growing impatient.

Finally, Drankla pulled himself up to his full height and said, "The Federation engineers aren't sure how stable the area is. They're trying to decide if they want to pack up and retreat to Capital Square now. Weight is an issue. We need someone small and light to go into the mine and check on the people down there."

Sarjenka swallowed hard. They wanted *her* to go into the *mine*? She'd been pursuing a career as healer to avoid just such an event. "What about the Federation healers? Do they have any transportation devices like the Exiles had? What if they could transport into the mine shaft?"

Nekara shook his head. With the gold-and-red patterned surgical cap covering his fore lobes, his rounded skull almost looked like a moon trying to rotate.

"They've attempted it already," Drankla said. "I didn't understand what the exact difficulty was, but they said something about the interference having the same effect as a dampening field. Their computers can't—what did he say? They can't get a lock."

"So, it's up to the miners to go down and get them." Sinterka said. She saw a resolution in his eyes that she couldn't recall ever seeing before. "We need people who can fit into small spaces, and the first person I thought of when the subject of healers came around was you."

She tried weighing the options. If she went down there, she could die in another collapse and never see her parents again.

The same could be said for just standing around on the surface. From the looks of it, the radius of the collapse had spread to at least two *kilopars* in every direction. It was just a visual estimate, but it certainly looked as though two of her could span the chasm.

And that expanse surrounded a five *kilopar*-deep hole. What was at the bottom of that hole? The top of another one—this time much deeper and much more dangerous. One that she'd have to crawl into and then try work on patients in *Traiaka* knew what condition, while the very real possibility of the roof collapsing on her literally hung over her head.

"Nnno problem. We fffind the pppeople."

In search of the source of the gurgling voice, Sarjenka looked down to see a small oddly shaped creature with a round head—the top being a little bit smaller than the bottom. Its yellow eyes opened sideways, the actual eyelids themselves vertical slits. It had—well, she wasn't quite certain what it had for an internal support structure, but it looked far more adaptable to small spaces than anyone else in the area. She could see some of that skeleton through the creature's pale, blue skin. If it wasn't bone as in a Dreman anatomy, the creature's weight would be very little, indeed.

Whatever it was, it was fascinating.

Its bright eyes looked up at her. *Or, is it sideways for you, little creature?*

"Wwwe go down ttto fix problem now?"

Its mouth never left an O-shape form as it spoke, and it sounded as though it were speaking underwater. It wore a black and yellow Federation uniform, and in one of its seven-fingered hands was a tool kit. On its back was a small pack. Sarjenka assumed it contained the tools the creature would need for the expedition.

A quick glance at Drankla and Nekara showed her something she didn't expect to see in the two men, revulsion.

"'Harm not,' Healers," she said chidingly. "Did you expect members of the Federation all to be human?"

The opportunity to observe this little creature certainly appealed to her curiosity. Was the risk to her life worth such a thing though?

She dropped to her knees, which brought her to eye level with the creature. Holding her hands out, she gave it the standard *leevka* fingertip greeting. "I am Sarjenka. What should I call you?"

The creature tilted its head to its right. "Lllolo. Lllolo fix machines."

"Lolo," she said. "Why are they sending you?"

"Ppput up juranium sssupports," it said, holding up a small, silver-black beam that was about the length and width of her arm. "Kkkeep mine safe."

She felt a slight pang of gratitude, hoping her father lived long enough to thank the Federation for taking care of his planet in such a manner.

"And fffind and fffix bbbombs."

They really think there may be more down there? Her stomach sank. "And what if there are no bombs?"

"Ttthen Lolo work on ttttransppporter ppproblem."

She looked at Lolo's bright yellow eyes and realized that she had been trying to do nothing more than come up with excuses for being a coward. If this little creature, with its strange speech and seven tiny webbed fingers on each hand could muster the courage to go into probable death, then how could she be so selfish?

Turning, Sarjenka found Sinterka still standing a short distance off. "All right," she said. "Let's go."

CHAPTER
17

Latik Kerjna, Drema IV
Pithead, Dilithium Mine Alpha
Day 2

Sarjenka wiped perspiration from her brow. Shifting her weight as little as possible, she turned to check on Lolo—who was still working behind her—fusing the new duranium supports which the Federation engineers had created for the mineshaft into place as they went. According to one of the officers, who had looked to be a human, but had pointed ears, hair as dark as the night's sky, and never smiled in the entire time he'd been helping Sinterka instruct them on what to do, the duranium supports also contained a small data pathway built in that would, as he put it, "Allow a targeting signal to get a firm lock through the dilithium's interference."

Sinterka had shown her the digging process, saying that this was what had been done since the collapse: One person dug, while another moved the dirt to a safer location. They needed to make sure that as little weight as possible was over the remnants of the shaft, as they couldn't be sure of the stability of the area around the pithead. Lolo had wanted to vaporize the dirt, eliminating it once it had been brought to the surface, but the creature was overruled by a very robust, good-natured

Federation officer named Walsh. The human male had been unsure of how the weapon's energy would dissipate within the dilithium, and they wanted to mitigate the risk to the rest of the planet as much as they could. He'd seen the reports, and the last thing he wanted to do was chance that the planet would try to tear itself apart again.

Sarjenka couldn't help but agree. As destructive as the Exiles had been, they had nothing on the tremors. The risk of bringing the superior technology to bear on the problem was just too great.

So, with Sarjenka digging and Lolo working in the supports behind them, they grabbed work kits, water, and headlamps, then walked into the pit to start work.

After what felt like hours of digging in silence, Lolo said, "Ssswim."

Sarjenka thought she heard a touch of lost spirit in that one word. "Swim?" she asked.

"Yes. Dddust in my gggills. Swim wwwould help. Belandros an ooocean planet."

Watching her movement, she turned toward Lolo. "Gills? What are those?"

"Bbbreathe in water," Lolo said, pulling down the neckline on the uniform. She could see what looked like slits in its skin, slowly opening and closing in a rhythm she associated with breathing. Curious.

"Didn't your people pack water for you to drink?" she asked. "Do your people *need* water to drink?"

Lolo cocked its head sideways, apparently thinking it over. Finally, it said, "Yes."

With that, the little creature dug through its pack, moving aside the ration bars the Federation people had given them both and digging out one of the five bottles of water they'd also packed. Lolo unscrewed the top, leaned back, and poured the bottle's content over its gills. While Sarjenka watched, the gills opened and closed several more times, and murky, dark green water flowed back down the front of its uniform.

The little creature's yellow eyes brightened, and it wiggled its fingers as if stretching them after a long rest.

"Eeeasy fix. Ttthank you. Tttoo tired to ttthink properly."

She fought the urge to smile. "Are all of the Federation officers as . . . different . . . as you are?"

It fixed her with a noticeably sharpened yellow gaze. "Hhhow different?"

Sarjenka pursed her lips, trying to figure out a way to rephrase the question. When one finally came to her, she said, "The other Federation officers that came with you—"

"SSStarfleet," Lolo said. "Wwwe are Starfleet officers."

"All right. The other Starfleet officers—they all look human. And there's you. What's Starfleet like?"

"One Vvvulcan. Wwwhen we finish dddigging, I tell you. Ooookay?"

Sarjenka's curiosity was dragged back to reality by that. "Okay," she said, turning back toward the pile of greenish-brown dirt that rested beneath her knees. They dug for a bit longer— she hadn't thought to bring a time-teller, so she wasn't really sure how long they'd worked—when her digging met with a bit of resistance. Her large brow furrowed. It didn't feel like anything she would have expected to find in a collapse. Placing the shovel aside, she began to gently pull dirt away by hand. Pebble by pebble, she began to uncover it and realized that it was a tube-like object.

Her eyes widened as she realized what, in fact, the thing most likely was.

"Lolo," she said, "we need to go back to the surface. Now."

"Nnnow? Wwwhy?"

She quickly reached back and grabbed the portable light. "See that?" she said, shining it on the object. "That's a bomb. Get to the surface."

Lolo's eyes widened. "Bbbomb?"

"Yes. I don't know if I triggered it or not."

"Nnnot eeexplode."

Sarjenka shook her head. "My father got the one he found all the way to the surface before it exploded."

"Nnno ppproblem," the tiny creature said, seeming to muster its courage. "Eeeasy fix. Gggo to surface in cccase."

"What are you going to do?"

"Fffix bomb." It cocked its head to the side, eyes narrowing. "Sssurface. Gggo."

"But—"

"Gggo!"

Sarjenka crawled back out of the series of supports Lolo had been erecting, stopping at the opening and turning back to see what it was doing. The little creature had closed its eyes, and was reaching its left hand down into the dirt. She could see the arm occasionally move, almost as if he somehow had muscles under the skin.

Seconds passed until Lolo appeared to get frustrated with something, and then raised its other hand to tap the portable communicator on its uniform. "Lllolo to *Tttrosper.* Lllock on mmmy signal with tttransporter. Bbboost lock signal as mmmuch as possible. Hhhighly explosive. Bbbeam to ccclear ssspace. Wide dddisperse. Ttthree sssecond dddelay."

A female voice said, *"Explosive, aye. Boosting signal one-hundred twenty-five percent. Three second delay beam out to clear space, wide dispersal."*

What was it doing?

Before she could figure that out, Lolo removed the communicator from his uniform, attached it to what little of the bomb it had unearthed, and reached a hand around it. In one quick, smooth motion, it pulled the bomb the rest of the way out of the ground and threw it straight into the air. A flash of gold told her that the communicator had somehow remained attached. Just as the bomb reached the height of its flight, at least two *kilopars* over the surface proper, a silver shimmer formed around it, and it disappeared.

Sarjenka could do nothing more than stare. Was that *their* transporter? She shook her head, attempting to send the fog she felt with the bomb.

When she finally regained her wits, she looked down into

the pit. Lolo was standing there, arms at his sides and . . . *was that its toe tapping?*

"Nnno problem. Eeeasy fix."

"Are you insane?" she said, walking back into the pit far more gingerly than she had before. "You could have been killed!"

"Bbbut I was nnnot," it replied, sounding as though nothing at all dangerous had happened. "Lllolo fix bomb."

Sarjenka's eyes went to the blue sky over them and then back to Lolo. "Yes, you did. Would you show us how? We've never been able to keep them from detonating."

The little creature's head cocked to the side. "Nnno problem. Bbback to work?"

Sarjenka looked down at the mound of dirt that was still beneath them. Shovel in hand, she mustered all of her resolve and said, "Back to work."

CHAPTER
18

Latik Kerjna, Drema IV
Bottom of Dilithium Mine Alpha
Day 2

Gold checked the chronometer. Eight hours since her break-down, and Kajana seemed to have recovered somewhat. She scooted a few inches away from the wall, but she was facing away from them, so what little light they did have from the tricorder's display didn't tell him much. She hadn't turned that panicked look on either of them for at least an hour, though.

He could hear Jakara and Eijeth working at the veritable mountain of dirt that had them trapped. They hadn't seen much of the two men since they began their work, apparently spurred on more after they realized Kajana's plight.

He reached down and grabbed another two fingers' worth of the dried meat. He finished off the bread an hour ago and was almost at the end of his first strip of meat. He'd been trying hard to stagger his nibbles, giving at least two hours between bites, but his arms were beginning to shake just moving to pick up the meat.

The sound of scraping at the dirt mound stopped for a moment, and then Jakara's voice said, "I think I hear more digging."

Liankataka pepped up at that. "Finally."

"I hear it, too," Eijeth said.

Kajana's head popped up from its resting place on her knees. "Thank you, *Traiaka*. How long have we been down here?"

"A little over a day," Gold replied.

Kajana feebly tried to raise her arm. "I feel weak."

"It's the lack of food," Gold began. "Eat a little bit more of the meat for now. We'll be okay once we can get to the surface and get a day or two of real food in us."

The sound of digging resumed. "Hello?" Jakara said, his distant voice raising. "Who's there?"

No sign of an answer. The digging doubled in intensity, presumably as Eijeth rejoined the effort, and Gold could hear the two men working faster than they had before.

That was when it happened.

A rumbling sounded in the ground around him. Pebbles began to fall lose from the cavern's ceiling, falling into the water until it almost sounded like a thunderstorm at work.

"What the—?" he started to ask, looking to Liankataka and Kajana to gauge their reactions. *Rumbling below the surface of a planet is never a good thing.*

Then the screaming began.

Sarjenka stopped digging, her heart leaping into her throat as the rumbling began. The memory of the collapse months before came immediately to mind. *It's over. We're too heavy.*

Behind her, Lolo stopped midway through fusing another piece of reinforcement into place. "Wwwhat ttthat?"

"If it's—"

She wasn't given a chance to finish that thought. No sooner did a shovel break through the dirt from the other side than everything underneath the spot she was kneeling gave way at once.

She tumbled down the mineshaft, somehow ending up going down the steep incline on her side. The stones felt like giant boulders, even though they were probably only a fingernail's width in size. When she thought it was going to go on forever, it stopped in a pool of water and a pelting of pebbles that felt as though she were being pummeled by an ice storm.

She expected Lolo to have been sucked into the mine after her, but when she raised her eyes, she discovered that the little creature had grabbed the rung of the last support. Lolo was hanging by both arms from the duranium pipe, out over the now far more open chasm. "Lolo!"

"Sssarjenka, help!"

She tried to scramble back up the incline, but tripped over something. Flipping her small wrist light around, she discovered an arm floating on the water. Moving the light further in, she realized that arm was attached to a very large Dreman. His eyes were closed, and his mouth hung open just enough for her to see that he hadn't gotten any water in there yet. "Lolo, hang on!"

The first thing Gold saw in the dim light was a bulk roughly Jakara's size hit the pool of water.

The second thing was something about half that size fall behind him, then try to crawl up the mineshaft, until they tripped. Judging by what little he could see of the young woman doing the yelling—Sarjenka, if what the voice he'd heard could be trusted—was barely big enough to be much help. However, even a little help was better than nothing.

He wasn't sure who Lolo was, but the last thing they needed was their would-be rescuers getting stuck along with them. There was barely enough food left as it was.

He could see a body floating on the surface, but then the young woman stood up, Gold began to get worried. "Sarjenka?" he said.

The young woman jumped back as though she'd been touched by the dead. She had what looked like a Starfleet-issued palm beacon in her right hand and flashed it back toward them. To eyes that had been in relative darkness for a day, the bright light hurt for a moment and then became the most welcome sight he could have imagined. He tried to scoot toward the pool of water, only to discover that his feet felt like nothing more than dead weight at the end of his legs.

"Could you check on Jakara please?" He gestured toward the figure floating face-up—he could now tell—in the water. "He hit the rocks hard."

Sarjenka leaned over the floating man, shining her light against his chest.

Gold saw what looked like breathing, but at that distance, it was difficult to be sure. "Does it look like he's breathing to you?"

"Yes, sir," she said. She reached down into the top of Jakara's work shirt, feeling for something. "He's got a pulse, so it looks like the fall just knocked him unconscious. Can you help me get him over there with you?"

"Can't move. My legs took some damage in the fall." With a shake of his head, Gold added. "There's barely enough room for the three of us as it is."

"Sssarjenka!"

She pointed the palm beacon back up the shaft. "Lolo, can you get a footing on something?" Her head jerked back. "What's that? Who's up there?"

"Me, ma'am. Name's Eijeth. I can help."

Sarjenka seemed to take in the situation and said, "Okay. Lolo, let Eijeth help you. Then we need help down here."

Shining the light once again at Gold, she said, "Who's injured besides you, Admiral?"

"I'm not Admiral Tucker, young woman," Gold said. "I'm Captain David Gold. Guardian Liankataka has some damage to his back, and Kajana here is suffering from what we call claustrophobia. If Dr. Katherine Pulaski is on the surface, she'll be able to help you with that. Up on Eijeth's level is someone with a bum ankle. I never saw him, but his name's Kajkob."

"We'll get you out of here, Captain Gold," she said before turning her attentions back to the still-floating Jakara. "All of you."

CHAPTER
19

Latik Kerjna, Drema IV
Uprising Memorial
Day 10

David Gold knelt beside Captain Don Walsh in the open field, both men bowing their heads in respect to the highly-polished terracotta red wall that was covered in inlaid dilithium-crystal glyphs and served as a memorial to those lost during the Dreman uprising.

Grabbing his knotted wood cane—a gift from Liankataka when Pulaski had insisted upon his not putting his full weight on his freshly-knit ankles—he pushed himself back to a standing position. The midday sun was warm, but after ten days either in a hole or in a hospital bed, it felt good to stand outside in the open air. A gentle breeze blew through the distant trees, carrying the verdant smell of the greenery with it.

"Well, Captain," Walsh said, extending a hand toward him. "I hear the *Progress* is due for reassignment. Same goes for the *Trosper.*"

Resting his weight against the cane, Gold shook the man's hand. "Good people you have there, Captain. Pulaski and Gom both briefed me on how you all worked with my people to get this done. It's going to be a shame to see them reassigned. Any idea where you're going to be posted next?"

Walsh shook his balding head. "Not a one. Waiting on the brass to send me a list of options. I'm not even sure if they're going to let me stay with the S.C.E. There's talk about the S.C.E. getting some of the new *Sabre*-class ships, though. Might be interesting to command one of those. They've got a little more firepower than the old *Oberth*-class."

Gold had heard about the *Sabre*-class project, mostly from a chief engineer who followed the comings and goings on Utopia Planitia like some people followed sporting teams, and while it sounded interesting, what got him more was the idea of a ship filled with predominantly engineers. *Sounds like it may be almost as boring as supply runs. But then, after today, I can't think of anyone else I'd want in a pinch.* "They really think the Borg'll be back?"

Walsh gave a cynical laugh. "Captain, if the Borg come back, a *Sabre* is going to need a lot more firepower than it's supposed to carry."

"Then it'll be good they've got so many engineers on board, won't it?" he said, half-smiling.

"Rrready to depart, Cccaptain."

Gold and Walsh both watched the tiny Belandrid pull himself up to his full height as he walked up to them and saluted. Gold looked down at the little creature and saluted in return. "Lolo, thank you."

"Fffor what, Cccaptain?"

Gold raised an eyebrow. "Doing your job, I guess."

"Yyyou're welcome, sir," Lolo said, inclining his head toward him.

"And thank that chief engineer of yours for coming up with the idea of routing the signal through the duranium reinforcement, Captain. Smart man you have there."

Walsh patted him on the shoulder. "Will do, Captain. Barreto will be glad to hear it. For a bunch of engineers, they're a good crew."

"Captain Gold!"

David Gold turned to find Sarjenka walking toward them,

her iridescent white tunic shimmering in the warm midday sun. She was accompanied by an older Dreman couple. The man was sitting in a wheelchair, had no hair, and his left arm was amputated. The woman was pushing the wheelchair. *Her parents? My God, that was her father?*

"Take care of yourself, Gold," Walsh said. "No matter where you end up, they're getting a good man."

"You, too, Captain. I hope our paths cross again."

Walsh smiled broadly before wandering off toward Barreto and the rest of his crew.

Gold hobbled forward, still not entirely used to using the cane. The ground in the field was more level than not, which helped the walking and, it seemed, piloting the wheelchair.

"Captain Gold," Sarjenka said, holding her hands out a fingertip's width over Gold's shoulders, then running them down his arms. "It's good to see you up and around after your ordeal."

Gold looked down at the man in the wheelchair. The man's face was covered in regenerated skin, which stood out in its slightly paler color than the typical cinnamon-red, especially when he tried to smile. His loose-fitting white trousers and shirt covered what he was sure was more regenerated skin. Pulaski had mentioned that she was going to try to attach a prosthetic arm, but it would take some time to perfect the process. "I could say the same about you. It's Eliatriel, right?"

"Yes, Captain. My daughter, she—"

"I want to go with you," Sarjenka said. "I watched Dr. Pulaski healing my father, and I want to learn your ways."

Gold gave her an apprising look. "Are you sure? It's not an easy place. You may not pass the entrance exam."

Her gaze hardened into that same one he'd seen in the cave, when she'd turned from a girl frightened by the fall into a healer sent in to administer first aid. She was resolute in her decision, and Gold got the distinct impression that if he didn't bring her, she'd badger Lieutenant Xavier to take her to the station and find alternate transport herself.

"All right," he finally said. "If your parents agree, I'll take you back to Earth with us. You can take the entrance exam at the facility there."

The smile that lit her face was one he hadn't seen since his daughter, Sarah, had been accepted into the conservatory.

He was already composing the letter of recommendation in his head, but he thought for sure he could get at least a couple of more letters out of people.

"Get your things, and meet me at Capital Square in three hours."

Without even so much as a "good-bye," she turned and sprinted off.

"Thank you, Captain," Eliatriel said. "All she's talked about for the last three days is Dr. Pulaski and your medical facilities. She loves to learn, that one."

"Well, she'll learn quite a bit," Gold said. "There's a big universe out there."

EPILOGUE

May 2377
Headquarters, Starfleet Medical

David Gold stood in one corner of the reception area, watching the internal broadcast of the ceremonies with far more interest than he'd ever shown on Drema IV, a fact he found himself regretting more by the day since he found out she was graduating. *Eight years is a long damned time.* He absently flexed his mechanical left hand. *A lot of things can change.*

Thanks to what she'd already studied on her home planet when she decided to go to the Academy, she'd been able to test out of a few courses, allowing her to shave almost a year off of her overall stay. Having a recommendation for bravery in the face of credible threat couldn't have hurt, either.

Gold made a mental note to send Liankataka a note thanking him for that memo. Lense needed help. There were no two ways around it. She'd get used to the idea of having an organic assistant CMO eventually.

Sonya Gomez walked up beside him, a small, content smile on her face. He hadn't seen that look on her face for far, far too long. "Bringing back memories, Gomez?"

His first officer nodded. "And none of them good."

"Then why are you smiling?"

She let out a small, nervous laugh. "I think this is the first time we've brought new crew on board, and it wasn't to fill some kind of void. It's about time we brought someone on for a positive reason."

"Huh," Gold said. "I think you're right."

"We don't have much extra space, so we shouldn't make a habit out of it," Gomez quickly added. "We'd end up with people sleeping in the hallways. And you *know* how well Domenica would take that."

Gold tried his best not to laugh. Instead, he said, "We haven't brought her on board yet, Gomez. The choice is still hers. We're just here to make the offer."

"May I ask you a question, sir?"

"Of course."

He could see Gomez scanning the rest of that year's graduating class. Gold had stopped counting after a while, adjusting his estimate of their numbers to somewhere between "enormous" and "ridiculous."

"Why did you back her application to the Academy?"

"He didn't." Rachel Gilman walked up, a glass of champagne in hand. Her short, graying brown curls still seemed a bit more matronly than the sleeveless, very fitted black dress she'd chosen for the reception. He still knew better than to try to change his wife's mind about anything, however, and hadn't even brought up the subject.

In the corner of his eye, Gold saw Gomez do a double-take. "Her record lists a letter of recommendation from you."

"Oh, I sent a letter of recommendation," he said, "but I wasn't the one who ended up backing her application."

Before Gomez could get another word out, a very familiar face approached. Her already gray curls had become a little lighter in the intervening years, and a couple more lines had etched themselves into her features, but Katherine Pulaski still looked much the same as when he'd left her on Drema Station years before.

No, she looks happier. Working in that institute must be doing her good.

"Captain Gold. Rabbi Gilman. Good to see you again. Commander Gomez, it's been a long time."

Gomez shook off the look of surprise. "Dr. Pulaski? What brings you in from the Phlox Institute?"

An enigmatic look spread across the doctor's features. "They asked me to give one of the commencement addresses. What brings the two of you to graduation ceremonies for Starfleet Medical?"

Raising one gray eyebrow, Gold gave Pulaski a sideways glance. Her name had been nowhere to be found on the commencement program. "We're here to discuss a staffing issue with someone."

Folding her hands behind the small of her back, Pulaski said, "I heard about your CMO, Captain. Good news travels fast. Elizabeth Lense is one of the best we have. Please give her my congratulations on the baby."

Gomez gave a curt nod. "Of course, Doctor."

On the monitors, student after student in vivid royal blue commencement robes passed across the dais and received his or her diploma.

"Cccaptain Gold?"

Gold nodded, looking down to find a tiny Belandrid in a formal operations-yellow uniform standing just to Rachel's right. "Lolo? Is that you? How have you been?"

"Nnno problems," it said, puffing with pride. "Assigned to the *Hhhood* now. Dddeputy Chief Engineer."

Gold introduced his wife and Commander Gomez to the little creature, and both women seemed intrigued with the Belandrid.

When the graduate finally walked over to them, her blue-and-black dress uniform was immaculate. Her commencement robe was slung over her left arm, and a small etched crystal cylinder was in her right hand. He'd heard they were redesigning the diplomas for both Starfleet Academy and the Medical Academy, but he hadn't yet seen one.

"Blue is your color," Gold said.

Sarjenka blinked quickly, then snapped to attention, but Gold quickly shushed her with a hand. "This is your graduation," he said. Quickly checking her uniform collar, he was pleased to see that she'd already attained a junior-grade lieutenant ranking. "Lieutenant," he added, "how does it feel?"

"Good, sir."

"Requested assignment to Drema Station, I see? Dr. Klesaris needs help already?" Gold raised an eyebrow and then shot Pulaski a glance. The look he got in return just said, "very funny, now get on with it."

Sarjenka looked down at the diploma in her hand. "I wanted to take this knowledge back to help my people, Captain. However, I understand that until Starfleet sees fit to allow me to leave, I'm obligated to serve."

Gold looked over at Gomez and Rachel, who had torn themselves away from asking Lolo questions. Rachel gave him that soft look that she always did when trying to encourage him to go through with something.

"I'm here to offer you an opportunity to go where you're needed, Lieutenant."

"Excuse me, sir?"

Raising his eyes back to Sarjenka, he said, "What would you say if I told you we need your help?"

"*We*, sir? What kind of help do you require?"

Gomez took a step forward. "The *da Vinci*'s CMO is expecting a child. She has come up with bad idea after bad idea to try to distract me from the fact that she desperately needs an assistant. We need someone who can stand up to her if necessary, who'll do what it takes to treat the patient, and who'll stand up to Captain Gold if he won't come in for his checkups."

Gold rolled his eyes at that. "I've been in for every one of my checkups, Gomez," he said, playing along.

"Of course you have, sir."

Rachel cocked one eyebrow. "And the messages they've sent me were nothing but social calls." Leaning over to Sarjenka, her voice took a more conspiratorial tone. "He may look like a teddy bear, but he *hates* being poked and prodded. He won't tell you that, but he does."

Sarjenka let out a giggle. Pulling herself back together, she said, "Are you asking me to join your crew, sir?"

"That's what I'm asking, Lieutenant."

She made a grand show of thinking it over, then smiled as broadly as she had that day he'd agreed to bring her to Earth, and said, "I'd be honored, sir."

THE FUTURE BEGINS

Steve Mollmann & Michael Schuster

Dedicated to the memory of James Montgomery Doohan

ACKNOWLEDGMENTS

Michael wants to thank his parents for their continuing support, even though they have no great love for science fiction. He'd also like to thank every one of his English teachers—most of all, however, his two favorite teachers, Ray Flanagan and Martina Friedrich. Finally, he wants to thank his very good friend Angelika Heininger, who has been there for him ever since they stumbled across each other on the original Psi Phi *Star Trek* Books Board.

Steve would like to thank his parents as well, without whom he would probably not exist. He would like to apologize to his mother, to whom this novel would have been dedicated if unfortunate circumstances had not intervened. He will make it up someday.

As this story would never have been written if there had not been contradictory accounts of what Scotty was doing in 2375/76, which we tried to reconcile, it seems only fair to thank the people responsible for these stories. They are: Peter David, for the *Star Trek: New Frontier* novels *Renaissance* and *Restoration*, and John J. Ordover and Keith R.A. DeCandido, for the creation of the eBook series *Star Trek: Starfleet Corps of Engineers* and the inclusion of Scotty as a recurring character in said series.

We would be remiss if we didn't also thank the writers of other stories and reference works which were used in the writing of this eBook. They include Christopher L. Bennett, Diane Carey, Gene DeWeese, Kevin Dilmore, Diane Duane, Julia Ecklar, Michael Jan Friedman, Robert Greenberger, Vonda N. McIntyre, Robert J. Mendenhall, Michael Okuda, Scott Pearson, Judith and Garfield Reeves-Stevens, William Rotsler, Kevin Ryan, Rick Sternbach, Dayton Ward, Howard Weinstein, and whoever wrote "A Page from Scotty's Diary" in the collections of the old Gold Key comics, as well as the aforementioned Mssrs. David, DeCandido, and Ordover.

Aptly enough for a series about futuristic technology and engineers, we also owe thanks to the inventors and developers of the Arpanet, which evolved into the Internet that we know and love today. Without instant worldwide communication in the form of email, this story would not have been written.

But most of all, we want to thank James Doohan for giving us such a memorable character in his portrayal of a Scottish engineer. He will not be forgotten.

Prologue

Stardate 53509.4
May 2376, Old Earth Time

Geordi La Forge materialized right in front of the Tucker Memorial Building, the beam having been ably targeted by *Enterprise*'s Vulcan transporter chief. The Tucker Building, adjacent to Starfleet Medical Headquarters, housed the Earth-based facilities of the Corps of Engineers. Those consisted of several offices, of course, and numerous labs where Starfleet's best engineers analyzed alien technologies, developed new ones of their own, and fixed anything that came their way.

Basically, it was a building full of very skilled tinkers.

La Forge quickly stepped up the flight of stairs leading to the building's front doors, which automatically swished open to admit him. The lobby of the building was dominated by a massive replica of Zefram Cochrane's *Phoenix*, which La Forge had not only seen in real life, but actually sat in only a few years ago. Around the circumference of the room were holoframes depicting many other great engineers who had served in Starfleet over the centuries, from the one that gave the building its name to George William Jefferies to Mahmud al-Khaled.

One of the holoframes was switched off, presumably out of a sense of modesty, as its subject was alive and well and presently berating another engineer by the lobby's main desk. "What do you mean, you don't have the report on the time corridor generator! You told me you would have it ready in a week!"

The engineer, a Vissian woman by the look of it, attempted to mount a defense. "Sir, that generator was buried on Mars for over two centuries, and is in *horrible* shape. A week was our minimum estimate—"

Captain Montgomery Scott, head of the Starfleet Corps of Engineers, shook his head mournfully. "Lassie, do they not teach you anything? Always multiply your estimates—your *maximum* estimates—by a factor of four."

La Forge cut in as he drew closer to the arguing pair. "He's right, Ensign. That way you look like a miracle worker."

Abruptly, Scotty turned to see the new arrival. "Geordi lad! 'Tis good to see you." He grabbed La Forge's hand and shook it most vigorously, then turned back to face the Vissian. "When I first met this lad, he was as bad as you. But I taught him how a *real* engineer works, so there's hope for you, too."

La Forge managed a weak smile at the Vissian. He admired and respected Scotty, and considered him a good friend, but the man's philosophy on reporting to one's superiors left something to be desired, in his mind.

"Now go on, and get back to work." The Vissian ran off for parts unknown.

Scotty turned to face La Forge once more. "What are you doin' here, lad? Not that I'm unhappy to see you."

"It's good to see you too, Scotty." It had been a few years since they had last encountered one another, aside from the occasional subspace communication. "The *Enterprise* is here for some repairs after that whole gateways mess, but I decided I needed some time off."

Scotty sighed. "I wish *I* could get some time off." He set off for one of the lifts at the far end of the lobby, indicating La Forge should follow him. "I thought the reconstruction work had us spread thin enough, but the gateways crisis has made everythin' twice as bad. Every one of my teams is tied up somewhere, and I've got a dozen admirals askin' me to move each of them to two other places, at the very least."

They entered the lift, which Scotty ordered to the appropriate destination. "How are things with you, lad?"

"Not much better," said La Forge. "It's been one crisis after another ever since the war ended, from Gemworld on."

"Captain Gold said you spent some time on the *da Vinci*."

La Forge nodded. "I joined them for a few missions. It was certainly different from what I usually do, and I enjoyed it, but I was happy to return to the *Enterprise*. Sure, both ships were just as hectic, but at least on the *Enterprise* I'm not horning in on someone else's turf."

"Gold and Gomez both said you were a wonderful addition to the team," said Scotty as the lift doors opened, depositing them in a nondescript corridor. Scotty led the way down it.

"I suppose so," said La Forge. "But anyway, working with an S.C.E. team made me think of you, so I decided to drop in next time I was in the area."

"It's good that you did, lad," said Scotty. "I could use a break."

The two reached a door marked COMMAND LIAISON which opened as they approached to reveal a small office. "Good mornin', Deg," Scotty said to the Blood Many male sitting at the desk.

"Good morning, Captain Scott," replied the aide. "Good to see you in the office today."

"Ah, be quiet, lad, I have a guest." Scotty gestured unnecessarily at La Forge. "Do I have any appointments today?"

"Only your interview with Dr. Ven this afternoon," Deg replied immediately.

Scotty frowned. "What's that about, again?"

"He's looking for a medical position on an—"

Scotty waved off the rest of the sentence. "Tell him I'm sorry, but I'm out for the day, and I'll have to reschedule." Deg nodded, and began typing into his computer console. "Oh, and hold all my calls." Deg nodded again, and Scotty gestured at the bright red door at the back of the room. "After you, laddie," he said to La Forge.

La Forge stepped up to the door, somewhat out of place with its drab surroundings, and it slid open automatically. What it revealed was no ordinary office.

Scotty's office had been thoroughly redecorated in the style of a twenty-third-century *Constitution*-class vessel. There were bright primary colors everywhere, including the red grate dividing the portion of the room with the desk from that with some antique chairs. The desk itself was topped with a period-authentic three-sided computer monitor, and next to it sat a pile of old-fashioned duotronic computer cartridges.

"Scotty . . . this is amazing," La Forge said, finally stepping out of the doorway. As Scotty crossed into the office as well, and the doors closed behind him, La Forge noticed they had done so with the pneumatic swish characteristic, once again, of the time period.

"Thank you, lad," said Scotty. He stepped past La Forge to the "lounge" half of the room, where he sat himself down. The other engineer picked a seat across from him. "When I finally decided to take the job as head of the S.C.E. back in March, I determined the first thing I would do is make myself an office I would be comfortable in."

Scotty reached for a squat table next to him, grabbing a bottle and a couple of glasses. As he poured the drink—Scotch, La Forge presumed—into the glasses, Scotty continued. "Everythin's fully functional, even the computer disks. They're really isolinear chips with a casing around them so they work in my 'antique' adapted reader." He shook his head. "You don't know how many antique dealers tried to peddle off bad merchandise. One tried to tell me his twenty-second-century desktop monitor was from *my* time. Sure, it was three-sided, but that doesn't mean it was what I wanted."

La Forge grimaced as Scotty handed him the drink; it was Scotch, all right, and despite the other engineer's repeated efforts, he had yet to develop a taste for it. "You seem to be enjoying yourself, Scotty."

"Oh, that I am, lad, that I am," said Scotty, quickly downing his own cup of the drink. "I definitely made the right move when I accepted Ross's offer."

La Forge took a tentative sip of his cup. "Actually, I've been meaning to ask you about that. Since the last time I saw you, you've left the *Sovereign,* become head of the S.C.E., quit the job *and* Starfleet from what I hear, and returned in the same capacity. What is up with that?"

Scotty chuckled. "It's quite a tale, Geordi." He drank some more Scotch. "I'd like to tell it to you, but it's a wee bit classified in parts." Scotty paused for a moment. "Ah, hell, what's that between friends?"

La Forge shrugged. "Your secrets will be safe with me."

"Of that, I have no doubt, lad." Scotty finished off his glass, and began pouring another. "In the final months of the Dominion War, I was tapped by Admiral Ross to take over the Corps of Engineers from John. A couple months after takin' my new position, I found myself called away from Earth by a very young laddie and his shuttlecraft, to be taken to the *U.S.S. Gorkon.* Her commandin' officer required me to help her humor some new alien friends . . ."

Situational Engineering

Stardate 52612.6
August 2375, Old Earth Time

Once the delegation materialized on the surface of Kropasar, inside a very nice-looking gathering hall, Scotty immediately lost sight of the others who'd transported down with him—except for Admiral Nechayev. Before he had quite acquired his bearings in the massive room, she was pulling him face-to-face with his first Kropaslin.

The Kropaslin were not normal humanoids by any stretch of the imagination. To Scotty's eyes, they resembled tall, bi-pedal lizards with feathers and a high forehead. They had four short arms which they usually kept close by their bodies, al-most as if to protect themselves. Their most peculiar attribute was the complete lack of any visual organs. In any case, Scotty didn't spot any, even though he did look hard. In fact, the only sensory organ he could make out was their nose, which sported huge nostrils where other beings had their eyes, and they opened and closed in quick intervals.

They possessed feathers, or at least something that *looked* like feathers. Most of them grew on their head, around the nostrils, although the Kropaslin's arms also sported a few. This particular one did not even come up to Scotty's shoulders, though looking around he noticed there were several taller ones about. All of them were clothed, which was a blessing.

"Captain Scott, this is Bendalion Iamor, a thane in the

Kropaslin Witenagemot," said Nechayev. "Thane Iamor, this is Captain Montgomery Scott, head of the Starfleet Corps of Engineers." She looked around the room and, noticing a Kropaslin trying to catch her attention, set off. "If you'll excuse me, I see High Cyning Forecic over there."

Scotty reached out and shook one of Iamor's four hands. "Good to meet you, Thane."

"Likewise, Captain Scott," Iamor replied. The Kropaslin's speech was heavily accented and very screechy; apparently he was speaking Standard directly, without the benefit of a universal translator. His voice box seemed to be unsuited for it.

"Thane, eh? Do you all think you're Ancient Scots or somethin'?" asked Scotty amusedly.

"Ah," said Iamor, "you refer to our political terminology: 'Witenagemot' for the legislature, 'thane' for its members, and 'high cyning' for its head. No, these terms were selected by a Federation translation team. They were considered most indicative of the fact that we possess a thoroughly democratic government that utilizes the trappings of an ancient feudal one."

Scotty simply nodded. As the conversation trickled on to a small pause, he finally took a good look at the hall they were in. It was certainly not a room designed for such receptions, that much was clear. However, quite for what purpose it had been designed was a question he did not have a ready answer to. The ceiling was a good five meters above the tallest Kropaslin's head, and in the center of it was a transparent dome that let in the murky light from outside. It seemed to be a cloudy day here in the planetary capital whose name he didn't recall at the moment.

The gathering hall sported a stone floor that must have been designed with a passion for art, because intricate patterns like these didn't come natural to those who did not enjoy their work. Abstract shapes wound their way across the shining marble floor, like cubist snakes jointly sculpted by Salvador Dalí and Yeros of Vulcan.

"Why did Nechayev so wish me to speak to you?" Iamor asked, changing the subject.

"Damned if I know," replied Scott, quickly adding a respectful "sir." It wouldn't do to cause an incident in the first ten minutes of the event. "You don't happen to work in biotechnological engineerin', do you?"

"Alas, no," Iamor said. "I am the head of the Agreement Party."

"Agreement Party?" Scott asked, a bit confused.

"Did you not read the briefings we provided your delegation?" asked Iamor. "I was told information on our political structure was included in your briefing packet."

It was very possible that that information had been on the padd that Commander Piñiero had given him, but if that were true, it hardly mattered, as Scotty hadn't even looked at it. He'd had too many technical journals to read. "Ah, I skimmed it."

"Well," said Iamor, "our government is dominated by two political parties, known as Agreement and Consensus. Presently, the Consensus Party holds a majority in the Witenagemot, but three years ago—"

"Sorry, Thane," Scotty said, interrupting Iamor's obvious enthusiasm for this topic, "but I'm an engineer. Politics is a wee bit over my head. I just know to show up on Election Day."

Iamor made a facial expression that Scotty was not sure how to interpret. "Very well then, Captain Scott."

"I don't mean to be offensive, Thane, but if you want to talk politics, I'm sure Ambassador Morrow over there would be very keen to hear it." Scotty gestured toward where the young diplomat he'd first met in the *Gorkon*'s transporter room was talking animatedly with a small group of seemingly very interested Kropaslin. "Now if you don't mind, I'm going to check out the bar."

Upon arriving on the *Gorkon*, one of the first questions Scotty had asked Fleet Admiral Alynna Nechayev—*the* first, actually—had been "Why am I here?" There were others more suited for this sort of thing, people with, well, a real diplomatic background. Admirals, members of the Diplomatic Corps . . . even Nechayev herself.

Her reaction had been dry and serious. "This is not a formal negotiation, Captain," she'd said. "It is more of a way of reminding the Kropaslin of what we have to offer—and the other way around of course—in preparation for the actual negotiations. One of the things they have to offer us is their expertise in biotechnology."

Biotechnology—the one thing the Kropaslin could offer the Federation where they could be sure that the Federation would pay any price to obtain it. Despite extensive research in that field, Federation scientists still lagged behind species such as the Breen and the Azziz. They managed to incorporate elements of it in their technology, certainly—the bioneural gel packs used on some of the newer ship classes were evidence of that—but that was a far cry from having entirely biological vessels at one's disposal, ships that you could basically grow in your own backyard while enjoying a quiet drink on your veranda, so to speak.

Scotty had become somewhat familiar with the technology while working on the construction of the newest *Enterprise*, and that was when he had first come across a reference to Kropasar. Nechayev must have known about his interest in those people's biotechnological accomplishments when she had picked him for this little "ice-breaker," an informal get-together of Kropaslin and Federation luminaries to ease tensions, now that membership negotiations were once again in full swing. Before the war, Kropasar had applied to become a member of the Federation, but then the revival of Klingon hostilities and the subsequent Dominion War had changed the Federation's goals. Since Kropasar was located a couple dozen light-years rimward of Omicron Ceti, far from the conflict zone, its admittance had fallen to the wayside, given the Diplomatic Corps had much more pressing matters to deal with.

But now, the president had decided the time was right to get things back on track, which was why Scotty was here on the fourth planet of a star system with no name, just a number, searching for a drink.

The bar, as Scotty had guessed, did not serve Scotch. However, one of the ambassadors, an El-Aurian, had recommended the Andorian ale, and Scotty soon held a glassful of that in his hands. Fortunately, it was a delightful vintage, possessed of a strong blue hue. Wandering over to the buffet, there was also an unsurprising lack of any good food. It seemed as though the Kropaslin had a big liking for foods imported from the Vega system, which was very unfortunate, as one of the many things he had disliked about Vega IX had been the food.

What he really wanted was some haggis, but he hadn't had a good plate of that for almost three years, since his time on the *Enterprise*-E; helping build a ship from almost the ground up meant you could hardwire the replicators just the way you liked. In the end, he reluctantly settled on a kebab of vegetables from Xaraka XII.

No sooner had he began to munch on the kebab than he was approached by another Kropaslin. This one was taller than Iamor, rising to about two meters. "I hope you don't want to talk politics, laddie," said Scotty. "You *are* a laddie, right?" He frowned, realizing he had no idea how the Kropaslin genders were differentiated.

"A what?" asked the Kropaslin.

From the way the translator rendered the person's voice, Scotty was willing to gamble that it was a she. Perhaps the taller ones were the females? "A laddie is a boy," he said, "but you seem to be a girl."

"I am a bit older than a girl," said the Kropaslin wryly. "Dr. Delasat Vantimor."

"Captain Montgomery Scott," said Scotty. "I'd shake your hand, lassie, but . . ." He held up his hands, each of which was presently occupied holding something, and shrugged. "Not enough limbs."

"Oh, I know who you are," Vantimor said. "I worked on the team that designed the special bioneural gel that was used on the *Enterprise* and the other *Sovereign*-class ships. Your reports and complaints made for . . . interesting reading."

"Lassie, let me tell you, interfacin' alien gel with isolinear computer systems is a tricky job." Scotty didn't recognize her name, but that was to be expected, as he had worked with far more people than he could recall on the *Enterprise* computer systems, most of them via subspace.

"Indeed it is," said a new voice. Scotty turned to see an older-looking human male had approached from his right without his noticing. "Sorry," the man said, "but I couldn't help but hear your conversation." Scotty recognized him as yet another member of the group from the *Gorkon* that had assembled in the transporter room that morning, though he hadn't been introduced to him. The man stuck out his hand. "Professor Andrews of the Timsonian Institute."

Scotty sighed inwardly and quickly transferred his kebab to the left hand, which was also holding his ale, and shook Andrews's hand. "I imagine you lot will have your hands full catalogin' all this new stuff, won't you, lad?" Located in Cluster Telpha-Z, the Timsonian Institute was a counterpart to the more famous Daystrom Institute, focusing less on development of new technologies and more on classifying and labeling ones acquired through trade, alliance, and the like.

"Indeed we will," said Andrews, moving over to the food bar, where he grabbed a spider tramezzino from Alpha Arietis. "I would appreciate it, Captain Scott, if you did not refer to me as 'lad.'"

"Ach, you may be older than me physically," Scotty admitted, "but I was realignin' dilithium crystals when you were in diapers."

"Oh, I remember hearing about this," Vantimor said excitedly. "You fell through a temporal rift in the Typhon Expanse, didn't you? Came from the twenty-third century to the present?"

"No, lassie, that was my good friend Morgan Bateson. My story is a wee bit different. I was on my way to a retirement colony on Norpin V, when the ship I was on, the *Jenolen*, encountered a Dyson sphere."

"A Dyson sphere?" asked Vantimor. "Is that a spatial anomaly of some sort?"

"No," said Andrews, "it is a massive artificial habitat constructed around a star to absorb all of its energy." He munched on his half-sandwich with a forlorn expression. "Unfortunately, before the Institute could mount an expedition to take a look at the one the *Jenolen* discovered, it up and vanished. Most perplexing and distressing."

Scotty had taken advantage of the interruption to take another swig of the Andorian ale. "Exactly," he said. "The *Jenolen* crash-landed on the sphere, killin' everyone aboard but me and an ensign. Knowin' rescue might be a long while in comin', I managed to put the two of us into transporter stasis, by loopin' our patterns through the buffer over and over."

"Really?" came a voice from his left. Scotty realized they had been joined by another Kropaslin. "That is extraordinary."

"Well, don't praise me all too quickly," Scotty said to the newcomer. "We were in transporter stasis for seventy-five years, until we were rescued by the *Enterprise*-D. But poor Franklin's pattern degraded too far for him to be rematerialized."

"That's sad. However, it's still an amazing piece of work," affirmed the Kropaslin. "A miracle of engineering."

Scotty shrugged. "Aye, you might say that."

Vantimor had what Scotty thought might be a puzzled expression, though quite honestly he wasn't qualified to judge Kropaslin faces. *No wonder—they have no sodding eyes!* "I thought you were on your way to a retirement colony. Why are you in Starfleet now?"

"Well, lassie," said Scotty, taking another sip of his ale, "that is another story."

"Tell it then," she said.

Scotty smiled. One of the advantages of being an old relic was almost always having a willing audience for a story—and having more than enough stories to tell. "After I helped save the *Enterprise*-D from a wee bit of a scrape they landed in, Captain Picard rewarded me with my own shuttlecraft. Instead of headin' to the retirement colony, I decided to roam the galaxy for some time." He fell silent.

"What happened?" asked someone Scotty didn't recognize, a Deirr. It seemed he was attracting a crowd.

"Well, warpin' around in your own shuttle sounds thrillin', but it soon gets lonely. Oh, I had my fair share of . . . excitement, but before long I'd entered into a sort of funk. Bein' seventy-five years out of time can do that to you. Fortunately, thanks to an odd dream about Captain Kirk and some advice from a Hermat lass on Argelius—"

"Hermat *lass*?" asked Andrews quizzically.

"Well, she was a lad, too, I suppose," Scotty acknowledged. "I try not to dwell on that. Anyway, she told me I needed to get back to doin' what I was good at, and her words hit home. So I signed up at Starfleet Academy for some courses to get me up to speed with all the new technology, and soon enough, Morgan took me on as chief construction engineer of the *Honorius,* one of two *Sovereign*-class starships being built at Starbase 12."

"That was the original designation of the new *Enterprise,* wasn't it?" asked Vantimor.

"Aye, lassie," said Scotty. "The *Enterprise*-D crashed on Veridian a few months after I joined the project, and so Starfleet redesignated the *Honorius* in her honor. I served as her chief engineer on her maiden voyage, and after helpin' Morgan with her sister ship, the new *Bozeman,* I signed on to the *Sovereign* as chief engineer for a couple of years, where I worked on testin' new technologies for implementation on other *Sovereign*s. Once that was up, Bill Ross asked me to take over the Engineerin' Corps, and so here I am."

Aye, and it's not really where you want to be at all, is it?

He drowned that thought with another swig of Andorian ale.

Tried to, more like. He didn't succeed. Involuntarily, he thought back to the conversation Nechayev and he had had in the admiral's ready room. At the start of it, she'd been pleasant and friendly, but her demeanor had changed quickly, giving Scotty the impression that it might have been just an act.

"Captain Scott," Nechayev had begun, "you know as well as I do that you have not stepped foot in your office at Headquarters for the last three months."

"I've been busy," Scotty had said defensively. He had been wracking his brains for what he knew of Nechayev. Not much. She was way up there in Starfleet Command—almost as high as you could be, really—but he had only met her once before, during the Amargosa crisis, and that had only been for a brief time. He was woefully uninformed beyond the fact that she was the one who had been at the forefront of the Cardassian negotiations and the mess in the Demilitarized Zone that had followed. "When your man Dramar caught up with me, I was just on my way to my office. I'd been helping the repair teams in San Francisco."

"Which is very admirable and fully understandable," Nechayev acknowledged. "But before that you and Admiral McCoy were on the *Hudson* conducting a monthlong inspection tour, I believe?"

"It needed to be done," Scotty said, still defensive. He had not expected to have his job performance evaluated on the *Gorkon*.

"Certainly," Nechayev said. "But almost anyone in the S.C.E. would have been qualified to carry out the task. It didn't exactly require superb engineering prowess to look at a couple of facilities."

Actually, it had ended up requiring quite a bit of skill on Scotty's part when the *Hudson* had been forced to make an emergency landing on Bakrii, but he didn't think the admiral would appreciate him pointing that out. "Well, it doesn't require 'superb engineerin' prowess' to manage the S.C.E. either.

Commander Leland T. Lynch is perfectly capable of doin' the job."

"It's not his job, though, is it?" Nechayev said. "When Admiral Ross asked you to take over for Harriman, I think he expected *you* to do the work. Not your *assistant*."

Truth be told, Scotty hadn't really wanted to assume the position of liaison between Command and the Corps of Engineers. But when his tour on the *U.S.S. Sovereign* had come to an end, Scotty hadn't had anything lined up. He'd been thinking of retiring again. While he had enjoyed the time he'd spent constructing the *Enterprise*-E with people who understood his plight, his subsequent time on the *Sovereign* had made him feel like a relic once more. The crew of the ship, from Captain Sanders down to Chaplain Blackwell, had treated him like a curiosity. A revered and respected curiosity, granted, but still a curiosity.

But before Scott could bring himself to actually do the deed, Admiral William Ross had come to him with the offer of heading the S.C.E. Scotty had leapt at the chance to do something useful but, not keen on becoming an administrator, insisted it only be on a temporary basis, until someone who actually wanted the job could be found. His first month had not endeared him to his new duties: it had been signing off on orders, approving requests, dictating reports, and more of the same. When a chance had come to get out of the office and do some work on a communications array at Tsugh Kaidnn, he had taken the opportunity without a thought. And the next opportunity to get out of the office, and the one after that.

The only thing that kept him in the job were the words Harriman had spoken to him a few years back, when Harriman had been contemplating retirement himself and offered his job to Scotty: *They only gave it to me to keep an old admiral busy. But an engineer like yourself, you could really do something with it.* But every time Scotty called Commander Lynch back at the office and learned how much more paperwork had built up, he doubted Harriman's words more and more.

Returning to Earth after the inspection tour on the *Hudson*, he had thrown himself into helping with the reconstruction efforts repairing the damage caused by the Breen attack on San Francisco. But having wrapped up what he could at the moment, he had been dreading returning to his office. Fortunately, Ensign Dramar had happened along. At the time, he had thought that even a meeting with the notorious Admiral Nechayev would be better than confronting his paperwork.

He'd been wrong there.

"What was it like on the *Sovereign*?" asked Professor Andrews, diverting Scotty from his momentary bit of introspection.

Scotty, not letting his doubts about his choices show, said, "It was pretty tricky workin' new technology like that, but I adapted quickly. When you've been an engineer as long as I have, you start to learn that some things never change."

"How long *have* you been an engineer?" asked Vantimor, her interest obvious despite her alienness.

"Over one hundred fifty years if I cheat and count my time in the transporter," said Scotty with a grin. "All my life, really. I think I've served on over a dozen starships. Three *Enterprise*s, of course, plus *Sovereign, Excelsior, Starstalker, Kumari, Gagarin.*" He continued to recite his impressive pedigree, enjoying himself for the first time in a long while.

That evening, Scotty returned to his quarters, quite pleased with himself. He had spent the rest of the day swapping stories with Vantimor, Andrews, and the other engineers, and he could think of few things more pleasing than that, except maybe reading technical journals.

Speaking of which, he was still behind in his reading of the *Kropasar Journal for Applied Biotechnology*, not to mention the several hundred papers published by Federation journals on the issue. Tomorrow, he was scheduled to tour a gel production plant with Dr. Vantimor and some of her colleagues; he needed to be well informed if he didn't want to look like a relic from another time.

After cleaning himself up and changing into some Starfleet-issue pajamas, Scotty had the computer download his reading material onto two isolinear chips, loaded one of the chips into his padd, and settled down on his bed to read until he fell asleep. He hadn't done anything like this since cramming for his last history final at the Academy. He was rather enjoying himself.

Just as he was getting to the exciting part of the second paper—a discussion of realigning the nanotech processors to more efficiently process the neural-based output of gel packs without a loss in data density—he was interrupted by a beeping from the computer terminal on the room's desk.

Sighing, he heaved himself up out of bed, and crossed the room. "Scott here," he said, pressing the appropriate button on the terminal.

Commander Esperanza Piñiero, the *Gorkon*'s first officer, appeared on-screen. *"Captain Scott, Admiral Nechayev has taken ill."* She seemed to be in sickbay.

Scotty was puzzled. "I'm sorry to hear that, lassie. What's wrong?"

"It appears something she ate on Kropasar disagreed with her," said Piñiero.

Scotty nodded. "Probably those meatballs from Vega. I always thought Vegan food was disgustin'."

Piñiero shrugged. *"Dr. Ezeafulukwe isn't sure exactly what did it yet."*

"I don't mean to be rude, lassie, but I don't know what this has to do with me. I can't do much more than offer my sympathy. I'm an engineer, not a doctor."

"Admiral Nechayev was scheduled to meet with some members of the Witenagemot tonight," said Piñiero. *"She has selected you to take her place."*

"Me?" Scotty asked, astonished. "Surely one of the diplomats would be more suited for the task?" He couldn't imagine why anyone would want him to talk to a group of politicians. "Send that nice Morrow lad."

"Captain Scott, the admiral explicitly instructed that you go in her stead. The meeting's at 2100 hours. I'm sending the location of the meeting to you now. Send me your padd's network address; sealed orders will be encoded into it that you will be able to access at the appropriate time."

Scotty sighed. "Aye, aye. Tell the admiral I'll be there." He keyed his padd's address into the terminal.

Piñiero smiled. *"Thank you, Captain Scott. I'm sure the admiral will be most grateful."* Her image blinked away, and Scotty checked the chronometer to realize he had a couple hours before he was due back on Kropasar.

"What's she playin' at?" he asked himself. Well, he'd know soon enough. In the meantime, he had better replicate himself a nice, strong Mythran coffee. It wouldn't do to doze off while he listened to some politician natter on.

Scotty materialized in an empty corridor in the Kropaslin Curia. The lights flicked on in response to his presence. Checking his padd, he determined the room he was headed for was a little bit down the hall.

Damn and blast, why am I doing this? He'd been thinking for almost two hours, and had yet to come up with a reason why he would be the best replacement for Admiral Nechayev at a meeting with some alien politicians.

He reached the door, and he tapped the control on the wall next to it, causing it to slide open. Inside the room were seven Kropaslin gathered around a large round table. The table was mostly featureless gray metal, except for some computer terminals on the edges and a white ring in the center. As he stepped across the threshold, the door slid shut behind him with a *clink* he recognized as the activation of an electronic lock.

"Take a seat, Captain Scott," said one of the Kropaslin. Scotty recognized him as Thane Bendalion Iamor, the small fellow Nechayev had forced him to speak to briefly that morning.

The chair closest to the door was empty; Scotty sat himself down in it. There was a small computer terminal embedded in the table in front of him; it appeared to be one of the most recent models to come out of the design facilities here on Kropasar. "Why am I here, lad? Why am I meetin' with your government?"

"We are not the government," replied Iamor. "Not anymore, that is. As I mentioned to you this morning, I am the leader of the Agreement Party. High Cyning Forecic is a member of the Consensus Party; they currently lead Kropasar."

"I don't understand what all your political wheelings and dealings have to do with me." Scotty shifted in his chair; it had been designed for the unusual Kropaslin anatomy, and thus was rather uncomfortable to him.

Another Kropaslin, this one a woman, spoke up. "Patience, Captain Scott. We will explain." Scotty vaguely recognized her as someone he had been introduced to during the day.

Iamor continued. "It was my political party that held power when we applied for Federation membership four years ago. In the intervening time, however, there was an election, and we lost our majority in the Witenagemot, though only just barely."

"The Consensus Party," the woman went on, "is somewhat less . . . tolerant than us. They place stricter qualifications on freedom of speech, open less of their policies to public review, and tend to favor members of certain ethnic groups. It is just on the edge of what the Federation considers acceptable in a member government, and in all honesty, our application could end up with a rejection now that negotiations are on again."

"Why is President Zife pursuing your membership *now*, then?" asked Scotty.

"There is a very good reason for that," said another of the Kropaslin. "Allow me to introduce myself: Thane Dreso Miculamor." This new fellow tapped a button on his terminal. The white ring embedded in the center of the table suddenly lit up, revealing itself to be a holoprojector. An image of a strange, asymmetrical spaceship came into being in midair.

Scotty recognized the ship immediately. It was a Breen frigate. "The Breen?" he asked. "What do they have to do with your politics?"

"I see you recognize the ship, then, Captain Scott," said Miculamor.

"Of course I do!" Scotty snapped. "Three of them attacked Earth. We haven't stopped fightin' them since."

"Indeed," said Miculamor. "Several months ago, a Haradin trading vessel came across one on the outskirts of the Helaspont Nebula. All the escape pods had been jettisoned, but the ship was largely intact, with only some minor damage. We still have no idea why it was abandoned. I am sure you know Breen ships are biological in nature, and their level of expertise is rumored to exceed even ours. The traders could not make use of it themselves, but they sold it to our government—for a hefty sum."

"You have a Breen frigate!" Scotty exclaimed. "Starfleet would die to have one of those. The specs on that blasted energy-dampenin' weapon alone could change the course of the war!"

"Regrettably," Miculamor said, "this ship does not appear to be equipped with one. In every other way, however, it seems to be identical to those Starfleet has faced in battle."

"Still worth a king's ransom, then," said Scotty. "If we knew everything about those ships, we would have a major tactical advantage."

"Yes," said Iamor. "However, High Cyning Forecic and the Consensus Party believe the existence of the Breen ship should be kept as secret as possible, to maximize the economic and business advantages access to the superior biotechnology will bring our planet."

"I'll bet Starfleet Intelligence still found out, though," said Scotty. "No wonder the president suddenly made Kropasar's admittance a priority."

"That is most likely," said the female Kropaslin.

"You may now access your sealed orders from Admiral Nechayev, Captain," said Iamor. "The password is R0-XX4-HT33-L."

Scotty typed the code into his padd, causing a file to suddenly appear and open. He quickly read through it. "You want me to *what*?"

"Captain Scott, your superiors want that ship, and we want them to have it," said Iamor. "If they are going to . . . acquire it, they will need the coordinates of the spacedock where it is being analyzed."

"But why do you *want* Starfleet to steal from you?" Scotty shook his head. "These orders have only made everythin' make *less* sense."

"The Federation does not honestly want Kropasar as a member," said the female. Scotty suddenly remembered her name was Gilvatac. Or maybe Gilvatas. Not that it mattered much. "There are not only the democratic problems the Consensus Party presents, but a planet that will not disclose the existence of a ship that could change the tide of the war is obviously not the ideal member. The reason membership is being pursued now is the Breen ship."

"And we don't want to become a member," Iamor said. Before Scotty could state his confusion once more, he continued. "Federation acceptance at this time would provide an enormous validation to the Consensus Party in the eyes of the public. As the leader of the opposition, I cannot let that happen if we ever want to control the Witenagemot again."

"But why *me*?" Scotty asked, his voice almost a whisper. "Surely one of your people could provide the coordinates."

"No," said Miculamor sharply. "They are known only to the handful of pilots that make the run between the spacedock and here. There is not a single member of the government, in either party, who knows them. They are, however, stored in our government's most secure computer core. As your orders should indicate, that computer core is multitronic in nature, for security reasons."

That made sense, Scotty reflected. Multitronics was an

evolution of the old duotronic technology that had been used in the twenty-third century. The Federation had abandoned the development of multitronic technology like most of the peoples of the galaxy and eventually moved in a totally different direction, to isolinear technology. Though multitronics had its advantages, isolinear computers had come to dominate because it was immensely difficult to create a stable operating system for a multitronic system.

Scotty had seen the results of that problem himself. Dr. Richard Daystrom had used his own memory engrams as a model for the M-5 multitronic unit, which had resulted in the computer going mad and damaging several Federation starships before Captain Kirk had managed to shut it down.

But according to the orders provided by Nechayev on his padd, the Kropaslin had managed to create a stable multitronic computer core. This made their data storage virtually invulnerable, as no one outside of the few Kropaslin who had designed it had the necessary knowledge to tap into it remotely. Every other computer on the planet was isolinear/bioneural in nature, and interfacing one of them with a multitronic system was something no one knew how to do.

Except Scotty, of course. He had been there when Daystrom had installed the M-5 on the *Enterprise,* and he still knew exactly how it had interfaced with the standard Starfleet systems. "I'm the only person who can do it, aye," Scotty said quietly. "Daystrom's dead; the M-5 and its predecessors long disassembled. Everyone who worked with him is gone, too—except for me."

"Exactly," said Iamor. He tapped a few buttons on his computer panel, and suddenly the one in front of Scotty lit up with blocks of code. "This is as far as our own programmers have been able to get; none of them have been able to make sense of the data."

"Everyone who worked on the multitronic computer is kept with it, well away from outside contact," Miculamor explained. "We are a secretive people where our technology is concerned." He made a gesture with his upper arms that Scotty interpreted as a shrug. "This is a necessity in today's competitive market."

"You may begin now," said Iamor.

He, and with him every other Kropaslin in the room, looked expectantly at Scotty.

Though outwardly he may have looked calm, inwardly Scotty was furious. He had been set up! Manipulated by Nechayev, by Piñiero, by Iamor and the other opposition politicians. This whole diplomatic function was nothing more than a ploy to get him into this room so that he could steal from the Kropaslin government just so the Federation Council could avoid taking on an undesirable member, just so these politicians' precious bid for power wouldn't be jeopardized.

It was sickening. He could feel the vegetables from his kebab churning in his stomach, along with the ale and the coffee he'd consumed. He desperately wanted to visit waste extraction.

Yet here he was. The door was locked, and he had his orders from the almighty Fleet Admiral Alynna Nechayev right in front of him, clearly signed and dated. Oh-so-conveniently, she wasn't here. He couldn't argue with her. And he had no doubt that the door would not be unlocked until he had extracted those blasted coordinates from the multitronic computer.

There was no way out. He sighed, and cracked his knuckles before leaning down to take a good look at the screen on his terminal. "Well, I'll have to give it my best shot, laddies and lassies, haven't I?"

At least it would be an interesting challenge.

He could take some small comfort in that.

When the beam released Scotty into the *Gorkon*'s transporter room, the first thing he noticed was Admiral Nechayev standing before him; Commander Piñiero was operating the console. "Glad to see you're better, *Admiral*," he said as he stepped off the transporter dais.

Nechayev held her hand out. "Your padd please, Captain Scott."

Scotty slipped his hands behind his back, the padd still

clutched in them. "I don't think this is right. We can't just *steal* from another planet."

"Captain Scott," said Nechayev with a sigh, "I had hoped this would not happen. You know as well as I do that if the Federation wants to stop losing this war, we need that ship."

"Admiral, I don't deny that! I just don't think we should be stealin' from potential member planets—or any other planets—just because it's more *convenient* for us!"

Nechayev shook her head. "Captain Scott, it's not as though you don't know Starfleet can be a little . . . underhanded at times. I seem to recall you once joined a commando squad on a mission into Romulan space to steal a prototype vessel?"

"That's not the same—" began Scotty.

Nechayev cut him off. "And of course, you had no problem with stealing from the Federation itself when you conspired with Captain Kirk to sabotage the original *Excelsior* and steal the *Enterprise* out of spacedock." She motioned to Piñiero, who stepped forward to right in front of Scotty, her hand extended. "Captain Scott, hand over that padd. That's an order."

Just as when he had read the sealed orders earlier that night, Scotty couldn't refuse a direct order like that. He brought his hand from behind his back, and dropped the padd into Piñiero's hand. Piñiero flipped it on and skimmed through the data. "It's all here, Admiral," she said. "The coordinates, the layout of the facility, everything."

"Get to the bridge and break orbit," ordered Nechayev. "The *Catherine Mary* is waiting at Delphi Ardu for that information."

"Yes, Admiral." Nechayev held out her hand, and Piñiero gave her the padd. Nechayev gave some further orders about sending an apology to the high cyning for the abrupt departure, and then Piñiero left.

"You don't have to be rude to them as well, Admiral!" exclaimed Scotty. "At least do them the courtesy of finishin' out your commitment here."

"I can't afford to waste any time here, Captain Scott. Captain Wrightwell needs that information as soon as possible if his strike team is going to capture that Breen frigate, and we can't risk transmitting it, even in code." She skimmed through the data on the padd herself. "Good work, Captain Scott. I think you'll understand if I can't put you up for commendation, though." She began to head for the door.

"Now wait just a second, Admiral," called Scotty, halting her in midstride. "I want to tell you somethin'."

Nechayev turned, a look of curiosity evident on her face. "And what's that, Captain Scott?"

Scotty paused for a moment, not sure if he really wanted to go through with this, not sure if he really wanted to say the words or not. Then he thought, *The hell with this.* "Admiral, I quit."

For the first time he had ever seen, Nechayev looked like she was at a loss for words. "You *what*?"

"I quit," he repeated. "I resign."

"Captain Scott," began Nechayev, "surely—"

"This has nothing to do with the stealin'," said Scotty. "Well, it does, but that's not the reason. The reason is that you manipulated me, Admiral. You deliberately engineered the entire situation so I would have to obey those orders." Scotty wasn't the type to disobey orders.

That's not true, Scotty thought. *How many times did you disobey orders under Captain Kirk?* But there was a difference. Under Kirk, Scotty had never been the one initiating the disobeying. He had always been following orders, really; it was just that they had been the captain's orders and not Starfleet's. And now the captain was dead . . .

"What about your job with the S.C.E.?" asked Nechayev. It was clear that she still couldn't quite believe that Scotty would end his Fleet career for such a reason.

"Admiral, you yourself told me I've not been doing that at all," said Scotty. "There's nothing to tie me to Starfleet anymore." In truth, there hadn't been since he finished his work on the *Enterprise*-E, if even then. "This century's Starfleet isn't for me if this is the way it treats its officers."

He reached up to his chest, removed his communicator badge, and put it on the transporter console with a thump.

★ ★ ★

"Where to, sir?"

"Laddie, don't call me 'sir' anymore. I resigned."

Ensign Dramar nodded absently as he ran through the shuttlecraft *Irenic*'s preflight checklist. "Sorry. But where do you want me to take you?"

Scotty shrugged. "Earth, I suppose." At the very least he would now need to clear his belongings out of his Starfleet-issued apartment in San Francisco.

The ensign nodded and as he continued doing the checklist with one hand, began plotting the course with the other. "What are you going to do now that you're retired?"

"I don't know, lad. This'll be my second time, but I didn't really know then, either." The retirement colony on Norpin V was definitely out. The last thing he needed was to be with a bunch of old-timers all reminiscing over bygone days. He had enough history of his own to wallow in. "I'd return to wanderin', if I could."

Unfortunately, when he had reenlisted with Starfleet, Scotty had donated his old shuttlecraft, the *Romaine*, to the Starfleet Museum as a form of recompense for stealing a starship from them. Brennad Odymo, the museum head, would surely never part with it now, since the former shuttlecraft *Goddard* was the only sizable intact remain of the wrecked *Enterprise*-D.

"I didn't particularly like wandering much, really." Though there had been some interesting encounters on the way—renewing his friendship with Morgan, rescuing the Narisian refugees, tangling with Koloth one last time, rescuing Spock from Romulan captivity—most of the time he had just felt aimless. Much like he did now, much like he had since transferring to the *Sovereign*.

But the engine room was no longer a home to him. Starfleet was no longer a home for him.

Right now, aimless wandering is all I have.

Interlude

Stardate 53509.5
May 2376, Old Earth Time

Geordi La Forge set down his glass, his first drink still unfinished. "Well, that's Nechayev for you," he said. "The things I've heard about her, from the captain and elsewhere . . ."

"Oh, I know that *now*, laddie," said Scotty. He reached for his bottle, but evidently reconsidered yet another glass of Scotch, as he withdrew his hand only partway there. "If only I'd known earlier."

"So you resigned?" La Forge asked. "I thought I'd heard you went on inactive duty."

"I *wanted* to resign," Scotty said, "and I certainly filed my resignation. But Command—specifically Admiral Ross—wouldn't take it, and he managed to talk me into goin' on 'inactive duty.' I was maintained in an 'advisory capacity' to the S.C.E. or some similar nonsense, and Commander Leland T. Lynch took over as temporary head until a suitable replacement could be found."

La Forge nodded. He knew Lynch, and had never been impressed by the man's engineering prowess, but from what he heard, he made a capable administrator.

Scotty stood up. "I don't know about you, lad, but I fancy goin' somewhere else than this office, as nice as it is." He nodded at La Forge's glass. "I suspect you would like to do the same, so you can have a drink more to your taste."

Geordi smiled. "That would be nice. I haven't been to Worlds in a while."

"Laddie, I don't think I've been there since I retired the first time, and I'd certainly like to see how the place has been doing in the past eighty-odd years." La Forge stood and followed Scotty out of his office, back into Deg's.

"I'm goin' to be takin' the afternoon off, Deg lad," said Scotty. "Anythin' I need to hear before I leave?"

"Admiral Koike would like to send the *da Vinci* to Maeglin to deal with a situation there once they've completed their mission to Tellar Prime," replied the Blood.

"Gateways related?" asked Geordi.

Deg nodded. "There are few other types of crises these past few days."

"Those Petraw fearties are about to give me an everlastin' headache, I'm tellin' you! Thank goodness for your Captain Picard," said Scotty. "Otherwise we would be facing even worse. Tell Koike he's free to send the *da Vinci* wherever he wishes," he said to Deg.

"Yes, sir," said Deg, beginning to tap into his computer once more. "That should be it for the day."

Scotty led the way out of the office, as Geordi followed. "It won't be, of course. It never is."

Strange New Worlds, the full name of the bar commonly called "Worlds," was an ancient Starfleet institution, supposedly older than the Academy itself. According to myth, it was here that Admiral Jonathan Archer had been offered the position of Chief of Staff of the fledgling Federation Starfleet.

La Forge had never quite bought that one. The bar was old, but it wasn't *that* old. Regardless, it had been popular with Starfleet personnel for over a century now, and that showed little sign of changing. La Forge had been coming here on and off since he was an Academy cadet, and had always liked it. The bar was filled with Starfleet memorabilia, from dedication plaques to model starships to used self-sealing stem bolts.

Once they were settled in at a nice corner booth—Scotty with an Aldebaran whiskey, and La Forge with a nice Saurian brandy—the younger engineer prompted Scotty to continue his tale. "Did you return to wandering, or what?"

"I suppose so, laddie," said Scotty, "but wanderin' of a more limited sort. I returned to Scotland, revisiting my old homeland for the first time since I left on the *Jenolen* back in '94. But soon I found myself called away to a far more . . . *pleasurable* destination."

Damage Control

Stardate 53194.6
March 2376, Old Earth Time

As he made his way to the lift of the observation tower, Montgomery Scott managed not to bump into a single tourist, which in itself was a small miracle. Usually, they didn't care whether they were in his way, only to later complain quite loudly about his obvious inability to walk without distracting others from observing the scantily-clad natives.

Even if the visitors were forgettable, Risa itself always was a lovely spot to spend your downtime, and it hadn't changed a bit in the years he'd been . . . offstage, so to speak. There were still those large wooden *horga'hn*s everywhere, almost forcing you to get yourself some *jamaharon* while there was still some left.

Scotty was glad that he had found this job. He just wasn't the kind of man to sit around lazily all day long, reading books, and solving 3-D crossword puzzles. He wished he had figured that out just a few years earlier (relatively speaking, of course), because then he wouldn't have been on the *Jenolen*, on course to that bloody retirement colony, which had resulted in him skipping seventy-five years cleverly ensconced in a transporter buffer.

It had had its upsides, however—not only had he escaped a depressing number of wars and armed conflicts, but also some unnecessary revivals of outrageous fashion styles. Yet what had survival brought him? Nothing, except the knowledge that the galaxy hadn't improved. People were still as stupid as they had been in the twenty-third century.

Case in point—suddenly, someone big and heavy bumped into him, mumbled an excuse and continued down the corridor. Scotty looked at the quickly moving back of the person—who seemed to be a Megarite, judging from his drysuit—and thought about thanking him for his consideration, but somehow he got the impression that sarcasm was wasted on the peculiar aliens who used song to communicate their ideas and opinions.

Finally, Scotty made it to the lift; it made the one hundred twelve-story journey in less than thirty seconds. He stepped out of the turbocar and onto the observation deck of the Tolari Tower, the tallest structure on this continent. Even from up here, the main building of the nearby El Dorado Resort resembled a fake Aztec pyramid consisting of real Risian basalt, and it looked authentic, from what Scotty could tell. But then again, he didn't know all that much about ancient Aztec architecture.

He went to the railing and took a deep breath. The view was outstanding as always. He had heard that Risa's peculiar geological history was responsible for the abundance of beaches and lagoons, but he suspected that the Risian government had helped nature along. For more than two hundred years, the planet had been one of the Federation's most popular holiday destinations, together with Wrigley's Pleasure Planet, Casperia Prime, and Phloston Paradise, but if the Risians hadn't begun to interfere with their natural environment centuries ago, the planet would have rivaled Ferenginar in humidity.

However, some people didn't like the way the visitors to Risa behaved. They claimed that the Risian lifestyle was the cause of complacency, vanity, and extreme hedonism. In response, they had founded the New Essentialists Movement and tried to show people the error of their ways. Nobody would have complained if they had done it by holding rallies and handing out pamphlets, but no, they had had to switch off the entire weather control grid and the tectonic stress regulators. Who in their right mind believed that was more likely to convince people to change their lifestyle?

Anyway, that was long past. The Risian Ministry for Planetary Affairs had realized that they needed a better weather grid, one that couldn't easily be controlled by a small handheld device, so they had installed a new one and hoped it would solve all their problems.

It had not. In fact, it had created more of them. Some satellites stopped working for hours or even days at a time, and their memory cores had to be completely wiped before they could be reactivated. Visitors to Risa had to cope with incredibly localized gales and thunderstorms—if they stayed. Most of them left when they discovered that the planet no longer was the paradise they'd been promised.

As it so happened, a Starfleet admiral was spending his vacation in the Temtibi Lagoon Resort. He had contacted the local facilitator and told her that he knew just the person to solve all their tech-related problems. A number of calls later, Montgomery Scott was packing for his journey to the oldest pleasure planet in the Federation, ready to prove once more that he was the original miracle worker.

Admiral William J. Ross had been right. He had known that Scotty would enjoy his time there, even after he'd repaired the weather grid. The government had even offered to make him honorary citizen of the Risian Hedony, but he'd declined politely, telling them—and himself—that he'd be content if they let him stay on the planet just a little bit longer.

Luckily, a reason to stay had cropped up—there were other problems that needed his attention. The management of the El Dorado Holiday Resort contacted him about some computer trouble they had and asked him, since he was on Risa already, if he could help them out.

He hadn't said no. After all, the resort had a very nice bar.

Another deep breath, another look across the lagoon, taking

in all the sights that Hanotis Harbor offered. He made a point of coming up here every now and then; seeing fantastic sights like this was part of the reason he'd gone into space in the first place, and he wouldn't let retirement stop him from doing it.

Even from here, he could still see the big *horga'hn*s that symbolized the attitude toward sexuality held by the planet's three billion Risians (not to mention more than a billion visitors that came every year). The majority of them had a rather . . . open approach to intimate pleasures. Not that he minded, of course. Not at all.

Ah . . . Belunis. He was sorry that she'd left so soon after he met her. She was a lovely woman, and he wouldn't have minded spending more time with her. Being a living Starfleet legend could get pretty lonely after a few years, not to mention boring. So it had come as a pleasant surprise that there was at least one woman who didn't know who he was or what he'd done. She liked him nonetheless. He had believed that she even loved him, but he would never find out now, would he?

A sigh escaped his lips before he could stop himself. Melancholy and self-pity wouldn't help him. That Hermat he'd met on Argelius II had told him as much, and it was still true.

Right. Abruptly, he turned around and headed back for the lift.

Scotty's shift began at eight in the evening and lasted four hours. Now it was past six, and he was feeling quite a bit peckish indeed. Once he left the Tolari Tower, he began heading back toward the grounds of the El Dorado, where his bungalow was situated.

After a number of failed attempts, he'd tuned the replicator in his apartment the way he needed it to be to produce an acceptable Forfar Bridie. Now, however, he wanted something simple and sweet, like a piece of Dundee cake or a Caledonian cream.

It was remarkable. The older he got, the more he longed for

traditional dishes, the ones he'd grown up with. His mother, despite her Danish ancestry (or perhaps *because* of it), had been the best cook in Aberdeen—and indeed in Scotland.

And then he joined the Fleet and discovered all the splendid cooking that was done on other planets. The unimaginable, the impossible happened: he liked it better!

Perhaps it had something to do with changes of ingredients and different preparation methods. Perhaps it was the fascination of the unknown. Possible . . . but perhaps it was simply the joy of finally getting away from all the history and tradition and cultural background that threatened to crush him like a bug whenever he was in Aberdeen.

At least, that was how he'd felt as a teenager, when he hadn't known that there really was no place like home.

Now, however, he was on Risa, on the paved road leading to his fake Aztec bungalow. When he arrived at the front door, he keyed in his security code, and the door swished open.

He flicked on the lights, replicated himself a double-sized piece of Dundee cake, and sat down at his computer terminal. He was greeted by the blinking words: *You have twenty-three new messages.*

A sigh was followed by acceptance of the unavoidable.

He quickly scanned the message titles and their senders, and eliminated seventeen of them by way of being unknown and/or clearly identifiable as tribblecoms. That left six messages that got a second chance.

A couple were business-related—one from Theodore Quincy, Scotty's manager, about a meeting and another from the head waiter about a contingent of Withiki visiting tonight—and these he quickly read and digested. Three others he eliminated mere moments after opening them, realizing they were tribblecoms more cleverly disguised than most.

The sixth message was the one he'd expected, but not in a positive sense. Still, he had to listen to what it said.

The visage of Admiral Ross, formerly of Starbase 375, Kalandra Sector, now attached to Starfleet Headquarters, Earth, filled the terminal screen. He seemed calm and relaxed, and yet his messages always had a touch of desperation to them.

"Good day, Captain Scott." He still called him "Captain," despite the fact that Scotty was supposedly out of the Fleet. Scott guessed it had something to do with respect, or maybe Ross just didn't know better. He didn't really care either way.

"I know it's quite likely you haven't changed your mind in the last nine days, but nevertheless I want to ask you to reconsider. Starfleet needs you, now more than ever. The Corps needs you. I need you.

"Commander Lynch has now officially submitted his resignation as Corps liaison; his position will be vacant a month from now. Last week, all I could tell you was speculation and rumors, but now it is official. We need a replacement, and I can't think of anybody better suited for this task than you—considering that you worked closely with him until recently."

While it was surprising that Lynch had now actually resigned, the rest of the message wasn't all that different from what Ross had said in last week's message, or in the one from the week before, or the one before *that. Are there no other engineers who could sit behind a desk at HQ instead of me? Starfleet must really be desperate if they can't think of anybody else. Me, a retired,* slightly *overweight, gray-haired man with a bad case of nostalgia! What bloody times are we living in?*

Unaware of Scotty's thoughts, the recorded Admiral Ross continued. *"On behalf of Captains Xentalir and Gold, I have to thank you for your recommendations you sent last time. Apparently, the candidates you picked fit their needs perfectly."*

Hrmph. Not much of an accomplishment. Even the thickest admiral would have seen that Lieutenant Borosh and Commander Gomez were the best of the best. It didn't take a genius to realize that. Okay, so Borosh had a bit of a popularity handicap there with his transparent skull, but he certainly made up for it with his engineering talent. And Sonya Gomez was simply *brilliant.* Her Academy paper about subspace accelerators had impressed Scotty very much—still did—which was the reason why he'd recommended her for the post of S.C.E. team leader on the . . . what was the ship's name again? He only knew the former leader had been a Vulcan. Killed in the war, in a Cardassian attack.

"There are four other senior posts to fill. I'll send you the files of the people we think would be ideal for their respective jobs."

Remind me again why I let myself be talked into this? It still feels like I'm part of the Fleet, even though my brain tells me I am not. But there he was, helping Ross and the soon-to-be-replaced (though not by him) Lynch, choosing candidates for leading S.C.E. positions. This went far beyond gratitude to Ross for steering him to Risa—that debt was long since paid. *How stupid am I? Didn't I promise myself never to work for these people again?*

But some part of him had never really left Starfleet, not even after last year's incident. Some part believed that the organization he'd been a member of for more than half a century was still the same, always looking for something to explore, not exploit. Back when his parents had convinced him to undergo command training even though he had always known he wanted to be an engineer, he'd thought that Starfleet was interested only in acquiring as much knowledge as possible, be it technological, social, medical, or something else. As it turned out, he'd been wrong.

Oh, how wrong he had been.

"I ask you to consider this latest offer. Maybe next time we can talk face-to-face without me having to leave a message for you. That way, you'd get to voice your concerns, and I can provide you with answers to any questions you might have. Good-bye, Captain Scott."

Next time, Ross had said. Yes, it *did* feel as if he were still serving in the Fleet. He'd originally thought that agreeing to help find some S.C.E. candidates would satisfy the top brass on Earth. Once again, he immediately got the proof that he knew better how to deal with machines than people.

The screen changed, and Ross's visage disappeared. The list

of received messages returned, reminding Scotty of the calls the admiral had made in the weeks past. It had all started on a Tarnday about two months ago. Scotty had just finished his work on the El Dorado computer system when the computer announced that Starfleet Headquarters was asking him to call Ross back at his convenience.

Scotty had assumed it had been to see how he was enjoying Risa after he recommended him for the job of fixing the weather system.

As it turned out, there was an ulterior motive: Ross wanted him back in the Fleet.

That was never going to happen. But kindhearted man that he was, Scotty offered to help Ross out by finding fresh blood for the S.C.E., the one Starfleet institution that he still trusted implicitly. Ever since his first close contact with it—then a ragtag group of dirty engineers on a decommissioned starship— he'd felt sympathetic to its cause: solving technology-related problems, wherever they might occur.

Now, however, he was content with his work at the El Dorado. His job consisted of standing at the entrance of the Engineering Room and waiting for prospective patrons. If they decided to enter the establishment, he was to approach them, shake hands and do some small-talk. Pretty straightforward, really—and just what he wanted to do at this stage in his life. Certainly there was better work available for an ex-Starfleet officer, especially one of Scotty's status, but he wasn't doing it for the money; that had been understood both by Scotty and Quincy at the beginning of their employer-employee relationship.

No, what he did it for was the chance to meet people. Despite his being more comfortable with machines around him, Scotty still enjoyed the company of others, and he relished the chance of seeing new faces every day. It was too bad that he rarely had time for longer conversations. Usually, he just approached the newcomers and spoke the magic words—"On behalf of the management of the El Dorado Hotel and Vacation

Resort, I welcome you to the Engineering Room," or a varia-
tion of that. Only sometimes did he manage to actually involve
somebody in a talk that lasted longer than a simple handshake.

Deep down, Montgomery Scott knew he didn't need to resort to fiddling with machines and engines in order to live a
fulfilled life. No, he could just as well do that by interacting
with his friends and acquaintances. However, he preferred to
keep this part of him a secret. It took a very special person to
get past that wall that he'd built for himself, early in his childhood.

His sister, bless her, had been that kind of person, but Clara
was long dead. She'd eventually moved to Neu-Stuttgart after
the death of Hamish, her first husband, having married a
Dr. Hoffmann. Perhaps one day he'd find the time and spirit to
travel to Neu-Stuttgart and visit her grave.

Mira Romaine had been another, and she, too, was no longer among the living. Her fate had been one of the first he'd
checked up on, after his long-overdue rescue from the pattern
buffer.

Belunis had also belonged to this select group of people,
who all happened to be female. She had been Scotty's first
friend on Risa, and soon became much more than that. He'd
worked closely with her when the situation with the weather
control satellites had arisen, and the day after he'd finished the
repairs of the control grid, he'd asked her out, in that special
way of his. She hadn't said no.

Then followed five wonderful weeks of love, happiness
and . . . yes, of pleasure. While many people who'd reached his
age—in actual years he was long past his prime, even though
a bit of transporter trickery was involved—preferred to live a
quieter life in certain respects, Montgomery Scott had never
been one to shy away from anything that gave him pleasure.
It didn't matter if it was food, drink, music, the love of a wonderful woman; when he opened his heart to something, it was
opened wide.

Eating the last bits of Dundee cake, he switched off the

computer terminal. Then he walked back to the replicator to recycle both plate and fork. A quick glance at the antique Canopian timepiece on the wall opposite his desk told him that it was still over half an hour until his shift started, but he decided to be there early. He walked over to the sofa, grabbed the maroon uniform that was lying on it, and put it on.

The uniform was replicated, but it was in all possible ways identical to the one he'd worn for over twenty years. True, most of the time he'd just put on the white turtleneck and his favorite engineer's jacket, but on special occasions he had slipped into his standard uniform.

After dressing he left his bungalow, sealed the entrance by voice command, and began walking toward the imposing pyramid of the El Dorado Hotel and Vacation Resort.

The Engineering Room itself looked just like its real equivalent on an average starship—to the uninitiated eye, at least. A much-decorated chief engineer like Scotty, however, noticed a great number of mistakes and inaccuracies ranging from the placement of the power transfer conduits to the lack of any security measures that would have been standard on any ship of the Fleet. Sure, there was the obligatory railing around the main reactor chamber, but that was about it. Besides, it appeared to only be there for show, not for safety.

There was no need for force fields, as the swirling colors inside the vertical pressure vessel toroid—looking for all the world like a poor man's version of the warp core he'd used on the refit of the original *Enterprise*—were not a result of a constant mixing of both matter and antimatter but different kinds of alcohol, fruit juices, and other ingredients. The PTCs leading away from the reactor chamber supplied a number of taps from which the bartenders drew their drinks hurriedly. The bar was bustling with people already, even though it was not even night yet.

Technically, "night" was something that Risa in its natural

state rarely experienced. The cause for this was the existence of a second sun that had an entirely different revolutionary rhythm. To avoid almost eternal daylight, the Risians had installed gigantic screens in orbit that would blot out any unwanted rays from the larger, reddish star on the "nightside" hemisphere. Of course, they didn't want a large, starless field in their sky, so they also installed simulated stars that mimicked their real counterparts. This was but one example of the trouble the Risians went to to satisfy their visitors as well as themselves.

Now he was standing outside the hotel, watching the steady throng of people coming down the boulevard. Many of them were obviously attracted by the music and the kaleidoscope colors that were pouring outside through the open hotel doors. Many of them were humans, or at least humanoid, but there were a few aliens that had almost nothing in common with those. Scotty saw a few Escherites, those horizontally-oriented creatures that he'd first met on the refit *Enterprise*, and they were still extraordinarily strange to look at, even though he had served another three decades in an ever-expanding Federation. Scott also spotted the occasional Mizarthu, and if he wasn't mistaken, there was a Horta slowly disappearing behind a group of Gnalish.

Presently, Montgomery Scott found himself staring at two shapes that moved along the promenade with the other tourists, and when he realized which species they belonged to, he was quickly thrown out of his nostalgic reverie, only to land on the hard floor of reality.

Two Kropaslin were among the various aliens attracted by the sounds of laughter and joy that came out the hotel's open doors. The couple, a male and a female, was actually taking a left turn, walking slowly and magnificently down the paved road that led to the El Dorado's main entrance.

Scotty was using all the power at his disposal not to utter a particularly profane Gaelic curse. There was so much time in the universe, so why did these two have to show up *right now*? Who they were or why they were here didn't matter; what mattered was *what* they were, and that they reminded him of something that he still hated himself for.

It had happened only about half a year ago, and the memory was still fresh. He'd tried to drown it in many a glass of Scotch, Saurian brandy, and genuine Romulan *kalifal*, but it hadn't worked. No matter how much alcohol he imbibed, Nechayev's order was still as present in his mind as if everything had happened yesterday.

Of course, he was intellectually aware that he was, as a member of an originally military organization, expected to follow the orders of his superiors, no matter what those orders might be. That wasn't the problem.

The problem was that he was also morally aware that some of those orders were just stupid—or worse, they were totally and utterly *wrong*. Nechayev's order had struck him as one of the latter sort, no matter how often she told him it was for the good of the Federation. She was a much-decorated Starfleet admiral, that was true—but, as Tarbolde had once said, "even the gods have erred," and Nechayev clearly was not a god.

The good of the Federation. What a bloody excuse to throw away your ideals and integrity.

Great. Now he was angry *and* nostalgic at the same time. Not the best of moods to be in while working. He needed a distraction, and he needed it quickly.

There seemed to be only one way out of this dilemma. He had to engage the Kropaslin in a conversation.

"Good evening to you both. On behalf of the management of the El Dorado Hotel and Vacation Resort, I welcome you and invite you to the Engineerin' Room. I'm sure you're going to have a nice evenin'."

Later that night, he came close to forgetting the Kropaslin and what they reminded him of as they left the ER soon after they'd entered. Apparently, it was not their kind of bar, and they endeavored to look elsewhere for adequate entertainment.

While the bar was open until six in the morning, Scotty's shift ended earlier. Usually he left the ER at twelve; sometimes he stayed on for another couple of hours. Occasionally, he even placed himself on a stool at the bar, watching the bartenders draw their drinks. That Guinan woman he'd met on the *Enterprise*—the *Enterprise*s, plural, to be exact—would fit right in here.

Tonight, he got home at about one, tired and a bit dizzy from all the welcome drinks he'd organized for new guests (of course he'd had to drink some himself; it simply wouldn't do to let the guests down them alone). When he unlocked the front door by voice command, he experienced a short memory flash, as if something in his mind had been activated by an unknown stimulus.

Not only did he suddenly remember the two Kropaslin, but also every bit about the mission to Kropasar last year, the repercussions of said mission, his decision to wander once more, and the call for help from the Risian officials.

It seemed there was no escaping the past, no matter how hard he tried. A Takaran spiced ale seemed to be in order, as it would enable him to accept the inevitable onslaught of regret, anger, and general helplessness.

Belunis had not been very fond of his drinking habit at all. She was of the opinion that he was an alcoholic, but she was mistaken. If anything, he appreciated the taste of alcoholic drinks, but he did not imbibe them for the single reason that they contained alcohol.

The most important thing was the taste. The alcohol was just a nice side effect. That blasted synthehol those greedy little cheaters had introduced a few years before his return to a physical existence just wasn't good enough, and he'd told a great number of people what he thought about that Ferengi swill.

"Light."

The computer obeyed and illuminated the interior of the bungalow Montgomery Scott had occupied for the past two months. It was not as spacious as the one he had lived in after he moved out of his parents' house, but it was more than just acceptable. Most important, there were enough shelves for all the engineering textbooks, technical manuals, starship guides, and engineering briefs that he'd collected over the years. It was a quite impressive collection, and it moved with him whenever he changed residences. Those books had been in Aberdeen— albeit in not so great a number—first in his room on the second floor of his family's house, then in his flat; they had been in his room on the San Francisco campus, and they also had been in his quarters on all the *Enterprise*s. He'd even taken them with him when he'd moved into his sister's house just some months before he boarded the *Jenolen*. Thank goodness he'd left them there when he left for the retirement colony, otherwise they'd be so much debris on the side of a Dyson sphere right now.

There was a small hallway that led from the entrance to the back of the building, with two rooms on either side of it. It contained a row of coat hangers as well as a clothing replicator integrated into the wall also containing a companel and computer access. The first room on the left was his office/bedroom; opposite it was the bungalow's kitchen, whose reduced size was due to the big living room adjacent to it. The final, fourth room was the bathroom, which contained a sonic shower and a real bathtub, a toilet and an Antedean soaking spot.

The bungalow was small, especially if one compared it to some of the others Scotty had been offered by Quincy, but it was perfectly suited to his needs. A single man did not need as much space as two people did. Belunis had never mentioned moving in with him, nor suggested *he* move in with *her*. Scotty had the feeling it wasn't only because their relationship had not lasted long enough to give her a chance to think about this major step, it was also because Belunis wasn't the type for such relationships. She was passionate and caring, but deep down she wanted to be free of commitments. She was what was now called a "free bird," flying wherever she wanted and settling down only when needed.

Scotty, however, was all too happy to settle down

permanently. He was ready for retirement, had been ever since before Khitomer. There were some in Starfleet who thought it a good idea to get him back into action, but they simply had not found out yet that they were wrong.

Granted, working until they dropped dead might be all right for some, but it wasn't for him. He was no Leonard McCoy—still an active Starfleet admiral at nearly 150, occasionally commanding a starship on a mission, visiting starbases and cruising around the Federation in a small runabout.

That inspection tour he'd joined McCoy on had been a lot of fun, even when they had almost met their fate on Bakrii at the hands of a Breen warship. It was better than paperwork, at any rate. Afterward, though, they had seen the damage wrought by the Breen on Earth, and learned how fragile some things really were.

The Breen. Of course.

His mind was going in circles, never straying too far from the subject that was at the heart of the matter. It all came down to the orders Nechayev had given him, the ones that had forced him to betray the trust of a planet full of innocent beings, simply because she thought it a good idea.

Blast the Breen.

Blast Nechayev.

Abruptly, Scotty moved over to the desk upon which the computer terminal sat.

"Computer, patch me through to Admiral Leonard McCoy's office."

"Working."

Seconds passed, and even though he hated the cliché, they seemed much longer—though not quite like hours.

Then, finally: *"Unable to comply. Admiral McCoy's office is closed."*

"Why?"

"Admiral McCoy is not in his office," the computer said, almost mockingly.

What? Where would Leonard be at this time of year? And

why would he *close* his office? The last time they'd spoken face-to-face—which had happened shortly after their return to Earth, in the aftermath of the Breen attack on San Francisco—McCoy had intimated that he'd refrain from ever leaving his home planet again, "unless it turns out to be absolutely necessary and impossible to avoid."

"Locate Admiral McCoy. Authorization: Scott-Psi-Three-Phi-Tango."

"Authorization accepted. Locating." A few more moments passed. *"Admiral Leonard H. McCoy is currently on Arcturus."*

"Patch me through to Arcturus, then. And better make it quick, y'hear?"

"Working," the computer's male voice said, ignoring the angry undertone in Scott's voice.

While the computer contacted the planet via various subspace relays, Scott took another sip of the Takaran ale. It was a bitter brew, and even for him it had required some getting used to.

"Comlink to Arcturus established. Contacting Admiral McCoy."

"Finally. Next time I'll do it myself. Wouldn't be any slower than you, I'm tellin' you," Scotty grumbled.

Another sip, and he closed his eyes as the liquid made its way down his throat. Because of that, he was completely unprepared for what happened next.

"I'd sure like to know who has such a unique talent of calling at the worst possible moment!"

It was all Scotty could to do keep from sputtering his ale across the computer screen. He'd been successful!

"Hello, Admiral," Scotty said, using the formal address that Len so despised.

"Scotty! I should have known it was you. I'm doing something very important, and I don't want to be disturbed. Why do you think I closed down my office?"

"And a good day to you, too, Len."

"Oh, don't pretend to be so awfully polite. Doesn't get you

anywhere, y'know?" McCoy said, looking distracted. Scotty couldn't quite make out where his friend was, except that it was a room with a giant emblem of Starfleet Medical on the wall. A medical conference? But they usually took place on holiday planets, didn't they?

"I'll try to remember it for the future. So, what is it you're doing, and why did you close your office in Krung Thep for it?"

"Because this is the presentation of this year's Carrington Award winner, and I've been chosen to announce the winner. Having won the award twice before, I must've seemed like the logical choice," McCoy said with a glint in his eye. Something amused him, though Scotty did not know what.

"And the office?" he asked.

"Is closed until further notice. Rank hath its privileges, you should know that by now. It's not like I'm actually responsible for running the place—Yerbi does that, even if everything would fall apart without me. And after all I've done for him, he can't deny an old fart like me a little pleasure. Look at me, I'm older'n Sarek was when I met him for the first time. Every day I am surprised that I'm still alive. I take it you know the feeling?"

Scotty only nodded.

"The Krung Thep office, which you tried to contact without success, is closed because I took my staff with me. They're hard workers, and they deserve to have some fun now and then."

"But—"

"But me no buts, Scotty. I'm an admiral; I can damned well do as I please."

Admiral. The rank that Jim Kirk had never wanted to have—because it brought power with it, both political and military, and, as everybody knew, power corrupted. Even McCoy wasn't immune to its effects.

"So, hurry up, old-timer. What is it that you want from me?"

Scotty pretended not to have heard the bit about the "old-timer." "I just wanted to have a nice, quiet conversation with an old friend of mine, but I realize this is a bad moment . . ."

"That's right. I've only got a few more minutes before they drag

me onstage. I really have no time to talk now. Later, maybe, but not now."

"I understand, Len. Have a nice day."

"I'll make sure that I do. Good-bye, Scotty, and behave yourself. That's an order."

"Aye, Admiral." As the line was cut, Scotty leaned back in his chair and sighed. McCoy was much too busy for his own good. A man his age—and McCoy had aged the old-fashioned way, without tricking Time—should slow down a bit. Relax. Enjoy life. Not necessarily sit on his bum all day long, but at the same time not ask more of himself than his body was willing to give.

It hurt Scotty to look at his fragile friend, his extremities supported by a duritanium and plasteel framework, not dissimilar to those worn by members of species native to low-grav planets. The seventy-five years that had been taken from the engineer had not been overly kind to McCoy, even though the doctor had made use of any and all medical innovations and advantages that had become available to him.

McCoy was probably the best friend Scotty had left— certainly the one he'd spent the most time with since he'd been revived on the *Jenolen*. Sure, some of his other old shipmates were still around, but most of them kept busy. Uhura still had her Intelligence job, but that meant that she had a lot on her plate, with little time for old shipmates. She was working with others at shaping the fate of the known galaxy, although she herself would most likely never have put it quite so dramatically. Some years ago, he'd even got a call from Chekov, who'd wanted to say hello. Now a desk-jockey admiral, the former security officer had an enormous amount of work, but he'd made some time.

Scotty would contact any of them if he was sure enough that they'd be able to spare an hour for him. Unfortunately, he wasn't. Not at all.

Grumbling, he switched off the computer terminal and stood up. The truth was, McCoy's lack of time for him, regardless of his reasons for it, hurt the former engineer. He'd awaited—*expected*—a jovial talk about the past, some friendly advice, maybe even the promise of an inquiry into the legality of the Kropasar mission. Yet he had received none of this.

So perhaps it's time I bloody well took matters into my own hands. Why rely on the possiblity of McCoy looking into things—or asking Uhura or Chekov to—when he could do it his own self? He needed to know what he'd done, what he'd caused to come to be, and there was no reason why he couldn't have a look into the Federation's xenosociological and xeno-historical databases himself.

Standing there, staring at the display, he was clueless as to why it had taken him over half a year to do this. He should have done so immediately after the Kropasar mission. He should have performed weekly checks to find out what had happened to the planet after he had left. The truth was that he had been afraid of what he might discover.

Blast it. It was no use thinking about what he *should* have done; only people afraid to actually try to undo the damage they caused did that, often while downing one drink after another.

And I'm no alcoholic, so I won't do that.

With newfound enthusiasm, Scotty searched the databases for any bits of information about Kropasar. It took several hours to compile it all, but after a time, he had collected enough data to form a picture in his mind.

It was not a pleasant picture.

Apparently the government had lost credibility with the public following the rejection of the planet's bid for Federation membership—a rejection that almost immediately followed the Breen cruiser's being purloined. After all, there was no need to be nice to the aliens if the Federation had what it wanted out of them. The Consensus Party had lost its majority in the Witenagemot; High Cyning Forecic lost her position as its head.

But Thane Iamor and his Agreement Party had been unable

to rise into the gap. According to the public record, a dispute over some action of Iamor's—Scotty had a good idea what action *that* was—had split the party asunder, meaning no one was able to achieve the majority in the Witenagemot necessary to create a functioning government. Unfortunately, one of the planet's many provincial cynings had taken advantage of the lull in authority to revive a long-standing grudge with another cyning, weapons had been fired, and any chance of a unified Kropasar reemerging had died in the ensuing chaos.

He couldn't have imagined it if he had tried. He had known betraying the Kropaslin by stealing their cruiser and rejecting their bid for Federation membership would have had to have *some* effect on them, but *this*? According to reports, the multitronic computer so important to the continued functioning of several government services had been one of the first fatalities of the provincial cynings' squabbling. With that computer gone, vital government secrets relating to the production of bioneural circuitry had been lost, and without that vital export, the entire planet's economy was plunged into ruin.

Things only got worse from there.

This was bad. This was really bad. And it was partially his own fault—though not his alone. Fleet Admiral Alynna Nechayev shared the responsibility for these developments.

Which was why the next thing he did was contact her.

"Admiral Nechayev is currently not in her office."

Blast and double-blast! Was nobody willing to go to work today? First McCoy, now Nechayev. He'd thought that a call by a living Starfleet "legend" like himself would cause Starfleet Command to immediately establish a connection. Instead, he was given the usual evasive gibberish about Nechayev being incredibly busy and thus unavailable.

"Well. That's too bad," Scotty said, restraining himself from telling the admiral's Andorian secretary what he really felt. "Can I leave her a message? It's rather urgent, I'm afraid, and I'd like to hear her take on it."

"Of course you can leave her a message, Mr. Scott. I'll make

sure that she sees it," the secretary said, her antennae probing the air as she spoke.

"Thank you. I'd like to record and encrypt it, so if you don't mind, I'll get back to you in a few moments."

"Of course, Mr. Scott. The admiral will contact you later. Have a nice day."

With that, the connection was cut, and Scotty found himself staring at an empty computer screen, barely containing his anger. Was Nechayev really not in her office? He knew from experience that she was not above lying when it suited her needs. After all, she'd claimed to be sick once already, at a time when it would have been uncomfortable for her to suddenly have him calling her, complaining about the orders she'd given him. Instead, she'd claimed to be ill, a ruse that should have been as transparent to him then as it was now.

Silly him. He'd really expected her to be honest with him, when her day's work consisted of making up stuff as she went along? Nechayev belonged to the upper echelons of Starfleet Intelligence, which was just like any other secret security agency. There certainly wasn't much of a difference from the Tal Shiar or Imperial Intelligence.

He was certain that you had to give up your soul when you got recruited by any of them. Even Uhura, whom he still thought of as a friend, had changed in the decades since he'd last seen her in the twenty-third century. She'd become more serious, more distant, more . . . secretive, than the woman he'd once fancied.

He quickly recorded a short message to Nechayev, ambiguous enough to confuse any listener not familiar with what really had transpired on Kropasar last year, but at the same time detailed enough to let the admiral know what he wanted. Then he encrypted it, using a particularly clever technique; Scotty had found out years ago that many Starfleet codes were based on engineering protocols and warp-field physics. Using this knowledge, he chose a particularly difficult code to give Nechayev's grunts an interesting time—after all, he was certain that she wouldn't attempt to decrypt the message herself. She knew how to delegate.

Oh yes, she did.

He sent the message without establishing a direct comlink to Nechayev's office on Starbase 395, because he didn't want to talk to *Zha* Obnoxious again. Even though he wouldn't have admitted it to anybody, he felt a certain smugness when he hit the SEND button.

Having accomplished what he'd set out to do, he went on to clean up his office. There were unrecycled glasses everywhere, a painful reminder of last week's drinking excesses, even more so because he'd told himself that he had stopped drinking alone. Stretching his arms, he grabbed as many of the replicated crystal tumblers as he could, all the while telling himself that he wasn't an alcoholic. After all, he'd know if he was one, right?

The glasses weren't the only thing he had to clear off his desk. There were a number of padds lying there as well: detailed analyses of the computer system the El Dorado used, some technical manuals, a number of data files he'd found lacking and started to amend to fit his own needs.

He was barely done with it when the computer beeped.

"You are receiving a real-time communication."

"Well, on the soddin' screen with it! What are you waitin' for?"

A face appeared on the display screen. However, it was not the stern, angular face of Fleet Admiral Alynna Nechayev. Instead, it was that of Theodore Quincy, who—for reasons unknown—asked the people he considered his friends to call him "Thomas."

"Good evening, Mr. Quincy."

"Scotty, I don't know how often I've asked you to—"

"—call you Thomas. I don't know, either."

"Ah, so you do remember. But what about this morning? Have you forgotten about that?" asked Quincy, clearly agitated about something.

"What? When—" he interrupted himself. "Computer, what's the time?"

"Eight hours, twenty-six minutes and eleven seconds."

"Thank you. You were sayin', Mr. Qui . . . Thomas?"

"This is exactly why I'm calling. It's already past eight o'clock! Today's a Varasday, in case you aren't aware."

"Oh." Bloody sodding hell. Varasday was Risa's equivalent of a Sunday, the last day of the weekend, and thus something special. It had been Quincy's—Thomas's—idea to have the Engineering Room open on a Varasday morning and serve breakfast as usual, but with a twist.

The twist consisted of a simulated warp core breach, which was achieved by flashing lights within the M/ARA and colorful smoke being released from the ceiling. To top it all off, Scotty was supposed to pretend to do his best to stop the core breach. However, he was not supposed to be entirely successful. The breach was the special weekly event that drew in an additional two hundred or so visitors that put the money into Quincy's pockets, the manager had told Scotty at the beginning of their relationship.

"Don't worry, Thomas," he said, "that only means the breach'll happen a wee bit later than usual. It's not as if those usually happen at a specific time, anyway."

"This is the financial future of the El Dorado we're talking about! If there's no core breach today, our customers will immediately flock to some other hotel on the other side of the harbor. This is important, Scotty! I do hope you'll be here in a matter of minutes, otherwise I don't know what we should do!"

"Have you considered doin' it yourself? Really, all I do is run around and play prevent-the-core-breach. You could do the same, I'm sure."

"I have better things to do than pretending to be a headless chicken!" Quincy shouted. *"I'm the manager of this establishment. I hired you to attract more customers, in case you forgot. At the moment, I can't say you're doing your job."*

"Okay, okay, don't get your knickers in a twist just yet. I'll be there before you can say 'asymmetrical peristaltic field manipulation.'"

"I'll be waiting for you," Quincy said and ended their conversation.

Bugger. Was it really past eight already? He hadn't noticed the time slipping away like this.

Scotty found that he didn't really care either way. While angering Quincy was something he didn't mind all that much, he also could do without it. It made working for him much easier.

So it happened that, roughly ten minutes later, he was on the paved road again, walking through the carefully kept jungle toward the gold-covered walls of the El Dorado Hotel and Vacation Resort, mentally preparing himself once more for the unspeakable terror that was the Varasday morning warp core breach.

At ten o'clock, the smoke had long since cleared, most of the patrons had left the ER, and Scotty was on his way back to the bungalow. Quincy's mood had immediately improved the second he'd seen Scotty in his ancient uniform. From then on, everything had progressed as it always did. He'd pretended to be not quite the miracle worker people told him he was, running around like a headless chicken indeed, and he'd even shocked quite a number of patrons by having some of the "warp plasma" blown in his face.

When he unlocked the door, he was greeted by the computer's voice that told him he was receiving a real-time communication.

Hurrying toward the office, he shouted, "Well, put it on, you *glaikit* heap of isolinear rods!"

Just as Scotty reached the room at the far end of the corridor, the computer obligingly activated the screen on the wall near his office desk, displaying the Starfleet emblem for a short moment before changing to the countenance of the one member of the Fleet he most seriously wished never to have met.

Admiral Alynna Nechayev stared at him with the same serious look on her face that he had expected to see. Not even once
in all the time he'd had the dubious pleasure of working for
her had he seen her crack a genuine smile.

Which was probably for the best. For all he knew, her face
would split apart, and the top of her head would fall off.

"*Mr. Scott,*" she said in lieu of a greeting, "*I hope I didn't contact you at an inopportune moment.*"

"Oh, you most certainly did not, Admiral. Ever since leavin'
the Fleet I've had more time on my hands than is good for me."

"*I see. I do have to admit that I am surprised to see you wearing this.*"

"What? Oh," he said, realizing that he was still wearing his
old engineer's radiation suit, a replicated one whose design
dated back to the same era as his standard duty uniform that
he usually wore when playing the greeter at the ER's entrance.
"What can I say? Those were better times. You can't fault an
old man for doin' a little reminiscin', can you, lass?"

"*Mr. Scott, I remember telling you on numerous occasions
that I resent being called a 'lass.' Surely your memory is still as
remarkable as it was?*"

"Ach, would that it were. There's things that I can't seem
to remember even if my life depended on it, and yet there's
things that I will quite possibly never ever forget," Scotty said,
deliberately choosing an ominous way of phrasing his reply.
Why shouldn't he remind Nechayev of what he knew? Maybe
one day he'd tell everybody how she'd maneuvered him into
betraying his oath and everything he believed in. The Federation newsnets would eat it up like Kaferian apple pie. After all,
they liked stories about Starfleet scandals. He remembered the
fuss the media had made about Jim Kirk's death on the *Enterprise*-B. Poor John Harriman had had to bear the devastating
reports that put all the blame on him, and not on an unpredictable ribbon of flashing energy, not to mention a headstrong,
stubborn guest of honor.

"*Splendid. Now, in your message to me—whose encryption, I*

have to admit, was quite a puzzle to my specialists, at least at the beginning—you mentioned something about Kropasar? I believe you even said you were concerned about its people."

"Indeed I am, *Admiral*," he replied, using her rank like an insult. "You see, I spent some time last night gatherin' information about Kropasar. You are aware of the situation on the planet, I trust?" Not giving her any time to reply, he continued, "Never mind. I'll tell you. Kropasar's fallen to pieces. The government's collapsed, the economy's on the way out, disasters are ragin' unchecked. And all of that happened because you and your pals decided to flout the basic principles not only of the Federation, but also of decency itself."

Nechayev's face was made of stone, her lips a thin line. Then, finally, she opened them to answer. *"So you've done your homework, Mr. Scott. Bravo. But let me show you that I've done mine as well. Going over your file, I didn't notice any filed complaints of yours when your revered Captain Kirk and Commander Spock went over to that Romulan battle cruiser and acquired its cloaking device. Neither did you protest in the least when the* Enterprise *fired on that colony of Axanar insurgents. You did not have any objections to Kirk's rather unconventional solution to the Pelosians' extinction problem that violated the spirit, if not exactly the letter, of three of Starfleet's General Orders. What's more, you even participated in that* Starstalker *project whose goal was to create the ultimate fighting cruiser.*

"Are you going to tell me that these instances are in no way comparable to what happened on Kropasar? Because I get the feeling that Kirk never did anything wrong, or you would have said something."

Losh, that woman certainly knew how to push a man's buttons, didn't she? "It may surprise you, but Captain Kirk did make the occasional mistake. Still, he certainly was no thief. He did what he was ordered to—"

A laugh—or was it a snort?—from Nechayev interrupted him, but he regained his composure quickly enough.

"He sometimes interpreted the rules a tad too generously,

that is true, but what he did was always in the best interest of Starfleet and the entire Federation. And as for the events you cited, let me tell you that the Romulans were our enemies back then. I seem to remember that the Kropaslin were supposed to be our tradin' partners and a potential member! We're not supposed to steal from our *allies*!

"Those Axanar rebels, they deserved nothin' better, and if you've read my file, you know. As for the Pelosians, let me just say that history vindicated our actions, just as it did with regards to the Talin incident. Nobody was found guilty of violatin' a single General Order."

"Have I touched upon a sensitive subject? If so, let me apologize, Mr. Scott. However, you have not explained your involvement with the Starstalker *project."*

"And I shan't. The S.C.E. asked me to help them out, which I did, mainly because I was asked *politely*."

Nechayev surprised him by smiling, even though it was not a kind smile. It reminded him of the expression usually found on the face of a Gorborasti palmsnake before it dislocated its left and right jaws to devour its victim.

"A pity you chose to be an engineer, Mr. Scott. You would have made a decent intelligence operative. Your evasive reasoning is on par with that of my best agents."

Now he became really angry—even though he didn't know what about, to be honest. "What is that supposed to mean, Admiral?"

"Mistakes are always the others' fault, aren't they? If you or your friends break the rules, there's always a good enough reason to pacify your conscience. Somebody else does the same, it's an outrage. How dare they treat the principles of the Federation like that, et cetera."

"Now that is simply not true, and you know it! Frankly, I'm appalled that an officer like you would resort to makin' petty remarks like these. Stealing anythin' from the Kropaslin is an extraordinarily serious crime, and I hate myself for havin' been moved into participatin'."

"*I remember you telling me as much just after the mission ended. Why did you choose to contact me at this exact point in time?*" asked Nechayev, her face deadly serious.

"I . . . I simply had to. The disgust is eatin' me up inside, and I just can't bear it any longer. Eventually, though, I will be able to speak with others about all this, not just with you. The truth will out, Admiral, there's no denyin' it."

Nechayev leaned forward, so close to the optical sensor in her comm terminal that her face filled the entire display. "*Are you threatening me?*"

Scotty shook his head. "No. I'm not willin' to incur your eternal wrath by leakin' Starfleet secrets to the press. However," he began and took a sip of the now stale *kalifal* he'd replicated earlier today, "be assured that I know of no secret that remained exactly that. Somethin' always goes wrong, somebody always blurts somethin' to his 'friends,' and pretty soon there's no stoppin' it. I'm a patient man, Admiral, I can wait. But when the Kropasar mission becomes public knowledge, I certainly won't be helpin' you to save your precious hide."

"*Mr. Scott, far worse than you has threatened me during my Starfleet career. You can do whatever you like, but I would advise you to remember your manners when you speak to your superiors, even if you are on . . . 'inactive duty.'*"

"Manners, my arse. You had better start preparin' a plausible explanation for your actions, because people *will* ask questions. Lots of them. Good-bye, Admiral. Rest assured you won't be hearin' from me in a very long time. Scott out."

Before Nechayev had a chance to reply, the connection was cut, and the El Dorado logo replaced her thin face.

"Computer, do not establish a two-way connection to Admiral Alynna Nechayev's office until further notice, no matter how urgent she makes it out to be, you hear me?"

"*Acknowledged.*"

"Good. Now switch off and let me take a nap."

★　★　★

The following day lacked any unforeseen events, thus being the first "normal" working day for months. Not even Ross decided to call, which was . . . interesting, to say the least. In fact, the day's uneventfulness was suspicious, but Scotty couldn't well complain about experiencing a boring day every now and then, could he?

Despite his misgivings about the lack of unexpected happenings, the day progressed and ended without a surprise of the bad sort. He went to work, drank a few drinks with new and returning patrons of the Engineering Room, and spent some time talking to Beltz, one of the regulars, about the romantic prospects of a middle-aged, balding Klingon on a Federation pleasure planet.

Over the past few weeks there had been almost regular communications with HQ, mostly because of Ross's repeated calls. However, the next days did not bring any news from that corner of the galaxy. No pleading calls to change his mind, no requests for more officer recommendations, nothing. Not even Commander Lynch tried to contact him, which was a miracle in itself. If ever there was a person most certainly *not* suited for the job of S.C.E. liaison to the admiralty, it was Leland T. Lynch. Of course, this made his calls much more frequent than they would have been if Lynch had actually been competent. Despite what he'd told Nechayev and Ross before, Lynch was about as perfect for the job as a Klingon was for writing juicy romance novels.

By the end of the second week, Scotty had almost gotten used to the lack of attempts to contact him. At the very least, he didn't constantly expect to receive a call from Ross or somebody else at HQ any longer. Yet just as he was making small talk with all four members of an Andorian quad, one of the bartenders ran toward him.

"Sorry for the interruption, Scotty," said the bartender, whose name was Geren'zrix, "but there's a message for you. Somebody from Starfleet, apparently. He said it was urgent."

"It's always urgent, Zrix. It always is." Scotty sighed. "Please excuse me, *zhutanii*," he said to the quad.

There was a comm terminal near the faux warp core, to be used by the ER staff whenever they needed it. When Scotty arrived there, it was active, displaying the bulldog face of William J. Ross. What was the old gadgie up to now?

"I apologize for disturbing you at work, Captain Scott, but there's something I have to tell you, and it can't wait. If this wasn't urgent, I wouldn't have called you, trust me."

Scotty felt that a sigh was in order right now, and he did not try to hide it. "I do have to say you didn't pick an ideal time, Admiral. But I'm here, listenin' to you, and so we had better continue this. What is it that you want?"

"I have made inquiries," said Ross, leaving Scotty to wonder what on Earth he was talking about. *"Somebody told me that you are not very fond of a certain member of the admiralty. Is that true?"*

True to the old Fleet proverb, rumors did travel at warp ten, it seemed. "Who told you that?"

"Never mind. I have people who tell me things I need to hear. Mind you, I also have people who tell me things I want to hear, but those are not as welcome as the others." Ross allowed himself a quick smile before his face returned to its usual state of stony seriousness. *"In any case, I know of your, let's say, 'discussion' with a certain female admiral, and I believe I have a good idea of what this is about."*

A short, deprecating laugh escaped Scotty's mouth before he could stop himself. "I'm sorry, Admiral, but I don't believe you do. And even if you know somethin', you most likely don't know *everythin'*."

"Then why don't you tell me? I'll be in-system in a couple of days. I suggest we meet on Epsilon Ceti Outpost."

"I don't know. If this is just another trick of yours to get me back into action, then forget it. All due respect, Admiral, but I'm not a toy to be played with as you see fit."

"I am quite aware of that, Captain Scott. Let me assure you that I'm not trying to trick you into returning to the Fleet. While I make no secret of my interest in getting you 'back into action,'

as you phrase it, I consider myself honest enough not to resort to scheming and plotting like a power-hungry madman."

"And I never accused you of bein' one."

"I know. Now, what say you to a meeting, Scotty?"

"Well, I don't think it can hurt," the former engineer said carefully, not wanting to sound too eager. The fact of the matter was that he welcomed the idea of meeting with Ross face-to-face, but for completely different reasons. Some things just didn't have a big enough impact when said on a subspace channel. "Let me know when you're here."

"I will. Scotty, I'm really looking forward to this meeting," the admiral said, apparently satisfied. *"Ross out."*

When he returned to his place near the ER's entrance, Scotty began to realize that a visit from Ross, no matter what the reason, could only mean trouble.

Crivens, what have I got myself into now? he asked himself. Ever since Ross had got wind of his resignation, he'd tried everything in his power—short of bribery and blackmail—to make him change his mind.

Was it Scotty's fault if Ross didn't realize he didn't have a chance?

True to his word, Ross called him a mere two days later, asking him to be on Epsilon Ceti Outpost at noon, Central Risian Time. The *U.S.S. Cerberus,* Ross's flagship, had arrived in the system, ready to beam the admiral onto the outpost. After telling Quincy that he really needed to do this, Scotty was allowed to borrow his private impulse flitter, which he piloted across the binary system toward the Starfleet outpost orbiting the smaller star of the pair at a distance of roughly four hundred sixty million kilometers.

The outpost had been established toward the end of the twenty-second century, shortly after the Risian government had agreed to ally itself with the fledgling Federation of Planets that had been founded only a few decades before. The Risians had hoped for an increased influx of visitors to their planet, and they had not been disappointed.

Of course, the structure now orbiting Epsilon Ceti B was not the same one that had been built almost two centuries ago. The station had been overhauled, repaired and upgraded many times, so much so, in fact, that it no longer resembled a dark gray cylinder but a disc with a slightly blue tinge.

EC Outpost, as it was commonly named, featured a breathtaking observation center. Five levels tall, it served as a general recreation area, complete with trees, ponds, lakes, hills, even a river and a waterfall. Ross had asked him to wait at the Littlejohn Monument, a statue of the famous Earth president that had been erected near the central lake. On three sides of the monument, a number of comfortable benches invited passersby to sit down and enjoy the view—and perhaps think about the time of the founding of the Federation, back when Lydia Littlejohn had been Earth's president.

Those had been bad times, almost as bad as these last few years, Scotty was sure. The Romulans had been the twenty-second century's Dominion, provoking Earth into a war by means of their minefields and crudely disguised ships. Earth's wounds from the Xindi attack had just begun to heal when a new threat had made itself known. However, although they were trying to destabilize relations among Earth, Andor, and Tellar, the pointy-eared xenophobes managed to strengthen them instead, which directly led to the foundation of the Federation only a few years later.

The sound of approaching steps on the graveled path behind him disrupted his train of thought, and he turned around to look at the newcomer. It was Ross.

"Good day, Captain Scott," the much-decorated war veteran said. "Thank you for coming."

"A good day to you, too, Admiral. Why don't you take a seat?"

"Oh, I will, don't worry. I have a lot to talk about with you, and I'd much rather do that with a nice hardwood bench beneath me."

"A lot, you say? I thought there's only one thing we need to discuss," Scotty said, confused. What had Ross planned for this meeting? He mentally prepared himself for the worst and expected dozens of S.C.E. captains looking for new crew members, letters of recommendation to be written, speeches to be given, and all the other tasks that so far had been dutifully fulfilled by Leland T. Lynch.

"One *major* thing, that is correct," Ross said, his face once again serious as usual, the welcoming smile of seconds before gone without a trace. "But before we start, let me just show you this."

Ross held up a small metallic-looking ball between his thumb and forefinger and showed it to Scotty. It was an electronic device, that much was certain, but its function was not as clear. However, Ross had chosen a particularly public spot that, while currently being remarkably devoid of other visitors, still was not as suited for discussions of a very secret subject as both of them would have liked it to be. Most likely, this device's purpose was to change that. Indeed, it did have some similarity with a comm scrambler that Nyota had shown him once, about a century ago, if he wasn't mistaken.

Ross seemed to read his thoughts. "This here is a little gadget to ensure the privacy of our conversation. Nobody will be able to listen in, so you may talk as freely as you like."

"That depends," Scotty said and leaned back, crossing his arms across his chest.

"On what?"

"Will you do the same?" he asked and looked Ross in the eyes. Scotty's level of candidness depended heavily on Ross's reaction, so he observed intently.

The answer came at once. "Of course I will. I have no reason to lie to you."

"That's very good to hear. So, let's cut to the chase, lad. Why are we both here?"

"I thought that was obvious. I know of your connection to Alynna Nechayev, and of your journey to Kropasar last year."

So his fears had *not* been unfounded. Had he been a cynic like McCoy, he'd have been happy about that, at least. Still, there was no reason to immediately spill all the beans. "What are you talkin' about?"

"Oh, don't play the innocent here, Scotty," Ross said impatiently. "I know what the *Gorkon*'s mission was said to be. I also know what her mission really was, and I know that Alynna doesn't think as highly of you as she did before you set foot on her ship half a year ago."

"Oh, she doesn't? That's a pity."

"Sarcasm doesn't suit you, you know that?"

"I happen to think otherwise, but let's stop the small-talkin'. You know what she ordered—*forced* me to do. All right. Still, what is it to you? Are you goin' to expose her for what she really is: a threat to the Federation?"

"Honestly, no. I can't do that."

Scotty harrumphed. "I should have known."

"Probably, yes. But tell me, if her orders went against everything you believed in, why didn't you simply disobey them? Correct me if I'm wrong, but didn't Kirk do the same repeatedly, not caring about what happened to him and his career, because he did what he thought was right?"

"Don't lecture me on what Jim Kirk did, Admiral, I know that better than you. Better than most of today's SFHQ, even. I was serving in Starfleet before their grandfathers were born, so—"

"Don't give me that speech again, Scotty! I've heard that so often now that I've lost count. You're older than I, that's right. You're even older than Admirals Akaar and Mondolen. So what? Does that give you the right to be obnoxious and stubborn?"

"It bloody well should," Scotty grumbled, angry at Ross for preventing him from complaining about the inadequacies of today's Starfleet top brass.

"Let me tell you something. People were making mistakes even in your time. Does the name Cartwright ring a bell?"

Scotty nodded silently.

"How about th'Zhalin? T'Vreen? Usbek-Wran? Almodóvar? Ortolappin?"

"I know a few of them."

"Good. Suffice it to say that Alynna Nechayev is only one in a long line of people doing seemingly 'bad' things for the good of the Federation, and I—"

Scotty's disgusted snort caused Ross to interrupt himself.

"What's the matter? Don't you think that she gave you the order because she wanted the Federation to survive this war?"

"Is our survival a good enough reason to sacrifice our principles? Where would we be if those in charge did what they thought was necessary, disregardin' everythin' from common sense to general standards of morality and everythin' in between? This is wrong, Admiral, and I will not accept it."

Ross observed his outburst in silence and then said, "You still haven't answered my question, Scotty."

"Hm? What question?"

"If you found those orders so appalling and downright wrong, why didn't you disobey them? Surely the result of such a decision could not have been worse than what you actually did shortly afterward. In both cases, the result would have been the loss of your Starfleet commission."

"So I have to defend myself against you now, is that what you're aimin' at?"

"No, it isn't, and you know it. Granted, I'm no psychologist, but I believe that you did what you were told to—instead of telling Alynna where to put her orders in a not very polite manner—because deep down you felt it was necessary, even though you tried to convince yourself of something else. Maybe now your bad conscience is trying to punish you for not listening to it then?"

"Oh, that's a load of dreck, Admiral, and you know it!"

"Do you have a better explanation?"

"Of course I do, but I don't see why I should tell you."

Ross sighed. Scotty was close to doing the same, but he held himself back.

"Captain Scott," Ross began, using the formal address as if to underline the importance of what he was going to say, "let me tell you a story."

"I hope it's a short one," Scotty said in a low voice.

"I'll certainly try to make it as short as possible. So. There once was an idealistic Starfleet officer rising through the ranks, on his way to being an admiral, just as in those dreams he'd had as a child."

"This is goin' to be about you, isn't it?" Scotty asked mischievously.

"Maybe. Just be quiet for a moment and listen, okay? So, there was this man, and in the fifties he was assigned as second officer to the *Leonov*. It did not take long for the troubles with the Tzenkethi to intensify. One day, the ship was caught between two Tzenkethi troop transports that fired on it. The enemy fire caused the warp core to breach. There was barely enough time for the *Leonov*'s crew to get to their lifepods and leave the ship before the core exploded, taking the ship with it. The fight had been initiated by the transports near an L-class planet, so the crew's only chance was to land on that planet and fight for their survival. Unfortunately, the Tzenkethi fired on the slowest pods, killing roughly half of the remaining crew. The ones that managed to make it to the planet's surface fought the enemy for over two weeks before reinforcements finally came.

"A few months later, the officer found out that the location of the *Leonov* had been leaked to the Tzenkethi by somebody in the Federation. Not somebody from Starfleet, but somebody who was working for an autonomous agency. The officer was enraged, of course, because that somebody was directly responsible for the destruction of the *Leonov* and for the deaths of three hundred sixty-four able men and women. He swore that he'd hunt down the person responsible and bring him to justice.

"So he spent month after month on the search, using all his contacts both inside and outside the Fleet to find clues as to the person's whereabouts. Eventually, he was successful and caught him on a remote moon in the Arias sector."

Unable to avoid being interested in how the story ended, Scotty asked, "And then what happened?"

"They talked. They talked for a long time, and during the conversation the officer realized that, while the deaths of the crew were a very high price to pay, everything the other man had done had been in the best interests of the Federation."

And to think it had actually been interesting until now! "You've just lost me here. He's the one that could just as well have killed your crew himself, and you're defendin' him?"

"That officer was angry, I will admit as much, but he did not let his anger cloud his mind. He listened to what the other man had to say, examined the proof, eventually spoke to some other people involved, and in the end he saw that there would have been many more deaths if the *Leonov* had not been attacked."

"Why? What makes you say that? What sick, twisted mind can listen to all that hogwash and still be able to keep down his lunch?"

"The *Leonov* would have received orders to destroy a presumed industrial complex on Gauran Ja-Tem, a Tzenkethi border world, about two days later, had the attack not taken place. Many innocent people, mostly civilians and scientists, would have been killed. The repercussions of this assault would have been enormous, and the autonomous agency the man worked for had judged them to be grave enough to try everything in their might to avoid them."

"And you're actually believin' that? You're dafter than I thought, pardon my Tellarite."

"Oh, I've had my doubts, rest assured. Still have them, as a matter of fact. But whenever I feel like I'm not doing the right thing, I walk over to the nearest mirror and look myself in the face. Never have I had cause to turn away. And not once have I regretted my decision not to report the man to the Fleet authorities."

Ross apparently hadn't noticed slipping from the third into the first person. Scotty wondered if that was significant.

"Is that all? Did you come here to tell me this story? I'm sorry, but you haven't made me change my mind. If anythin', you've strengthened my resolve not to have anythin' to do with the likes of Nechayev and yourself for the rest of my life. Expect my final resignation to grace your desk when you get home," he said and made as if to get up.

"Wait," Ross said, placing a hand on the ex-engineer's shoulder. "There's more I have to tell you."

"I'm not in a mood to listen, Admiral. I don't think there's anything you can tell me now that would make me change my mind about you."

"Then it won't hurt you if you listen to me, right? Last year, I was given a similar task to the one that Nechayev gave you, except that in my case it wasn't an order, it was more of a friendly request."

"That 'autonomous agency' you were tellin' me about before, I suppose."

"Indeed, yes. They needed somebody higher up in the Starfleet hierarchy to help place a mole in the Continuing Committee on Romulus. Because of my previous association with them, they thought of me. Just as I did that other time, I asked them to present me with all the documentation I needed to make up my mind. Scotty, I'm not one of those mindless fools with their finger constantly on the trigger who blindly follow orders, no matter how wrong those orders may be. However, if I can do something to save the Federation I love, then I'll do it, and damn the bad conscience."

Despite himself, Scotty was actually interested once more. Ross had . . . well, charisma, and besides, he'd heard rumors about that bilateral conference on Romulus last year that coincided with the ascension of Tal Shiar chairman Koval to the Committee.

"I have a relationship with Alynna that enables me to get her to tell me things she wouldn't tell any other admiral, mostly because of the similarities of our professional lives. We met for lunch a few days ago, and she told me that you were a, and I quote, 'real pain in my back end.' Apparently, we both made use of the same tactic—pretending to have fallen ill quite suddenly."

"An old trick, that was, and I really should have known better," Scotty admitted, his logical self insisting that having a mole in the Continuing Committee was a tactical advantage, while his emotional self was jumping up and down, shouting that the ends did not justify the means, no matter how good one's intentions were.

"Ah well, don't chastise yourself because of it. The person I was forced to play that trick on also fell for it," Ross said, "and he was not happy about it, not at all.

"If this was an ideal world, I would never have agreed to work with these people. You should know me well enough by now to believe me when I say this. I was idealistic once, when I was a raw cadet, but I soon realized that I had no reason to be that 'daft,' as you put it. The world was a bad—and a mad—place, and it still is. Yet the Dominion War is over now, the threats to the Federation reduced to a minimum, which is their only goal, you know. Keep the Federation safe, regardless of the cost."

"And that is exactly the problem I'm havin' with their actions. And Nechayev's, for that matter." As he spoke the words, something in Scotty's mind clicked. "Wait a minute . . . is she working for *them*?"

"Even if I knew, I wouldn't tell you. There's a reason why keeping the organization a secret is of the utmost importance. If they knew about me telling you this, they'd be rather angry, to put it mildly."

Scotty had a wee bit of trouble digesting all the information Ross had heaped on him, and while the image of the war veteran was changing into something of a somewhat unpredictable top-level operative sometimes working on the wrong side of the law, he also had to admit that it made Ross somewhat more . . . well, truth be told, more of a *person*. Before, Ross had been flat, unremarkable, the perfect soldier, with an altogether incomprehensible affection toward Scotty. Now, however, he had faults, he had dubious motives, just like every other human in the galaxy.

Come to think of it, that affection toward him was still as incomprehensible as ever. What better time to ask Ross about it than now?

"I can't say you've won me over, Admiral, but at the very least, you've given me somethin' to think about."

"I should hope so. Now, let me ask the obvious question: is there really a chance of you returning to active duty?"

Okay, that had not come all that unexpectedly. "I really can't say. Give me time to think about it, about everythin'. But please tell me: why me? Why not some other, younger genius of an engineer who's currently workin' on the *U.S.S. Lollipop*?"

"I'll tell you why, Scotty. Because you're different. You're old-school, you know what a ship is made up of. You know how to work engines. However, you also know how to work people. That's even more important for the job as S.C.E. liaison. You have to interact with people, you have to make them work with each other."

"I'd be the one handin' out assignments, just like Blackjack Junior did, right?"

"Right. I believe Commander Lynch was assigned this duty by yourself when the two of you took over from Harriman, is that correct?"

"'Tis, indeed."

"Care to tell me why?" Ross wanted to know, concern still etched into his face.

"It just didn't feel like the kind of job best suited for me. I've always felt more confident with machines and computers than with people," Scotty admitted, secretly amazed at how his mood had changed ever since Ross had more or less confessed to having been part of an organization that had no compunctions about working outside the law. "Don't get me wrong, I *like* people. It's just that . . . I don't know . . . it is easier to find out what makes a warp engine tick, if you know what I mean, than doin' the same for a person. People are a Daluvian puzzle to me, most of the time."

"Ah, I don't believe that. You're working as a greeter on Risa, for goodness' sake! If you don't get along with people, you should have moved elsewhere. Friends tell me there's a lump of rock orbiting 36 Ursae Majoris that offers its visitors spectacular views of the entire star system."

"Now you're just makin' fun of me. I can't say I'm in the mood for that right now."

"I'm sorry, Scotty," Ross said and stood up from the bench. He straightened his uniform, turned and asked, "When can I contact you again?"

"There's no need to. I won't change my mind," Scotty replied, certain now that Ross was only wasting his time. But that was *his* problem, and not Scotty's. An important admiral from Starfleet's upper echelon wanted to spend hours, even days, trying to make him reconsider, so what? Let him. It certainly wasn't Scotty's responsibility to make Ross happy. Ross was a grown man who should have learned how to deal with disappointments.

Yet, deep down inside of him, Scotty also knew that Ross was a man who was eager to give more to the service than he expected to get back. The people of Starfleet were more important to William Johannes Ross than his own life and career. By his own admission, protecting the Federation from coming to any harm was his top priority, and he would do almost anything to achieve that.

There weren't that many differences between Ross and himself, Scotty realized. They both had the same approach to their work, and they really cared about the people they worked so hard at protecting. It was only a matter of where one drew the line. Admiral Ross had found out for himself that he could draw it quite a bit further off than the retired Captain Scott.

Still standing on the same spot as before, Ross said, "I

realize that you are still mad at Alynna, and you even have a good reason for it, unlike many other people. You didn't want to hurt the Kropaslin, but by following her orders, you had no choice but to harm them and their civilization." Stated like that, so matter-of-factly, it seemed extremely neutral and distant, rather like coming from an android than a human person.

"As I said, I had a conversation with Alynna a few days ago, and she told me that, while she understands the reasons for your 'emotional outburst,' as she called it, she does not in any way understand how you can hold her responsible for changes in Kropaslin society that the Kropaslin themselves are to blame for."

Now that was too much, indeed. "What? How dare she! The carnaptious hag! If she hadn't come to steal that cruiser, Kropaslin society would not have fallen apart!" *Calm yourself down, Scotty! Do you want to get yourself sued by calling a Fleet admiral names?*

"Maybe not. Maybe, however, it would still have done so, only at a later date. Who knows? The truth is, Scotty," Ross said, playing with the com scrambler in his right hand, "the past is just that: the *past*. We can't do anything about it, as Regulation 157 tells us. However, we can do something about the *future*. And that is where you come in."

"Me?" Scotty had no idea what Ross was talking about.

"Yes, you. If you agree to become the full-time head of the Starfleet Corps of Engineers, leaving Commander Lynch free to retire, then you will have enough power and resources at your disposal to assist the Kropaslin with rebuilding their societal structures."

"You're havin' me on, Admiral!" he said, unbelieving. "Aren't you?"

"Oh, you'd know if I was. This, however, is serious. Just about as serious as I can make it."

"That . . . that is . . . temptin', to say the least. Still, I do need to think about it all. You said you'd give me some time for cogitatin'?" Scotty asked, realizing too late that he sounded vaguely optimistic. Ross didn't deserve that much, certainly not.

"Yes, I did say that. Contact me when you have reached a decision, say, within the next month or so?"

"That's acceptable. It might take the whole month, though."

"I understand. Thank you for listening to me, Captain Scott. I appreciate that," Ross said, and he sounded serious. He might have been an idealistic man once, but he had let himself be pulled over to the dark side by the evil forces that were at work within the Federation.

That sounds much too dramatic for an old tinker like me. I really must do something about that.

Scotty remained seated on the bench and watched Ross walk down the path that, some thirty meters from the Littlejohn Monument, was lined with tall trees on both sides. They had slightly orange leaves that prevented any light from reaching the ground. As he observed Ross disappearing in the shadows, he thought that this was an apt depiction of the admiral's dilemma.

But Ross had made his decision long before. From the look of it, that had happened roughly two decades ago, during the Tzenkethi situation. Now he had to live with it.

Scotty didn't know if he could do the same.

There was only one way to find out.

The following days were agonizingly long, which was mainly due to the fact that Scotty didn't make it easy on himself. He still worked in the Engineering Room, and every time he walked by the artificial waterfall in the middle of the hotel lobby, directly underneath the artificial sun at the top of the lobby's magnificent dome, he thought that it was not the worst kind of work he was doing here. Sure, there were almost no machines involved, and certainly no warp drive— unless you counted the ER's cleverly disguised drink dispenser column—but that was not a major issue for him anymore. The truth of it was, he was content with his current job, and there would have been no reason at all for him to ask for a change if things had been normal.

Except that things were not normal. They actually never were, so that was not much of a surprise.

Ross, despite his flaws and questionable connections, had made him an offer that was very, very tempting. To take over the S.C.E. full-time, throw out Lynch, and take an active hand in organizing things was a huge task. He'd realized that when Harriman had talked to him about it in '71, and today it wasn't different.

As S.C.E. liaison to the admiralty he'd be the one handing out the assignments to the various ships and their crews, all the while making sure that the best of the best were working for the Corps. He'd be a sort of talent scout, constantly on the lookout for new engineers that seemed perfectly suited for Corps work. Most important, however, he'd be in the position to actively influence the Fleet's technological development, as he'd have a say in their ship design policies.

Ah, the agony of making life-changing decisions! He could almost hear his sister scold him: *Face it, Scotty, this is a prestigious job, and you'd be a real dobber if you said no.* Clara, in addition to being the only one back then to call him by his future nickname instead of his proper name, had been the one to always tell him the truth outright and without embellishment.

Ah, the hell with it. He could think about it all later today, when his job was done. Indeed, today was a busy day at the Engineering Room. He'd shaken many hands and tentacles already, downed many drinks—in company, of course.

From the corner of his eye he saw the main doors open and two humanoid females enter. Promising the Hekaran in front of him to drop by later for a short talk, he started to walk toward the pair. They looked remarkably like mother and daughter, but he'd learned early enough that appearances were deceiving. They could just as easily be two lovers, or two friends. And besides, what *looked* like a female person didn't always have to *be* a female person.

And the older of them looked rather familiar. He approached them swiftly, all the while concentrating on the face of the woman, trying to remember the person she reminded him of.

"Welcome to the Engineerin' Room, on behalf of the management of the El Dorado. I'm—" he began, but had to stop himself because now he realized who the woman was.

It couldn't be.

It simply couldn't be.

She looked just like Christine Chapel, except that she didn't. Her hair was different, and she was a bit younger than Christine had been the last time he'd seen her—the last picture of her in her Starfleet file, to be exact. It had to be a remarkable coincidence, finding somebody who looked so much like her, even if that was just as unlikely as having her really be here.

The younger of the pair, a thin lass with a round face and dark-brown hair, watched him closely, he noticed.

Get hold of yourself, Scotty!

"You are . . . ?" she asked, offering him an encouraging smile.

"Scott. Montgomery Scott." It was impossible for him not to study the face of the woman who was and was not her. "Christine?" he whispered before he could stop himself. The moment the word left his lips he felt the blood rush to his cheeks, caused by shame about the foolishness of actually thinking that this woman here was the real Christine Chapel, late of the *Excelsior*. Losh, his face must look like a port formation light! He suddenly felt as stupid as he had when he'd just been liberated from transporter stasis and he'd asked his rescuers if Kirk himself had managed to devise a means of saving him.

The young'un looked from him to the other one and back to him. "Who?" she asked, obviously not comprehending. Not that he could blame her.

"You have me confused with someone else, I'm afraid," the older woman said kindly. "My name is Morgan, Morgan Primus. This is my daughter, Robin. She's with Starfleet."

Of course. Yet another young soul to be corrupted by the machinations of the Powers That Be. "So was I," Scotty admitted, letting his tone slightly indicate just how happy he was he'd left.

Despite her name, this Morgan looked and even sounded so much like Christine, it was uncanny. Ignoring the still increasing redness of his face, he admitted as much. "The hair is different, but . . . you could be her twin."

Morgan stared at him. "I'm afraid I don't know what you're talking about."

Just like that, she brought him down onto the hard, cold floor of reality. For a moment there he'd thought there was a chance, unlikely though it had been, to catch up on old times, asking her how her life had been after she'd left the *Enterprise*.

It was not to be. She might have looked like her, but she was an entirely different person.

Realizing he was being a little rude, Scotty did his best to explain his mistake and then introduce himself again. Robin was a little skeptical of his claim to be *the* Montgomery Scott, given his "well-preserved" state, and suggested he was a clone.

"No, no . . . the original item," he said, smiling at her while attempting a quick bow. "Perhaps you ladies would allow me to buy you a drink." Social drinking, that was the key. After all, who knew? Perhaps there was a way to make him forget not only Nechayev, but Ross as well. He certainly wouldn't regret it one single second if he never heard of Starfleet ever again.

Besides, this Morgan woman seemed rather . . . interested in him, so to speak. It was best to strike the iron while it was hot, as they said, so he couldn't let this chance pass without trying to make use of it. "I wouldn't have it any other way," she said, waiting for him to lead the way to the bar, where he ordered her a screwdriver.

The young'un called Robin joined them, mumbling something incomprehensible that surely was of no importance to Scotty. He decided to enjoy this evening.

Perhaps there was even a reason to enjoy the night.

★ ★ ★

As it turned out, the relationship Morgan was interested in was of a friendly nature, but not as intimate as Scotty would have liked. Perhaps it was his own fault, talking mostly about machines and computers and not about things that interested her. In hindsight, he'd pretty much killed any chance of getting anywhere with Morgan Primus on their very first date—if "date" was the correct word for it.

However, the following days turned out to be the best since Belunis had decided to look elsewhere for the adventures that were absent in her life. Scotty and Morgan had fun getting to know each other more closely, talking about a broad variety of subjects that ranged from starship propulsion (as it turned out, Morgan had served on a Starfleet ship herself) to native Risian cuisine.

They had long since left the greeter-guest relationship behind for something better when a new player entered the game: some no-good shaan gadgie who reeked of money. His name was Rafe Viola, and he proclaimed himself an entrepreneur. When Scotty discovered that Viola was making advances toward Morgan, his alarms went up. The man was not good enough for Morgan in any case, and then there was the fact that Scotty had a bad feeling about him.

He said as much to Morgan, but she accused him of being jealous when all he wanted was to prevent her from being hurt. *Women. "Can't live with 'em, can't live without 'em," indeed.*

In the end, when Viola turned out not only to be what he'd suspected but also a cold-blooded killer, Scotty had felt no satisfaction over having been right in the first place. A mere two weeks after his first meeting with Morgan Primus and her daughter Robin, Scotty's life had been turned upside down, the quietness of the past few months gone as if it had never existed.

At least I'm still alive, he thought. Poor Mr. Quincy was not. Viola's son Nik had killed him—although "son" wasn't the correct word. "Clone," however, was. Later, after everything had calmed down, Morgan had told Scotty everything he'd missed. He'd missed a lot, apparently.

But his temporary absence was understandable. After all, you don't get thrown into a shaft inside a multiple-level computer core only to miraculously appear mere seconds later. He had to thank the Great Bird of the Galaxy that he'd had the common sense to put on antigrav boots before he went to inspect the core together with Mr. Quincy.

Mr. Quincy—*Thomas*—wasn't the only victim of this madman's killing spree. Part of the resort—mostly trees and other plants—had been destroyed by a computer virus that caused the wave generator at the beach to malfunction. Out of control, it threatened to flood the entire hotel complex and drown every adult and child in the vicinity. Working together with Morgan, he'd managed to undo the damage, and within one hour the water had begun to be pulled back into the lagoon, where it couldn't hurt anybody any longer.

The resort's owners had contacted Scotty soon afterward, offering him the post of manager of the El Dorado. Unlike so many other corporate creatures, they knew what a loss the death of a manager like Theodore Quincy was to them. They were genuinely sorry, which was a point in their favor. However, they also saw the need to go on, and in order to offer the visitors a perfect holiday, they needed to repair the damage to their computer system, their wave generator, and—most important—their public image. A Starfleet legend such as himself would be a brightly colored feather in their cap, they reasoned, and they even offered him everything he ever dreamed of, including his own boat.

The owners of the El Dorado Hotel and Vacation Resort were not the only ones to advance an offer. Others from all over the planet did the same, some even going so far as to say that he could have his own private island if he agreed to work for them.

He politely declined every offer.

The truth was, he did not feel he needed to remain on Risa

a single day longer. Ever since Viola's sabotage had been repaired, he'd felt restless, as if something was calling to him, telling him to move on.

One evening, a twelvenight after Quincy's funeral, he sat in the wicker chair on his small veranda, holding a glass of Scotch in his right hand. He watched the fireworks on the horizon, a colorful display of happiness that marked the end of the Lohlunat Festival over in Suraya Bay. Melancholy was washing over him like waves at high tide, and it was not a pleasant feeling.

When he lifted the glass to his lips, he was surprised to discover that it was empty. He didn't remember finishing his drink, nor did he remember drinking it, for that matter. He supposed he should be worried about that, but at the moment he just didn't give a damn.

Another plume of fireworks, then nothing. After a while, the muffled sound of the explosion reached Hanotis Harbor, but the sky was dark once again, only illuminated by the constellations of the stars and the two moons.

In a weird, morbid way, the fireworks reminded him of exploding ships in planets' atmospheres, and this, in turn, reminded him of the story that Ross had told him. A person's mind was a strange thing. So utterly abstract, yet there was no denying its existence. And the worst thing was, it operated in mysterious ways. Nobody could tell what dreadful memory of the past it dredged up next.

Ross and his offer, though, were not all that unexpected. Scotty had thought about them on an on-and-off basis during the last two weeks, and he grudgingly admitted to himself that it was indeed rather tempting. Yet he didn't know if he shouldn't just make a clean break now, leave Starfleet forever and buy himself a house on Caldos Colony, far away from SFHQ.

Absentmindedly, he took another sip of his Scotch only to notice again that the glass was empty. Something was wrong with him—had to be—because he normally never failed to consciously enjoy a drink.

Oh, sod it.

He abruptly rose from his wicker chair and entered his bungalow. Once inside, he went into his office and activated the comm terminal there.

"Computer, do me a favor, will you?"

"Please state your request."

"Get me Admiral Ross's office. And better make it quick, before I change my mind."

"Working."

"You're a good lad."

Epilogue

Stardate 53509.7
May 2376, Old Earth Time

"I *knew* the planet Kropasar rang a bell," Geordi La Forge said, setting down his glass. He was on his third drink—yet still, the taste of Scotty's Scotch lingered. "I remember some of the *da Vinci* crew talking about the S.C.E.'s relief efforts there."

"Aye, laddie," Scotty said. "We're only just beginnin', an—"

He was cut off by a chirp from his combadge. "I hate these bloody things," he grumbled. "No damn off-switch." Despite his complaints, he tapped it. "Go ahead."

"Sir, this is Deg," came the voice of his aide.

"What is it, lad? I thought I told you I was out."

"There's a bit of a crisis in lab seventeen that . . . needs your touch."

Scotty shook his head. "Fine, beam both of us over."

"Aye, sir." Scotty stood up, and Geordi followed suit just before both of them were swallowed by the blue sparkles of the transporter beam.

When they rematerialized, they were in what seemed to be the cockpit of a Starfleet runabout. It resembled the *Danube*-class La Forge was used to, but seemed more advanced. Alarms were blaring, and red lights were flashing.

There were two engineers already in the cockpit, though

La Forge didn't recognize them. "What have you done, lads?" Scotty shouted. Both engineers were furiously tapping buttons on the runabout's control panels.

One of the engineers, a human man, looked up from his work to reply. "I'm not sure, sir!" he shouted above the din of the alarms. "We just switched the reactor on to see if we'd fixed the dilithium fracture, and now the power won't stop building!"

"Did you try an emergency shutdown?" La Forge asked, joining the man at his console and looking over the readouts.

"Of course!" he shouted back. "First thing!" The other engineer, a Guidon, looked up from its panel just long enough to let off some agitated squeaks in the typical manner of its species.

Scotty shook his head. "Lasca, what have I told you, over and over? Get your hands dirty!" He moved to the rear of the runabout. "Give me a hand, Geordi!"

La Forge helped Scotty remove an access panel from the wall next to the transporters. Immediately, Scotty plunged his hands inside and began yanking out and rearranging bits of circuitry.

"Power is still building!" called Lasca, watching his screen. "It's at one hundred forty-seven percent and rising! In another thirty seconds, the warp core will explode!"

La Forge briefly considered telling Scotty to hurry up, but years of unnecessarily being told that by his own commanding officers meant that he knew better.

"I cannot do it!" Scotty was frantically pulling bits out of the wall now, with no apparent regard for what he was doing. "I need more time!"

La Forge joined Lasca once more. "It's no good," he said. "The tetryon flow is continuing to multiply."

"Slow it down, lad!" Scotty ordered.

"I cannot change the laws of physics!" La Forge shouted back—doing his best Scottish brogue. The Guidon engineer looked up from his console to stare in amazement. La Forge supposed not many of the people here would dare to mock the "living legend" that way.

Lasca was still watching the clock. "Fifteen seconds!"

Scotty grinned. "No, you can't do that! But I can!" With that he jerked his left hand out of the mechanics compartment, and reached across the runabout to the opposite wall, where a finger stabbed down on a single button.

As La Forge watched, the power overload suddenly disappeared, the meters dropping down to zero.

"You did it!" shouted Lasca. "If that had overloaded, it would have taken out the entire Tucker Building!"

"At the very least, laddie," said Scotty. "I knew lettin' you lot run tests on the surface was a bad idea. I shouldn't have let you start up the whole tetryon plasma experiment again in the first place."

"But aside from that, the *Yellowstone* is flawless," protested Lasca.

"Aside from that, the *Yellowstone* is like any other runabout," said Scotty, "so it would be, wouldn't it? Well, except for your precious retractable sensor pod, but *that*'s bloody useless."

The Guidon engineer waved his hand for Lasca to join him at his panel. The two conferred over the readouts briefly in hushed tones, and then Lasca looked up. "I don't understand, Captain Scott. How'd you do it?"

Scotty shrugged. "Sure, I *could* tell, you, laddie. But who would want to hear me spout off a load of technobabble?"

"Are you sure you have to go, laddie?"

La Forge and Scotty were in the lobby of the Tucker Building once more, in front of the holoframe depicting the eponymous engineer. "Captain Picard has called me," the younger man said, "and so I must go. Sorry I won't get to hear the rest of your story."

Scotty waved his hand dismissively. "There wasn't much left, just a wee bit."

La Forge looked around at the massive room, engineers and other Starfleet personnel streaming in and out. "You've done well for yourself here," he said. "You're enjoying yourself."

Scotty shook his head. "It's only been two months," he said. "Give me time to be unhappy again, lad; it'll come."

"I don't know . . ." said La Forge. He noticed the Vissian woman Scotty had berated this morning rush past, her head ducked to avoid attention. "I think you're enjoying passing your knowledge on to the next generation."

"I suppose so, lad," Scotty admitted with a smile. "Someone's got to whip them into shape—their professors certainly don't."

"You're being challenged. That's good for you." La Forge tapped his combadge. "La Forge to *Enterprise*. One to beam up."

"*Acknowledged. Thirteen seconds, Commander,*" replied the clipped voice of the transporter chief.

"Good-bye, laddie—Geordi. Hopefully, I see you again soon. It's been too long between visits."

"Sure has," La Forge said. "Good-bye, Scotty." He continued to speak even as he felt the beginnings of the transport sequence. "Maybe someday you'll get a chance to finish telling me that story. . . ."

Future Construction

Stardate 53426.4
April 2376, Old Earth Time

The visitor on the starship's bridge silently observed the goings-on that characterized every single vessel of the Federation's exploration/defense fleet, amusing himself with comparisons of single crew members to friends of times long gone.

In the center seat of the bridge sat a lean Bolian man, his collar pips clearly identifying him as the ship's captain even though his posture alone did a very good job at doing the same. His name was Bor Loxx, and he commanded the ship that Scotty himself had picked as the vessel to extend a hand of friendship toward the people on Kropasar who had been so deviously relieved of their prized possession of Breen origin.

The ship's name was *Akarana*, and it belonged to the class of transport vessels named for the city of Istanbul on Earth. Usually when Scotty needed a ship to send somewhere, he just tapped one of the four *Saber*-class ships that carried around the S.C.E.'s mobile teams, but this time all he needed was a ship capable of transporting a group of people from one place to another. The mobile response teams were better deployed elsewhere, considering all the postwar reconstruction going on, and so Scotty had called on the crew of the *Akarana*.

"Entering Akiganel sector," the Vulcan at navigation announced.

"Thank you, Mr. Lorin," Loxx said.

Scotty sat on an empty chair at one of the science stations aft of the captain, next to the starboard turbolift. From there, he could survey the entire bridge, watching everybody there doing their jobs, accompanied by the sounds the computer made reacting to command inputs.

Their mission here was simple: help the Kropaslin rebuild their society by lending what technological help they could.

Of course, this was not simply a Starfleet mission—it couldn't be. This was a matter of immediate concern to the entire Federation, which was why Scotty had had to address the entire Council in the Palais de la Concorde, and not just once, but twice in as many weeks. Despite his recently increased influence as the head of the S.C.E., he was sure it would not have worked if President Zife had not supported his petition.

Yet why exactly the Bolian had done so was beyond him—just as it had been beyond him when Nechayev had told him about Zife's decision to reopen negotiations with the Kropaslin. Then, the numpty had had an ulterior motive: technology. It was highly likely that there was such a motive now as well.

But Scotty didn't care. As long as they let him help the people on Kropasar pick up the pieces of their society and start anew, he didn't give a tinker's cuss about what the president thought he'd get from it.

In the time between the petition and now, Scotty had feared he'd strangle himself with red tape as there was a googolplex of forms and documents to fill out and sign, a myriad of people to talk to and practically beg on his knees for their support.

But all that was now a thing of the past. Now Scotty was on his way, aboard the *U.S.S. Akarana*, to deliver goods, technology, and a shipload of engineers and ambassadors to Kropasar so that the people there had a fair chance of survival, despite all the pain and sorrow Starfleet had caused them without their knowledge.

"Captain Scott?"

"Hm? What is it, lad?" he asked the Bolian captain.

"Now that we're almost on their doorstep, I believe we

should contact the Witenagemot. Maybe you want to do that yourself?"

"That I do, lad, that I do. Thanks for indulging an old man."

"Oh, it's no problem, Captain Scott. It's your project, so it's only fair that you get to do the talking," Loxx said, grinning.

"I beg your pardon?" said Scotty, not quite understanding what he was going on about.

"The fact of the matter is that I'm not all that comfortable with talking to heads of state. You, on the other hand, seem to have a bit of experience with that."

"Not as much as you'd think, Captain, but yes, you're right."

"The captain is *always* right," Loxx said, laughing. He turned to the Tiburonian standing at the tactical console. "Open a channel, Lieutenant Ramaijif."

The large man nodded. "Shouldn't take too long, sir. It's not as easy as shooting things, but it's not *that* hard."

Loxx waved Scotty over to where he was sitting in the center of the bridge. "Ignore Ramaijif," he said as Scotty stood up and crossed the bridge. "He's been moaning ever since the Fleet decided to make the tactical officer responsible for communications."

"I have managed to open a channel to the high cyning of the Witenagemot," Ramaijif reported just as Scotty reached the area in the center of the bridge.

Loxx stood up and gestured graciously to his now empty seat. "It's all yours."

Scotty sat down. *Nice,* he thought. It seemed that after centuries of spaceflight, Starfleet had finally developed a comfortable captain's chair. Loxx nodded to Ramaijif, and the distinctive face of a Kropaslin appeared on the main viewscreen. "This is Captain Montgomery Scott of the Starfleet Corps of Engineers," he said.

The Kropaslin answered back, the sound of her voice revealing her to be a female. *"I am Sunanios Gilvatac, high cyning of the Kropaslin Witenagemot. I take it you are here to begin the promised relief efforts?"*

Scotty realized he recognized her; she had been one of the

members of the Agreement Party there on that fateful night. "Aye, ma'am." He knew enough diplomacy not to call a head of state "lassie," at any rate. "We're here to provide whatever technological help we can, startin' with the weather modification net." Maintenance of the net had been one of the casualties of the collapse of the Kropaslin government, and now drought was raging across several continents.

"Thank you, Captain Scott. All of Kropasar will be in your debt—this government has only been up and running for a few weeks now, and just the news that the Federation was sending aid went a long way in establishing our credibility with the public."

"It's only fair," said Scotty, "given what the Federation's rejection of your membership did before."

"None of us could have foreseen that chain of events," said Gilvatac sadly. *"No one."*

Scotty quickly glanced at a readout below the main screen. "The *Akarana* should be entering orbit in thirty minutes," he said.

"I look forward to seeing you again," said Gilvatac. *"Witenagemot out."*

Her image was replaced by the stars streaking by, their light split up in rainbow colors, as the *Akarana* sped toward her destination. Scotty was eager to repair the damage caused by the previous visit of a Starfleet ship and almost couldn't wait to set foot on Kropaslin soil.

There was just so much to do.

Monty Scott in the 24th-and-a-half Century!

A Timeline of Scotty's post-"Relics" Journey

In writing *The Future Begins*, we found it necessary to weave together the bits and pieces various novels, eBooks, comics, and short stories had given us about Scotty's life in the twenty-fourth century into one continuous narrative. Previously, we had only received snapshots of his journey; our goal was to combine these into a coherent whole, and *The Future Begins* would serve as the culmination of this whole.

The following timeline lays out what we know of Scotty's twenty-fourth-century (and beyond) odyssey. Not everything is here: we tried to fit what would work together, and not every story can. Indeed, it is possible that not everything that is here works together without contradiction, but we tried our best.

Thanks to Geoff "Wersgor" Hamell for his assistance in compiling this timeline, as well as the ever-helpful folks at Memory Beta.

Bracketed abbreviations: *TOS*=original *Star Trek*. *TNG*=*The Next Generation*. *NF*=*New Frontier*. *SCE*=*Starfleet Corps of Engineers*. *SNW#*=*Strange New Worlds* anthologies. *TDW*=*Tales of the Dominion War* anthology. *NL*=*New Frontier: No Limits* anthology.

2369

Starfleet Captain Montgomery Scott (ret.) is rescued from the wreck of the *U.S.S. Jenolen*, where he has been existing in a transporter loop since 2294, by the crew of the *U.S.S. Enterprise*-D. Captain Picard gives Scotty extended loan of the shuttlecraft *Goddard,* and he sets out to wander rather than retire to Norpin V. ("Relics" [*TNG*])

2370

Blaming himself for the "death" of Captain Kirk on the *Enterprise*-B, Scotty travels back in time on a derelict Klingon bird-of-prey in an effort to prevent it, accidentally changing history so that the Borg dominate most of known space in the twenty-third century. History is eventually restored, and no one remembers the alteration. (*Engines of Destiny* by Gene DeWeese)

Scotty meets an old acquaintance, Captain Morgan Bateson of the *Bozeman,* who was also displaced almost a century in time. They fight over the memory of Mira Romaine but put their differences behind them when they realize that they are still friends. ("Ancient History" by Robert J. Mendenhall [*SNW6*])

Koloth engages Scotty in battle to settle a final score before heading to Deep Space 9 to track down the Albino. ("Old Debts" by Kevin Ryan [*TNG* Special #3])

Scotty renames the *Goddard* the *Romaine* in honor of his former love. (*Crossover* by Michael Jan Friedman [*TNG*])

2371

Scotty steals the old *Constitution*-class *U.S.S. Yorktown* in order to help rescue Spock from Romulan captivity. (*Crossover* by Michael Jan Friedman [*TNG*])

Inspired by an encounter with Burgoyne 172 on Argelius II, Scotty reenlists in Starfleet, donating the *Romaine* to the Fleet Museum as recompense. After taking some refresher courses to get up to speed with the new technology, Scotty joins Bateson at Starbase 12 to assist in the construction of the *Sovereign*-class *U.S.S. Honorius*. (*The Two-Front War* by Peter David [*NF*]; "Through the Looking-Glass" by Susan Wright [*NL*]; *The Future Begins* by Steve Mollmann & Michael Schuster [*SCE*]; *Ship of the Line* by Diane Carey [*TNG*])

On leave at Earth to join Admiral John Harriman and his wife at their sixtieth anniversary dinner, Scotty learns of the crash of the *Enterprise*-D and the reappearance and death of Captain Kirk. Harriman, who is considering retiring from command of the Corps of Engineers, tries to persuade Scotty to replace him. ("Full Circle" by Scott Pearson [*SNW7*])

The *Honorius* is redesignated the *Enterprise*-E in honor of the fallen ship, meaning that this is the third vessel of that name Scotty has served on. (*Ship of the Line* by Diane Carey [*TNG*])
On the 77th anniversary of his disappearance on the *Jenolen*, Scotty makes an appearance on the newscast *Terra Tonight*. The broadcast is interrupted by an emergency situation on the *U.S.S. Hood*, and Scotty talks Cadet Ella Rose through resolving the situation during the live broadcast. ("Terra Tonight" by Scott Pearson [*SNW9*])

2372

Scotty serves as chief engineer of the *Enterprise*-E on its maiden voyage under Captain Morgan Bateson. Afterward, the ship is turned over to Captain Jean- Luc Picard and the former command crew of the *Enterprise*-D. (*Ship of the Line* by Diane Carey [*TNG*])

Scotty assists Bateson in completing construction on the *Bozeman*-A, another *Sovereign*-class vessel being assembled at Starbase 12. Once it is completed, he begins a tour on the *U.S.S. Sovereign* herself as chief engineer under Captain Sanders. (*Ship of the Line* by Diane Carey [*TNG*]; *Spectre* by William

Shatner with Judith & Garfield Reeves-Stevens [*TOS*]; *The Future Begins* by Steve Mollmann & Michael Schuster [*SCE*])

2374

While the *Sovereign* visits Earth, Scotty helps Ensign Dorian Collins come to terms with the loss of her shipmates from the *Valiant*. ("Dorian's Diary" by G. Wood [*SNW3*])

2375

His tour on the *Sovereign* completed, Scotty is contemplating retiring when he is invited by Admiral William Ross to take over for Harriman as the head of the Starfleet Corps of Engineers. (*Interphase* by Dayton Ward & Kevin Dilmore [*SCE*]; *The Future Begins* by Steve Mollmann & Michael Schuster [*SCE*])

Scotty temporarily assigns his duties to his assistant, Commander Leland T. Lynch, so he can take part in projects outside the office, including joining his old shipmate Admiral Leonard McCoy in making an inspection tour on the runabout *U.S.S. Hudson*. ("Safe Harbors" by Howard Weinstein [*TDW*]; *The Future Begins* by Steve Mollmann & Michael Schuster [*SCE*])

The *Hudson* returns to Earth just after the devastating Breen raid on the planet. Scotty throws himself into assisting with the reconstruction efforts, continuing to neglect his duties with the S.C.E. ("Safe Harbors" by Howard Weinstein [*TDW*]; *The Future Begins* by Steve Mollmann & Michael Schuster [*SCE*])

Scotty is summoned to the *U.S.S. Gorkon* by Fleet Admiral Alynna Nechayev to take part in a diplomatic mission to Kropasar. Afterward, he resigns from Starfleet. Leland T. Lynch takes over as the head of the S.C.E. (*The Future Begins* by Steve Mollmann & Michael Schuster [*SCE*])

Scotty returns to Scotland briefly, until he is hired by the Risian government to rebuild their weather control network. After finishing the job, he sticks around, and eventually ends up employed as a greeter by the El Dorado Hotel. (*Renaissance* by Peter David [*NF*]; *The Future Begins* by Steve Mollmann & Michael Schuster [*SCE*])

2376

Scotty sees two Kropaslin at the El Dorado, inspiring a confrontation with Nechayev. Following this, Admiral William Ross meets with Scotty to discuss the Kropasar mission in one more attempt to get him to return to the Fleet. (*The Future Begins* by Steve Mollmann & Michael Schuster [*SCE*])

Scotty is assisted by Morgan Primus and Robin Lefler in stopping the plot of Rafe Viola to sabotage the El Dorado computers. Afterward, he finally formally returns to Starfleet. In his capacity as head of the S.C.E., he begins pushing resources toward the reconstruction of Kropasar. (*Renaissance* and *Restoration* by Peter David [*NF*]; *The Future Begins* by Steve Mollmann & Michael Schuster [*SCE*])

Scotty, in his capacity as head of the S.C.E., is heavily involved in coordinating Starfleet's response to the crisis precipitated by the mass activation of Iconian gateways across the galaxy. Even once the gateways are deactivated, the S.C.E. must engage in various cleanup operations. (*Doors Into Chaos* by Robert Greenberger [*TNG*]; *Here There Be Monsters* by Keith R.A. DeCandido [*SCE*])

During the gateways cleanup, the *Enterprise*-E returns to Earth, and Lt. Commander Geordi La Forge is able to see Scotty for the first time since Scotty's resignation and reinstatement. Scotty tells La Forge the whole sordid tale. (*The Future Begins* by Steve Mollmann & Michael Schuster [*SCE*])

Scotty assists the *da Vinci* crew in responding to the appearance of Shanial spheres in the middle of San Francisco. (*Aftermath* by Christopher L. Bennett [*SCE*])

2377

Scotty is part of a covert mission to the Watraii homeworld aboard the *U.S.S. Alliance.* (*Vulcan's Soul* Book 2: *Exiles* by Josepha Sherman & Susan Shwartz)

Two S.C.E. missions send Scotty into the field, where he works alongside the *da Vinci* crew once more: stopping space tycoon Rod Portlyn and repairing the cloud city of Stratos. (*The Art of the Comeback* by Glenn Greenberg [*SCE*]; *Signs from Heaven* by Phaedra Weldon [*SCE*])

2379

Scotty is part of an inspection team assigned to the *Enterprise*-E. (*A Time for War, A Time for Peace* by Keith R.A. DeCandido [*TNG*])

2381

In the wake of the Borg invasion, the S.C.E. undertakes Project Reassimilation, an effort to reverse-engineer the scraps of remaining Borg technology. Scotty wants the project to be open, but the views of Starfleet Security and project head Kareem Mussad win out, and the project remains classified. (*A Singular Destiny* by Keith R.A. DeCandido)

2380s

Scotty perfects the equation for transwarp beaming, a problem he has been grappling with since the beginning of his Starfleet career. This allows for matter transportation over interplanetary distances, even to vessels in warp drive. (*Star Trek* [2009 film])

2422

The Montgomery Scott Engineering Sciences Complex of Starfleet Academy is dedicated. Scotty is present to officially cut the ribbon. (*Engines of Destiny* by Gene DeWeese)

ECHOES OF COVENTRY

Richard C. White

To Joni: I can never tell you how much I appreciate all those late nights helping me edit this beast into something close to a story.

To James Blish and Alan Dean Foster: The adaptations you did of the original Star Trek *and the animated series reintroduced me to the series and got me back into reading science fiction/fantasy again.*

To Gary Huggins: Thanks for all the help with naval terminology and for putting up with this old Army guy's questions.

To Steve Roman: You introduced me to the concept of writing professionally, and after all these years, you still put up with me. That, dear people, is friendship.

To Keith R.A. DeCandido: Thanks for taking a chance with me and letting me play in the Star Trek *sandbox. (Psst . . . got any more work out there?)*

And finally, to Mom and Dad: See, all that time I spent on the couch reading finally paid off. Thanks for always being there.

CHAPTER

1

2377

"A single bulb hung from a wire, dimly lighting the hallway, creating flickering shadows. Toby Scholtz pushed the door open slightly and peered across the hall through the cracked doorway. He could see a figure fumbling with the lock on his office door. Reaching into his pocket for his .38-caliber snub-nosed revolver, Toby decided to approach the figure now, rather than wait for him to ruin a perfectly good lock. Slipping into the hallway, his soft leather shoes made no noise as he crossed the worn wooden floor . . ."

Bart Faulwell rolled his eyes and shook his head, slowly lowering the padd onto the table in front of him. Now that he was no longer concentrating on the novel he'd been reading, the familiar buzz of voices in the mess hall came back into focus. Reaching out for his cup of coffee, he rubbed his eyes and stared up at the ceiling. "I can't believe Anthony recommended this to me," he muttered.

"Recommended what?" a strange voice asked.

Startled, Bart nearly fell backward out of his chair, before catching himself on the table. Turning his head, he found himself looking into a set of piercing blue eyes. Scooting back a few inches, he saw the blue eyes belonged to a young ensign who was standing patiently beside his table. She realized he hadn't heard her approach and retreated several feet, blushing all the way to the edge of her blond hair.

The moment stretched into an uncomfortable silence before Bart finally found his voice. "Oh, this?" he asked, indicating the padd. "It's a novel a friend recommended to me. It was supposedly a genre popular back on Earth in the mid-twentieth century. I think he said it was called 'noir.' Personally, I don't know what he sees in it." He paused for a second, scrunching his mouth up as if he'd tasted something unpleasant. "There's really not much to the plot, the characters are one-dimensional, and the writing is just atrocious."

"Oh," the ensign said, pausing as if uncertain how to continue, her hands nervously playing with the braided ponytail that hung in front of her shoulder.

"Please, sit down, ma'am." As the ensign joined him at the table, he continued, filling in the awkward silence, "I don't believe we've met. I'm Bart Faulwell. I'm the ship's linguist and cryptologist." He raised his cup to her in a welcoming salute. The more Bart looked at her, the more he was convinced she was fresh out of the Academy.

The ensign blushed even more and then looked up, "I'm sorry. I'm Martina Nemeckova. I transferred to the *da Vinci* a few days ago. I'm assigned to communications, gamma shift."

Bart smiled at her, his brown eyes twinkling. "Well then, welcome to the *da Vinci* and to the S.C.E. I hope you're ready for anything, because that's what we tend to find." His face twisted as an acrid taste filled his mouth. The coffee had gone stone-cold while he was reading. *Hmm, must have been more intrigued with the story than I thought,* he admitted to himself.

"I'm sorry," Martina said quickly. "I didn't mean to disturb you."

He gave his head a quick shake and then went over to the nearby replicator to get a fresh cup of coffee. "Coffee, French roast, half-and-half, no sugar." He waited for a second as his request was filled, then turned back to Martina. "No, you're not disturbing me. However, was there something you wanted to ask?"

"Well, it's rather personal, so if you'd rather not talk about it, I understand."

Bart groaned on the inside, trying to keep his composure. He glanced around the mess hall, trying to see which one of his "friends" had sicced the young ensign on him, but none of the usual suspects were in sight. "What would you like to know?" he asked, waiting for the inevitable questions.

"I was told you were in the Dominion War as a linguist. As fourth-year cadets, we were taught about the importance of communications security. They liked to use examples from the war to scare us."

Bart nodded. He knew that drill too well.

She continued as if afraid she'd lose her courage if she stopped. "They also tested all of us for language capabilities our second year to see if any of us would like to transfer to intelligence."

"How did you do?" Her last comment raised his hopes. Martina's predecessor had been more interested in the technical aspects of communications technology than the linguistic end; it would be nice to talk a little shop with someone else who'd been through the same training as Bart.

A disappointed look crossed her face. "Not very well, but I really was interested in the field after that chief warrant officer talked to us. Anyway, I know what the instructors taught us at the Academy about security, but I don't think many of them saw duty. I was just wondering what it was like—being in the war and all?" Martina finished up, her words pouring out like a runaway warp engine.

Bart lifted his cup to his mouth, letting the hot coffee wash over his embarrassment. That certainly was *not* what he thought she was going to ask. His relationship with Anthony and its recent troubles were well known on board the *da Vinci*, so that was what he'd expected to be asked about.

A sudden frown ran across his face as he thought about

those troubles, but quickly took another sip of his coffee and turned his attention to the young ensign. He eased himself back into his chair and watched her with amusement. She acted like she was still in the Academy, perched on the edge of her chair and waiting intently for him to start speaking.

"Oh, you'd be bored with my stories. It's not like I was on the front lines or anything. I've probably seen more excitement here on the *da Vinci* than I saw the entire war. My battle experience pretty much consists of sitting in a dark, windowless room trying to translate documents and old subspace messages." Seeing the disappointed look on her face, he decided to take another tack, "Although, come to think of it, there was this one time back at Starbase 34. . . ."

A half hour later, Martina's eyes were filled with tears from laughing so hard. Faulwell finished up the last story about sending the poor petty officer to the supply officer for a left-handed magnaspanner, warp envelopes, and liquid to refill the particle fountain. Looking up, he saw he'd drawn quite a crowd in the mess hall, including the entire gamma-shift bridge crew, three of Corsi's security people, and Nurse Wetzel. Loud applause broke out as he stood and took a bow to his appreciative audience.

"Thank you, thank you! You're a lovely audience." Grinning from ear to ear, Bart bowed to the crowd and begged off, despite repeated requests for one more story. Grabbing his padd with the unfinished novel, he retreated from the dining hall.

After taking the turbolift down to his quarters, he stepped inside and turned on the lights. He set the padd down on the small table next to his bunk and started getting ready for bed. He had some time before he was required to be anywhere and a nap would be just the thing to recharge him. After hanging up his uniform, he flopped down on the bed, staring up at the ceiling.

Ah, if the poor ensign only knew, he thought as memories came unbidden from his tour of duty in Starfleet Intelligence. *I've got stories that would curl her hair permanently. However, since I'm not really interested in being court-martialed and spending the rest of my life making big rocks into little rocks, I think I'll keep them to myself.*

That little bit of hyperbole brought another grin to his face. Starfleet prisons weren't into corporal punishment any more than regular Federation prisons, but that phrase had been part of military folklore long before the first space flight.

His grin faded as a less pleasant thought ran through his mind. Running a hand through his thin brown hair, he remembered when he first transferred to the S.C.E. from Starfleet Intelligence after the armistice. He'd sat through several rather thorough debriefings and thumbprinted several nondisclosure agreements swearing he'd never reveal anything he'd ever seen, done, talked about, heard, or imagined. He was surprised they hadn't run a large degausser over his head, just to be certain.

There were times he was glad he couldn't talk about things. In fact, there were some things he'd rather not even remember.

CHAPTER

2

2375

The small shuttlecraft eased its way into the docking bay at Starbase 375 and settled into its berth. A soft hissing told Bart the walkway was attached and they'd be disembarking in a little bit. Ill at ease, he pulled at the collar of his uniform and waited with as much patience as he could before the airlock cycled open. When he heard the familiar sound of the door opening, he finally relaxed and started his trek through the starbase.

He wasn't quite certain why he was being transferred. Then again, the way the war was going, this sudden temporary reassignment didn't surprise him. The unexpected orders had only given him four days to report to this starbase. That was barely enough time to wrap up what he'd been doing with the latest batch of translations and pass the keys for the Cardassian Fifth Fleet's encryption system to the analytic section before he had to pack and catch a ride on the *U.S.S. Sutherland*.

SI's linguistics department was already short-handed and getting shorter by the battle. According to scuttlebutt, one of their scout ships had been either destroyed or captured by the Cardassians during a scouting mission near the Badlands. As guilty as it made him feel, Bart sincerely hoped for the former. The last thing anyone in intel wanted to do was meet a Cardassian interrogator on *his* terms.

"Excuse me, are you Petty Officer Bart Faulwell?" a gruff voice asked, shaking him out of his reverie. Bart turned and saw two burly security officers standing there. The shorter of the two was staring at Bart over the padd he held in his hand. The other security officer was scanning everyone else coming off the shuttle.

"Guilty as charged," he quipped, and then sobered up when the officer's lack of a humor gene became painfully obvious. "What can I do for you?"

"I'm Ensign Thomas. You'll need to come with us," the one holding the padd said in a tone of voice Bart recognized. There was no questioning the implied "or else." Bart simply gave him a nod and fell into step, with Thomas leading the way and the quiet one following close behind.

By the time they reached their destination, Bart was glad for the escort, humor gene notwithstanding. They'd changed directions, gone up and down different turbolifts, and doubled back more than once. At this point, he had no idea where he was. Finally, they stopped in front of a door in a fairly deserted hallway.

Using a special passkey, Ensign Thomas motioned Bart through the door. Curious, Bart looked inside and saw a standard briefing room. Sighing, he stepped in, jumping as the door suddenly closed behind him. Looking at it, he noted it required the same type of key to exit also.

"Welcome to the party," a warm voice called out to him. Bart turned around to see a human sitting in the corner. He'd been so quiet and still, Bart had missed him when he first walked in. The man exuded confidence as he rose from his chair and strode across the room to shake hands. He was older than Faulwell, with a shock of white hair darkened only by a few flecks of brown, but his grip was sure and firm. "Pleased to meet you. I'm Chief Warrant Officer Cruz."

"Bart Faulwell, Petty Officer First Class, and it's a pleasure to meet you too, sir. Any ideas what's going on here?"

"Not a clue," the warrant officer said, sitting down at the

conference table, putting his elbows on it and resting his chin in his hands. "I've been teaching an advanced course in communications analysis at the Academy the past couple of years. I finally got to take some leave at home on Alpha Centauri and then next thing I know, my leave gets cancelled and I'm on the first starship heading this way," Cruz said, giving a huge mock sigh, before grinning up at Bart. "All I know is, if someone's going to all this trouble it must be good."

The door slid open again, cutting off Bart's sardonic reply as a Vulcan entered and quietly took a seat near them. He carefully rested his arms on the table, relaxed but alert.

Faulwell paused for a bit, but the Vulcan seemed content to simply sit there. Finally, Cruz broke the silence and introduced Bart and himself to the newcomer. The Vulcan looked at the two men and nodded slightly to each in turn, his piercing dark eyes taking in the situation. "I am Chief Petty Officer Sabran, most recently assigned to the *U.S.S. T'Kumbra*. And to answer the question you're about to ask, no, I have not been informed of the nature of our summons either."

"The *T'Kumbra?* Isn't that an all-Vulcan ship?" Cruz asked, curiosity evident in his voice.

"You are correct, sir."

Bart ran a hand through his scraggly brown beard and piped up, "So what other ships have you served on?"

"I am completing my second tour on the *T'Kumbra*. In between tours, I was detailed to the Vulcan Science Academy for a research-and-development project."

"Well, damn, it just seems strange they'd snag the three of us for whatever they've got planned. So, what did you do on that ship of yours, Chief?" Cruz asked, leaning back in his chair, staring at the door.

"I am a technician, specializing in computer languages. I was testing a new piece of communications security protocol when I was ordered to report to this starbase. Unfortunately, the test was about to finish in another week."

"Well, we'll have to see if we can make it up to you, Chief

Sabran," a voice sounded from the door, almost drowning out the "Attention on deck," Thomas sounded out with. The three men inside the room immediately jumped to their feet as a human rear admiral entered, closely trailed by a human commander, and a Bajoran in one of their militia uniforms. *Curiouser and curiouser,* Bart thought.

As quickly as they cleared the door, a dour-looking Andorian lieutenant wearing a security uniform shouldered his way past the two security guards. A quick motion from the admiral sent the guards out of the room. They gave the Andorian dirty looks behind his back as they left. As the door slid shut, the admiral sat down, motioning for everyone else to take a seat.

"I'm glad you all were able to get here so quickly. I'm Admiral Hazlitt," the senior officer began, his deep bass voice carrying through the room. After the requisite greetings were exchanged, he continued, "This is Commander Jonathan Mwakwere. He's here to assist me with the briefing, and this is Lieutenant Priya Chantrea from the Bajoran Militia. She's been assigned to work with the three of you on the upcoming mission. Also, this is Lieutenant Zarinth, who'll be in charge of the security team that will be accompanying you. Commander Mwakwere, if you please."

Bart watched as the large, dark-skinned man stood and pushed a series of buttons on the computer console, calling up a holographic map. Faulwell's quick glance confirmed it was the current Dominion/Federation front lines.

"Thank you, Admiral Hazlitt," he said, then turned to the rest of the people in the room, his dark eyes fierce and intimidating. Bart found himself shrinking back into his chair as the commander sized up the assembled group. Taking a deep breath, he began, "I'm required to inform you this briefing is classified top secret. You've been chosen based on your records and skills for a special temporary duty and have been assigned to this Starfleet Intelligence project." Listening to him speak, Bart placed the commander's birthplace somewhere near the Great Lakes region of the United States of Africa.

"Roger that, sir, but what exactly is this project?" Cruz asked, leaning forward in his seat and staring at the map that was slowly rotating in front of him.

"Ahem . . . yes, I was just getting to that." Commander Mwakwere refocused the map to highlight a specific section. Raising the magnification, it was easy to see the outlines of Cardassian, Breen, and Federation space. "This is the current situation as of four hours ago. This sector has been relatively quiet." He made some adjustments and a small planet began to glow. "We'd like to keep it that way."

Looking closer, Bart noted that it was just beyond the Rolor Nebula. "Excuse me, sir, but that's definitely outside of Federation space."

"Yes, we know, which is why this mission is so sensitive. We've taken advantage of that fact by establishing a listening post *here*." He enlarged the map again, showing a rather nondescript planet with an ice-covered moon circling it. "Right now, the Cardassians have not made any moves in this direction and by keeping our footprint in this system as small as possible, we're hoping to keep their eyes turned to a different direction. There is occasional traffic through the system en route to the Bajoran colony of Dreon, which is how we'll insert you."

"Insert *us?*" Cruz asked, drawing out the last word to encourage Commander Mwakwere to expound on that thought.

"Yes. You're going to be assigned to Project Mungin. We've managed to deploy a number of listening devices into Cardassian space as well as in between the Cardassians, the Tzenkethi, and the Breen Confederacy. They periodically dump their information to the listening post we established here."

He pushed another button on the console. The moon began to expand, showing a cutaway schematic of a post buried beneath the surface. "The actual listening post is designed to allow a small team to process and analyze everything they pick up without drawing attention to themselves. If the team discovers anything of interest, they'll review the intercepted subspace messages or other anomalies, decipher and interpret them, and periodically report their findings here or to Starbase 621 as an alternate."

The admiral broke in. "We have it on good authority that the Dominion is trying to bring the Breen into the war. I know the Breen are currently neutral and the Diplomatic Corps swears up and down that there's no reason to suspect they'll change their stance. However, you know and I know, Starfleet Intelligence cannot take that chance. If the Breen were to enter the war on the Dominion's side, an already ugly situation could quickly become untenable." He ran his hand through his close-cropped white hair and refocused on the holographic projection. "Mungin's purpose is to ensure we don't get caught off guard."

"Begging the admiral's pardon," Bart said, as the admiral paused, "but there must be some mistake. I *am* a linguist, but I'm barely familiar with Cardassian."

"No, Mr. Faulwell, there's no mistake. We're well aware of your scholastic achievements before you joined Starfleet, but your skills as a cryptanalyst are why you were chosen for this mission. You'll have plenty of time to brush up on your Cardassian, but that's why Lieutenant Priya is going to be joining you on this mission. She's an expert on the Cardassian language as well as a number of the Gamma Quadrant races that are serving in the Dominion's forces."

Commander Mwakwere added, "The lieutenant has been fully vetted and cleared. Even though Bajor's signed a nonaggression pact with the Dominion, the Bajoran Militia has been quietly working with Starfleet Intelligence since the start of the war. Mr. Cruz, you'll be in command of the cryptography mission. Lieutenant Priya will be your second in command, and Lieutenant Zarinth will be in charge of security."

"Folks, I don't have to tell you how important this mission is," Admiral Hazlitt said as Commander Mwakwere powered down the computer console. "You'll be given full documentation on the mission once you leave the base. Your mission is scheduled for six months, with a possible extension of another six months. The base has been equipped with the finest state-of-the-art technology and highly classified systems. In case of discovery, the base cannot, I repeat, cannot fall into the hands of the Dominion. Do I make myself clear?"

Lieutenant Zarinth spoke up for the first time. "Perfectly, sir. You do not have to worry about that. My people fully understand their duty."

Somehow, I'm not really comfortable with how well his people understand their duty, Bart thought. *If we get into trouble, are they likely to shoot the enemy . . . or us?*

Admiral Hazlitt and Commander Mwakwere headed for the door. "You'll remain here until an escort comes to retrieve you. You should be leaving for Mungin in approximately two hours." The admiral paused at the door and raised an imaginary glass to toast the room, "Here's hoping you have a very uneventful six months."

CHAPTER

3

Bart thought back on the admiral's final words. *Obviously he cast a curse on this entire mission, because "uneventful" is exactly what's going on.*

Bart sat at the terminal in the operations section of Mungin watching as the computers downloaded another transmission from Probe 13. Looking up, he scanned the room, painted in a standard eggshell white, with light gray floors and track lighting overhead. There were several computer terminals stationed at various locations in the room, one for each of the team members. Two large screens flanked the walls near the exit to the room. They were set up so the analysts could work together on projects as well as doubling as a communications viewscreen.

Bart let his thoughts wander as the transmission from Probe 13 was being processed by the station's computers. Operations was on deck two, while security and communications were located on deck one. The deck immediately below them held the rec room, gym, and holosuite. Farther down were the decks that held the living quarters, sickbay, armory, life support, and other sundry functions. The lowest deck, which they had dubbed "the boiler room," was where the powerful generators that kept the entire system running smoothly resided. The base was very utilitarian, with minimal design for comfort.

Even that wouldn't be a problem if we were kept busy. Given the lack of work though, plain walls and such become depressing over time. He stared at the walls, trying to motivate himself. He knew he ought to get up and start working on the recovered data, but he was having a hard time convincing himself anyone really cared what they were collecting here.

Looking across the room, he saw Priya listening to a recording they'd made a week ago. She looked up and noticed him watching her.

"Is there something you needed to bring to my attention, Petty Officer?" She spun in her chair to face him, removing her earpiece. The modified communications device was partially hidden beneath her red hair.

"No, I was just thinking about how boring it's been lately. From the way the admiral had built this assignment up, I was really expecting a lot more than just this. If that Cardassian cruiser hadn't transited through the system, I'd begin to think the rest of the universe was an illusion." Bart stretched, feeling the tension in his shoulders and neck. "What in the world is so important about this site?"

"We were told to monitor specifically for any communications between the Dominion and either the Breen or the Tzenkethi." She rose from her chair and straightened out the earring she wore on her right ear. She followed his lead and stretched also before retaking her seat. Just before she buried her head in her work again, she smiled wistfully at him. "The commander did point out this was an inactive sector of the conflict, Dr. Faulwell."

"Inactive is right and please call me Bart." Bart groaned as he stood up from the stool he'd been sitting on. "We could probably all pack up and go home and no one would notice. I don't know how you keep from going insane, Priya. I mean, the highlight of my shift is getting to listen to that repair facility near Delavi. I swear, I know more about Cardassian freighters and tugs than I ever thought was possible."

"True, there hasn't exactly been a pressing need for a Cardassian language expert. You've had more than enough time to brush up on your language skills." She paused for a moment, and then said in a softer voice, "Even if you do still speak with an accent."

Bart simulated tossing a grenade at her and turned back to the computer terminal. An all too familiar noise announced the transmission from Probe 13 was completed. He called up the results of the transmission, his fingers flying across the touch pad and, as expected, it was the weekly transmissions from Cardassia Prime to various outlying bases discussing upcoming personnel transfers and supply requests.

He noted with a passing interest the Cardassians had changed their encryption system again. He transferred the data to his padd and walked over to the replicator to get a cup of coffee. Armed with fresh caffeine, he sat down at the small table nearby to see whether this was simply an updated system or if they'd actually done a communications change.

"It could be worse." Priya's voice broke through his concentration. Her almost cheerful voice caught his attention and he turned to see her resting her head on one arm, looking at him.

"Oh? This I have to hear." Bart chuckled, setting the padd down.

"We could be sitting on top of this rock. Nothing like temperatures averaging around twenty below zero to help you appreciate how good you've got it," she said. Bart felt his skin crawl at the thought of being out in the almost permanent blizzard conditions that existed just beyond their lair. Priya continued, "Of course, it'd beat being on Antros III itself."

"It'd be a little tougher being stationed on an airless world, I must agree." Antros III might have been a Class-M world once, but something had stripped it of any atmosphere it had long ago. In a way, it reminded Bart of being on Earth, only in reverse. Here, the moon was habitable (if only barely), but the planet was a huge ball of rock, hanging over their head. "Remember when we first got here and Jamie was spending all that time examining Antros with the short-range sensors? I thought Zarinth was going to have a conniption fit if he didn't quit messing with the settings."

"Serves him right. I thought I had some tough trainers when I first joined the militia, but Zarinth is incredible. I'm surprised his people haven't killed him yet." Priya shook her head in amazement.

Jamie Cruz entered the room just then. "Well, he's trying to keep them sharp. A bored security guard is a dangerous security guard, especially around all this equipment. I've already had to explain to McKenzie why he can't take over the zero-g racquetball court and turn it into a target range."

"Oh, don't tell me he's on that kick again," Bart said in an aggravated tone of voice. "I thought Zarinth got through to him last time."

"I thought so, too. I guess they're as bored as we—"

Cruz was cut off in mid-sentence by a sudden chime from the computer. *"Incoming message from Probe 42."*

"Forty-two? Have we ever gotten anything from that one?" Cruz looked from Priya to Faulwell apparently hoping someone would have an answer.

Bart rushed over to his station and typed in a few queries into the main computer. "No, in fact, Mungin shows no traffic of any type ever coming in on it. I'm getting a preliminary reading now." While he examined the results the computer was sending him, Priya started running a diagnostic on the traffic. After a few minutes, Bart looked up at Jamie. "I've never seen anything like this before. This is seriously strong encryption on this message."

"I've been looking at the message logs," Priya said, following up on Faulwell's initial report. "There was no preliminary chatter, nothing that would tell me who might have sent it or why. It just started at a specific time and stopped at a specific time. No acknowledgment from whomever received it either. I honestly can't say if it was Cardassian, English, or straight binary."

"Bart, any chance these might be Jem'Hadar communications?" Cruz asked, sitting down with the Bajoran officer to go over her preliminary analysis.

"I don't think so. This doesn't resemble anything we have on record for them."

Bart was busy typing in a new diagnostic test when Cruz came over and tapped him on the shoulder. "Okay folks, I know you were just getting off shift, but if you don't mind . . . ?"

"Mind? Are you kidding?" Bart looked up at the warrant officer with a surprised expression on his face. "After the past few weeks, this is definitely worth losing a sleep shift over." The cryptanalyst got up and started pacing around the room, his fingers interlaced behind his neck. "The only problem is, there's only this one piece of traffic. We're going to probably need a lot more if we're going to break it. The sample is too short to run most of the tests I know."

"Well, that's not exactly up to me, Bart." Cruz smiled at the linguist's enthusiasm. "However, I'm sure we can dedicate a link to monitor this probe." He moved back over to his workstation and tapped his combadge. "Sabran, we've got a new signal down here. If you wouldn't mind, could you come down here and run some tests?"

"Why would I mind, Mr. Cruz?" The Vulcan's confusion was evident even over the link. *"Is that not why I was assigned to the team? I will be down there shortly."* Bart watched as Cruz started to explain further and then apparently decided it wasn't worth the effort. Sabran would be in the operations center before he could finish.

The group quickly divided up to begin analyzing this mysterious signal. Bart began by getting a printout of the signal. Taking a look at the entire message, he punched some commands into the computer to begin looking for any anomalies or sections that repeated. He was looking for anything that would give him a chance to start identifying the encryption system. In addition, the computer would provide a frequency count of individual letters as well as groups of two, three, four, and five.

"Priya, any luck identifying what language this is?" Looking up, he realized two hours had passed while he had been analyzing the results the computer had given him.

The Bajoran looked up from the padd in front of her and pinched the bridge of her nose. "No, but there's nothing here besides this message. As far as I can tell, it's machine code of some kind. We'll have to break into it before I can find the actual language. How about you?"

"Nothing. The first rule of cryptanalysis is to know what the target language is," Bart admitted, stretching his arms over his head. "It makes it a heck of a lot easier to set up your diagnostics if you know what you're going after."

Sabran looked up from his scope, "So, she needs you to break the encryption before she can identify the language and you need her to identify the language before you can break the cipher? Most unfortunate."

Bart laughed, "Well, I *can* break it, eventually. I've translated a few artifacts without having a clue who made them or what their purpose was. It just helps if you know something about the culture. The more clues you have, the better your chances are."

Priya looked over at Jamie. "How are you doing over there, Mr. Cruz?"

He looked up from his station and smiled. "Please, call me Jamie, okay? I'm patching a range of subspace frequencies into Probes 24 and 38, since they're the two closest to 42. If we pick up another unidentified message, it'll alert those two and we'll try to triangulate the message. If we're lucky, we'll catch the receiving station acknowledging and we can see where this message is going."

"How long will that take, Mis—Jamie?" Priya asked, picking up her padd again, and touching a few symbols on the page with her stylus, isolating them for further study later.

"Reprogramming the probes? Already done. How long will it take to find where these messages are coming from? All depends on if and when they transmit again. I can't find what's not out there. I've filed the initial report with Starfleet. I forwarded a section of what we picked up for them to do some crunching on those big computers they've got back there."

"Do you believe they'll have any more success than we?" Sabran asked. "I'm having difficulty even identifying the transmission method for this message. It's akin to nothing I've ever encountered."

A silence settled back over the room while they continued to examine the message. After a little while, the silence was broken by a beeping coming from Jamie's console. Touching a control, a fuzzy picture appeared on a small communications screen set in the wall.

"This is Raven, over," Jamie replied to the hail. When they had arrived, their orders explained that even over secure comms, they were to use cover terms. If the Federation was able to break Cardassian codes, there was every reason to believe they could return the favor.

"Raven, this is Tiger. Reference your last message. Drop all else. Ironclad coverage on lone wolf in the pack. Forward all reports to this station every twelve hours. Out."

The message faded out as the transmission was cut off, leaving an eerie silence in the room. *What in the world have we discovered?* Bart wondered.

CHAPTER
4

A week later, Bart was almost wishing they hadn't found that signal. "Sabran, have you had any luck at all?" he asked as he reviewed his padd for what felt like the thousandth time.

"I am quite capable of understanding orders." Even in the dim light, Bart thought he could see a faint hint of frustration on Sabran's normally stoic face. "My silence implies my lack of success."

"I can't help it! I'm going out of my mind with boredom." Bart snarled, almost tossing the padd across the room. "This bloody signal isn't due for another six hours, thirty-two minutes. Every day, it's the same; a quick microburst and that's it for the day."

"Ironclad coverage does not allow us to deviate our attention to other signals of interest nor can we commit any of our equipment to other tasks. While I'm not certain I understand the logic in ignoring other signals to listen for this specific one, we have our orders."

Deciding this conversation was over, Bart sat at his workstation fuming for a bit. Looking around the operations area, he noted the chaos that had descended on it; stacks of printouts, padds, and reference material were scattered everywhere. Even though most of their work was done on computers, sometimes they found it easier to deal with a schematic or a long piece of analytic work when it was printed out so they could observe the whole thing at once. He had a number of the messages pinned to the walls with lines of varying colors going from one side to the other, looking for commonalities.

"I don't mind the orders so much, but I'm growing tired of Admiral Hazlitt's staff checking up on us all the time. I'm pleased they're interested in what we're doing, but I wish they weren't trying to tell us how to do our jobs." Bart could hear the tone of annoyance in the feminine voice that sounded in the hallway. A few seconds later, Priya appeared in the room. "You're relieved from your shift, Sabran." She took her place at her workstation and brought her console to life. As he started to stand, she continued, "Although if you want to hang around, you're more than welcome."

The Vulcan immediately settled back into his chair and called up a new set of equations on his workstation. "If you would not mind. There is something in this latest communication we intercepted that is proving interesting. I would enjoy an opportunity to pursue it further." Before Priya could respond, he turned around and returned to his task, the images changing on his computer screen faster than she could follow.

"Good evening, Bart. I'm glad to see you're in such a good mood. Are you ready for another racquetball match after our shift?" The sly grin on her face told Bart this wasn't as innocent a question as it sounded.

"Of course I am. After the drubbing you gave me yesterday, I fully intend to get my pound of flesh." Bart grinned back at her. "Oh, Priya, could you look at this bit of traffic with me? I think I'm starting to make sense out of a few sections. Make sense in the most generous terms, that is."

The Bajoran lieutenant moved over quickly and began examining the sections of code Bart had highlighted on his padd. Her eyes flicked between the padd and the scribbles he had made on the papers lining the wall, slowly nodding to herself. "That's promising, Bart. The same section of code occurs here in group 21 on this message and group 17 on the fourth message. Have you been able to identify the particular code yet?"

"No, the messages are still too short. We're starting to get enough of them to begin making comparisons. Up until now, I've been mainly applying brute force methods to them, trying different Cardassian words and seeing if I could force something in. Heck, I've even tried Jem'Hadar and Bajoran military terms to see if anything fit. Not that I think the Bajorans are helping," he quickly added, spotting the look on her face. "It's just that at this point, I'm trying anything the Cardassians *might* use to see if I can crib something in."

They spent the next couple of hours working on the problem, discussing different possibilities and discarding more theories than identifying ones worth pursuing further. Bart felt his mind and throat getting worn out about the same time and decided a cup of coffee was exactly what he needed. He looked up and saw Sabran and Jamie huddled over a computer whispering excitedly to each other.

"Good God, sir, what are you doing up? I thought you'd gone to bed hours ago." Bart grabbed the steaming cup of coffee from the replicator. "I didn't even see you come in."

The Alpha Centaurian turned to him with a harried look. "I was lying there almost asleep and all of a sudden it hit me. I had to come down here and check it out." Jamie's voice was slightly slurred and from the hunch of his shoulders, Bart could tell his body was fighting with his will about sleep.

"What hit you?" Priya spun around in her chair to look at the analyst. Her dark brown eyes showed concern for Jamie's condition, but there was no mistaking the excitement creeping into her voice.

Jamie continued his slurred explanation, as if he'd never heard Priya's question. "Sabran is helping me run the statistics. I don't trust my eyes right now, but I think I've figured out a way to determine where the messages are going to and coming from. That might give you guys the break you need to get into those messages." From the way his eyes were glazed over, it was obvious to Bart the immediate question was would the computer finish its analysis before Jamie fell asleep on them.

"Jamie, have you been skipping your sleep sessions again?" Priya's expression showed a hint of irritation as she ordered up some hot chocolate for the drowsy analyst. "I thought we discussed this obsession you have with working until you pass out."

"We did discuss it. It's just hard once I get my teeth into a problem to *not* work on it," Jamie admitted, before gratefully accepting the steaming mug. After nearly scalding his lips, he compromised by taking a deep whiff of the chocolate smell before setting it aside to cool. "However, I think I've really got something this time."

"And as soon as you're certain, one way or the other?" she asked in a threatening tone.

"As soon as I'm certain, I'm going straight to my bunk. No questions asked."

"We're getting something," Sabran announced to no one in particular. Bart and the others crowded around the workstation as the Vulcan brought up the results on the large projection screen.

"I was right, the first message is originating in Cardassian space." Cruz almost crowed as he grabbed a padd off a nearby table and started paging through it. "According to that last bit of information I requested from Starfleet, there's something . . . ah, an abandoned Cardassian naval yard is located at those coordinates. I guess we can inform Starfleet it's been reoccupied. Sabran, can you pull up a map with those coordinates highlighted?"

"Certainly, Mr. Cruz." Sabran never looked up from his screen, continuing to work on Jamie's calculations.

"Sabran . . ." Jamie stretched the Vulcan's name out, ensuring he had the chief's attention.

"Yes, Mr. Cruz?"

"*Will* you please call up the map with those coordinates highlighted?" he asked the literal-minded Vulcan.

Bart stifled a chuckle as Sabran turned without saying anything and nonchalantly brought the requested scene up on the large monitor. He wondered sometimes if Sabran was as literal as he appeared or if this was his subtle way of encouraging

Jamie to be more precise with his language. Pulling himself back to the here and now, Bart noted the coordinates were on the "northern" edge of Cardassian space. There were only a few inhabited systems nearby and none of them were important enough to warrant much interest. It was a great location for a base if you didn't want to draw much attention.

"Here comes the tricky part, Sabran. How close do you believe the second set of coordinates are to being correct?" Jamie asked, a small waver in his voice. He picked up the hot chocolate again to steady himself.

"I have no way to be certain, Mr. Cruz, but from examining your proposed test, the mathematics are sound and the proposal is highly logical. I see no reason to doubt the results at this time." Sabran's voice was carefully neutral as always.

"All right then, let 'er rip." Jamie said, the excitement in his eyes blazing, his posture straightening as the next wave of adrenaline hit.

Bart watched as a series of formulae flashed over the screen. He wasn't sure what the computer was searching for, but he could tell the mathematics involved were more advanced than anything he'd taken either during his abortive time at Starfleet Academy or after that in the three different universities on three different planets where he'd done his studies leading to his doctorate.

After a few minutes, the computer announced it had arrived at an answer.

"Put it on the main screen," Jamie said. As they watched, a star system was projected on the wall in front of them. "Magnify and identify." Bart could hear the excitement in the mission commander's voice as his idea had apparently paid off.

Finally, the recipient of the mysterious transmissions was identified. As soon as it became clear where the messages were going, Bart felt a cold shiver run down his back.

The Breen Confederacy.

"Well, that explains a lot of things," Priya said, a forced nonchalance in her voice. Bart took a quick glance at her and could see she was unnerved by this sudden turn of events.

"No wonder it didn't match up with any word patterns I was applying to your recoveries, Bart. I was applying the wrong language."

"Don't look at me. I hope you speak Breen. I know just enough to order a beer and find the bathroom if I got stuck in one of their space ports."

"We certainly didn't have contact with them on Bajor, but I'm certain someone's got a Breen dictionary we can access somewhere."

"Is it wise to concentrate on the Breen language?" Sabran asked, his quiet voice breaking into their congratulations. "Since these messages are going *to* the Breen homeworld, is it not possible it's communication aimed at someone else? It could still be Cardassian, or one of the Dominion species such as the Vorta or the Jem'Hadar."

"Ah, Sabran, always the voice of reason," Jamie said. "Well, let's get this information off to Starfleet. It'll take a little while for them to digest this lump of gristle and inform everyone who needs to be informed. They'll probably request further directional shots to be certain we know how to read a computer screen."

"You think they won't believe us? Why would Starfleet put us out here if they won't accept what we find?" Priya's questions were accompanied by a disbelieving frown.

"Didn't say they won't believe us, but some old Earth scientist stated something like 'extraordinary claims require extraordinary proof.' If I were you, I'd certainly enjoy my next few shifts off. I expect things to get really busy around here very soon." Jamie raised a hand to his mouth, stifling a yawn.

"And you need to get back to bed, Mr. Cruz," Priya said, threatening the half-asleep Alpha Centaurian. Bart chuckled in spite of himself as she assigned Sabran to ensure Jamie got to his quarters before he passed out. Turning back to his padd, he started to go over all his data again.

The Breen.

CHAPTER
5

The insistent buzzing of the intercom woke Bart up out of a deep sleep. Groggily, he reached out and found the speaker button on the second try. Trying not to fall out of his bunk, he finally made himself intelligible. "Faulwell here."

"Bart, this is Cruz." A familiar voice slowly filtered into his sleep-fogged brain as he forced himself to sit up on the edge of his bed, staring into the darkness of his room. *"You need to get down to operations as quickly as possible."*

"What's going on? The power plant threatening to blow up? The Cardassians are attacking? Ow!" Stars exploded in his head as his shin rammed into the nightstand next to his bed. "Computer, lights." Fully awake as the room became illuminated, he grabbed his leg, trying not to plunge forward on his face. Expelling a few choice curse words under his breath, he headed for his closet.

In the background, he could hear Jamie's response. *"Priority One message from SI headquarters. They want all of us present. Preferably in one piece."* Bart could hear him suppressing a laugh.

So much for them taking their time to digest the information. He grabbed a fresh uniform out of the closet, giving himself a second to calm down before replying. "You're hilarious," he called back toward the intercom, struggling to put his tunic over his head. "Be there in about five minutes."

As Bart entered operations, he noted everyone else seated around the various workstations that dominated the room, waiting for him to arrive. To his surprise, even Lieutenant Zarinth was there. *Someone must have held a phaser to his head. He never comes down to operations unless he absolutely has to.* Bart responded with a cheery smile as the Andorian greeted him with a humorless nod. Zarinth had taken over the security center and converted it into his office/personal quarters, preferring to ignore the intelligence personnel as much as possible.

As soon as Bart placed his chair where he had an unobstructed view of the screen, he nodded to Jamie, who dimmed the room lights and brought up the signal. The transmission was weak and fuzzy, but there was no questioning the concern on Commander Mwakwere's face.

"Excellent work so far. The analysts here at Headquarters agree with your findings. It corroborates some reports we've been receiving from other sources. Prepare to receive supplemental tasking for your mission."

"Standing by, sir," Jamie said.

"Your first priority is to determine exactly who is sending and who is receiving these messages. We need as much information as you can possibly derive from any and all sources at your disposal. Secondly, we need to know exactly what is being transmitted in these messages, so we'll need full reports on not only the encryption system and its keys, but also complete translations of all messages that you can recover."

"Should we continue forwarding everything we intercept to your location for analysis?" Bart noted there was a serious tone in Jamie's voice he'd never heard before.

"Yes and no." Commander Mwakwere ran his hand through his close-cropped black hair. *"There's no question about the value of the information we're receiving from you. We have no historical equivalents to the cryptosystem you've encountered. The head shed thinks it's probably a unique system and probably some very high-level stuff going back and forth on this channel. However . . ."*

"I'm not certain I like where this is going," Bart said, not realizing he'd spoken aloud.

"You're going to like this even less, then, Petty Officer. We have reason to believe the existence of your mission has been compromised. We're not certain, but the counterintelligence guys tell us there's a good chance that one of the Mungin receivers was discovered, based on their own sources. The Dominion probably doesn't know where they're routed to, but you can be damn certain they're going to devote a lot of time trying to find out."

"Understood, Commander. We'll make preparations just in case," Jamie replied.

"I'm certain you will, Mr. Cruz. However, to minimize your signature, it would be best if you limited communications with us. That's why Mungin will have to do the majority of the heavy lifting on this project. The more traffic you feed us, the more likely your site will be compromised. In fact, unless absolutely necessary, maintaining radio silence unless you have a solution would probably be best."

A feral grin on his face, Zarinth said, "My people are quite prepared for any possible encounters with the Dominion, Commander. We've arranged a few surprises should they attempt to penetrate this site."

"Let's hope you don't have to test their training," the commander replied, rubbing his hand over his eyes. Even through the fuzzy picture, Bart could see Mwakwere probably hadn't had much sleep lately. *"Good luck and keep us informed if anything develops. Tiger out."*

As the screen went blank, a sudden quiet settled over the room. Looking up at the chronometer, Bart saw there were only three more hours before his shift started. Even though he had always been able to survive on catnaps, here lately he'd appreciated getting in a full night's sleep to recharge. He knew he was in that no-man's land, but if he went back to bed, he'd just get into deep sleep about the time his alarm went off.

Pondering his options, he looked back around the room and noted everyone, except Zarinth, was still there. The Andorian had wasted no time escaping back into his own cocoon. *Probably dreaming up new ways to torture his people in the name of training.*

"So, what's next?" Priya asked, stretching back in her chair.

"We get back to work," Jamie said, grinning like the Cheshire cat. "And you two, get back to bed. I want my two linguists as sharp as possible when they're on duty. Sabran and I can handle things for now."

Bart nodded to Jamie and wedged himself up out of the chair to leave. He shook his head in mock dismay as he saw Jamie and Sabran already huddled together, examining something on the Vulcan's terminal. He slipped out of the room without disturbing them. Before he had gotten very far down the corridor, Priya fell into step with him as they made their way to the turbolift.

"So, what was your impression about the conference?" the Bajoran asked, pinching herself on the ridges just above her nose to fight off a yawn.

"I think Commander Mwakwere knows more than he's telling us. I don't know if it was because he was worried about the conversation being monitored or if there's something else going on, but he seemed to be holding back. Either way, it's a concern." Bart touched a control, summoning the turbolift to their level.

"I agree. Personally I think it was a little of both. If we have been compromised, there's a chance the Dominion could be listening in. However, I have a feeling we'd be considered 'acceptable losses' in case we came under attack. I doubt there's a Starfleet ship close enough to come to our aid if we needed it."

"Now, there's a comforting thought." Bart gave a mock groan as the doors to the turbolift opened. They stepped inside and he called out, "Deck four."

As the doors hissed closed, Priya turned to him and grinned, "So, how are you with a phaser, anyway?" Her brown eyes twinkled mischievously at his sudden discomfort, as the lift began sinking in the tube.

"Well," he admitted grudgingly, "last time I qualified, I managed not to shoot myself or any of the range cadre. Let's just say there's a reason why I'm in intel and not security. Just hope it doesn't come down to me saving the day with a fancy shot. I'm more likely to hit the life support than the attackers."

"That bad, huh?"

"Pretty damn close." As Bart finished his confession, the lift reached the end of its trip. They walked into the dimly lit corridor toward their quarters. "Now, Zarinth is a different matter. I'd be surprised if he isn't running a snap drill right now. He seems to live for a chance to scrap with the Cardassians."

"To be quite honest, I've got a few scores to settle with them myself. However, unlike Zarinth, I'm not so gung-ho that I want to take on a battle cohort by myself. I'm happy helping direct some of your Federation ships to deal with them for me." The sudden ferocity in her voice caught Bart off guard.

As they paused in front of her quarters, Bart changed the subject. "I have to admit, Chantrea, I was surprised when you were introduced to us. I thought Bajor was neutral in this conflict."

Priya stopped, her hand arrested just millimeters short of her door. Turning back toward Bart, she glanced down at the floor as if unsure how to continue. Finally, she looked up at him, coming to a decision.

"Officially yes, Bajor has signed a nonaggression pact with the Dominion. The Emissary requested that, to keep us from becoming a Dominion target."

Bart frowned. "The Emissary?"

"The one sent to speak the words of the Prophets to the Bajoran people. I believe you know him as Captain Sisko, the commander of Deep Space 9."

Bart soundlessly mouthed "Oh," having no idea what she was talking about. He wasn't up on Bajoran mythology, but it was obvious whatever the Prophets and the Emissary were supposed to be, Priya was a true believer. The real surprise was that Benjamin Sisko was apparently part of that mythology.

Bart knew of him as the commander of DS9, the station that had been at the forefront of the war, as it stood proximate to the wormhole to the Gamma Quadrant, through which the Dominion forces had come to this area of the galaxy. *Didn't realize he was also moonlighting as an emissary.*

Priya continued. "In any case, we know who our friends really are, so a select group of militia officers resigned our commissions and, well, disappeared. Then we contacted Starfleet surreptitiously and offered our services. This way we can keep helping the Federation while giving the government deniability with the Dominion."

Bart leaned up against the corridor wall, stunned by this revelation. "So, you're not officially part of the Bajoran Militia after all?"

"No, not officially. Don't get me wrong, this is my uniform— I was a lieutenant serving in Dakhur Province up until I volunteered for this." The pride in her voice was obvious.

"Well, for what it's worth, I think their trust was well placed in you." Bart's arm snapped upward to stifle his own yawn. "However, if Starfleet is trusting me to be awake on shift, I better get to sleep now. See you in about three hours."

"Thanks, Bart. I appreciate the vote of confidence," she said just before she slipped through the door into her quarters. Bart stood there, staring at the now shut door and pondering the events of the past thirty minutes. Slowly he returned to his quarters, lay down on the bed still dressed, and shut off the lights.

The alarm buzzer went off two and a half hours later with him still staring up at the dark ceiling.

CHAPTER

6

The days following the conference with Mwakwere blended together into a painful memory for Bart. After a while, the concept of shifts devolved into endless sessions in operations with everyone catching sleep as they could. Tempers began to run short and they found themselves having to go back over and over their work to make certain they weren't overlooking anything in their exhausted states. After about a week, things were reaching their breaking point.

Bart looked up from his padd after another unsuccessful attempt at breaking the code to find Jamie standing in the doorway. Jamie's fierce look swept across the room and Bart could see the Alpha Centaurian start to say something at least twice before thinking better of it. Finally an idea lit up Jamie's face as he made a decision.

"All right, folks, everyone follow me. Team meeting." His voice broke through the silence in the room, causing Priya and Sabran's heads to pop up as if someone had set off an explosive charge in the door.

"But, Jamie, I'm . . ." Priya's voice quickly trailed off as the analyst cut her off with a withering look.

"That was an order, not a suggestion. Let's go, people. We need a break and we're taking one *now*!" he repeated and then spun around. Slowly the others rose from their workstations and followed him out of the room. Jamie stood at the end of the hall, holding the door to the turbolift open until he was certain everyone was there. He followed them into the lift, calling out deck three to the central computer.

Once they reached the requested deck, Jamie led them past the gym and the rec room into the holosuite. As the door shut behind them, he called out, "Program Alpha Six-Two."

There was a slight wavering and the team found themselves standing on a tropical beach, surrounded by palm trees and looking out over a crystal blue sea that stretched to the horizon. Bart looked behind him and found four chaise lounges arranged there, with their own individual umbrellas and coolers.

"Grab a seat, people. We're going to relax, review what the hell we've been doing here lately and then I'm ordering some mandatory R&R." Jamie plopped down on one of the chairs and adjusted the umbrella to cut down on the sunlight hitting his face.

"Hang on a minute there, sir. Who's monitoring the situation if we're all down here?" Bart asked, confused. "We might miss something vital."

"I've instructed the computer to deal with any incoming traffic. Zarinth has someone monitoring the subspace radio in case Starfleet finds it necessary to break radio silence. He knows we're going to be down here for a while. If anything *really* important happens, he knows the pass code to get in here. For the next couple of hours, our only mission is to soak up some rays, do some swimming, or simply walk along the beach and enjoy the ocean breezes. And for the next couple of hours, drop the 'sir' stuff. There'll be enough time for that once R&R is over."

"Mr. Cruz, I'm afraid I don't see the wisdom of this. Wouldn't our time be better spent continuing to work on the problem at hand?" Sabran asked, a hint of curiosity and irritation in his voice.

"Chief Sabran, you may enjoy the ocean or you may sit here and do nothing. That is your choice." Jamie turned slightly in his chair to face the recalcitrant Vulcan. "However, once we finish the review of our mission, there'll be no more work on the project until the simulation runs its course. There are a couple of cabanas a few meters in that direction. You're all to change into the beachwear you'll find there and reconvene back here in ten minutes for the staff meeting." Seeing the hesitation, Jamie sighed and continued. "That's an order, folks." He leaned down and snagged a glass bottle filled with an amber liquid out of his cooler.

"Sir, I really do not see the need to change our clothing to have a staff meeting," Sabran continued.

"Of course you don't. That's exactly why you need to do it." Jamie shaded his eyes from the sunlight that broke through the light clouds in the sky. He got up off his chair and headed inland. "Nine minutes left, folks."

A few minutes later, the group reassembled in their bathing gear, except for Sabran, who had chosen a T-shirt and shorts. Jamie motioned for them to pull their chairs together in a circle. "Ah, this is better. I want you to know I've noticed how hard everyone has been working on this project and I really appreciate it. I guarantee it'll be reflected in the report I submit at the end of the mission. However, I think we've hit the proverbial wall. Our efficiency has been going down like a *ptarn* bird that's been hit by a stunner. So, I made the command decision that we were going to take this break." He paused long enough to take a drink and then turned to Sabran. "In a nutshell, what have you discovered about the communications system we're targeting?"

Bart noticed the Vulcan looked positively uncomfortable out of uniform, but he gamely tried to accept the unusual situation with grace. "It does not appear to be a standard subspace communications system. In fact, it does not match up with anything we have on record. I would say there is a 92.54 percent chance we are intercepting a Gamma Quadrant communications device."

"Priya, does that match up to what you're seeing?" Jamie asked.

The Bajoran leaned back in her lounge. "It's as good an assumption as any. Nothing about the code we're examining seems to match up with any frequency rotas for any known Alpha Quadrant language. I've even compared it against every Beta Quadrant language I could find on record, just in case, but no luck. If it's from the Gamma Quadrant, it wouldn't surprise me." She paused, and then sat up slightly in her chair. "It's possible that it's an unknown dialect, but until we break the encryption, I'm not going to be able to isolate enough of the language to accurately identify it, much less start translating it."

"That throws the ball back into your court, Bart." Jamie lifted his bottle toward the cryptologist.

"I'd throw it right back at you if I could," Bart said, letting go with a self-deprecating laugh. "It's been a very frustrating situation. Every time I think I've found an in, it turns out to be a dead end. However, there is a section that's starting to look promising. I've got the computer running an analysis against it while we're down here."

"Keep plugging away, Bart. If we're going to get anywhere, you're going to probably be the linchpin. Once you get us into this thing, the rest should fall into place." Jamie leaned back in his chaise, staring up into the blue sky.

"Thanks, Jamie. No pressure. I like that." Bart laughed at him.

Jamie took another drink, finishing off his bottle and then tucked his hands behind his head. "Well, I've been concentrating on what little external chatter I've been able to get from the messages. We've only seen the receiving station in Breen space reply twice. Hard to say who or what's going on there based on such a small sample. However, the originating station is another story."

"How so?" Priya asked, her curiosity piqued.

"There's been some ship-to-ship communications that the sensors have picked up at the 'abandoned' naval yards. I'd say there are at least four Jem'Hadar battleships there and a number of supporting craft."

Bart sputtered. "*Four* Jem'Hadar battleships?"

"Yep. I was thinking that's an awful lot of firepower simply to secure an abandoned site. In addition, the way the war's going, why would you tie up *one* battleship on something as simple as transmitting a message, much less four? I'd say there's someone pretty damn important there to rate that kind of an honor guard. Anyway, I've got a few more things to check out and then I'm going to give you the results of my investigation, Bart. Hope it'll help you." Then he hopped up out of his chair. "So, who's up for a swim?"

Bart and Priya turned and looked at each other. Shrugging, Bart slowly got to his feet. "Might as well. You said the simulation wasn't going to end for a while."

"You'll pardon me if I don't join you, Mr. Cruz?" Sabran asked.

"Your loss, Chief, but if you're more comfortable here, knock yourself out. As I said earlier, this is your 'vacation,' however you want to spend it is fine with me," Jamie replied, and turned to sprint toward the water. He hit with a long, shallow dive and surfaced several feet out. Priya and Bart waded out until it was deep enough to begin swimming and slowly stroked out to where the warrant officer was treading water, waiting for them.

They'd been swimming for a few minutes when the sound of a siren caught their attention. Before they realized what had happened, they found themselves standing on a blank floor, with Zarinth standing in the doorway to the holosuite.

"Sorry to interrupt your session, Mr. Cruz. However, our long-range sensors have picked up a possible intruder entering the system. Mayhew is comparing its signature against any known ships, friendly or enemy. I felt it was best to alert you as quickly as possible." The Andorian kept his eyes aimed just over Jamie's shoulder, trying not to notice the analyst's current choice of attire.

"You did exactly the right thing, Lieutenant. We'll get changed right away and meet you here. If you find out anything more, let us know as soon as possible." Jamie nodded to Zarinth and then turned to head toward the dressing room that had been disguised as a cabana earlier.

After a quick shower and change of clothes, they met up with Zarinth. Before Jamie could ask him anything, Zarinth's combadge started beeping. "Zarinth, here. Report." The Andorian's words came out in a sharp staccato reminding Bart of an old-fashioned projectile weapon.

"Mayhew here, sir," a voice crackled. *"We've identified that intruder. It's a Cardassian scout ship. However, there are five more intruders approaching this system in a slow, looping approach. I'd say it's the rest of the scout's unit. Estimated time to Antros III, one hour for the scout ship, four hours for the five unknown bogies."*

"Roger. I'll be back up at the command center in about five minutes. Defense posture Bravo for right now. Keep a close eye on that scout. Zarinth out." The security chief turned to Jamie. "Mr. Cruz, I'm going to have to insist we go to minimum power usage to lower our signature. Please go up and begin shutdown procedures. Your people will be restricted to the bottom four levels once you've accomplished your mission."

"Excuse me, Lieutenant. I believe the admiral put me in charge of this mission."

"You are in charge of the cryptography mission, Mr. Cruz. And I am in charge of the *security* of that mission. If your people are down here, minimizing our electronic signal and not in the way of my professionals, we're more likely to get out of this alive. I think my instructions on this matter from the admiral were quite clear. If you object, you have the right to protest to Admiral Hazlitt *after* this situation is resolved. Provided we're still alive to contact him."

The Andorian let Jamie chew on that for a few moments. Bart could see Jamie's jaw moving as if he were trying to form some words, but nothing was coming out.

After a few minutes staring at each other, Zarinth spun around on one heel and disappeared in the direction of the turbolift. Jamie slowly turned to face the group, his face flushed with anger and embarrassment. "All right, you heard the man. Let's get up there and go to minimal operations. If you have printouts, grab them and meet back down here. We can use the open area to set up a secondary operations area."

"What about that program I have running?" Bart asked, a worried tone in his voice. "If we interrupt it now, I could lose everything it's recovered up till now."

"Can't be helped, Bart. Try to save what you can, but get that computer shut down. If Zarinth isn't overblowing the situation, losing the data could be the least of our worries."

The team quickly headed up to deck two and began shutting everything down. Bart saw the computer was about eighty-five percent through the process, but he had no clue if it was getting anything useful. With a lump in his throat, he hit the interrupt key, placing the diagnostic program on standby and saved what he had. He had to hope the computer system would be able to restart from the saved point, but there were no guarantees, especially once they powered the computers down.

Looking up from his work, he saw Jamie and Sabran talking. With a curt nod, the Vulcan headed out of the room toward the turbolift. Bart knew Jamie was still steaming about the incident with Zarinth, but he could see their leader was in no mood to speak to anyone about it.

Snagging his padd and all his printouts, he headed toward the door. Priya was waiting there and he could see Jamie was making one last check through the room before shutting everything down. Finally, as operations went dark and silent, they made their way down the corridor to the turbolift and returned to deck three.

As they entered the holosuite, Bart saw Sabran had already set up several folding tables and was busy setting up a portable communications system. He turned to Jamie, "I thought we were supposed to shut everything down. What's with the comms equipment?"

"If they break through into the compound, I plan on dumping everything we've got on file here as long as the subspace antenna is intact," the Alpha Centaurian said, a wry tone in his voice. "That blasted Andorian isn't the only professional at this site."

Bart grinned back at him. "Remind me not to get on your bad side." Looking over to his left, he saw Sabran handing a phaser and a couple of spare power packs to Priya. "What's up with the weapons?"

"No sense in taking chances. I requisitioned the weapons and borrowed enough stuff to make some rather nasty booby traps, just in case," Jamie replied, setting a large satchel on one of the tables by the door. He opened it up, showing Bart a number of devices with a series of lights on them. "Pressure activated bombs, remote activated bombs, and a rather nasty electrical field generator. Zarinth would have a fit, but some of his people thought it was funny to teach the 'old professor' something about things that go boom."

"Tears of the Prophets . . . did you build those yourself?" Priya asked, looking over his shoulder.

"A few of them. M'thanga helped with the trickier parts. We tested a few of them outside, so I know they work in theory." Jamie beamed down on the devices as if they were his children.

"Outside? When the—? Those sleep shifts you were missing. You weren't working on this, you were out goofing off with the security guards!" Priya yelled at him, the veins in her forehead becoming pronounced.

"Not all of them," Jamie confessed. "However, I figure a few hours of missed sleep may just pay off for us. And if we don't need them, at least it was fun learning about this stuff." Priya looked at him like he'd lost his mind, but she finally just laughed softly and walked away. Bart noticed Jamie was so busy checking and rechecking the devices he'd designed, he never saw her leave.

A sudden chirping caught everyone's attention. Jamie reached up and tapped his combadge. "Cruz here."

"Mayhew here, sir. The Cardassian scout ship has transited the Antros system, but the rest of the Cardassian fleet has moved into orbit around Antros III. Don't know what they're up to; we're passively monitoring the situation. Will keep you informed."

"Understood. Cruz out." Jamie turned around and looked at the group. "Well, that's it for now. We hunker down and wait."

CHAPTER
7

Bart stepped out of the holosuite after another frustrating shift. He'd gone over and over the readouts he'd brought with him when they shut down operations, but he was no closer after this shift than he'd been two days earlier. He knew without a doubt the answer was waiting for him in the memory buffer of the main computer, but they simply couldn't chance turning it back on.

Mayhew had informed them that the ice-covered moon had been probed at least four times in the past two days. Apparently the shielding Starfleet Intelligence had used to hide the underground facility had done its job, but knowing a single barrage from one of the ships floating near Antros III would completely obliterate their spider hole kept everyone on edge. Bart gave Zarinth credit, though. Whatever his personal feelings were toward the SI personnel, he did a great job of keeping them updated as things began happening.

"Hey, Bart, you awake there?" He glanced up to see Priya standing over by the entrance to the zero-gravity racquetball court. "You're just staring off into space."

"Oh, hey, Priya. Sorry, I was just thinking about those cruisers up there. It's just tough knowing we don't even have a good spitwad shooter to fire back at them if they decided to take a few dozen feet off the surface."

"Welcome to my world. When the resistance was fighting

with the Cardassians, we had no navy and very little air support to speak of. We learned to appreciate caves with high concentrations of magnetic rocks. The Cardassians knew we were using them to hide from their sensors, but there were too many caves and tunnels for them to guard all of them all the time. I swear, there were times I wondered if the sun was still in the sky. It felt like I lived most of my life underground."

The earnest look on her face made him smile. "That sounds familiar. Not so much the hiding in caves, but working for SI, I spend way too much time in windowless buildings, hiding behind sensor-resistant screens. We called the place I was just at 'the mushroom farm' because we were always kept in the dark and fed a lot of manure."

Priya laughed. "So, are you up for a quick set of racquetball?"

"Ah, trying to work off some of your stress by picking on my minuscule racquetball skills?" Bart teased.

"Oh, please. I mean, you actually scored seven points last match."

Bart retrieved the racquetball as it hovered in midair. Floating about five feet above the floor, his measured movements helped keep him stationary, letting him savor the moment. The current score was 14–11 and for the first time since they'd started playing against each other, he felt confident he was about to win a match. He turned his head, trying to estimate where Priya's trajectory was going to take her before he served.

"All right, quit gloating and serve, would you?" He finally located her, floating near the ceiling. She was positioning herself to kick off to try to retrieve his shot.

"Gloat? Me?" he asked in a shocked voice. "Perish the thought." Bart drew back, trying to counter his body's inertia as he pushed the ball downward. If he'd done it right, he should hit the ceiling just about the time the ball struck the floor and they'd meet about the center of the room.

Just as the ball hit the ground, he felt himself growing

heavier and he started floating down toward the ground as the dampeners kicked in. Before he could turn around, Jamie's voice rang out from the control room. *"Sorry about the game, guys, but we need you in here now."*

"Dammit, Jamie! Couldn't you have waited one more minute?" Bart called back as his feet settled to the ground and normal gravity returned to the room. "I was finally going to beat her. It was game point!"

"In your dreams, cryppie boy," Priya muttered, just loud enough for Bart to hear.

"Sorry, but it can't be helped. The Cardassians just launched a small shuttle toward our position. Zarinth wants everyone in position, even us nonprofessionals."

The smile fled from Priya's face. "What's the shuttle's ETA?" From the tone of voice and the way she held her body, Bart was reminded more of Zarinth than the racquetball partner he'd had a moment ago.

"Best estimate is one hour before they touch down. You've got a little time to shower and change, but we need you in the holosuite as quick as possible." The concern was easy to hear in Jamie's voice. Bart realized their leader might try to keep the atmosphere light but Jamie took the responsibility of his command seriously.

A quick shower later, Bart found himself being issued an additional hand phaser, just in case. As Jamie went over a series of strategies, the door to the holosuite slid open without warning and Mayhew walked in. The blond-haired noncom's eyes bugged out and his hands involuntarily rose skyward at the sight of four phasers being pointed in his direction.

"You know, you could knock and let us know you're coming, Mayhew," Priya said, an aggravated tone coloring her voice as she realized her mistake.

"Uh . . . yeah . . . sorry. Lieutenant Zarinth wanted me to issue you these." He handed each member of the team a wide belt. Each belt had a large bulge in the middle and a covered button on the buckle.

"And these would be?" Sabran asked, gingerly holding the belt in one hand.

"Those are your last-ditch weapons. If it looks like you're about to be captured, flip open the cover and hit the button. Five seconds later, the phaser power packs mounted on your belt will go critical." Mayhew's voice showed no more emotion than if he were explaining how to perform maintenance on a turbolift. He raised an eyebrow as his ice-blue eyes scanned the shocked faces in the room.

"Are you crazy? Why would we do that?" Jamie sputtered.

"Sir, with all due respect, I'd rather you do that than fall into the hands of the Cardassians. Besides, if they manage to fight their way all the way down here to where you are, we've probably hit the self-destruct button. I'd rather go like this, quick and painless, than have several tons of rock and ferrocrete land on me. But, that's just me."

"A very sensible precaution, Mr. Mayhew," Sabran said, buckling on the belt. "What is the status of the approaching enemy?"

The rest of the team eyed the belts like they were handling live snakes. After everyone had put them on, Mayhew continued. "The shuttle just landed. We lost visual on them as soon as they got within half a klick of the surface, but it appears they landed just north of this site. We have a few micro-sensors out there, but for now, we're keeping them in their shelters. The lieutenant thinks trying to acquire them isn't worth the chance of them spotting the sensors."

"That makes sense," Priya said. "Surely we have other methods for tracking anyone trying to approach the base, though."

"We have a few, but this site was designed for concealment. I don't think when they built it they were considering defending against an enemy on the surface of the moon. We're going to have to rely on the pressure grid and the passive sensor system to give us a heads-up. Odds are, we won't know where they are until they're right on top of us," Mayhew said, rubbing his hand on his chin. "Oh, and we're shutting down the turbolift as soon as I get back upstairs. You'll have to take the ladders if you need to get anywhere. We'll keep you up-to-date as best we can."

"Thanks. We appreciate your candor," Cruz said.

The noncom nodded sharply to the chief warrant officer and beat a hasty retreat out of the holosuite.

"Well, that certainly puts a different light on things," Bart said, patting the power pack resting in the small of his back. "I didn't realize our sensors were so limited."

"We have additional sensors, but cannot use them," Sabran responded, inspecting his phaser once again. "They're all active sensors. They'd show up on the Cardassian monitors the instant they were turned on. We have to rely on passive sensors, which are notorious for their short range and lack of sensitivity. They'd pick up a ship flying overhead, but probably not a human-sized target using a jet pack."

"You're not making me feel any better, Sabran."

"I didn't realize you were ill. Do you require something from the medical supplies, Petty Officer?"

Bart started to say something and just shook his head no. Jamie tried to suppress a smile and failed miserably and Priya spun around, giving Bart the impression she was trying to hide her amusement also. Once he regained control, Jamie told Sabran and Priya to go grab some sleep while Bart and he settled in to take the first watch.

They spent the first half of the watch setting up some barricades where they could keep an eye on the turbolift. After Jamie was comfortable with their efforts, he sent Bart in to get back to work on his project, while he sat out in the hallway on guard.

Six hours later, Sabran and Priya relieved them. After Jamie and he showed them the improvements they'd made, Bart climbed down the emergency ladder to his quarters on deck four. He smiled at his pillow as he flopped down on his bunk and dropped off into an exhausted sleep.

All too soon, his alarm went off. Making his way back up

the ladder, he was surprised to see Sabran working at a portable monitor. Looking over his shoulder, his eyes widened even more as he saw the Vulcan technician had acquired a picture of the security office. It was easy to make out the complement of guards on duty, monitoring various stations in there.

"I thought we weren't supposed to be using the computer. How'd you get that signal?"

"While I was on duty last night, I realized, even with the main computer offline, the computer that maintains our life support system was still operational. It's a much less powerful system, but a computer is a computer."

"And, you are a computer expert," Priya said, grinning.

The Vulcan looked at her and gave her a small nod to acknowledge her compliment. Turning to face Jamie, who'd just arrived, he continued. "All I had to do was tap into its systems and I was able to bring this up. This device can receive signals that are only available through the life-support monitors to minimize bandwidth. It's crude, but it'll be more effective than sitting here staring at the turbolift door."

"A commendable solution, Chief Sabran," Jamie said, a broad grin spreading out over his face. "However, I wouldn't make a big deal about this. I'm not certain how well Lieutenant Zarinth would take it."

Sabran started to say something to Jamie and then paused and nodded. "I see your point, Mr. Cruz."

The next three days crept along for the quartet. Bart was going over the printouts for what seemed to be the thousandth time when he heard the familiar chirp of a combadge.

"Cruz here," Jamie said.

"*Mr. Cruz, this is Zarinth. Sensors indicate the Cardassian shuttle has left the surface of the planet. From what we can ascertain, it appears the fleet is making preparations to leave the Antros system.*"

Bart thought he heard disappointment in the Andorian's

voice. *He's actually upset they didn't get to fight the Cardassians,* he thought as Jamie acknowledged Zarinth's transmission.

"We'll stay on minimal functions for another day until we're certain they've actually left the system. This will give my people sufficient time to do a sweep and see if they left any monitors on the surface. We'll be restoring turbolift functions in a little bit. You can tell Chief Sabran he'll have to keep using his sensor for a bit longer."

"Why that son-of-a—He knew all along," Jamie said, a smile of admiration forcing its way onto his face.

"Apparently they have their own computer experts," Sabran said. "I was not trying to hide my intrusion, but then again, it wasn't an obvious program I was running. I wonder if they spotted it, or if they've been observing us on their own terms?"

"Their own terms, meaning they've bugged the compound?" Bart asked, letting the others draw the same conclusions he was reaching.

"It's possible, since they work out of the security office. It would make perfect sense for there to be hidden sensors. Remember, there have been rumors of changelings infiltrating Starfleet. A saboteur could easily threaten the safety of this mission. Of course, if there had been a spy in our midst, transmitting messages to the Cardassian ships overhead would have been just as effective."

Jamie agreed, nodding to himself. "If the Dominion could gain control of this site without Starfleet's knowledge, they could feed false data directly to SI. They could trick us into maneuvering our limited reserves to meet a nonexistent threat, opening up entire sectors to be exploited. I certainly don't think any of us is a traitor, and I'm pretty darn confident that Zarinth's people are solid, but from a security standpoint, Zarinth can't afford to take any chances."

"That's a pretty damn cynical attitude to take, Jamie," Priya said, shaking her head and looking up at the ceiling for any telltale signs.

"Thirty-eight years in Starfleet Intelligence will do that to you, Chantrea. I've seen some peculiar things and met some peculiar people, but the men and women in counterintelligence are the most paranoid, anal-retentive, everything-by-the-book bastards you'd ever meet. However, they're also the people I most want watching my back."

"Even so," Priya said, "I dislike Zarinth flaunting his abilities like that."

"He does seem to have an attitude about SI that goes beyond the typical combat arms mentality. However, as long as he does his job and lets us do ours, I don't have the time to let his petty games get to me. Grab your stuff, guys, and let's get ready to head back upstairs. There's work that needs to be done and we're the people to do it."

CHAPTER
8

The near-miss by the Cardassian vessels seemed to spur everyone into a higher gear. As Bart had feared, shutting down the computer system had corrupted his data. However, Sabran was able to do a partial recovery, so the cryptologist didn't have to start from square one again.

They found Probe 26 had managed to record much of the Cardassian's ship-to-ship chatter during the transit of the Antros system. Jamie immediately set out to incorporate this new information into their databases and compare it against earlier intercepts. As he suspected, it was a different system than the one they were most interested in, but he noted a few similarities that might be worth pursuing.

Bart examined the messages while he was waiting for the newly reactivated computer to finish the program he'd started seven days ago. A cursory examination didn't find anything that jumped out at him. It was a straightforward Cardassian encryption system; his diagnostic program identified it as a pre-Dominion cipher that Starfleet had broken a few years ago. Priya took his decrypts and began translating them in case there was anything useful to report when the next opportunity arose.

After a few hours, Priya went over to Jamie's station and physically escorted him out of the operations center, muttering dire threats about what would happen if she caught him out playing with the security guards. He put up a halfhearted protest, but he knew she was capable of following through on her threats, so he acquiesced in the end.

"I swear, Bart, sometimes he's just like a kid," Priya said as she reentered the room. "He knows he needs to eat and get some sleep, but he'd be in here 26/7 if he thought we'd let him."

"I think this is the first time he's been in the field in a long time. He's starting to get to the age where they're not going to want to deploy him much more and he knows it. He's trying to squeeze everything he can out of this assignment." Bart looked up at Priya over his padd. He turned to push a few buttons on the computer terminal next to him and annotated the information on his padd before continuing. "He sees this as his swan song."

"Swan song?" There was no questioning the confused tone in her voice. "What would a bird have to do with this mission?"

"One of the most pervasive of swan legends back on Earth is it sings a beautiful song just before dying. Over time, it's come to mean the last great act a person does in their life."

"You think Jamie will die after this mission?" Her shocked voice echoed in the ops center.

"No, but he'll probably go back to the Academy and teach there until he retires. He sees this as his last chance to do something really meaningful. That's why he's doing all the extra stuff, playing commando, et cetera," Bart confided, keeping his voice low before returning to his computer.

Looking up a while later, he saw Priya sitting at her terminal, staring over the top of her monitor at the wall beyond her. "Is something wrong?"

She jumped, startled by Bart's sudden question. "No, I was just thinking about what's going to happen to us after this mission is over."

Bart laughed, "Well, I don't know about the rest of you, but I fully expect to wind up in some dull, boring, and very safe assignment after this war is over."

"I imagine I'll go back to Bajor, but in a way, I'm not looking forward to it." She sat at her terminal, tapping the end of her stylus on the table in front of her.

"I thought you were fighting to liberate Bajor?"

"I am." There was pride in her voice, but sadness was visible in her eyes. "It's just that it's only been a few years since we liberated ourselves from the Cardassians, and now this. I don't know what Bajor's going to be like when the war's over."

As they reached the end of their shift, the computer finally spit out the results Bart had been waiting for. His eyes lit up as he saw there was a positive match with several of the groups of code he'd been targeting. As he turned around to pass the good news on to Priya, he saw Sabran standing in the doorway to operations. It was obvious the Vulcan had something on his mind, but Bart had the feeling he wasn't certain how to ask.

"Chief Sabran, would you check this out for me and make certain I'm interpreting the data correctly?" he asked, hoping it would give Sabran the opening to say whatever was bothering him.

The Vulcan moved across the room with a catlike grace, taking the padd from Faulwell. His brown eyes gazed at the computer's results and then he began comparing the recoveries and the original text. "Very good, Petty Officer Faulwell. It appears you have begun to make good progress against the unknown code."

"It's a start. I just wish it didn't take so long to run this program. There's no guarantee the Cardassians won't return before I get the entire message broken out." Frustration was visible on the cryptologist's face. "It takes too long even to prove something's wrong."

"I believe I can help there."

"Oh?" The Vulcan's hesitation had gotten Bart's attention. Sabran was usually so confident when he spoke.

"I noted certain . . . inefficiencies in the diagnostic program you were using. I have been working on a suitable upgrade if you are interested in testing it out. I realize using an untested process is against regulations—"

"—but given the current situation, I take full responsibility," Jamie said, appearing behind the two of them out of nowhere. "What makes your program so much better, Chief?"

"Well, the original program was designed to look at only a small number of messages, comparing statistical and various other attacks against the traffic. It is extremely thorough, but it requires a large amount of the computer's capabilities, even one as advanced as this station's, which is why it can review only selected messages." The Vulcan's voice grew stronger as he warmed to the subject.

"I understand the limitations of Bart's current analytical programs. What are you going to do to improve that?" Jamie asked, waiting for Sabran to get to the point. "And, in plain terms. My head still hurts from the last time you tried to explain that damn subspace signal."

"Very well, sir. My process will allow the computer to skim all the traffic we've intercepted, and at the same time we can easily include any new information that might arrive once the process starts. It looks for commonalities rather than examining it at the micro level. My initial thought was to attempt a brute force attack, but since Petty Officer Faulwell has made these possible recoveries, that simplifies things. The program can be modified to take advantage of his recoveries and use all known attacks against the intercepted messages as well as every possible variant. We'll be putting a strain on the main computer, but I believe there's an eighty-six percent probability it'll lead to a recovery sooner than our current methodical process."

"My head's starting to hurt again, Sabran. However, unless Bart has an objection, go ahead. We can always continue using Bart's diagnostic programs if your system doesn't work." Jamie smiled at the Vulcan and then turned to walk over and get a cup of coffee from the replicator.

"Thank you, Mr. Cruz." The Vulcan took his position and began to type away on his console.

Turning to Faulwell, Jamie gave him a big smile. "Nice work

on that possible recovery, Bart. I know you were chomping at the bit when we were shut down."

"Well, it's only a partial recovery, if it *is* a recovery. For all I know, it's strictly coincidental. Until I have readable text, it's still a theory."

"I've got a good feeling about it." Cruz carried his coffee over to his console. Entering a few commands, he made annotations about the Cardassian fleet that had just moved beyond the Antros system. Looking back up at Bart, he gave him a wan grin. "You're a cryptanalyst; I'm a communications analyst. Sometimes you just *know* something's right, long before you can prove it. I *know* you're on to something here."

Looking around, Bart saw Priya had already left the room. He hurried toward the door to see if she was up for a match before shift, when Jamie's voice stopped him.

"Oh, by the way, I'd keep a low profile. I had a talk with Zarinth. He's concerned the Cardassians may return in force. He wants to issue defensive armor and weapons to everyone, just in case. Unless you want another thing to have to hand-receipt, I'd make certain he didn't find you."

"Me hand-receipt something? I'd hate to think how much stuff you've signed for just in improvised explosives," Bart laughed.

"No comment. Now, get out of here and get some sleep." Jamie's voice followed Bart down the hall as he hurried toward the turbolift.

As the turbolift door shut, Jamie's final comment finally sank in with him. *Oh sure, you're a great one to be giving sleeping advice.*

Three days later, Bart slid open the door to his room to find Priya waiting for him. He noticed she was looking over his shoulder into his room at the pile of equipment lying in the corner. "Yes, one of Zarinth's minions found me. I've got more military hardware resting in my room than I've ever owned in my life."

"Don't feel bad; he caught me earlier too. I've never used a phaser rifle before, so Mayhew was kind enough to give me a training manual. At least I don't think he's going to expect me to field strip it blindfolded yet." Priya's eyes twinkled as they shared a laugh. "However, knowing Zarinth, it's just a matter of time before we're drilling right along with his troops."

"I know the Andorians are a martial race, but Zarinth is taking this to extremes. Are we certain he's not part Klingon?" Bart joked as they made their way to the lift. "It's too bad we don't have time for another match."

"After the way I trounced you today, I'm surprised you're wanting a rematch so soon." As the door to the lift opened, they discussed the match as the turbolift rose toward deck two. The conversation lasted all the way down the corridor toward operations, with Priya showing Bart some of the things he was doing to tip her off on what he was trying to do.

"So, I've been giving myself away this whole time?" he asked, playfully slapping himself on the forehead. As they walked through the door, a sudden snoring halted her response and they both turned to find Jamie laying sprawled across his terminal. They rushed over but, after a quick examination, they decided there was no medical emergency here.

"That goofball," Priya said. "I'll bet he stayed up all night doing something with M'thanga again and fell asleep before his shift was over. I swear, if they don't blow themselves up, it'll be a miracle." She pointed toward a clear spot on the floor by the far wall. "Help me move him over here. At least he can be comfortable while he's asleep."

Bart grabbed Jamie under the arms and began to lift so Priya could get a grip under his legs. As Jamie's torso came upright, a sudden intake of breath from the Bajoran nearly caused Bart to drop Jamie. He turned his head to look and she was nodding her head at a portion of his workstation that had been hidden beneath Jamie's slumped torso.

A single red light was flashing.

Shifting Jamie's body carefully, he positioned himself so he could reach the screen without dropping his commander. Bart quickly ran his hand over the touchpad to take the terminal out of snooze mode, and carefully typed in the password with one hand to get past the security layer. A broad smile crossed his face as he examined the information that sprang to life on the screen.

They'd broken the code!

CHAPTER
9

Bart stood there staring at the results on the computer before Priya's strained voice broke through the fog, "Ah, Bart, I know you're excited about this, but Jamie's really getting heavy. Could we finish moving him first?"

Quickly muttering an apology, he reacquired his grip on the recumbent analyst. They moved him over by the wall, being careful not to slam his body into anything and eased him onto the floor. Bart toyed with the idea of getting one of the gurneys from sickbay, but he knew the medic would insist on reporting this to Zarinth. He was *not* in the mood to deal with the Andorian right at the moment.

"Priya, can you see if you can contact Sabran. I'm surprised he's not here." He made certain Jamie was comfortable before moving over to his station. Priya tapped her combadge as Bart routed the information from Jamie's workstation to his. He could hear her conversation in the background, but he immediately lost himself in the information flashing on the screen.

"Yes, see here, we've got matches all across the board!" Excitement rose in his voice as he motioned her over to the screen. "We're getting plain text now. Do you recognize the language?"

"I've never seen anything like this before, but it's definitely a language of some sort, Bart." She spun him around in his chair, a huge grin on her face. "We've done it, *you've* done it! You broke the encryption. Now it's just down to doing the translations."

"Time to earn your keep, Lieutenant." Bart began going through the parameters of the encryption, preparing the short explanation of the system. He would do a more formal report later, but right now, it was important to get the basic information about the encryption ready to broadcast. Cryptanalysts had their own shorthand for describing encryption systems; with a good description, any analyst would be able to re-create the cipher without ever having to see the original message.

The room remained quiet as Bart and Priya buried themselves in their work, only Jamie's soft snoring echoing above the familiar hum of the computers. After a few hours, Priya projected the images from her screen onto the large viewscreen mounted on the wall. She began manipulating the symbols on the screen as Bart looked on in amusement.

"I've never seen letters that looked like that," he said in a confused tone as she replaced one set of symbols with another to begin building an alphabet of unknown origin.

"Well, these aren't real letters." Priya never took her eyes off the screen as she shifted several symbols around into a new progression. "One of the tricks with dealing with an unknown language is to use symbols. If I started out using Bajoran letters for similar sounds, I could talk myself into assigning meanings to words that have nothing to do with their real meaning. By using these generic symbols, I can concentrate on trying to decipher the words on their own merits."

"Makes sense. It's too easy to talk yourself into thinking something is 'X,' whether it is or not, in cryptanalysis also. You've got to keep an open mind and not assume anything."

"These words here are probably proper names, since they occur near the first and last of the message." She ran her stylus over the padd she was using, highlighting several symbols on her terminal screen. "I'll leave them alone for later, but I'm certain these groups of symbols here are words based on their repetition in the message. Now, if the computer just has something that matches up with these possible word patterns, we'll be able to cross-reference it against the original alphabet and voilà, we've identified the language."

"That's great . . . if the computer has a match. After all, there aren't that many languages spoken in the galaxy, are there?"

Priya frowned at him and then realized he was picking on her. "Arrgh! Well, luckily, the Federation's universal translator technology has proven very flexible. All we need are enough samples and there's a very good chance we'll get somewhere. It would be useful if we could identify the language, though."

As Priya manipulated a few more symbols, a section of the screen began to glow blue and an unknown alien writing began to appear in the blank spaces directly beneath the symbols. Just below the writing, a translation began to appear also. Bart moved over and began to read the translation as Priya continued to manipulate the symbols, causing more and more of the alien writing to appear.

"You've got something here, Priya. It's still disjointed, but you're on the right track," he called back over his shoulder. He could see her furiously punching on her terminal as the number of unidentified symbols rapidly converted into the alien symbols. "Has the computer identified the writing?"

"I believe you'll find that it's Vorta," came Sabran's voice from the doorway.

"Vorta?" Bart asked, quickly turning around to see the Vulcan standing there.

"They are administrators for the Dominion and serve as ambassadors to non-Dominion governments."

"I'm familiar with *who* the Vorta are, but why do you think this code is theirs? Usually their codes are easy to decipher because their language is very simplistic, since the Founders never needed vocal speech. They just created one to speak to us. This is a significantly high-level code."

"It would not surprise me if after all is said and done that this is actually a Breen encipherment system given to the Dominion. After all, the Breen have very little love for the

Federation. However, with regard to the Vorta, it would only be logical to find them behind these communications. Although the Cardassians do have an embassy on the Breen homeworld, I began to suspect the Vorta based on the unknown communications system."

"How long have you suspected the Vorta?"

"It was always one of the possibilities. Since the Vorta maintain a high position in the Dominion, it was the logical solution. However, I did not want to prejudice Lieutenant Priya's work. There was a slight probability it could have been any of a number of other races that serve in the Dominion's forces or even the Founders themselves. From my research, I determined the majority of our knowledge of the Founders and the Vorta language come from the reports which are on record at SI headquarters—"

"—which, of course, we can't access because we're on radio silence." Bart and Sabran turned to see the Bajoran staring grimly down at her terminal. "Even though Vorta is a fairly simplistic language, we don't have much in the linguistic databases. Bart, I'm going to need your help on this one. We're going to have to do this the hard way. Maybe it's a good thing Admiral Hazlitt added an extra linguist to this project."

"That's why he gets all the perks, I guess. Sabran, we may need some computing help here. We're going to be stretching some of these programs to create a Vorta dictionary in a hurry. We may need you to write some patch code as we go along."

"Very well, Petty Officer," the Vulcan replied. "While I am here, there are a few scenarios I want to run against those subspace transmissions. Some are really quite fascinating and I'd like to include more data about them when we make our report."

"Knock yourself out, Sabran. We'll call if we need you," Bart said, turning back to his terminal. Priya and he continued to hammer on the translation. They followed a few rabbit trails here and there before realizing their mistakes. After several hours, they had resolved most of the kinks in their program with some assistance from Sabran.

The first few messages they translated were fairly innocuous, providing little information about the Vorta representatives in Breen and Cardassian space outside of their names. Apparently negotiations with the Breen had progressed slowly. However, the message they'd received yesterday was much more ominous.

Greetings Veydek,

Our efforts appear to have begun to pay off. The Breen have expressed interest in an alliance with the Dominion. We agreed there is much to be gained by both sides in such an alliance, both militarily and economically. Their forces are fresh and would help compensate for the losses our forces have sustained.

However, they still wish to be convinced that our forces will prevail. They point out that they gain very little if they back the wrong side in this war. While there is little love between the Breen and the Federation, there is also no real rivalry. They desire to see something more convincing before they will agree to ally with the Dominion.

Please coordinate with the Founders and inform me of their desired response to the Breen.

In service to the Founders,
Lithara

After they'd read the message, Bart and Priya turned toward each other. "That does *not* sound good," she said, touching a few controls on her terminal. Bart nodded in agreement as she continued. "I'm going to run that through the translator one more time. I want to be certain those words match up against the other messages."

"A very logical course of action," Sabran said, looking up from his work.

Bart scratched his beard thoughtfully. "Maybe we should see what today's message says before you do that. If we're correct, it should be a response to this message. We could even do it as a blind test by running the translation program on it without input from us. This way, we could be certain it was really what the message was breaking out to instead of us filling in what we thought we'd see. I think we've recovered enough to understand what was being said even if a few words were missing."

"Might as well. I'm as curious as you are about what the reply might have been." Priya turned to the terminal and poked in a few commands. "Given the length of the message, it'll be a few minutes before the computer has an answer for us. Want to grab something to drink while we wait?"

"I think a quick stretch and a cup of coffee would be just the thing. Actually, a quick session in the gym and a long jog would be even more useful, but that'll have to wait."

By the time he rejoined her at the computer, the program had run its course. Calling up the message, they stared as the words scrolled across the main screen. As the enormity of the message sank in, Bart felt his blood run cold.

Lithara,

The wisdom of the Founders never ceases to amaze me. The Founders have just arrived at Naval Repair Station Delta Seven, bringing the Breen ambassador to Cardassia with them to tour the Jem'Hadar battleships at my disposal. I had no more brought your latest message to their attention before they summoned the Breen ambassador to the conference room. We discussed several points that might serve as a basis for a treaty with the Breen. It would call for them to set aside their neutrality in return for certain concessions by the Dominion in the way of resource-rich planets currently within the Federation.

The Breen ambassador did mention he was impressed by the latest counterattack we'd launched against the Federation/Klingon combined fleet. The Founder had a situation map brought in and showed him the purpose for our fleet to be assembled at Delta Seven.

We are prepared to attack Federation Starbase 11. If our attack on the starbase is successful and we can drive off their

*defenders, we are to proceed toward Benecia. No doubt, the Fed-
eration will have to move their forces to ensure an important system like Benecia does not fall to the Dominion. If the Federation
reacts as our analysts believe they will, they will have to weaken
their forces around [untranslatable]. We will use this opportunity to seize [untranslatable] which will make their position in
the [untranslatable] system untenable.*

*The Breen ambassador was impressed by this plan. If our mis-
sion is successful, your mission should easily come to fruition.
Wish us luck.*

In the service of the Founders,
Veydek

As the last words scrolled across the screen, a deathly silence settled on the room. Finally, Bart pried his eyes away
from the screen to turn and look at Priya, who had paled reading the translated message.

"We've got to get this information to Starfleet, now!" Bart
said, the urgency unmistakable in his voice. "What planets
were they discussing?"

"I don't know, Bart, the computer didn't recognize the
names. I don't know if those were code words, if they were recoveries we simply haven't made yet, or if the Dominion have
their own name for those planets, similar to the Cardassians
calling Deep Space 9 'Terok Nor.' Either way, you're correct.
We've got to get this forwarded as quickly as possible."

Bart spun around in his chair and went over to where Jamie
was sleeping. "Rise and shine, bossman. Time for you to earn
your keep," he said, poking Jamie to wake him up.

Slowly Jamie's eyes opened and he blinked them furiously to
try to focus them. "Wha . . . what the hell are you do—" As he tried
to sit up, he banged the side of his head against the wall. "Ow!" He
reached up to rub the sore spot and looked around confused.

"Yes, you're still in ops. I wasn't going to haul your carcass
all the way down to your room just because you can't be bothered to go to bed when you should have." Bart helped their

sleep-addled leader to his feet. "Come on, we've got something hot here. We need you to send it out."

Jamie finally stood up, stifling a yawn with the back of his hand. He shook himself all over, trying to get the blood flowing again and slowly made his way over to his terminal. "Quick, hot chocolate, a status report, and more hot chocolate in that order." Easing his way into his seat, he winced as he sat down and arched his back, obviously trying to get a kink out from where he'd slept on the hard floor. He heard Priya's sympathetic chuckle and looked over at her. "Remind me to requisition softer floors the next time we go out on one of these damn-fool missions."

"You'd better look this over, Jamie. If we don't get this information out soon, there may not be any more missions, damn-fool or otherwise."

Accepting the steaming hot chocolate from Sabran, he blinked several times getting the last of the sleep out of his system and then turned to the main viewscreen. The hot chocolate paused just short of its intended destination as Jamie's eyes began running down the message on view there. He eased the untouched cup back down onto the table and began calling up additional information about the message, correlating the new recoveries with the message externals.

"Incredible! I knew there was something going on, especially once we saw there were four battleships there, but to think the Breen ambassador was actually visiting," he said in an awed voice. "This is incredible. Time to break radio silence. Send me everything you have on this. I'll need a few minutes to get everything together that they're going to need back at SI HQ. This ought to spin a few heads, once they get a load of this."

Sabran looked over at Priya, who smiled at him and nodded. "I believe he's saying they'll be pleased with this," she said. Sabran merely nodded and raised an eyebrow as he looked back at the Alpha Centaurian who was frantically typing his report at his station.

The room was strangely quiet, except for the tapping sound

coming from Jamie's position. After a few more minutes, he raised his right hand with a flourish and brought it down on the button next to his terminal. "And, kids, that's a wrap!" He beamed at his team with obvious delight. "Now it's all up to the guys back at HQ. With any luck, they can maneuver a fleet to intercept the Jem'Hadar. That would deliver a crushing blow to the Dominion and keep the Breen out of this war once and for all."

Several hours later, as they were finishing up their celebration, a buzzer went off in the room. *"Incoming message from Starfleet,"* the computer's voice rang out over the dying conversations.

"On-screen," Jamie called out, as they moved quickly over by the main transmission screen. It took the signal a little bit to focus, but shortly they could see Commander Mwakwere sitting there. "Sir, we hope you received our message."

"Indeed. Let's just say you've kicked over a beehive here. I just wanted to call and let you know everyone is very proud of the work you've done." The commander's huge smile said more than any words could. *"In fact, we have new orders for you."*

"Standing by," Jamie said, picking up a nearby padd.

"This target is being assigned to another collector. You are only required to maintain logs when this target transmits and only report on it if there is a major change in their communications. Report any signs of ships moving into that region or departing. Otherwise, resume standard sweeps looking for new targets of interest."

"Sir?" The hurt and confusion was visible on Jamie's face. "We have a strong signal from the target and we've just finished adapting a translator for the messages. With all due respect, I think we've earned the right to continue providing information on this target."

The commander's face became serious as he shifted uncomfortably in his chair. *"I understand your feelings, Chief Warrant Officer, but these orders are not open to negotiation. This is no reflection on your team's competency. In fact, word of your discovery has already been forwarded back to Starfleet Command. They are the ones who issued the orders for you to discontinue the current mission. Don't know exactly what they've got planned, and I didn't ask."*

Jamie let out an audible sigh. "Understood, sir. Wilco on the new orders."

"At least I have some good news for you, Mr. Cruz. Admiral Hazlitt has decided to relieve you at the six-month mark. Looks like you'll be saying good-bye to that place pretty soon." Mwakwere's smile returned as he passed that information on to them. *"Tiger out."*

As the screen faded to black, everyone sat there pondering what they'd just heard. Bart felt the tension they'd all been under for the past several weeks begin to fade away a little bit at a time. He felt himself physically slumping in his chair, letting his back relax.

"Well, folks, you know what this means?" Jamie asked after a short while.

"No, but I'm certain you'll tell us," Priya teased.

"I think it's time we got back to that well deserved R&R on those sandy beaches. Last one to the holosuite is a rotten egg."

CHAPTER

10

The rest of the time spent at Mungin was uneventful and the repetitive shift work helped mask the passage of time. They found themselves retreating to the holosuite more and more often as their tour wound down. To everyone's relief, the next shift of analysts arrived at Antros III on schedule. Jamie's team briefed the newcomers and boarded a tramp freighter with their gear, all under the watchful eyes of Zarinth's people.

Their flight back into Federation space was quiet. In fact, a little too quiet. The only member of the crew they saw was the steward who brought them their meals. The freighter's captain had restricted them to their quarters, which didn't even have their own replicators, stating his ship was too cramped for a bunch of passengers to be wandering about, interfering with his crew's work. Bart and the others were too excited to care about their accommodations as long as they were leaving the ice-covered moon that had been their home for the past six months.

Once they were deep in Federation space, the freighter rendezvoused with an *Excelsior*-class Federation starship. After a quick exchange of information on the communicator screen, they were beamed aboard the starship. Instead of materializing in the ship's transporter room however, they found themselves in an isolation ward in the ship's sickbay.

"All right, this is starting to get ridiculous." Bart tested the door to find it sealed.

Jamie paced around the room like a caged tiger. "If I didn't know better, I'd think we were under house arrest."

"But why? What's going on? If we're under arrest, why are we here and not in the brig?" Priya asked.

"I do not believe we are officially 'under arrest,'" Sabran said, looking at Priya. "If I have begun to understand Mr. Cruz's dialectal use of language, I believe he means we're being kept away from the crew for some unknown reason rather than being held for criminal matters."

"Either way, this stinks. If we've done something wrong, they should just come out and tell us." The frustration of the situation pushed Bart's words out like an explosion.

Before he could continue with his rant, Priya broke in, "Has anyone seen or heard anything from Zarinth? Do we even know if he left on the freighter when we did?"

"I saw some of Zarinth's security personnel when we were boarding the freighter, but I had no way to ascertain whether or not they actually boarded once we were in our quarters," Sabran said, sitting down on one of the examination tables.

Bart started to ask the Vulcan if he knew how to answer a question with a simple yes or no, but managed to rein in the sharp reply. Sabran was not the enemy and this was not the time to make him one. He went over to the communications terminal and activated it.

"*Nurse Orisaka,*" came a feminine voice over the intercom. "*How may I help you?*"

"You could let us out." Bart knew what the response would be, but felt he had to try.

"*I'm sorry. We've been ordered to keep you in the isolation ward until we reach our destination. We can't risk the possibility of infection,*" came the sympathetic reply.

"Infection? What infection?" Jamie's voice broke in over Bart's intended question. "There has to have been some mistake here."

"Again, I'm sorry. Our orders stated we were to pick you up from that freighter and transport you. You'll have to ask Dr. Mac-Donald for more information. I thought you knew why we'd been sent to retrieve you."

"Could you please summon Dr. MacDonald for us? We'd like to speak to him as soon as possible," Bart asked, shushing Jamie with his left hand.

"I'll have him come to your ward so you can speak to him personally," Nurse Orisaka said. *"If you're hungry or thirsty, there is a replicator in the ward set up for your needs."*

Bart turned off the intercom. "Well, they've thought of everything. A nice little gilded cage we find ourselves in."

"I'm not certain what's going on, but there's nothing we can do until Dr. MacDonald arrives," Priya said. "I recommend relaxing and enjoying the trip. After all the things we've been through the past six months, some enforced inactivity is not the worst that could have happened to us."

Bart and Jamie looked at each other, and took seats at the one table in the room with little grace. Bart had just gotten up to get a cup of coffee when Dr. MacDonald appeared at the door. They rose as one to move toward the door, but he casually waved them back to their seats. He pulled up a chair outside their door and hit the communications button beside it.

"The communication system in the isolation ward is set up so that we can hear you wherever you're resting. There's no need to crowd around the companel," he said, a slight accent coloring his voice. He brought his long fingers up in front of his face, forming an inverted *V* with his hands as he looked them over. Bart felt the gaze from his green eyes boring into him and knew, without a doubt, what a specimen felt like beneath a microscope.

Jamie recovered first. "We'd like to know what's going on, Doctor."

The tall, lanky figure on the other side of the door slowly turned his head to look at Jamie. *"Mr. Cruz, we received orders from Starfleet to rendevous with the* S.S. Kristen's Luck *to assume responsibility for transporting three Starfleet members and one Bajoran officer for medical attention."* He paused, looking at a padd before continuing. *"According to the information we received, you were examining alien artifacts when the containment field failed. Each of you had been contaminated in the incident. Your last station had been unable to isolate the cause of the illness, so you needed transportation for further medical examination. I am not to enter, nor examine you for fear of contaminating this ship. Is this not correct?"*

Bart started to open his mouth when Jamie quickly stopped him. "You have to understand, Doctor, it's just we were surprised about the transfer. When we left, we thought the freighter was going to take us all the way."

"Understandable, given the current situation and all. However, we were already headed back to Jupiter Station. Diverting to meet the Kristen *only took us a few hours off course. We'll be able to make up the lost time, now that you're safely aboard."*

"Do you have an estimate of when we'll arrive?" Priya asked in a small voice.

"It shouldn't take more than a couple of days. We received some damage in our last battle and can't quite make maximum warp. As long as we maintain this speed, though, we should be all right. The captain wanted me to reassure you we'll do everything in our power to get you there in plenty of time."

"Just one moment, Doctor, I want to make certain everyone is feeling all right." Pulling the others into a tight huddle, the Alpha Centaurian whispered as he made a show of checking pulses and foreheads, "I don't know what's going on, but we still have to maintain operational security. At least, we know where we're headed now. Just play along and let's see where this leads."

"Is everyone all right in there, Mr. Cruz?" Dr. MacDonald asked, brushing a lock of his red hair out of his eyes. *"I do not like the idea of not being allowed to examine you. Just seems very inappropriate, but my orders were very clear."*

"I'm not a doctor, sir, but I'm certain if Starfleet sent out those orders, they must have a very good reason for doing so. We certainly appreciate your concern, though."

They chatted with the doctor for a bit longer, letting him talk about the ship and its crew, and some of the battles they'd been in. Dr. MacDonald was a likeable person and they felt bad about having to make up a story about what they'd been doing and the artifact they'd found. He excused himself after a short while to make his rounds, promising to check back with them once in a while.

After they were certain he was gone, Jamie had everyone search the isolation ward for transmitters. After a thorough search, they were unable to find anything, so they had to assume they could speak freely. Jamie called them together and whispered, "I don't know why we're going to Jupiter Station and not back to Starbase 375. Something is very strange here. Everyone hang loose, keep your thoughts to yourself and enjoy the ride."

Three days after their transfer, they arrived at Jupiter Station and were beamed into a security center. They were allowed to clean up and change clothes before being escorted to a large conference room. They meandered through the ornate room toward the large podium in the front and Bart noticed everyone was keeping their thoughts to themselves. He could tell by the way everyone moved they were all as nervous as he was.

They'd been there for a few minutes when Jamie broke the silence. "I wonder what's keeping them. I wonder if Commander Mwakwere will be here to debrief us?"

"I don't know, but I want to know how badly we beat that Jem'Hadar fleet. I'll wager we didn't let a single one get away," Priya said, a small sharklike grin crossing her face.

Just then, a whistle rang out in the room, and the door at the far end slid open. "Attention on deck!" a security officer called out as two officers and a master chief petty officer came into the room. Bart looked in amazement as he realized Admiral Marta Batanides, the commander of Starfleet Intelligence herself was the first one in the door. As the officers took their seats, the master chief motioned for the four to sit down also. Bart and the others quickly complied.

Admiral Batanides looked them over, her elfin features making it appear she was ready to break into a smile at any moment. Finally she began, "Let me start by saying the Federation owes the four of you an incredible debt of gratitude. Your efforts were invaluable in helping to turn the tide against the threat from the Dominion."

She paused for a second, pouring herself a glass of water from the silver pitcher sitting on the table. "The Vorta have been very generous in letting the Breen ambassador use their circuit to transmit information back to his government. He's proven to be quite a talented observer and has gone to great lengths to inform his countrymen about the size, composition and strengths of the Dominion forces he's observed. He's also made heavy use of that encryption system you identified." She took another sip from her glass and continued. "When the Breen entered the war, I have to admit the ferocity of their attacks caught us off guard. However, we were able to maneuver our forces to meet their counterattacks and as the Dominion withdrew even farther into Cardassian space, the ambassador was quick to keep his government informed with the latest news from the front."

"Begging the admiral's pardon," Jamie said, as she paused. "*When* the Breen entered the war? Wasn't Starfleet able to stop the Jem'Hadar fleet from attacking Starbase 11? There must have been time to put together a flotilla to stop them."

"Yes, Mr. Cruz, *when* the Breen entered the war. Once we started getting the field reports from the Breen ambassador, it was determined that the value of the information was too great to lose. There's no question we could have intercepted the Jem'Hadar forces. However, there was no way we could have done so without having exposed Mungin and the fact that we were listening in on the ambassador's private network."

"But, the people on Starbase 11 . . . ?" Bart's soft voice broke the ugly silence.

"We gave them as much warning as we could," she admitted, letting her emotions show through for a second, running a hand through her still dark brunette hair before she reimposed her professional demeanor. "Once the Jem'Hadar fleet attacked, we sent out a fleet we had pre-positioned and drove them off before they could complete the attack. Unfortunately, the Breen then announced their new alliance with the Dominion by attacking Earth."

Bart swallowed. He no longer had any family on Earth—or much of anywhere, truth be known—but he had friends there.

"You seem to be using the word 'unfortunately' an awful lot here, Admiral," Jamie said, a hostile tone creeping into his voice.

"Mr. Cruz, you more than anyone else here should understand the need to protect the source," she replied sharply, then caught herself. "Yes, the attack on Earth was unexpected. We had no indication of that on any of the messages we intercepted. And the loss of life at Starbase 11 and in the reserve fleet was higher than anticipated. However, there is no question the information we've been getting directly from the Breen ambassador ever since has shortened this war, saving the lives of hundreds of millions."

Bart and the others exchanged looks as the admiral softened her expression and continued. "In the twentieth century, there was a rumor that during their second World War, a Terran leader was faced with a terrible decision. His intelligence people had informed him his enemy was going to bomb one of his cities in the middle of the night. However, the enemy was communicating with what they believed was an unbreakable encryption device."

She let that sink in for a second and then continued. "If he evacuated the city, he would without a doubt save hundreds of lives, and if he maneuvered his dwindling air support, he could shoot down a number of the enemy's bombers before they could flee. But, if he did that, there was no doubt he would tip off the enemy that his intelligence people were listening in on those 'undecipherable' networks and they would change to a new system. Loss of this information would endanger a proposed invasion and prolong the war by an unknown number of years. What do you think happened?"

After a short pause, Sabran looked up. "He had to let the enemy bombers go through. Logically, it is the only answer. The needs of the many exceed the needs of the few."

"Yes, Chief Sabran, that's exactly what happened, except the rumors weren't quite accurate. The truth was there were five possible targets that night and his intelligence people couldn't identify which city was the target until it was too late to intercept the bombers. The city of Coventry was almost obliterated in the attack. However, we have reason to believe that even if he had known, he wouldn't have compromised the fate of the war to save a city."

"We regret the loss of life on Earth and at Starbase 11, but if their sacrifice brings the war to a close one day sooner, then it was worth it," her aide spoke up for the first time. "If the Breen or the Dominion had changed that cipher system, we might have lost thousands more lives than we have taking the fight to the Cardassian homeworlds."

Admiral Batanides brushed her hair back and gave them a sad look. "Believe me, these decisions were not made without a lot of sleepless nights. There hasn't been a night that I haven't questioned myself, wondering if there was another way to do what we did. However, that's why we brought you directly here. I wanted to be the one who informed you about Starbase 11. Also, I wanted to be the first to thank you for what you did at Mungin. Your efforts were in the highest tradition of Starfleet and SI."

Her face turned sober as she continued, the chill evident in her voice. "However, I have to once again inform you that what happened while you were on this temporary assignment is highly classified. Under no circumstances are you ever to talk about Mungin, what you did, where you were, nor who you were with during this time period. This prohibition extends even beyond your service in Starfleet. This program is not likely to be declassified during your lifetimes and therefore must be protected. Do I make myself clear?"

"Yes, sir," the four of them answered in unison.

"Very well. There is a reception in your honor being set up in the room next door." She motioned toward her aide. "Captain Abundez will be your point of contact here on Jupiter Station. He will be working with you to get your next assignment set up as well. As of 2400 tonight, you begin thirty days admin leave. Enjoy, go home, relax, and report back here in one month for reassignment."

The others sprang to attention as she stood up. "At ease. You're the honored guests here. If you'll please accompany me . . ." she said, motioning them toward a side door. As they passed through, they found a group of senior Starfleet officers and nearly the entire command of SI waiting for them. The master chief led them down to their seats on the front row as the admiral and her aide moved up to the dais in the front of the room.

A smattering of applause from the assembled staff officers and senior enlisted caused Bart and the others to exchange embarrassed looks. After a short pause, the admiral began, "Thank you all for coming. We're assembled today to honor the four members of Project Mungin for their invaluable contribution to the security of the Federation. Without their dedication and commitment to this cause, there is no doubt the Federation would be in truly dire circumstances."

The rest of the evening was a blur to Bart. He shook hands with more people than he knew were assigned to SI and made small talk with some who promised great things were ahead for him. All he could think about was Starbase 11 and Earth and the fact that for all his work and all his brilliance and all his ingenuity, they were still as dead as if he'd never solved the problem. All he really remembered about that night was getting stupid drunk with Jamie as quickly as possible before being given two stimtabs and being poured into a shuttlecraft to take him on his "well-deserved" leave.

EPILOGUE

2377

Bart sat up in his bed as the soft chime from the alarm sounded in the darkness. "Computer, lights," he said as he sat up and tapped the chronometer to shut off the insistent chime. Shaking his head to clear the cobwebs, he saw a rueful smile on his now clean-shaven face in the mirror. That was a memory he hadn't had in a long, long time.

He made his way over to the shower to start getting ready to go on duty, and thought about his companions. They'd all planned to get together, but it seemed that something or other always came up. It just never happened.

After he'd returned from leave, he'd been assigned to Starbase 92, which had been a rather interesting assignment in its own right. However, when he'd been approached about transferring to the S.C.E. and told about the type of work he'd be doing, he'd jumped at the opportunity to do something completely different.

Jamie Cruz and he had kept in sporadic contact. Jamie had gone back to the Academy afterward, becoming a chief instructor, before finally retiring a few months back. Bart smiled, thinking about the pictures Jamie had sent him from his home on Alpha Centauri. According to one of the latest notes, he was devoting himself to being a full-time grandfather and spoiling the grandkids rotten. In his spare time, he was working with another instructor, writing a history of Starfleet Academy, just

to keep his hand in. Bart knew Jamie might claim to be retired, but he couldn't imagine his old leader just sitting around
not doing anything.

As Bart pulled his tunic down over his head, he thought
about his much put-upon shift mate, Priya Chantrea. Smiling
fondly, he knew she'd returned to Bajor after the conclusion of
the war, and was present when Bajor joined the Federation last
year. She'd rejoined the militia formally, with a well-deserved
(in Bart's opinion) promotion to major. The last he'd heard, she
was teaching linguistics at one of the universities on Bajor. She
was very active on the faculty council as well as working with
the student ambassador program, getting young Bajorans to
travel to other Federation worlds to study.

Sitting down on the edge of his bed, his face sobered as he
thought about the remaining member of the quartet. A few
weeks before the end of the Dominion War, Jamie had sent
him a message. He'd heard through channels that Sabran was
killed. He'd been assigned to one of the ships involved in the
invasion of Cardassia Prime. Apparently, his ship had come
under attack from a Jem'Hadar ship trying to break through
the blockade and the section Sabran was working in took a direct hit while its shields were down, leaving no survivors.

Looking around the room, he continued letting his thoughts
wander. He remembered how angry he'd been, how stupid and
wasteful it had seemed at the time. *It's amazing how naïve I
was back then. I think I understand it better now, especially
after Galvan VI. I remember being so guilty afterward. Why them
and not me? Why were so many of my friends killed or injured
when I escaped virtually unharmed? It really made me appreciate friendships and love more than ever. Life's too damn short to
be afraid to reach out to each other.*

Bart paused, looking at himself in the mirror. He ran a hand
over his naked chin, debating once again the wisdom of having shaved his beard off. He had to admit his smooth cheeks
made him look about ten years younger than when he'd had
that salt-and-pepper beard. As he ran his hand down his chin,

he thought about the reluctant member of their little group. *I wonder whatever happened to Zarinth? We never saw him or his team again. Mayhew, M'thanga—it's like they never existed at all. Of course, knowing Zarinth, I'm certain he's still in Starfleet, terrorizing a new batch of recruits or making some noncom's life a living hell just because he can.*

Checking the chronometer, he saw it was about time to report for duty. He paused as he reached the door to stare at a black wooden statue. A raven sitting on a rock that looked suspiciously like the moon of Antros III stared back at him. Admiral Batanides technically couldn't give them an award for their accomplishments because their mission had never actually happened as far as Starfleet was concerned. However, if an admiral wanted to give out a few mementos to some personnel in her command, there was no harm in that, was there?

Bart patted the raven on the head a couple of times for good luck and quietly shut his door. He was supposed to meet Commander Gomez in a few minutes, so he needed to get moving. As he headed down the corridors of the *da Vinci* toward the turbolift, he had a sudden thought.

I need to check to see when I have some leave coming up. I know Anthony may be disappointed, but for some reason, I'm really in the mood to play some racquetball.

DISTANT EARLY WARNING

Dayton Ward & Kevin Dilmore

THE
TAURUS REACH
2265

CHAPTER

1

Turning from where he knelt next to an open access panel that revealed a maze of circuitry and conduits hidden behind the nondescript gray bulkhead, Lieutenant Mahmud al-Khaled rose to his feet and dashed toward the row of consoles lining the opposite wall of the environmental control substation. The room, like its nine counterparts scattered throughout the massive space station, was crammed full of computer workstations and display monitors as well as banks of gauges, dials, and switches.

"Try it now!"

Lieutenant Isaiah Farber, one of the more talented members of al-Khaled's team, tapped several buttons arranged in multicolored rows across the console's polished black surface, the controls looking almost tiny beneath his massive hands. Muscled and broad-shouldered, Farber appeared on the verge of ripping through the gold uniform tunic stretching across his chest and back.

Looking up at one of the display monitors set into the bulkhead just above eye level, Farber grimaced. "Nothing. We're still locked out of everything."

"Damn it," al-Khaled snapped. "This doesn't make any sense." According to every diagnostic conducted by him and his team, the environmental control system should have been operating within acceptable parameters. There was no reason for it not to be, as it, along with everything else aboard Starbase 47, was practically brand-new.

"Report!" said Lieutenant Curtis Ballard, the station's chief engineer, from where he worked at another station. "Is that section sealed off yet?"

From an adjacent console, a female ensign nodded, her own face a mask of anxiety. "Yes, sir," replied the young Asian woman, who al-Khaled remembered was named Tamishiro. "Ventilation ducts and all hatches leading to those areas are locked down."

Ballard nodded, and al-Khaled saw the sweat running down the side of the man's face. The report was short and terse, but al-Khaled knew, as did everyone else in the room, what it meant. Anyone still occupying those sections was now trapped, unable to escape the poison rapidly taking the place of breathable atmosphere.

"Environmental control's treating it like it would any section of the station with differing atmosphere requirements," al-Khaled said. "It won't let us just open a door without an adjacent section configured to act as an airlock." Shaking his head, he added, "Trouble is, it won't let us do that, either."

"Get computer control on that lockout," Ballard ordered, slapping the console with the heel of his hand as he continued to work. "How many people are still in that section?"

It took several seconds for Tamishiro to call up the relevant data from the station's internal sensor network. "Thirty-six, sir."

Pointing to another of the display monitors, Ballard said, "Tell the maintenance teams to start cutting through the doors. We'll force them open manually and seal off adjacent sections once we get those people out of there." With the sleeves of his gold tunic pushed up above his elbows and smudges of some unidentified substance dirtying his otherwise pale, unremarkable features, the man looked every bit like a harried mechanic frustrated with his inability to understand why the machines under his care were refusing to cooperate.

Al-Khaled sympathized with his fellow engineer, particularly in light of the current situation. Of course, the dilemma they now faced was only the latest in a string of problems that had plagued Ballard and his staff for weeks as they struggled to ready for operation Starfleet's newest deep space outpost, designated Starbase 47, or its more colloquial name, Vanguard.

For reasons currently surpassing understanding, systems across the mammoth Watchtower-class station were beset by irregular yet frequent malfunctions. Sensors, communications, life support, computer interfaces, and their related components all had fallen victim to such troubles, sometimes two or three times within the same twenty-four-hour period, and each time requiring repeated readjustment, realignment, or retuning. In short, none of the station's more sensitive systems had worked properly with any consistency since their activation. The spate of anomalies had tested Starbase 47's talented cadre of engineers to the point that the base's commanding officer, Commodore Diego Reyes, had called for assistance in the form of Starfleet's Corps of Engineers, specifically, Lieutenant al-Khaled and his team assigned to the *U.S.S. Lovell.*

"Atmosphere mixture continuing," Tamishiro reported, shaking her head. "Methane concentration increasing. Ambient temperature three hundred eight degrees Kelvin and rising."

Before today, the malfunctions had been merely annoying— all while evading resolution with relentless determination. Now, for the first time, they were proving to be life-threatening.

It had happened without warning, the first sign of trouble coming as someone reported a foul odor permeating the air on one level of the station's civilian residential district. Environmental sensors designed to detect such anomalies had not caught the problem, at least not until the strange pollutant began to spread throughout the section. The quick actions of a station maintenance worker had prevented other decks from becoming contaminated, with the affected area now completely sealed off from the rest of the station. Only then was the cause identified: internal environmental sensors—for reasons as yet unknown—had determined that the normal Class-M atmosphere which supported most humanoid life-forms in that section of the residential zone needed to be replaced with one similar to that found on Class-Y planets.

"Unless everybody up there has suddenly turned into a Tholian," Ballard had commented as the situation continued to worsen, "we're in big trouble." Anyone trapped in the affected section would be cooked alive, assuming they survived the toxic atmosphere currently replacing the oxygen-nitrogen mix favored by those living on that deck.

"Sir," al-Khaled heard Tamishiro call out, the ensign turning from her workstation to regard him and Ballard, "Lieutenant Soral reports they've begun cutting through the hatches. The hospital's been alerted and medical teams are on standby."

Even as he listened to the report, al-Khaled's attention was drawn to one of the monitors dominating the young woman's station. It displayed an image of at least a dozen men and women grouped near a hatch that remained stubbornly locked. Even though the picture was somewhat obscured by the gray haze that had begun to permeate the air in that section, he still could see some of the people pounding on the door with their fists. Audio pickups transmitted the sounds of flesh beating against metal, along with the calls for help as the victims shouted at the engineers they doubtless could hear working just on the other side of the barrier.

"Even with cutting lasers," Farber said from where he stood to Ballard's right, "it'll take too much time, Lieutenant." Looking to al-Khaled, he added, "We could try an emergency site-to-site transport."

His brow furrowing in concern, al-Khaled shook his head. On the face of it, the notion was not altogether outlandish, though there would be no room for error, and the operation would require the transporter system to be properly calibrated to exacting specifications. He doubted that the station's transporters had been so balanced, not if the condition of many other onboard systems was any indication.

As if confirming his suspicions, Ballard said, "On any other day, Lieutenant, I'd jump on that suggestion in a heartbeat, but given everything we've dealt with to this point, I'm not ready to trust the transporters."

"We're running out of time for being cautious," al-Khaled pressed, feeling his jaw tightening as he remembered he was addressing the individual in charge of engineering duties aboard the space station. Given the sheer magnitude of the responsibilities with which Ballard had been shouldered while trying to get Starbase 47 to full operational capability on what could only have been a tremendously accelerated schedule, it was doubtful the man was accustomed to people coming into his realm and telling him what to do.

His frustration mounting, al-Khaled looked back to the one viewer, which with cold dispassion displayed the alarming image of those still trapped in the affected section. The haze lingering about the corridor was denser now, and the engineer could see at least six people lying on the floor, having already succumbed to the toxic atmosphere from which they could not escape. Others were holding towels or pieces of clothing over their faces in feeble attempts to filter out the poisonous gases collecting around them. There was no mistaking the victims' labored attempts to draw increasingly tortured breaths, and al-Khaled felt his own respiration increasing and his pulse quickening as the stress of the situation continued to weigh on him.

Find the answer!

The demand echoing in his mind, al-Khaled forced his gaze from the scene and returned his attention to the monitors of the adjacent workstation, all of which were collaborating to give him the current status of the station's recalcitrant environmental control systems. There had to be something here they were overlooking, he decided, something that could be reconfigured, rewired, or simply hijacked long enough to help them: an idea outside the box, beyond the boundaries of normal problem resolution, outlandish in theory and perhaps even reckless in practice.

Where is it?

Then, as if heeding his silent pleas, the jumble of information cascading past his eyes seemed to ebb and clear, just enough for him to see . . .

"Purge the atmosphere!"

The words all but exploded from al-Khaled's lips as he moved toward one of the workstations, and both Ballard and Farber turned to regard him with matching expressions of unfettered disbelief.

"Are you out of your mind?" Ballard asked, reaching up to swipe at a lock of sweat-dampened blond hair that had fallen forward into his eyes. "We're trying to save these people, not kill them!"

Ignoring him, al-Khaled tapped a sequence of colored buttons on the control console before pointing to one of the station's display monitors. "Part of the fire suppression system allows for the emergency venting of the atmosphere from targeted areas anywhere aboard the station in extreme situations." *It's so simple,* he realized, mentally kicking himself. *How did I miss it before?*

"That takes care of getting rid of bad air," Farber said, frowning. "But it doesn't get those people out of there."

Al-Khaled waved a hand as if to fan away the lieutenant's doubts. "The computer's been kicking us in the teeth, reminding us of how it's on top of the environmental control systems, right?" He pointed to one row of status gauges. "The internal sensors are still online in that section, so the computer knows there are living humanoids there. If we vent the atmosphere from that section, the computer should interpret that as a hull breach or other failure and automatically initiate emergency protocols."

"That means sealing the section," Ballard added, "which the computer already did, and restoring internal atmospheric conditions to their designated norms." His scowl deepening, the

engineer shook his head. "That's assuming the system is working correctly."

Fingers already moving across the control console, al-
Khaled paused only long enough to wipe sweat from his forehead. "We're out of options. I'm initiating the venting now."
Even as he spoke the words, he knew the quite understandable
reaction they would provoke.

"Now hang on, Lieutenant," Ballard said, stepping forward.
"What if this doesn't work?"

Pausing for only a moment, al-Khaled turned until he
locked eyes with his fellow engineer. "You know what it means,
but they're dead anyway if we don't try," he said before returning to the console.

Ballard looked away long enough to regard the scene
playing out on the display monitor. Returning his gaze to al-
Khaled, he swallowed nervously before slowly shaking his
head. "Damn it, Lieutenant," he hissed through gritted teeth, "I
hope you're right about this."

His hand slamming down on the control that would initiate the emergency venting procedure, al-Khaled hoped he was
right, as well.

CHAPTER
2

"Your man got lucky."

There was no mistaking the disapproving tone in Commodore Diego Reyes's voice. Fortunately for Captain Daniel Okagawa, he was long past the point in his Starfleet career where the stern words of a superior officer alone could intimidate him. He also had, long ago, overcome the inclination to erupt in hearty laughter when confronted by someone unfamiliar with the capabilities of the men and women attached to the Corps of Engineers—particularly those assigned to his crew.

Instead, seated as he was across from Reyes in the commodore's office, itself situated high atop the command tower of Starbase 47, Okagawa merely chuckled.

"Not sure I see the humor in this, Captain," Reyes said, the words coming out more a growl than actual speech. His scowl deepening, he added, "I can appreciate unorthodox thinking and pulling miraculous solutions out of thin air in the nick of time. I just don't like them employed when the safety of my people is on the line."

"Lieutenant al-Khaled isn't some sort of show-off, I assure you," Okagawa replied, letting his smile fade. "In addition to being one hell of a gifted engineer, he's also one of the most thoughtful and dedicated people I've ever met. He purged the atmosphere only when it became his last, best option, and it worked just as he thought it would."

"I'm thankful it did, don't get me wrong," Reyes said, "but I don't need a stunt show next time."

As the commodore emitted a deep, irritated sigh, Okagawa could not help but note the similarities as well as the stark differences between them. Reyes was a bit older, with only a few more years of service to Starfleet. Physically, the two were matched in their salt-and-pepper hair that boasted closely cropped regulation styles, but where the shorter, stocky Okagawa had kept much of his round, boyish face, Reyes's lean, muscular body and somewhat weathered visage seemed as put-upon as the man's attitude. There was no mistaking at first glance that Diego Reyes was all business, and Okagawa's nature just could not prevent him from verbally jousting with the commodore, if only slightly, in spite of that observation.

"Sir," the captain said, "I get this feeling that you're not upset so much about al-Khaled's irregular approach to problem solving as you are to my people needing to be here in the first place."

Cocking his head, Reyes narrowed his eyes. "Quite the judge of character, Captain. Were you a psychiatrist before taking the command track?"

Okagawa chuckled again. "More like I skipped the class on nurturing my control issues." Seeing renewed irritation in the commodore's eyes, he added, "Sir, I know you've got a lot going on out here. I don't know all the specifics, but it doesn't take much to figure that it must be important to put a project as big as this station on the fast track to completion. I'm not here to get on your nerves, Commodore. I just want to do my job, which in this case is bringing my people in to assist your crew to get this place up and running so that you can do *your* job, whatever the hell it is. Once that's done, we're off to another glorious assignment carving a tunnel through an asteroid or fixing the toilets on some remote outpost."

He had come to enjoy the act of disarming superior officers. Such situations almost always began in much the same manner as his meeting with Reyes, with the other officer giving him the same combination of raised brows and suspicious frown that the commodore displayed. A lot of them also folded their arms across their chests and regarded him warily even as they began to sway to Okagawa's side of the table.

Leaning back in his chair, Reyes now studied him in just that fashion.

"I'm not unappreciative," the commodore said. "It's obvious that your people know their jobs. I knew that even before you got here." He waved a hand in Okagawa's direction. "That repair and salvage job you did at Outpost Five near the Neutral Zone was a very nice piece of work. But, you're right that I'm not thrilled with the idea of your crew running around my station and putting out our fires. We should be able to do that ourselves."

"Never thought otherwise," Okagawa replied, settling back into his own seat. Since the *Lovell*'s arrival at Starbase 47 the previous day, nearly every member of his engineering staff had been involved with the numerous systemic problems afflicting the station. He had reviewed status reports from his first officer as funneled upward from the engineering teams and so was well aware of the proficiency and effectiveness of the station's own complement of engineers. "The ability of anyone— from either team—to carry out their respective responsibilities isn't the problem here, I think."

Reyes offered a tired, humorless chuckle of his own. "The problems are pretty simple: *Nothing* works."

Lacing his fingers together, Okagawa replied, "Ah, but nothing works all at once. You've read the reports from your own chief engineer and his staff. While they started out hammering away at individual issues as soon as they cropped up, it didn't take them long to figure out that they were only treating symptoms. You don't have hundreds of problems, Commodore, you have one. We need to concentrate on finding the overall cause."

Reyes nodded, listening to the observations. "Not seeing the forest for the trees, you mean?"

Shrugging, Okagawa said, "Well, you're in the middle of a lot of trees here."

The commodore reached up to rub the bridge of his nose, closing his eyes as if mounting a futile attempt to ward off an onrushing headache. "You have no idea." After a moment, he exhaled loudly. "I'm sorry, Captain. Operational security, need to know. I'm sure you understand."

Okagawa already knew enough about Reyes to dissuade himself from requesting too many details about Starfleet's intensifying interest in the Taurus Reach. Starbase 47's sheer size and commensurate command of resources and personnel was an unquestioned asset to the Federation's colonization and exploration efforts in this region. Still, Okagawa had to wonder: *Why now, and with so much apparent verve?* Though he had seen the official reports detailing the station's construction and its accelerated schedule, they offered no insights as to the reasons behind the initiative.

Curiouser and curiouser.

"I imagine it's a handful," he offered with more than a hint of sympathy.

Reyes sighed. "Let's just say that I know I've got problems when the easiest thing I have to deal with at the moment is theft from a couple of my cargo bays." Shaking his head, he added, "Seems that either the station's civilian population is harboring a criminal element, or I've got at least one member of my crew who's gone missing and maybe even looking to score a few extra credits by selling Starfleet matériel on the black market, or a combination of the two."

Such petty crime was commonplace on border outposts and remote colony worlds, Okagawa knew, particularly those located adjacent to neutral territory such as that traveled by vessels of the notorious Orion Syndicate or the incongruously named Merchant's Guild operating on and near the nonaligned planet Arcturus. It was no surprise that Reyes would be dealing with similar problems out here, far from the Federation's typical security and protection. That a Starfleet officer might be involved was surprising, of course, though unfortunately not completely unprecedented.

"You should consider yourself lucky," Reyes added after a moment. "Right now, I think there are worse career options than traveling from outpost to colony to starbase, trying to keep that rattletrap ship of yours from blowing apart at the seams." For the first time, there was a hint of good-natured ribbing in his expression.

Okagawa offered a mock salute. "Quite right, sir. The *Lovell's* an awfully tempting target for comics and pundits alike, but at least her onboard systems are working." Naturally, he at first had been horrified upon learning the particulars of his newest command. It, like its two counterparts currently attached to the Corps of Engineers, were without exception relics from a bygone era. According to Starfleet records, the last *Daedalus*-class vessel had officially been retired from service nearly seventy years previously.

"I understand those *Daedalus* ships are all Starfleet would give the Corps," Reyes said.

Okagawa replied, "Not exactly. They didn't give anything except permission to scrounge around a few storage depots for whatever the engineering teams thought would work best for hauling their equipment from place to place. It was decided that the *Lovell* and two other *Daedalus* tubs best fit the bill from what was available. Still, with a crew of engineers tinkering their little hearts out between assignments, you can be sure the *Lovell* is about as close to its original specs as you and I are compared to our Academy portraits." He wiggled his eyebrows mischievously. "I'd be happy to give you the two-credit tour, Commodore."

When Reyes laughed this time, it was with genuine humor. "Fix my station and loan me an environmental suit while I'm there and maybe we have a deal."

"You seem pretty worried for someone who served on an old *Drexler*-class frigate," Okagawa said. "Those weren't too far removed from their *Daedalus* predecessors, and I'm sure Captain Matuzas would choke on his Dramian weed tea to hear you speak ill of the *Helios*."

His brow furrowing in confusion, Reyes regarded him with renewed interest. "Seems you've done your homework, digging up that old posting of mine."

"Didn't have to do much," Okagawa replied. "You and I were posted to the *Helios* at the same time." Shrugging, he added, "Of course, our tours overlapped for a grand total of twelve days. You were a short-timer when I arrived, on your way to the . . . *Belleau Wood,* if I recall correctly."

"You do," Reyes said, nodding in appreciation. "I'll be damned. Another graduate of the Matuzas School of Starship Command. That's interesting to know."

Okagawa laughed. "We'll have to trade some stories. I guess his command style rubbed off on me."

Reyes narrowed his eyes. "Afraid I can't say the same."

Well, that does make a lot of sense, Okagawa admitted to himself. Captain Matuzas's very relaxed approach to command had run contrary to just about everything in every Starfleet rulebook Okagawa had ever come across, a character trait that had given many superior officers cause for concern. Still, the man had gotten results, had produced numerous officers who in turn had gone on to outstanding careers of their own, and his record of accomplishments was such that there had never been any real justification for taking issue with his leadership approach.

For his part, Okagawa had thrived under those conditions while serving on the *Helios,* but he wondered whether Reyes—given his own distinct demeanor—might have found such an atmosphere discomforting during his early career and as a result sought a transfer all those years ago to another starship with a more traditional captain.

Another bit of "need-to-know" information, I'm sure.

What had become an uncomfortable silence between the two men was broken abruptly by the whistle of the internal communications system. *"Cooper to Commodore Reyes,"* said a voice from the intercom unit set into the top of Reyes's desk.

"My exec," the commodore said as he reached across the

polished surface and pressed the control to activate the unit. "Reyes here."

"I'm down in sensor control, sir," the station's first officer said. *"We've just lost alignment on the lateral sensor array again. Long-range telemetry and processing are offline, and short-range is twitchy, too."*

"Damn," Reyes growled as he rubbed his temples. "Same thing as before?"

"Affirmative," Cooper replied. *"One minute they were fine, the next they were out. It's like someone flipped a switch. I've already issued a hold on all scheduled incoming and outbound traffic."*

Reyes shook his head, his expression one of disgust. "Keep me updated. Reyes out." Terminating the connection, the commodore turned to look at Okagawa. "Your crew just got a new 'job one' on the shopping list, Captain. I need that sensor array up and running yesterday. Everything else is secondary priority."

Sensing he was about to be dismissed anyway, Okagawa rose from his chair. "I'll notify Lieutenant al-Khaled and have him report directly to Commander Cooper. By the time my people are done, this station will be running like a top, and those sensors will be able to read the hull number of a starship two sectors away." It was a flagrant boast, he knew, but one he did not mind making. When it came to solving any manner of technical problem or anomaly, he would stack al-Khaled and his team against any engineers in Starfleet.

No sooner did the words leave his mouth than the overhead illumination in Reyes's office flickered before going out altogether. He and the commodore stood in near darkness as the emergency lighting mounted over the door activated, casting the room in muted ruby shadows. For the first time since his arrival, Okagawa became aware of the gentle whir of the ventilation system.

Reyes's laugh echoed in the darkened office. "An omen, of course."

"Oh, of course," Okagawa replied.

CHAPTER

3

"Now this is my kind of place."

Lieutenant Jessica Diamond looked over to see Commander Araev zh'Rhun actually slap her hands together as she made the comment, her eyes wide as she took in their new surroundings. It was atypical behavior on the part of the *Lovell's* Andorian executive officer, who in Diamond's experience normally maintained a reserved demeanor. In all the time she had known zh'Rhun, the commander's only professional lapses had come as presented by her understated, deadpan sense of humor, which she often used to scathing effect. Seeing her now, her expression one of near wanton amusement, was a refreshing change in Diamond's eyes.

In contrast, the weapons officer struggled to keep her own expression neutral as she surveyed the gambling deck of the *Omari-Ekon*, an Orion merchant ship and one of a handful Starfleet and civilian vessels currently making use of Starbase 47's external docking ports. Unlike even the liveliest of the establishments the two women had visited during their tour of Stars Landing, the station's commercial, entertainment, and residential district, the current surroundings appeared to be all but consumed by a festive atmosphere.

Music filled the room, complementing rather than drowning out the chorus of electronic gaming machines and those who played them. A haze of smoke lingered in the air, a combination of various tobaccos—some faint and pleasant, others thick and noxious. Diamond's eyes moved about the expansive parlor, studying the people gathered around tables and playing or watching assorted games of chance. She heard both the laughter and celebration of the winners and the groans of disappointment and frustration of the losers. Scattered among the crowd of revelers were several scantily clad females—most of them Orion, though Diamond thought at least one or two might be human—fawning mostly over male customers but also more than a few of the female clientele as well.

"Disgusting," she said, mindful to keep her voice low lest her criticism carry to unwelcome ears. Still, the idea of anyone—male or female—objectifying themselves in the name of entertaining a client was not something that normally sat well with her.

Glancing sideways at her, zh'Rhun offered a sly smile, her white teeth contrasting with her powder-blue skin. The look of mischief was only enhanced by the slow, curving decline of the twin antennae sticking out from beneath her pallid hair. "Why, Lieutenant, you never struck me as a prude."

"I'm not," Diamond replied, to her ears perhaps a bit too quickly. "If all involved parties are consenting, I'm all for anything." She nodded toward where one sultry Orion woman sat in the lap of a burly Tellarite, with only a single strap and perhaps a rogue gravity flux keeping her wisp of a dress attached to her toned, taut body. "Those women aren't doing this because they want to."

Her frown deepened when she heard zh'Rhun laugh. "Lieutenant, if you really believe that, then you've got a lot to learn about Orion society and social mores." Looking around for a moment before apparently seeing whatever it was she sought, the Andorian touched Diamond on the arm. "This way."

"It also occurs to me," Diamond said as she followed the commander deeper into the room, "that we're the only Starfleet personnel here." Indeed, she had scanned the room for signs of familiar uniforms, but found none. Only Commander zh'Rhun and herself, both dressed in regulation gold tunics and black trousers, appeared to be representing Starfleet within the confines of this establishment on this particular evening.

For her part, zh'Rhun shrugged. "It's early, yet. Maybe things will pick up after the shift change. It's not as though this establishment is off limits."

Diamond nodded, reaching up to push a lock of her shoulder-length brown hair from her eyes. Before departing the *Lovell*, she had reviewed Starbase 47's regulations regarding the various civilian establishments and seen no notices preventing Starfleet personnel from visiting any of them. Likewise, there had been no restrictions on any of the vessels currently docked at the station.

"Besides," the commander said, indicating the gaming parlor with a nod of her head and another impish smile, "it just means we've got the place to ourselves for a while."

Looking in the specified direction, Diamond almost did a double take. Reclined atop a pile of cushions and pillows was a humanoid female, someone of obvious wealth or importance—or both—who at the moment was the focus of attention of four large Orion males, all of whom were shirtless and with an assortment of tattoos and piercings accentuating their well-defined physiques. Two of the men flanked the woman on the cushions, one holding a plate of fruit while the other rubbed her feet with some kind of oil. The remaining two Orions stood to either side of her, one holding a silver goblet while the other carried a tray atop which sat a pair of towels and a small basin.

"All right," Diamond said, shrugging as she took in the scene. "I could probably get used to that."

As they moved past the woman and her consorts, zh'Rhun laughed again. "Relax, Lieutenant. One of the disadvantages of being assigned to a ship staffed by engineers is that when there's a mission that requires only the engineers, the rest of us have to find something interesting to do. How often does a situation like that come along and we get a chance to do nothing but enjoy ourselves?"

Nearing the bar situated at the center of the parlor, they found space between two disparate groups of customers— some human and others not, but all taking full advantage of the gambling deck's joyous ambiance. After placing an order with the Arcturian working behind the bar, zh'Rhun turned to look at Diamond, leaning close so she could be heard over the boisterous patrons around them. "Enjoy yourself, Jessica. This'll be fun. Besides, you've more than earned a bit of down-time."

Diamond was forced to admit that the commander had a point. Most of the *Lovell*'s staff of engineering specialists currently was assisting station personnel to complete the plethora of tasks still remaining before Starbase 47 could be deemed "fully operational," as well as helping to identify and resolve the rash of heretofore unexplained problems with various on-board systems. Those few members of the ship's complement who were not otherwise engaged had been granted shore leave by Captain Okagawa. While Commander zh'Rhun was receiving regular reports from the ship's department heads via her communicator, Jessica Diamond found herself in the unusual position of having nothing "important" to do at the moment.

Okay, okay, she mused. *I'll take the hint.*

The Arcturian bartender placed atop the bar two squat glasses with thick bases and each filled with what Diamond saw was an almost luminescent yellow liquid. Taking one of the glasses, zh'Rhun turned and offered the other to her.

"What is it?" Diamond asked, her brow furrowing as she took the proffered drink.

"It's called *gredlahr,*" the commander replied, "from Andor. Similar to rum, though sweeter." Waggling her eyebrows as her antennae moved to point toward Diamond, she smiled again. "You'll love—"

The sentence was cut off as zh'Rhun stood almost ramrod straight, and Diamond watched her expression morph from shock to puzzlement to annoyance within the space of only a few heartbeats. A scowl crossed her features and she turned to glare behind her at the group of four human males, all of whom seemed to be making a point of not looking at zh'Rhun. Only the man standing nearest to her—big, bald, and with an imposing physique highlighted by the material of the dark shirt stretching across his broad chest—cocked his head in her direction and offered a sly smile.

"Did he just grab your—?" Diamond began.

"Yes," zh'Rhun replied, her expression stern as the commander turned back to face her. "Yes, he did." Shaking her head, she placed her glass back on the bar. "Watch that for me."

You have got *to be kidding me.* The thought screamed in Diamond's mind as zh'Rhun spun on her heel, turned, and grabbed the bald man's right arm. Diamond had only an instant to register his look of surprise before the commander twisted his arm up and behind his back, pulling him around and slamming him face-first into the bar. He emitted a single low grunt of pain before sagging like a limp doll and falling to the floor at her feet.

The effect was immediate. Nearby conversations ceased and dozens of patrons turned to regard the disturbance in their midst. Despite that, Diamond still heard the sounds of gaming and partying taking place elsewhere in the parlor, the majority of the gambling deck's clientele blissfully unaware of the happenings at the bar.

"Uh-oh," she whispered, setting her own drink down on the bar and stepping away from the press of people, suddenly wishing she were carrying a phaser as the rest of the bald man's party—recovering from the shock of zh'Rhun's sudden and effective attack on their friend—turned to face the Andorian with matching looks of growing menace that did not quite hide the obvious effects of intoxication reddening their eyes.

"Not smart, Starfleet," said one of the men, his words slurred and the corners of his mouth curled into a snarl that was almost concealed beneath his thick beard.

Stepping away from the bar to give herself some room,

zh'Rhun affected a dismissive shrug. "Your friend should watch where he puts his hands."

Diamond noted that two of the men wore dark green coveralls with the insignia of a civilian freight service contracted to deliver supplies to the different colonies that were being established throughout the Taurus Reach.

Wonderful, she thought. *Probably their first night back after a long haul.* After who knew how many weeks at low warp, the men had arrived at the station with money to spend and energy to burn. Combined with the alcohol they had no doubt already consumed, it was a recipe for trouble.

The man who had spoken to zh'Rhun moved forward, his hands low and away from his body and his intent evident. He managed only two steps before the commander reacted, lunging forward and closing the gap even before the man could bring up his hands. Lashing out, she struck his chin with the palm of her right hand. The man's head snapped up and he staggered backward a few steps, one hand moving to cradle his wounded jaw. The other two men stepped forward, and Diamond's eyes darted to each of their hands, checking for any sign of a weapon.

For her part, zh'Rhun seemed disinterested in that notion one way or another as she turned to face the new threats, the two remaining men separating in an attempt to flank her with the obvious intent of ganging up on the Andorian. It was obvious that awareness of their surroundings had been as dulled by intoxication as their reflexes, given that the movements of one man brought him almost alongside Diamond.

Idiot, she mused in the instant before the man tried to make his move. He caught sight of her out of the corner of his eye, and Diamond imagined she detected comprehension finally coalescing in his alcohol-dulled mind. Reading his body language, she saw him tense and decided she had no choice even as the man raised an arm in a pitifully slow attempt to lash out at her. Diamond intercepted the arm with no effort, twisting it down and away from her and pulling the man off balance. He crashed to the floor in a disjointed heap, leaving her to look up in time to see zh'Rhun still facing off with the remaining man, who was looking for his opening.

"That's enough."

The words, though spoken in a conversational tone, seemed to carry forth across the gambling deck and draw the simultaneous attention of everyone standing within earshot. Diamond turned to see the crowd behind her part to reveal a hulking, bald Orion male dressed in what looked to be a maroon toga. An array of gold piercings decorated both of his ears as well as the right side of his nose. His thick brow was furrowed in obvious irritation as he took in the scene.

Flanking him was another Orion male—this one of much slimmer build—and a Nalori. While the Orion was dressed in simple woven trousers and shirt and looked every bit the part of a muscled enforcer, the Nalori sported a precisely tailored dark suit and matching shoes that reflected the parlor's low lighting even better than his shiny black skin or the bottomless pools that served as his eyes.

Just looking at him made the hairs on the back of Diamond's neck stand up.

Pointing toward the man still facing off against zh'Rhun, the large Orion said, "Jaeq, Zett, show these gentlemen the door." As the other Orion moved to carry out his instructions, his boss added, "Make sure they've paid their tab first." The near-deadpan delivery almost made Diamond laugh.

She moved to stand beside zh'Rhun as the Orion's two henchmen set about gathering up the wayward quartet of drunken or unconscious freight haulers, both women turning to face their unexpected benefactor. "Thank you," Diamond offered.

"Sorry about the fight," zh'Rhun added. "It wasn't our intention to cause trouble."

The Orion bowed his head, his expression relaxing only the slightest bit. "It is I who should apologize. I don't normally tolerate that sort of conduct aboard my ship."

"Your ship?" Diamond blurted. "You're the captain?"

"In a manner of speaking," the Orion replied. "My name is Ganz, and I'm the proprietor of the *Omari-Ekon* as well as this gaming establishment."

Along with your role in weapons trafficking, Diamond thought, *assorted smuggling, and slave trading, and prostitution, and who knows what else.* While she was not familiar with Ganz's dossier, if he owned this ship, it was probable he had his hand in a variety of illicit interests. *Those freight runners might just be heading for the nearest airlock.*

"We don't typically have fights in here," Ganz continued. "My staff is usually on top of such matters before they can escalate. Unfortunately, not all of my customers are fans of Starfleet."

"An odd attitude to take," zh'Rhun said, "considering they're docking at this station and making use of Starfleet facilities."

Ganz shrugged. "Irony comes in many forms, Commander."

As he spoke the words, the lights throughout the gambling deck flickered, and Diamond even heard a skip in the music being piped through the room's sound system. It was momentary, but still enough to make several of the patrons look around in confusion and cause Ganz's brow to furrow even deeper.

He turned to his Orion companion. "Jaeq, tell the engineers that I'm getting tired of these problems. If they can't figure out what's causing them and fix it . . ." He let his voice trail off as he regarded Diamond and zh'Rhun, as though considering what he was about to say for the benefit of his current audience. "Tell them to fix it, or I'll be unhappy. Are we clear?"

Jaeq nodded. "Understood, Mr. Ganz," he answered before turning and heading off to deliver the message.

They're having tech problems too? Diamond mulled that. *Interesting.* Were the Orion merchant's issues related to whatever was affecting the station's systems? She would have to inform Lieutenant al-Khaled and see what he thought about that.

Returning his attention to the Starfleet officers, Ganz took a deep breath before nodding in their direction. "Now, as I was about to say, ladies, you might wish to consider seeking entertainment elsewhere."

"You're kicking us out?" Diamond asked, feeling her features tighten into a scowl. "The only thing we did was try to buy drinks."

"Remain as long as you wish," Ganz replied. "Your drinks— and anything else you might want for the remainder of your stay—are complimentary." He paused, giving Diamond a frank visual inspection from head to feet. "Despite my policies, however, I can't guarantee that another of the patrons might not . . . misplace his hands."

Stepping forward, zh'Rhun said, "We can handle that."

"Of that I have no doubt," Ganz said, smiling for the first time. "Suit yourself. Inform my staff if you need anything. Enjoy the rest of your evening, ladies." With that, the enormous Orion turned and walked away, the gaggle of onlookers once again parting to facilitate his sojourn deeper into the gaming parlor.

As the crowd returned to normal and the festive atmosphere resumed on the gambling deck, Diamond could not resist offering a playful smile to zh'Rhun as both women reached for their drinks, which still sat atop the bar.

"You're right, Commander," she said as she sipped her *gredlahr.* "This is fun."

CHAPTER
4

After just a few hours aboard Starbase 47, Lieutenant Isaiah Farber had come to a single conclusion: The station was, in a word, incredible.

He had taken in as much of the starbase's numerous aesthetic features as his duties had allowed, typically while passing from one problematic point to another either via the network of turbolifts or the tram tube that skirted the periphery of Vanguard's massive primary hull. The tram in particular offered the young engineer captivating views of the station's terrestrial enclosure—an unhindered panorama stretching more than eight hundred meters—complete with rolling hills, a pond, and even a small forested area. Across the enclosure, the view was dominated by the "skyline" of Stars Landing, the station's high-rise complex of civilian residences and support facilities, which Farber had been told were worth visiting if for nothing else than the collection of restaurants offering cuisines from across the Federation.

Despite all of that, it was not until he got his first look at the main control center for the station's primary sensor array that Farber could admit to being truly impressed.

"Now we're talking my language," he said as he stepped from the turbolift into the room. Located near the bottom of the station's long, cylindrical secondary hull, the control center sat immediately atop the oversized multispectrum sensor array and was awash in activity. Technicians moved among the thirty workstations ringing the chamber's perimeter, each console sporting multiple computer interface terminals and situational display monitors. The chamber reminded Farber of the upper deck of a starship's bridge, complete with a circle of red railing at the room's center. Inside the railing, secured by a series of force-field emitters, hung a massive duranium support arm for the rotating antenna dish, which extended beyond the deck beneath their feet from the bottom of the station's hull.

Taking in the scene and relishing every detail, Farber nodded in satisfaction. "This place is amazing!"

"This place is a wreck," said a voice from behind him, "and it'll stay that way if we spend all day standing in the turbolift."

Realizing he had stopped on the lift's threshold, Farber turned and offered a sheepish grin. "Sorry, Ghrex." He stepped aside, allowing his Denobulan shipmate passage into the control room. Like him, the ensign was dressed in normal Starfleet gold tunic and black trousers and carried a standard-issue engineer's tool satchel slung over her shoulder.

Walking farther into the room, Farber could hear several conversations taking place, all accompanied by a steady stream of computer tones and indicators. He could only imagine the sheer amounts of data that would be processed by this control center and channeled to the station's computer core when the sensor array was functioning at top capacity.

Of course, right now it was operating far below that level, which was why he and Ghrex were here. Sent by Lieutenants al-Khaled and Ballard, the engineers were tasked with assisting in the diagnostics on the sensor array as well as figuring out a means of realignment that would not be compromised inside of a day, as had been the case at irregular intervals since the array first had come online. There was no undervaluing the necessity of functioning sensors, situated as the station was far outside Federation territory and on the doorsteps of both the Klingon Empire and the Tholian Assembly.

"As I understand it," Ghrex said as she followed after him, "both the long-range sensors and the lateral arrays are malfunctioning."

Farber nodded. According to Ballard's situation report, given to him by al-Khaled during their hasty, succinct briefing, both systems had failed within moments of one another, and with no apparent crossover feedback. It was not a case of cascading failures, with one malfunction overburdening and finally overcoming subordinate systems.

"Ballard and his people already ruled out malfunctions in the station's power and data network that might be overloading the array," he said, "along with negative effects from ambient radiation or some other stellar phenomenon in this part of space. So, basically, that narrows it down to—" He paused for dramatic effect. "—something inside the station, or something *outside* the station."

Frowning, Ghrex hitched her tool satchel up higher onto her shoulder. "Sounds like a simple enough problem to solve."

Farber regarded her with a smirk. "It was a joke, Ensign. Just trying to get a smile out of you."

"You're like my second husband's third wife," the Denobulan replied, shaking her head. "Just because we're facing a complex problem to solve doesn't require you to boost my spirits. I'm typically a very upbeat and positive person, after all."

"Oh, absolutely," Farber said, trying not to laugh. "I never thought otherwise, not for a second."

Turning away from Ghrex, he looked about the room until his eyes caught sight of the officer he guessed was in charge here in the control center, an uncharacteristically slender Tellarite male dressed in a blue tunic sporting lieutenant commander's insignia.

"Briv," the commander said by way of introduction, the single word coming out almost as a belch rather than actual speech. "You've arrived just in time, it seems."

"We're here to help, sir," Farber replied. "Where do you want us?"

Offering a terse nod, Briv said, "I've ordered a new set of diagnostics on the array, but I doubt they'll be any more helpful in finding a cause than the previous half-dozen tests we've run. The rest of our time has been spent making manual recalibrations and adjustments." He shook his head, and Farber read his expression of disgust. "You never realize how much you rely on automation until it's not available."

Farber grinned. "The story of our lives, Commander."

Standing beside him, Ghrex said, "I have an idea, sir. I'd like to take a look at the previous sets of diagnostics results. If the problem is internal, I might find a pattern to the malfunctions that I can trace back to a source."

"I've already had people do that," Briv replied, "but a fresh perspective might just be what's in order." He indicated an unmanned console. "You can work at that station."

Farber nodded. "Sounds like a plan. In the meantime, I can run a scan of the main data hubs and routers leading from here and feeding the primary data network. If there's a breach or some other form of defect, it could go all but undetected in the kilometers of wiring and circuitry filling the innards of this station." Looking around, he asked, "The schematics showed service lifts accessing the data network conduits?"

Briv shook his head. "Engineering service turbolifts are offline for safety reasons until we get the problems resolved." He pointed over Farber's shoulder. "We have Jefferies tubes that will get you there, though." His gruff expression morphing into a mischievous grin, he added, "They should be big enough for you to fit."

Wonderful.

Crawling around the access conduits aboard a starship—even one as small as the *Lovell*—was one thing. Doing the same aboard a Watchtower-class space station would be something else entirely.

Guess I won't need the gym today, he mused as he made a quick check to see that his tool satchel's flap was secure. *Or tomorrow, for that matter.*

After first activating his tricorder and adjusting its scan field to search for fluctuations in the data processing network, Farber entered the Jefferies tube and found a familiar-looking orange, tri-sided service ladder. The ever-present hum of the station's massive power generators was very audible in the shaft's narrow confines, though it was not enough to drown out the low-pitched whine of his tricorder or even the sounds of his boots on the ladder rungs as he climbed.

While he often traversed the comparable crawlways on the *Lovell* as a means of exercise—doing so as fast as he could, of course—on this occasion he moved at a more leisurely pace so that the tricorder could conduct its scans. The going was slow and mundane, with Farber splitting his focus between the tricorder's miniaturized display screen and the access conduit itself. Service platforms were installed at regular intervals on each side of the ladder, and horizontal ducts intersected with the shaft in correlation to each deck within the station's secondary hull. Farber tried not to pay too much attention to the markings on the shaft's bulkheads at each juncture, as they only served to remind him that he was climbing ever higher and ever farther from the sensor control room. He was now ten decks up from the sensor array, past the station's immense primary energy reactors and moving upward toward the areas designated for cargo storage and maintenance facilities.

He was almost to the next deck when he saw it.

A trio of dark lines of varying thickness, running down the wall and contrasting with the light gray of the bulkhead to his left, standing out even in the shaft's reduced illumination. Following the streaks with his eyes, he saw that they ended at the bottom edge of a rectangular grille for one of the station's uncounted ventilation ducts, situated on the bulkhead a meter above a service platform. It only barely reflected the shaft's subdued lighting, at first glance appearing to be leakage from some kind of coolant or perhaps a hydraulic seal.

Stepping onto the platform, Farber reached into his tool satchel and extracted a work light. When he directed its bright beam onto the wall, he knew without question that he was not looking at a lubricant leak.

Blood?

He ducked down in order to see through the grill, moving the work light so that it could shine through the thin grating, and froze when the light washed across familiar gold material and reflected off gleaming braid.

"Oh my god," he breathed as he looked upon the body of a dead human male. The man's throat had been slit, and congealed blood stained his neck, uniform, and the bottom of the ventilation duct into which his body had been unceremoniously shoved. A pungent aroma of dull copper assailed his nostrils, the scent of death. How long had the man been here?

Casting frantic glances around the shaft to ensure he was still alone while trying not to drop his work light or stumble from the service platform, Farber reached with one shaking hand for the communicator clipped to his waist.

More than an hour later, Farber sat in a small, almost claustrophobic office. Before him was a utilitarian gray desk, the undecorated room's most prominent furnishing. Other than the standard-issue computer interface terminal, the top of the desk was free of papers, data slates, clutter, or personal possessions of any kind. He could not even detect a faded ring from where a coffee cup might once have rested. Everything about the office indicated that its current owner made a supreme effort to spend as much time as possible away from these uninviting surroundings.

Though he had washed his face and hands after his initial interview with the station's security chief, Lieutenant Haniff Jackson, Farber realized he once again was rubbing his hands as though trying to clean them. He had caught himself doing it several times since his grisly discovery, even though he had not touched so much as a drop of blood from the unfortunate soul he had found.

The door behind him slid aside, allowing Jackson to enter. He was a stout man, like Farber himself, well-muscled and moving with the confidence Farber had always found to be typical behavior for security personnel. Dark skin contrasted starkly with his gold tunic, the ribbed collar of which stretched around his thick neck. He was bald, though he sported a mustache and a small patch of facial hair just beneath his lower lip.

"Sorry to keep you waiting, Lieutenant," Jackson said as he maneuvered his compact, barrel-chested frame behind the desk and settled into the office's only other chair. He carried a data slate in his thick left hand, which he laid upon the desk before directing his attention to Farber. "I don't suppose you have anything to add to your original statement?"

Farber shook his head. "No," he said, recalling what little he was able to offer in the way of information during Jackson's first interview, conducted down in sensor control. Beyond his discovery of the body itself, he of course could offer nothing else. "I guess he and I weren't all that different," he added. "Just in the wrong place at the wrong time."

"One way of looking at it," Jackson countered. "Ensign Malhotra was last reported conducting an inventory in Cargo Bay Nineteen, but he's been missing since yesterday. At first we thought he might have been involved in some thefts we've experienced." Shaking his head, the security officer sighed. "It looks like he might have been."

"I wondered about that," Farber said, only realizing after he heard the words that he had spoken them aloud.

His eyes narrowing, Jackson leaned forward in his seat. "What do you know about it?"

Farber cleared his throat as he adjusted his position in his own chair. "I'm sorry, Lieutenant. I didn't mean to muddy the waters with that comment. It's just that I noticed that bay's cargo manifest was the last thing accessed on the computer station located inside that room. You didn't know?"

Obviously still confused, Jackson shook his head. "So far as we could determine, the manifests look completely legitimate, even though we know they had to have been altered by someone who knew what they were doing. Why were you reviewing them?"

Reaching for the tricorder still slung from his shoulder, Farber replied, "As I said earlier, I was making scans of the main data conduits as well as the transfer hubs and interface terminals while moving through that access shaft. It wasn't until after I'd found Ensign Malhotra and climbed back down to sensor control that I realized my tricorder was still activated. While I was waiting to be interviewed, I went over the scans, and noticed the discrepancy."

"Let me see that," Jackson said, reaching for the tricorder, and Farber watched as he spent several moments studying the information stored within its suite of removable data discs.

"Wait a minute," the lieutenant finally said when he finished his review. "Whoever altered the manifest did an exceptional job covering their tracks, but your scans show the modifications in the database as though they were painted on the bulkhead. How did you find this?"

"I'll admit they were good," Farber said, unable to resist a smug smile, "but I'm better. Add to that the fact that my tricorder isn't exactly standard issue, as I've made several modifications to its scanning diodes." He shrugged. "Consider it an occupational habit."

Leaning back in his seat, Jackson chuckled. "I've heard that about you Corps of Engineers types." He indicated the tricorder with a nod. "I'd appreciate a copy of that data as soon as you can get it to me." Then he smiled. "After that, I might ask you to tinker with some of our tricorders."

"Anything I can do to help, Lieutenant," Farber replied.

Jackson drew a deep breath. "For what it's worth, you may have helped to narrow the list of suspects quite a bit. Lots of people can steal from a cargo bay, but I'm betting only a handful can make those kinds of subtle database alterations, and fewer than that are currently running around this station." He nodded in satisfaction. "When this is over, if you're still here, remind me that I owe you a drink."

"Fair enough," Farber said. "It's rare for me to turn down such offers." As he spoke the words, both men looked up in response to a rapid flickering in the overhead lighting.

"Of course," the engineer amended, "that assumes we can ever fix your station."

CHAPTER
5

Unlike the main engineering room aboard the *Lovell*, one thing al-Khaled noticed most about Starbase 47's primary engineering control center was the near lack of background noise generated by engines. Whereas his ship's massive power plant was located in proximity to the work spaces inhabited by the small, fragile beings tasked with caring for it, the low thrum of Vanguard's power generators—ensconced as they were deep in the bowels of the station—was all but concealed by internal dampening systems.

He still was able to sense the reverberations, of course, as would any decent engineer.

The other thing al-Khaled observed about his current surroundings was that, considering the sheer size of Starbase 47, the station's main engineering center was downright claustrophobic.

"You'd think your fellow engineers would have looked out for you when designing this place," al-Khaled said, turning in his seat as Curtis Ballard walked toward him.

Vanguard's chief engineer shrugged. "They made up for it. This is the main hub, but there are five auxiliary control rooms spread across the station. Even if something happens here, we can oversee every onboard system from any of those locations. All six stations also have direct turbolifts and Jefferies tube access to the station's power grid."

Al-Khaled nodded. The design approach was but one of several innovations incorporated into the Watchtower-class stations, making them the most technologically advanced model of autonomous, self-sustaining space-based habitats. Once operational, Vanguard would be capable of supporting itself and its crew of twelve hundred for a decade without outside aid, and in addition to its ship-maintenance and repair facilities the station boasted formidable weapons and defensive systems that would allow it to face any threat that might present itself. It was an important consideration out here in the Taurus Reach, light-years from normal Starfleet patrol routes.

The only problem with that plan, of course, was that it required the station in question actually to have onboard systems that *worked*.

Settling into a chair at a console adjacent to the one al-Khaled occupied, Ballard rubbed his eyes before running both hands through his disheveled blond hair. "You know, I hate staff meetings on the best of days."

Al-Khaled offered a sympathetic nod. "Lieutenant Farber told me about the crew member they found. I was sorry to hear about that." While death in the line of duty was a possibility faced by every Starfleet officer, that normally did not extend to being murdered while carrying out regular, even mundane assignments within the supposed safety of one's own starship—or starbase—and while living and working among one's own trusted colleagues.

"Not something you expect, that's for sure," Ballard replied. "If I know Lieutenant Jackson and his security team, though, they'll tear this station apart to find who's responsible." Shaking his head, he turned to his workstation. "In the meantime, I've got my hands full here." As he spoke the words, he cast a wry, humorless grin toward al-Khaled. "Sorry, I meant *we've* got *our* hands full."

"No offense taken," al-Khaled replied. At first, he was concerned that Ballard might take issue with outside engineers being brought in to help him resolve the station's problems, but the lieutenant had not batted an eye at Commodore Reyes's decision. A consummate professional, Ballard knew that deploying fresh minds and eyes against a problem was an effective means of finding a solution.

"You know, Mahmud," the engineer said after a moment, "I've been in Starfleet for seven years. I've been on shakedown cruises for three different starships, and I was part of the team that got Station K-5 up and running when Starfleet needed it operational six months ahead of schedule." He shook his head. "That was a host of headaches, let me tell you, but it was nothing compared to the ulcers this place is giving me. I've never run into anything like the problems we've been facing here."

Repeated inspections of the hardware and software components that comprised those systems experiencing the irregular and unexplained malfunctions—sensors, the internal communications and computer network, power distribution grids—had found nothing. Even prior to the *Lovell*'s arrival, Ballard and his team had been working with the theory that something external to the station must be responsible, but scans of the surrounding region revealed nothing—natural or artificial—that might be the cause.

That hypothesis gained credibility when personnel still on duty aboard the *Lovell* began reporting isolated odd happenings with the ship's systems, though nothing as extensive as whatever plagued the station. Then al-Khaled received a surprise when Lieutenant Diamond contacted him with news about the odd power fluctuations aboard the Orion merchant ship, the only other vessel currently docked at Vanguard.

"I've never fully shaken the idea that the Klingons or Tholians might be covertly jamming us," Ballard said as he leaned back in his chair. "It would make sense, especially given what's happening aboard the *Lovell* and that Orion ship, but we haven't found a single shred of evidence to support the idea."

Al-Khaled frowned. "Even if they were capable of doing something like that without us finding it, they've got their own people on board. You'd think they'd want measures in place to protect their own communications and computer access."

As part of Vanguard's mission to safeguard diplomatic relations between the Klingon Empire and Tholian Assembly as the Federation continued its push into the Taurus Reach, the station also played home to embassies from all three governments. Both the Klingon and Tholian ambassadors were supported by a staff of attachés and aides, all of whom were in regular contact with their respective homeworlds and appropriate political entities.

"Their communications and computers have been having the same problems as the rest of the station," Ballard replied. "Of course, any such protection would be pretty obvious once we started looking for the cause. I'd like to think we had the edge on Klingon technology, but as for the Tholians . . ." He shrugged. "Hell, nobody really knows about them, do they?"

The door to the control center swooshed open to admit Isaiah Farber, who entered at a run, and al-Khaled swore he could feel the deck plates vibrating beneath his feet in response to the muscled lieutenant's heavy footfalls.

"I think I know what's going on," Farber said by way of greeting. "Remember Buquair III?"

Al-Khaled could tell that Commodore Reyes, while doubtless an intelligent and articulate man, preferred to concentrate on the larger, grander picture while leaving the trivial details to those he commanded.

It also was obvious that the commodore was not a man of great patience when it came to having to listen to such details.

"What about this colony?" Reyes asked from where he sat behind his desk as he reached for the coffee cup near his left hand.

From where he sat next to the commodore's intelligence officer, Lieutenant Commander T'Prynn, Captain Okagawa replied, "Two years ago, the *Lovell* was one of several ships sent to Buquair III after an underwater earthquake generated a tsunami and it slammed into the Glassner Colony established by the Federation."

Farber said, "While we were helping out with repair and reconstruction efforts, we discovered a very subtle power reading coming from somewhere just offshore. It turned out to be the wreck of an alien spacecraft that had crashed and sunk there decades earlier, and was buried beneath ocean silt."

"The earthquake unburied it, Commodore," al-Khaled added, "and we picked up the distress signal it was still transmitting, though it was on a frequency so low that normal communications channels couldn't detect it. We picked up the power readings well enough, but we had to recalibrate our ship's sensors before we could lock on to the signal."

Holding up his tricorder, its black exterior practically swallowed by his meaty left hand, Farber said, "I was recalibrating this after replacing its power cell when I picked up an odd reading. I had our people on the *Lovell* retune the ship's sensors in a manner similar to what we did at the colony, and that's when we found it."

Turning in her seat, T'Prynn asked, "You are alleging that something comparable to what you discovered on Buquair III is occurring here?" She shifted her gaze—stern and unwavering in typical Vulcan fashion—between al-Khaled and Farber, and for an odd moment al-Khaled found himself realizing that he found her quite attractive. She was dressed in the female officer's version of the standard Starfleet gold tunic, with its high, thick collar almost but not quite concealing her long, thin neck. Her dark hair was piled atop her head in a regulation hairstyle that left her small, pointed ears exposed while seeming exotic as it framed her lean features.

Clearing his throat as he returned his attention to the matter at hand, al-Khaled nodded. "Yes, Commander." Crossing the commodore's office to the viewer mounted on the bulkhead to Reyes's right, he added, "This is what our sensors picked up."

He touched the control pad set into the wall next to the viewer, and the screen activated to display a computer-generated silhouette of Vanguard station superimposed over a starfield. Dominating the image was a series of blue lines, uneven and rippling as they expanded from one edge of the star map toward the station.

"We're calling it a 'carrier wave' for now," al-Khaled said, pointing to different lines on the screen. "It's definitely an artificial occurrence, transmitting on a frequency so low that sensors in their normal configuration would never register it."

Reyes frowned. "But my people retuned the station's sensor arrays looking for something like this even before you arrived." Looking to where Ballard stood near the bulkhead opposite the viewscreen, he asked, "I'm not misremembering anything, am I, Lieutenant?"

"No, sir," the engineer replied. "We didn't pick up so much as a twitch."

Stepping closer to al-Khaled, Farber said, "The sensors aboard the *Lovell* have been modified with modern components like those aboard newer and larger ships, and our teams have also enhanced them to a significant degree beyond their normal operational limits."

"A consequence of hauling a shipload of engineers traveling from assignment to assignment and looking for ways to pass the time," Okagawa added. "Welcome to my world, Commodore."

Nodding, Reyes even smiled a bit at that. "Nice card to have in your deck, though."

"Even with our sensors," al-Khaled said, "we detected nothing until we made additional recalibrations, and then we only just barely picked up the signal."

"And you believe this to be the source of our technical problems?" T'Prynn asked. The thin eyebrow over her right eye arched as if to punctuate her question. Not waiting for a response, she turned to Reyes. "An interesting hypothesis."

"I don't understand," the commodore said, leaning forward in his chair and clasping his hands together as he rested forearms atop his desk. "If this signal, wave, or whatever you want to call it is so weak, how can it be causing all of this trouble, not only to my station but also the *Lovell*, that damned Orion's ship, and anybody else wandering through this area?"

Al-Khaled replied, "We're only just starting our analysis, Commodore, but our preliminary theory is that this carrier wave is like a hailing frequency, intended to be received and processed through a device operating along specific parameters similar to that of the carrier wave's source. The signal is cyclic, repeating approximately every twenty-four minutes, but it lacks any real complexity. Based on what we've learned so far, it seems that sensitive equipment such as computer interfaces, sensor arrays, and communications networks are susceptible to minor disruption."

"In some respects," Farber added, "it's not unlike the distress signals utilized by civilian transport ships several decades ago, which were designed to interfere with the navigational systems of passing ships and attract attention in the event the signal itself was too weak to be interpreted by proper communications systems."

As his colleague provided his analysis, al-Khaled glanced toward T'Prynn and saw that the Vulcan's attention appeared focused on the viewscreen and its representation of the carrier wave.

She noticed his scrutiny and cocked her head in his direction before asking, "Lieutenant, have you been able to locate the carrier wave's origin point?"

"No, Commander." Al-Khaled pointed to the image on the screen. "So far, all we've been able to determine is that it comes from somewhere in the Taurus Reach. According to the information at our disposal, the area where we believe the signal originates has only been charted by automated probes, and even that was done in the most cursory manner. Our analysis to this point also suggests it may only have been transmitting intermittently during the past several weeks, corresponding to the time you began experiencing stationwide malfunctions. We hope to learn more as we continue our research, of course."

Sitting back in his seat, Reyes said, "That won't be necessary, Lieutenant."

Though taken aback by the abrupt statement, al-Khaled still noticed the quick glance the commodore exchanged with T'Prynn. It was no doubt intended to be subtle, something shared only between them, but there was no mistaking the look that flashed only briefly in Reyes's eyes.

We just stumbled onto something interesting.

"Commodore," Okagawa said, "I don't understand. It seems my people are into the middle of something here." Though the statement did not reveal anything, al-Khaled was familiar enough with his captain's mannerisms and thought processes to know that he must have caught the look between the Vanguard officers as well, and was doing some fishing of his own.

"Don't get me wrong, gentlemen," Reyes said as he rose from his chair. "I appreciate everything you've done to this point, including what looks to be finding the source of our problems. What I need from you now is your expertise in figuring out a way for my station to operate in spite of this interference, sooner rather than later. We do have a rather compressed schedule to keep." He looked to Ballard. "Isn't that right, Lieutenant?"

"Absolutely, sir," the engineer replied.

Reyes nodded, then glanced at T'Prynn again before continuing, "As for the signal itself and where it might be coming from, I have a whole staff of scientists I can task with that. Transfer all information you've gathered to this point to Commander T'Prynn, and she'll take it from there."

The commodore was smooth, al-Khaled decided, so practiced and polished was his delivery that he almost certainly was a consummate poker player. His instructions were of course completely proper and—on the surface, at least—lacking any hint of ulterior motive. Still, there was no denying the swiftness with which he had reassigned responsibility for determining the source and content of the mysterious carrier wave.

What are they worried about?

Rising to his feet, Okagawa nodded. "Understood, Commodore. I'll have my engineers get back to helping your teams right away."

After departing Reyes's office and making their way across the operations center, it was not until al-Khaled, Farber, and Okagawa were in a turbolift heading back toward the docking bays and the core of the station that anyone said anything.

The captain broke the silence. "Is it just me, or did we just get hustled?"

Farber nodded. "Not just you, sir."

"I'm thinking I'm going to be very busy after dinner this evening," al-Khaled said. "I want to get another look at the data we've collected so far."

Okagawa held up a hand. "Not so fast, Lieutenant. For now, we play it the commodore's way. Transfer everything we've got on that signal to Commander T'Prynn. You and your team have a job to do. Let's help get this station up and running the way it's supposed to be." Shaking his head, he added, "Besides, after that mess with the environmental control system, I don't want my ship coming down with any serious troubles of its own."

Though he acknowledged his captain's orders and started turning the thoughts running through his mind toward his primary assignment, al-Khaled could not shake loose the feeling that there was much about the mysterious carrier wave in which to be interested.

He also was certain that Commodore Reyes and Commander T'Prynn held similar opinions.

It's as though they were waiting for something like this to happen.

CHAPTER
6

Lieutenant T'Laen preferred to work the overnight shift.

It was not that she was antisocial, of course. In fact, and though it was an action she herself would never undertake, she believed that an informal survey of the rest of the *Lovell's* crew would show that—by Vulcan standards, at least—T'Laen was more than genial toward her shipmates. However, she long ago learned that she preferred to work in relative solitude, freed from as many potential distractions as possible while going about her duties as the ship's primary computer systems specialist.

Gamma shift on the bridge offered her that environment, particularly now with the ship docked within the safe confines of Starbase 47. Captain Okagawa had granted shore leave to all personnel not currently assisting the station's engineering teams to resolve their spate of technical issues, a relative distinction considering that fully two-thirds of the *Lovell's* forty-two-person crew were involved in that effort, and assorted members from the remaining third had pitched in as helpers and assistants wherever they might be useful.

As a result, the bridge was deserted except for her, with only the omnipresent sounds of workstations set to passive or automated modes to keep her company. With the exception of her station and those displaying vital information about critical onboard systems, even the array of status monitors and viewscreens ringing the ship's nerve center were inactive.

T'Laen had volunteered to "mind the store," as the captain had put it, freeing Commander zh'Rhun and other bridge officers to enjoy some well-deserved shore leave and allowing the lieutenant herself to concentrate on her current task: continued analysis of the mysterious carrier wave emanating from deep within the Taurus Reach.

While Lieutenant al-Khaled had been tasked with figuring out how to nullify the signal's puzzling effects on the Vanguard station as well as the *Lovell*—which T'Laen had experienced as occasional disruptions in the ship's main computer—she had taken it upon herself to learn as much as possible about the transmission's origin.

Though she had spent several hours seated at the bridge's library computer workstation studying the odd frequency and patterns of the communication, she had gleaned precious little in the way of new information. Breaking down the signal was easy enough, given its relatively simplistic construction. What she had so far been unable to fathom was whether she was dealing with an alien language—one that simply defied even the persistent efforts of the universal translation software—or an elaborate form of encryption.

A thorough search of the *Lovell*'s databanks had found nothing on record as resembling the signal, and her request for a similar search to be conducted through Starfleet Command's larger and far more comprehensive repository of information was still waiting to be processed. If that failed, she had already drafted for the captain's approval a request for computer access to Memory Alpha, the vast storehouse of scientific and cultural information gathered from all of the Federation's member planets. T'Laen did not expect to find anything resembling a match to the carrier wave, but due diligence required following all available avenues of investigation.

"Any luck, Lieutenant?"

It required physical effort on T'Laen's part not to jump at the sound of Okagawa's voice from behind her. Swiveling her chair away from her workstation, the Vulcan saw the captain regarding her with the small, knowing smile that always seemed to highlight his features.

"Excuse me, Captain," she said as she rose from her chair in deference to her commanding officer. "I apparently did not hear your arrival." How had he managed to get on the bridge without her noticing it? She had not heard the turbolift doors or the captain's footsteps as he stepped onto the command center's upper deck. Had her work really been that engrossing? Or was she simply tired?

"I'm stealthy that way," Okagawa said, his smile broadening. "Good to know I haven't lost my touch." Waving her back to her seat, he indicated one of her station's display monitors. "Still chewing on it, I take it?"

It took a moment for T'Laen to comprehend the meaning of the captain's words before she nodded. "I have attempted to augment the computer's translation subroutines to invoke a host of atypical search parameters in the hope of facilitating a conversion matrix. The efforts have yielded some progress."

"Do you still buy Mahmud's idea that it's a hail of some kind?" Okagawa asked.

"In a manner of speaking, sir," the Vulcan replied. "Based on what the translation software has accomplished so far, I believe the signal to be an advisory message of some kind. In other words, a warning."

Okagawa's eyebrows rose at that. "A warning for whom? More importantly, a warning about what?"

Turning back to her station, T'Laen said, "I am afraid that is still unknown, sir. However, there is something else of interest." She entered a string of commands to the library computer via the rows of multicolored controls arrayed across her console, each button press emitting its own telltale sound and the sequence sounding almost lyrical as the computer processed her commands. A moment later, the rightmost of the two screens situated on the upper bulkhead above her station flared to life, displaying a cross section of the Taurus Reach, with Starbase 47 positioned near the upper left corner. A light blue wedge overlaid the map's gridlines, its narrowest point near the lower right corner and expanding upward and toward the computer's representation of the station.

"The carrier wave is not omnidirectional, as first theorized," she reported. "According to our analysis to this point, the transmission was intended for something or someone in this general direction with relation to the origin point, at least at the time the signal was initiated."

"That explains why every ship in the region isn't having problems like the station's," Okagawa said as he began to pace the bridge's upper deck. "But it certainly raises a host of new questions, doesn't it? So far as Starfleet probes have been able to determine, there's never been anything of consequence in this area, unless someone is curious about the station itself."

T'Laen nodded. "An intriguing theory, sir. The station would, of course, be of interest to many parties in this region of space."

Releasing a mild sigh, Okagawa said, "One more mystery for Commodore Reyes and his people to solve, I suppose."

T'Laen nodded. "Indeed." She had heard from al-Khaled about the meeting in the station commander's office, whereby Reyes had all but shut down discussion about the signal's possible origin and purpose, directing the *Lovell* crew to continue their efforts at annulling its troublesome effects on the station. She knew that Okagawa had in effect defied orders to leave the investigation to Reyes's own people, but she also understood that the captain was more than capable of handling that matter if and when it became necessary.

Still pacing the perimeter of the bridge, his brow furrowed in concentration and his arms folded across his chest, Okagawa said, "All right then. Assuming your theory's correct, what if we sent back an answer?"

The abrupt suggestion almost caught the Vulcan off guard. "I beg your pardon, sir?"

Okagawa shrugged. "If you and Mahmud are right and the thing's nothing more than some kind of automated transmission, we might get some kind of programmed reaction if we send a response."

"We have no way of knowing what form such a reaction might take, Captain," T'Laen replied. On the surface, the idea seemed to be fraught with recklessness, though she could not deny that it also carried with it a degree of logic. "However, if it is a warning, then a response that the message has been received may well engender a benign reaction, if not one which offers us new insight into the signal's originators."

Smiling again, Okagawa offered an approving nod. "Couldn't have said it better myself. What will it take?"

T'Laen entered a new string of commands to her console, pausing to examine the results of her request on one of her workstation monitors. "I believe I can take what the translator has provided and craft a crude reply which essentially will communicate that we have received the message and are awaiting further instructions. I will also require Lieutenant al-Khaled's assistance to reconfigure our communications array to transmit on the signal's original frequency."

Okagawa clapped his hands together, a gesture the Vulcan recognized as one the captain made when he was satisfied with a proposed plan and was ready to see it put into action. "Excellent. Do it, and let's see what happens."

Nodding, T'Laen nevertheless held reservations. "Sir, you realize that Commodore Reyes will almost certainly express disapproval at your decision."

"Almost?" Okagawa countered. "Don't be silly. The commodore is going to be three kinds of irate with me when he finds out about this." Once more, he smiled. "That's the beauty of commanding the lowliest vessel in Starfleet, Lieutenant. There's no worse place left for me to be transferred."

"What the hell did you do, Captain?"

For a brief moment, despite his earlier comment and as he regarded Reyes's stern, clouded features, Daniel Okagawa

wondered if perhaps he might have underestimated the commodore's response to the report he had just been given.

"It appears," the captain replied, "that my computer specialist has inadvertently solved our respective technical issues."
Seated once again in one of the two chairs facing the station
commander's desk, Okagawa watched as Reyes's expression
seemed to grow even darker as he digested the answer.

Sitting next to him, Lieutenant Commander T'Prynn turned
to regard him with cold eyes, her own features fixed and neutral. "Your crew's orders were to leave the study of the transmission to starbase personnel." The statement was delivered in
a taciturn manner typical of Vulcans, he knew, but it also was
a tone he was unaccustomed to hearing directed at him by a
subordinate.

"Actually, Commander," Okagawa said, hearing his voice
hardening, "*my* orders were to turn my people's expertise toward
finding a solution for the transmission's effects on starbase
systems. Lieutenant T'Laen's areas of proficiency include computer and communications systems, which she employed to
arrive at the theory she then executed on *my* authorization."

"And all she did was create a simple response message?" Reyes
asked, his mouth curling into a questioning frown. "As a test?"

Okagawa nodded. "Yes, sir," he said, before explaining in
broad strokes the gist of how T'Laen had studied the mystify-
ing signal's syntax and created what she believed to be a short,
straightforward reply that essentially communicated, "Message received."

"According to the lieutenant's status report," T'Prynn said,
"the *Lovell*'s sensors detected the apparent termination of the
original signal seven hours, forty-one minutes, twelve seconds
after she transmitted her message. Based on reports subsequently submitted by starbase department heads, no further
disruptions in onboard systems have been detected."

"You're welcome," Okagawa replied.

Clasping his hands atop his desk, his face still a scowl,
Reyes said, "Your lieutenant's reports said she thought it was a

warning of some kind. Now that you've attempted to acknowledge it, has there been any indication that any sort of response
to your message is forthcoming?"

"No, sir." The captain had not expected any such reaction.
"It's our belief that the original signal is automated, and that
our response triggered another preprogrammed reaction." It
seemed the likely explanation, given that the message's behavior indicated a predetermined protocol of some kind. Whatever technology was involved, its creators might even be long
dead, and it was entirely possible that nothing of any consequence even remained of their civilization.

So, why does Reyes look worried?

The commodore had been vague from the moment he
learned of the carrier wave's existence and its apparent point
of origin deep in the Taurus Reach. Though Reyes had been
subtle in his attempts to steer further study of the signal to his
own people, there was no denying that more was going on here
than met the eye.

"The big mystery," Reyes said after a moment, "is whether it
was supposed to be a warning about something bad happening, or maybe a directive to stay away." He looked up from his
desk, and Okagawa sensed that the commodore was reading his
curiosity and was weighing his next words with deliberate care.
"I know you've got a lot of questions, Captain. Truth is, your
people's efforts to this point—while exceptional and most helpful—have also raised several new questions. Unfortunately, even
if I had any answers, I couldn't offer them to you."

Okagawa figured that one was coming. Everything he had
seen and heard about this matter had been leading up to the
commodore's latest revelation, he decided. It only served to
solidify the thought that had been nagging at him since the
previous day's meeting in Reyes's office: Vanguard's true purpose extended far beyond simple establishment of a Federation presence and support of colonization within the Taurus
Reach, and its proximity to both the Klingon Empire and the
Tholian Assembly was only a factor of that mission.

It made perfect sense, of course, when one considered the station's construction and deployment within a remarkably short time frame, a fact that, so far as Okagawa knew, had not been made public knowledge but had been provided to him and his engineers as part of their briefing to understand the starbase's technical problems. Still, from a tactical perspective, the Taurus Reach appeared to offer precious little to justify the establishment of a Federation foothold in the region while risking the ire of either the Klingons or the Tholians. So what did that leave?

Another question for which Reyes is unlikely to offer an answer, Okagawa mused. *But is it that he has no answer, or that he simply* can't *provide it?*

"I understand, Commodore," he said. "If I may, do you intend to continue tracking the signal to its source?"

Reyes replied, "That would be one of those 'need-to-know' type questions, Captain."

I'd call that a yes. What the hell does he think is out here, anyway?

Having served in Starfleet for more than thirty years, Okagawa was more than familiar with the concept of keeping secrets. He also had learned to accept that his position as a captain of a ship that did not patrol the Federation's borders or carry out strictly military missions meant that there was much information to which he never would be privy.

Obviously, this was to be one of those occasions.

Not that it would bother him to any significant degree. Though he was naturally curious as to what might be unfolding in this heretofore unexplored area of space, Okagawa also knew that with the apparent resolution of the station's difficulties, someone else would carry out the investigation that was sure to follow. So far as Commodore Reyes was concerned, the usefulness of the *Lovell* and her crew of engineers was at an end.

Such is life when on the bottom rung of the Starfleet ladder.

The intercom built into the desk emitted an abrupt, shrill

whistle, followed by a voice that Okagawa recognized as belonging to Reyes's administrative aide, Yeoman Greenfield.

"*Commodore? Lieutenant Ballard and Lieutenant al-Khaled from the* Lovell *are requesting to see you and Captain Okagawa. They say it's urgent.*" Okagawa watched Reyes's eyes widen in surprise, and even saw T'Prynn offer a raised eyebrow at the report.

Punching the button to activate the intercom, Reyes replied, "Send them in."

The bright red doors leading from the commodore's office parted to admit Ballard and al-Khaled, and Okagawa noted their near-matching expressions of concern. The station's chief engineer was carrying a standard-issue data slate in his right hand, while al-Khaled wore a tricorder slung over his left shoulder.

"Apologies for the interruption, sir," Ballard said, crossing the room so that he could offer the data slate to Reyes, "but you need to see this. We've got a security breach."

That got T'Prynn's attention. "What kind of breach?"

By way of reply, al-Khaled moved to the viewscreen on the far wall and activated it, tapping a long series of commands into the unit's keypad. "We were running a final set of diagnostics on the sensor suites, to ensure no lingering interference from the carrier wave, when we found this."

The viewscreen now displayed a technical schematic that to Okagawa appeared as a data stream—highlighted in bright blue—as formatted by a sensor array for transmission to a computer's memory banks. What he did not understand was the presence of the additional red data stream, weaving in and around the sensor telemetry so closely as to appear like an echo or tracing.

"What the hell is that?" Reyes asked.

"An embedded comm signal," Ballard replied, "piggy-backed along the sensor feeds. We found similar configurations in five different sensor nodes."

Pointing to the intertwined data streams, al-Khaled added,

"They're designed to take advantage of the gaps in the scan cycle when the arrays reset after each sweep before transmitting in burst packages." He turned away from the viewer, and Okagawa noted the worry in the younger man's eyes. "Whoever put this into play knew what they were doing."

"A saboteur," T'Prynn said. "Have you determined who's receiving these transmissions?"

Al-Khaled nodded. "In all cases, the other parties were civilian merchant vessels."

Leaning forward in his chair, Reyes looked to T'Prynn. "What do you suppose are the odds that this is connected to the cargo bay thefts and Ensign Malhotra's murder?"

T'Prynn paused to consider the theory before offering a succinct nod. "That would be a logical hypothesis, Commodore." She turned to Ballard. "I assume you have compiled a list of the involved vessels?"

The engineer pointed to the data slate lying atop Reyes's desk. "We're still following the trails, Commander, but I've got a preliminary list ready to go."

"Excellent work, gentlemen," Reyes said. Tapping his finger on the hard, polished surface of his desk, he added, "This also means that at least one of the people involved may be responsible for killing a member of my crew." The commodore's expression hardened into a determined scowl as he turned to T'Prynn. "Find those people, Commander."

CHAPTER

7

The walls were closing in around him.

That was the sensation gripping Isaiah Farber, anyway, as he once again negotiated the narrow confines of yet another of the station's Jefferies tubes. His muscles felt as though they might seize whenever he passed a shadowy intersection or ventilation duct. Everywhere he looked, he saw the dead, fixed eyes of Ensign Malhotra. Every instinct told him to turn back or to push through the closest exit from the access crawlway and into the nearest corridor.

Instead, he pressed on.

The crawlway met an intersection, an orange tri-sided ladder at its center, and Farber checked his location against the station schematic he had loaded to his tricorder. Satisfied that this was the junction he wanted, the engineer stepped out onto the ladder and began descending. All the while, the tricorder continued to emit an intermittent series of tones telling him that it was continuing to scan in accordance with the parameters he had programmed, but that it had not yet found what he sought.

Examining one of the five compromised sensor nodes they had discovered, al-Khaled and Ballard were able to determine that the covert communications signals were in fact being routed through the station's comm and data networks. They also had determined that such clandestine measures would require additional modifications to those networks. Someone with the proper expertise would easily have been able to conceal the necessary hardware components among the networks' existing infrastructure.

Scans of the station's interior from sensor control had revealed clues as to the general location of what probably were unauthorized or subversive modifications to the comm network. Pinpointing those components would require proximity scans via tricorder, which meant going over the target area of the network centimeter by centimeter. A slow process, Farber admitted, but a necessary one.

It might even have paid off, he thought as the whine of his active tricorder changed both in tone and speed. Pausing his descent on the ladder, the engineer reached for the unit and studied its small display.

"No hiding from me," he said aloud, looking about the shaft until he found the data conduit access panel several meters below him and to his left.

After reaching the appropriate service platform mounted to the side of the tube's bulkhead, Farber pulled his communicator from the small of his back and flipped it open. "Farber to al-Khaled."

"Al-Khaled here," his friend answered a moment later. *"What have you got, Isaiah?"*

"I think I've found the data hub we're looking for," Farber answered. Kneeling so that he could get a better look at the access panel, he set his communicator down on the platform near his left foot before holding his tricorder up to the panel. "Mahmud, reset the array cycle and see if we can't trigger this thing."

"Stand by," al-Khaled replied. *"Resetting . . . now."*

In an instant, Farber's tricorder beeped in triumph, displaying the fluctuation in the communications network he wanted to see. "That's it. Hold on while I get this panel open." Deactivating the tricorder, Farber let it hang from his shoulder as he extracted a work light from his tool satchel. He cast its bright beam on the access panel's smooth surface, and his eyes were drawn to a series of small nicks and scratches surrounding the panel's magnetic locking mechanism.

"Somebody forced their way into this junction," he reported. It was the first evidence of sloppy workmanship they had yet encountered during their investigation of the illicit tampering to the communications system. *Interesting.*

Farber deactivated the work light and returned it to his satchel, exchanging it for his P-38. Though in reality nothing more than a glorified Starfleet can opener, the small tool emitted focused emissions of light and sound that were ideal for disabling the magnetic seals on doors and—in this case—access panels. Pulling aside the now unlocked panel, Farber peered inside to find the expected collection of wiring, duotronic circuits, and optical cabling that all combined to form the network data hub ensconced within the compartment.

He also saw the single element that was not part of the expected ensemble of components: a palm-sized metallic disc rimmed with muted amber lights.

"Well," he said to no one in particular, "there you are."

After first determining—to the best of his ability, anyway—that the transmitter was not in any way booby-trapped, Farber extracted the device before descending the rest of the way down the Jefferies tube until he met up with al-Khaled and Ballard, who both waited for him inside Cargo Bay 12. Though an immense chamber—one of many aboard the station—the bay seemed almost cramped thanks to the numerous transport containers of varying size and shape stacked throughout the room.

Ballard, unshaven, his uniform wrinkled and his blond hair disheveled—a consequence of having worked almost continuously for the past thirty-six hours—smiled in obvious relief upon seeing Farber emerge from the access shaft.

"I'll be damned," the station's chief engineer said as he held the transmitter in his hand and studied it with a critical eye. "This is Rigelian technology."

Nodding, al-Khaled said, "I know. I recognized the markings on the base plate, too. Nothing more than a signal pulse scrambler and burst transmitter, designed to relay data fed to it by whatever system it's hooked into. Pretty common stuff, actually."

"Which means it'll be almost impossible to trace," Farber said, wiping perspiration from his brow. The air in the Jefferies tube had been warm and humid, and he was thankful to be back in the cooler environs of the cargo bay. Though he did not say so aloud, of course, he also was thankful for leaving behind the cramped confines of the crawlways. Along with the image of Ensign Malhotra that still haunted him, an irrational fear of perhaps coming across the person responsible for the man's death had gnawed at him the entire time he was traversing the access shafts.

Still holding the device in his hand, Ballard crossed the room to where he had left his own tool satchel sitting next to the door. From the satchel he retrieved a small diagnostic scanner. "If I remember correctly, these things carry a chip that records between twelve and twenty quads of data about the messages it relays. There might be something we can give to Lieutenant Jackson for his investigation."

A short, sharp tone echoed in the cargo bay, and Farber and al-Khaled turned in Ballard's direction. Farber saw that a new series of indicator lights had begun to flash across the surface of the transmitter.

"What's that about?" he asked.

Ballard shook his head as he waved his scanner over the device. "I don't know. Its receiver just activated," he said, still scanning as he turned to walk back toward them. "I didn't think these things worked without being plugged into a network."

Frowning, Farber replied. "They're not supposed to. Maybe it's been modified."

"It'd have to be," Ballard said. "I'm picking up a power reading."

Then Farber saw his eyes widen in comprehension.

"Curtis!" al-Khaled shouted from behind him an instant before Farber felt his friend pull him backward just as a dazzling red glow flared from the transmitter. A piercing whine filled the air of the cargo bay as the energy flare expanded and washed over Ballard's body, consuming him in a rippling crimson sheath before fading into nothingness, taking the engineer and the transmitter with it.

The only sound Farber heard was his own frantic, rapid breathing. Spots danced in his vision as he stared at the spot where Ballard had stood seconds before. No evidence remained of what had just happened—or that the lieutenant had even existed in the first place.

"Oh my God . . ." was all he could muster, the words fading as they passed his lips. Then he felt a hand on his arm, al-Khaled's, as his friend helped him to his feet.

"That wasn't a booby trap," al-Khaled said, stepping to where Ballard last had been standing. "You heard what he said. That thing was receiving a transmission." Farber saw the other man's jawline tighten in harnessed anger. "Someone deliberately sent a self-destruct signal."

His hand trembling as he reached for his communicator, Farber nodded. "We have to notify security and Commodore Reyes," he said. "We've got teams out looking for more of those damned things, and whoever did this might trigger those, too." In addition to the obvious potential for further casualties, the transmitters might inflict additional damage to the station's data and communications networks if destroyed while still embedded within other data hubs and transfer points.

"Maybe we can jam any incoming signals," al-Khaled said, reaching up to wipe his brow, and Farber saw that his friend also was rattled by what they had just witnessed. "Or find a way to trace them to a source." Shaking his head, he grimaced in what Farber recognized as mounting frustration and perhaps even a bit of helplessness. "Something, I don't know." Casting glances about the cargo bay, he shook his head. "I need to think."

Giving al-Khaled a moment to compose himself, Farber

flipped open his communicator, but as he reached for the switch to activate the unit, he froze in mid-motion.

To his right, a shadow moved among the stacks of cargo containers at the same instant he registered light reflecting from something metallic.

"Mahmud!" Farber shouted as the shadow moved and then the reflective object was sailing through the air. Farber dropped to the deck without thinking even as he felt the rush of displaced air on his face before something struck the container behind him with a dull thud. Rolling to his left, the engineer was able to see the blade and handle of a long, rather nasty-looking knife, still vibrating from where it had embedded itself into the side of the container.

Pulling himself to his feet, Farber turned at the same moment he detected movement in his peripheral vision and nearly flinched in response to the dark-clothed humanoid bearing down on him. He had time only to raise an arm in defense as something hit his chest, pushing him backward and slamming him into another large transport case. Farber exhaled sharply at the impact, scrambling to maintain his balance as the shadowy figure again danced in his vision, but no follow-up attack came.

"Isaiah!" he heard al-Khaled shout from somewhere in front of him.

The assailant, cloaked from head to toe in a one-piece black bodysuit that served to accentuate his muscled physique, turned on his heel and bore down on al-Khaled. The engineer saw the onrushing attacker and tried to backpedal in a desperate attempt to give himself some maneuvering room, but the intruder closed the gap between them with uncanny speed. He was on al-Khaled in scarcely a heartbeat, lashing out with one thick arm to strike the lieutenant in the left temple. Al-Khaled staggered to his left, stunned by the blow and completely vulnerable to the next strike as his attacker kicked him in the chest, sending him falling to the deck.

Farber released a near-maniacal cry of anger and determination as he lunged forward. The outburst had the desired effect, startling the intruder if only for an instant as he turned to confront the onrushing engineer. Trapped between two stacks of cargo containers, he had nowhere to escape. He held his ground and Farber lowered his shoulder and plunged forward, ignoring the glint of light on new metal as he threw his entire body into the attack, catching the cloaked figure just under his chin.

He sensed the swing of his opponent's knife hand and lashed upward with his left arm, halting the downswing of the blade over his head even as he punched at the intruder with his other arm. Farber heard a satisfying grunt of pain as his fist sank into the soft flesh of the attacker's lower torso.

Still, the other man was faster, his arms and legs moving with incredible speed as he pushed himself away from Farber. The knife sliced forward again, and this time the engineer winced as hot pain lanced down his left forearm. Instinct pulled him away and he felt a dull throbbing in his arm, in synch with his rapid heartbeat as he looked down to the thin incision from his wrist to his elbow. Blood streamed from the new wound to stain the gold material of his sliced shirt sleeve.

Then he sensed movement and lurched to his right as his assailant jumped toward him again. In a blind grab, Farber managed to catch the attacker's arm in his own massive hand. With a furious growl he pulled the arm down and around until his opponent was forced to turn his back to him. The knife clattered to the deck and he howled in pain as Farber forced his arm up between his shoulder blades. With his free hand—the one now slick with his own blood—he gripped the back of the other man's head and pushed him forward to slam his face into the side of a nearby cargo container. The attacker cried out in renewed pain, but the engineer ignored it as he pushed his head forward again, repeating the blow to the intruder's face.

Despite all of that the assailant was still struggling to free himself. Still gripping the other man's wrist in his right hand, Farber pulled upward until he felt the arm separate from the shoulder socket with a dull pop. The attacker screamed, but the renewed agony only seemed to fuel his own movements. Pushing off from the cargo container, he spun with startling speed and lashed out with his good arm, catching Farber just below his throat. The engineer staggered back before tripping over the edge of a smaller cargo box and crashing to the deck in a clumsy heap.

His vision blurry from the force of the attack, Farber shook his head even as he rolled to his side and back to his feet. Arms out and away from his body in a defensive stance, he tensed for a new attack but instead heard only the sounds of footsteps running away from him. Looking around, he finally caught sight of the attacker dashing through an open doorway at the end of the cargo bay, disappearing into the corridor beyond.

"You could have gotten yourself killed, you know."

Farber nodded in agreement as he watched Ezekiel Fisher, the station's chief medical officer, tend to his wounded left arm. Dressed in the blue tunic of Starfleet's sciences branch, Fisher was a human male of African descent, perhaps eighty years old, who carried himself with a quiet authority that the engineer instinctively trusted. His black hair and beard were liberally laced with streaks of gray, and his dark brown eyes carried the wealth of professional and personal baggage that Farber would have expected from a man of his years.

Though al-Khaled had applied emergency first aid to treat Farber's wound, it had required the services of a medical professional. Farber was thankful that the cut, though running nearly the length of his forearm, was not at all deep. No tendons had been severed and the blade had missed hitting a vein. Fisher had made short work of things, cleansing the cut before treating it with a dermal protoplaser. Within twenty-four hours, there would not even be a scar.

Still, it hurt like hell.

"We found two knives," Lieutenant Jackson said as he stepped around a stack of cargo cases and approached Farber and Fisher, a data slate clipped to his left hip and a canvas carrying bag slung over his right shoulder. Of Farber, he asked, "You didn't get a good look at him?"

"Good enough to know he was wearing a body suit," Farber replied, "including a full face mask."

"A stealth suit," al-Khaled added as he moved to stand next to Jackson. "Used by Starfleet special operations personnel. They mask body heat to avoid infrared detection."

Frowning, Jackson replied. "Which would explain why he wasn't picked up on internal sensors." He released a tired sigh. "Wonderful." To the engineers, he said, "He was shadowing you while you searched for the data transmitter. For all we know, he was on his way to get the thing before you beat him to it, and he improvised from there." Looking back toward the center of the cargo bay, where members of his security staff were at this moment conducting a thorough investigation of the entire scene, he shook his head. "Damn. Ballard was a good guy."

Farber felt a pang of guilt in his gut as he nodded in agreement. Though he knew he could have done nothing to save Ballard, he was certain that the device would likely have claimed his own life but for sheer timing.

I'm so sorry, Curtis.

"We want to help you find who killed him," al-Khaled said as though echoing that thought, nodding with a conviction Farber knew only too well. There was no mistaking the set to his friend's jaw or the look in his eyes. Now, the matter was personal, and he wanted it resolved.

Jackson replied, "I'll take all the help I can get. Station security is one thing, but murder investigations and forensics are out of my league." Retrieving his data slate, the security chief

activated the unit, using its accompanying stylus to scribble
something on the slate's faceplate.

"I'm transferring the evidence to you, Doctor," he said as
he reached into the shoulder bag and extracted a pair of long,
thin blades—each inside its own sealed container. "I'd like to
know if a blade like one of these might have been used on Ensign Malhotra."

Nodding, the doctor replied, "I'll get on it right away, Lieutenant. I should know something in an hour or so."

Everyone in the room looked up as the lights flickered, and
for a brief moment Farber felt his stomach lurch—a familiar
reaction when moving from one artificial gravity field to another.

Life support's acting up?

"Now what?" Jackson said, squinting his eyes in response to
the still-blinking lights. Reaching for his own communicator,
he flipped it open. "Jackson to operations. What's going on?"

The voice of Commander Jon Cooper, Vanguard's executive
officer, replied, *"Cooper here, Jacks. Looks like a batch of new
trouble with that alien signal or whatever the hell it is. You still
with those engineers from the* Lovell?"

"Damn," Farber said, shaking his head in resignation. "I
thought we had that thing figured out."

"Apparently not," al-Khaled replied, sighing in irritation.

Nodding, though Cooper could not see it, Jackson said into
his communicator, "Yeah, they're still here."

A burst of static met his response before Cooper's voice
came back. *"Send them to main engineering. Looks like we still
need their help."* His statement was met with another bout of
crackling interference, sure indications that the mysterious
carrier wave was meddling with communications now, as well.

Farber's eyes met al-Khaled's as the lieutenant asked, "You
up for it?"

"Yeah," the engineer replied, feeling a sense of obligation to
assist in the tragic absence of Curtis Ballard. "Let's go."

CHAPTER
8

The workstation nearest to the door exploded just as al-Khaled entered primary engineering control.

Throwing up his arms to protect his face, the engineer ducked to his right to avoid the worst of the blast, feeling the heat of sparks and bits of plastic composite shrapnel peppering his uniform and exposed skin.

"Mahmud!" Farber called out as he entered the room behind al-Khaled, shouting to be heard over the alarm Klaxon echoing throughout the chamber. "Are you all right?"

"I'm fine," al-Khaled replied as he brushed still-warm pieces of small shrapnel from his tunic. Noting Farber's torn and still blood-stained left sleeve as well as his somewhat ashen complexion, he asked again, "Are you *sure* you're up for this?"

Farber nodded. "Don't worry about me. Let's see what we can do to help."

Al-Khaled looked about the control room and quickly found Lieutenant Shepherd, second-in-command of the station's engineering department, bent over a console, her hands moving frenetically over the array of controls before her. Working at adjacent stations were Ensign Tamishiro, whom al-Khaled remembered from the earlier incident with the environmental control system, and Ensign Ghrex from his own team.

"Supplement power from the auxiliary generators," Shepherd said, pointing to one display monitor at Tamishiro's workstation before reaching up to brush sweat-matted auburn hair from her eyes. "I don't want life support acting up on us again. And shut off that damned alarm!"

Stepping back from the station to consult another cluster of status monitors, the engineer caught sight of al-Khaled and Farber crossing the room toward her, and al-Khaled noted the strain, fatigue, and grief in her eyes. Word about Ballard's death doubtless had spread throughout the station's crew with undue haste, and he recognized the look of someone forced to set aside their personal feelings of sadness and loss in order to concentrate on the situation at hand.

"What's happening this time?" al-Khaled asked as the alert Klaxon faded. Without its blaring report bouncing off the bulkheads, the control center was quiet save for frantic movements and short, terse interactions between the ten or so engineers moving and working about the room.

"That damned signal," Shepherd replied. "Even worse this time, and it's not even trying to be subtle anymore. Now it's pushing and beating its way through everything in its way. If it keeps up, it'll tear the guts out of this station."

Farber asked, "But still the same frequency and modulation as before?"

Behind her, Ghrex turned and looked up from her console. "Yes, sir. The only difference now is the intensity. It's wreaking havoc on every sensitive onboard system simultaneously. Computer access has been compromised, the primary long-range sensor array is offline, and so is the intrastation communications network. Even our portable communicators are experiencing some measure of interference."

"We've got other problems, too," Shepherd added. "I've gotten word that the *Lovell*'s experiencing fluctuations in her warp engines. One dilithium crystal's already fractured, and your chief engineer is performing an emergency shutdown in the hopes of preventing more damage." She shook her head. "Thank God our support ships are all out on assignment, otherwise we might be looking at a quartet of warp engine overloads." Casting a glance toward Tamishiro, she asked, "What about that Orion ship?"

"Its main engines are offline," the Asian woman replied without looking up from her station. "Their mechanics aren't completely incompetent after all, it seems."

"What about the station's power generators?" al-Khaled asked. "Aren't you having problems with them, as well?"

Moving to an adjacent console, Shepherd nodded. "You don't know the half of it. We're picking up spikes in both main power plants, and our attitude control system is also starting to act up." She indicated one display monitor with a wave of her hand. "Maneuvering thrusters are firing at random, and I've had to assign three of my people to try and coordinate manual adjustments until we can override the system."

Al-Khaled pictured an image of the station in his mind, bobbing and weaving through empty space in response to its unruly attitude control thrusters. When overseen properly by designated automated processes, the collection of small thruster ports positioned across the outer hull of the starbase kept it stationary at its assigned coordinates and corrected for drift.

And what happens when they're not looked after?

"What can we do to help?" Farber asked, his attention splitting between Shepherd and the collection of status gauges and monitors behind her, far too many of which were displaying troublesome if not alarming information.

Blowing out a sigh of mounting frustration, Shepherd replied, "If you could pull one of those fancy Corps of Engineers miracles out of your pocket, that'd be great right about now."

As she and Farber moved to a nearby workstation, something groaned beneath al-Khaled's feet, channeling vibrations up through the deck plating and across the bulkheads. To him the sound was all too familiar: that of duranium and trititanium protesting at being pulled and twisted in manners with which they did not agree.

"That can't be good," Farber said, and al-Khaled saw the

expression of worry beginning to take hold on the muscled lieutenant's features. Shepherd turned to say something in response, but the words were lost as a renewed alarm Klaxon blared to life, its cacophonous, rolling wail once more filling the room.

Then al-Khaled felt it. Almost imperceptible at first, it took only heartbeats for him to identify the sensation of gravity pulling him in a different direction than normal. Recognition dawned in the instant before he felt the deck shift the barest fraction beneath his feet.

"The thrusters!" he called out even as his stomach registered the shift in his center of gravity. Lunging across the room, he gripped the edge of a console as the angle of the floor continued to increase. All around the control center, other members of the engineering staff were encountering similar difficulty. Those seated at workstations were able to anchor themselves against the increasing slope of the deck, while others like him scrambled and stumbled for something to which they might cling.

"Can't we just shut them off?" Farber shouted from the station he now staffed, sitting in the chair and holding on to the console before him.

Hitting a control to silence the current alarm, Shepherd replied, "Attitude control is unresponsive." She had wedged herself between the edge of one workstation and the narrow service ladder leading up to the room's second deck. "Random thrusters are firing intermittently." As she made the report, al-Khaled felt the deck plating beginning to tilt in a new direction.

Without instructions from the system's self-correcting algorithms, the thrusters, if left unchecked and if they fired in just the right sequence, conceivably could push the station into a frenzied tumble. While structural integrity and inertial damping fields as well as artificial gravity would—for a time, at least—keep Vanguard's inhabitants from suffering the worst effects of such chaotic movement, the truth was that the station simply was not designed to withstand this sort of prolonged stress for any great length of time.

In other words, we have a big problem.

"If this keeps up," Shepherd said through gritted teeth, "the station could tear itself apart."

That would be the problem.

"We're getting calls from all over the station," Tamishiro shouted from where she still clung to her console, a communications receiver inserted into her ear. "Injury and damage reports, the works."

"Forget all of that," Shepherd ordered. "Find me a way into attitude control, damn it!"

All around him, al-Khaled heard and felt the mounting strain on the very structure of the station, its support frame beginning now to protest with conviction the stresses being placed upon it. Still holding on to the edge of his console, he reached out and managed to enter a command string to request a diagnostic task for the structural integrity system, and was relieved to see that it still appeared to be functioning normally.

How long will that last?

A two-note tone chirped from the communicator clipped to his waistband. Retrieving the device, he flipped its antenna grid open and pressed the activation switch. "Al-Khaled here."

There was a pause before the connection was completed, and then a hiss of static burst from the communicator's speaker grille before he got a reply. *"Mr. al-Khaled, this is Lieutenant T'Laen."* Though the interference degrading the channel was still audible, it was not enough to drown out the computer specialist's voice. *"I have been analyzing this latest transmission and I believe I have a theory."*

"This really isn't the time, T'Laen," al-Khaled said, swiveling his chair toward the control console and planting his feet against the bulkhead underneath as the room began to tilt in yet another direction, though this time the angle and the speed of the shift was not as pronounced.

"I believe this signal to be automated," the Vulcan said, undeterred by al-Khaled's discouragement, *"much like the original carrier wave. Many of the linguistic algorithms involved appear to be similar, though there are new variables I have not yet been able to study. Still, my preliminary analysis suggests parallels which might—"*

"T'Laen!" al-Khaled snapped. "The concise version, if you please."

"Simply put, Mr. al-Khaled, I believe that the person or technology responsible for sending the original signal received our reply, and that entity is now responding in kind. It is my assertion that we are, in effect, being hailed and that the signal's origin point is awaiting our reply."

"Can we skip to the part where this helps us?" Farber shouted from where he sat, two consoles to al-Khaled's left.

In her typical fashion, T'Laen ignored the emotional outburst. *"I am attempting to create a new reply to send in much the same manner as we did earlier."*

"That will take too much time," al-Khaled said. "The station won't put up with these erratic positioning corrections long enough to wait for a change in the signal."

Farber said, "What about—"

"Emergency shutdown!" Shepherd called out, cutting off her fellow engineer.

Nodding excitedly, Farber replied, "Exactly!"

"I don't understand," al-Khaled said.

Turning in his seat and bracing himself against his workstation to keep from falling from his chair, Farber replied, "Think about it. The original signal reacted to our message. What if whoever or whatever sent it didn't just stop, but instead studied T'Laen's message and composed a reply? They could be looking for someone or something to talk to. If we don't give it an answer, maybe they'll stop transmitting their own signal."

"Not only do we not answer," Shepherd added, "but we make it look like there's no one here anymore." Her attention now was focused on her console and the rapid-fire sequences of commands she was making to the station's central computer. "Turn everything off and make like a hole in space."

Skeptical about what he was hearing, al-Khaled asked, "Can we do that? Shut down *everything*?" So far as he knew, an operational space station never had faced a situation whereby every onboard system was deactivated, especially if—at the time—said station was populated.

"We may not need everything," Farber said. "Battery power at minimum levels and only used in those areas that absolutely require it should be enough."

As the lieutenant and Ghrex set to work assisting Shepherd and Tamishiro, al-Khaled communicated the plan to T'Laen, with the recommendation that the *Lovell* follow similar protocols. That accomplished, and while doing his best to ignore the pitching and bouncing that were reminiscent of sitting in a small boat on the open ocean, the engineer pitched in with what quickly had become a long list of items to check and verify in preparation for Farber and Shepherd's unorthodox scheme. Al-Khaled himself drew responsibility for ensuring critical systems such as structural integrity and life support as well as the handful of special environmental habitats for the station's decidedly nonhumanoid contingent.

"All set," Farber reported, casting a thumbs-up gesture toward Shepherd, and al-Khaled noted that the brawny engineer's face appeared to have lost most of it color. Was his friend experiencing motion sickness, a condition perhaps exacerbated by his recent injury?

Hang in there, Isaiah.

Shepherd called out. "We're ready. Mr. al-Khaled?"

"Standing by," he replied. "I've coded bypasses for sickbay, environmental control, this room, and the escape pods." Both Shepherd and Farber turned to look at him in response to the last item, and he shrugged. "Just in case." He felt no need to complete the thought aloud, as everyone in the room knew what was at stake. A failure to arrest the station's increasingly unstable movements would almost certainly require evacuation.

"Here we go, then," Shepherd said, reaching to her console once more to key the power-down sequence she had just written. Without saying anything more, she pressed the control to activate the newly authored protocol.

The effect was immediate—on the room's collection of status monitors, at least. Multicolored lines representing power flow, short-range sensor telemetry, the ebb and flow of station-wide communications—one by one, the graphic representation of these functions morphed from spikes and valleys on their respective charts to flat, dull white lines. Far below the engineering deck, the faint yet still perceptible reverberations from the station's main power generators faded from perception, and the only clue offered when they finally did power down was the row of indicator messages on the monitor in front of al-Khaled going dormant.

Then the control center was plunged into darkness as primary power faded altogether, and even the comforting buzz of the ventilation system dissipated. Battery-backup illumination activated almost instantly, bathing everything in a warm crimson light that stretched and distorted the shadows now dominating the room. Then auxiliary power kicked in, returning the workstations to life.

"Thrusters are deactivated," Farber called out a moment later. "We're still drifting, but at least now we're not being jerked around all over the place. Just a nice, slow roll."

"Good thing we're not orbiting a planet," al-Khaled replied. Looking to Shepherd, he released a small smile. "Otherwise, your doctor would likely be tending to motion sickness for the rest of the day."

"What do we do now?" Ghrex asked.

Shepherd shrugged. "Now we wait."

Al-Khaled knew from T'Laen's earlier report that it could take as long as eight hours for any kind of response to be detected. Of course, such thinking assumed that the transmission possessed sufficient similarity to the original signal for such predictions to be anywhere close to accurate. What if it was

substantially different? What did it mean? Were the originators of the mysterious carrier waves really trying to communicate?

All questions worth pondering, he decided as he executed
another diagnostic task, which reported that the structural integrity system showed no fluctuations or other signs of trouble.
By all accounts, it should be able to hold its own until attitude
thruster control could be restored.

Assuming the field holds, or if this idea even works.

Even as the notion crossed his mind, al-Khaled decided that
he really would be better off if he ever could learn to stop harboring such negative thoughts.

CHAPTER

9

Farber's arm itched.

Seated in a booth adjacent to the front window inside Tom Walker's place—one of several bars located in Stars Landing—the engineer could not resist pushing back his left sleeve and scratching at the newly healed section of skin that had been treated by Dr. Fisher. It was not the first time Farber had received treatment for lacerations with a dermal protoplaser, and on each previous occasion he had experienced similar discomfort. In fact, his roommate on the *Lovell*, Lieutenant Paul LeGere, had teased him without mercy for a week following one particularly nasty—and embarrassing—injury.

Farber had gotten even, of course, and though his method of retribution had not been painful, it had eliminated LeGere's need for a comb for months afterward.

Glancing about the bar's interior, the engineer took in the cozy atmosphere permeating the room. All around him, conversations and laughter were the order of the day. Uniforms mingled with all manner of other attire, as members of the station's Starfleet and civilian complements enjoyed a meal and drink, be it after long duty shifts or following a long journey to the station from some far-off location.

Behind the bar, one employee was stocking the shelves lining the back wall, working to replace bottles of liquor and glassware damaged or destroyed during the station's recent bout with mechanical difficulty. Other than that, the tavern lent itself to relaxation, with its subdued lighting, dark wood furnishings, tasty cuisine, and a selection of libations from worlds throughout the Federation.

I could get used to this place, Farber thought.

He was reaching for the pint of beer situated near his left hand when a shadow flickered in his peripheral vision, followed by a hint of Starfleet gold. Looking up, Farber saw the face of Captain Okagawa.

"Good evening, sir," the engineer said, attempting to rise to his feet before Okagawa waved him back to his seat.

"At ease, Lieutenant," the captain said as he slid into the booth across from him. "I was just on my way to meet Commander zh'Rhun for dinner when I saw you through the window. We're eating at Manón's, if you're interested." Smiling, he added, "Commodore Reyes tells me the food is exquisite."

Shaking his head, Farber replied, "I took a look in there earlier, sir. Not really my kind of place." He indicated their surroundings with a wave of his hand. "This is more my style."

"Fair enough." Pointing to Farber's left arm, Okagawa asked, "How's the wing?"

Pulling his sleeve back into place, Farber replied, "Coming along nicely, sir. For a passing shot, it was a pretty nasty cut, but I'll be fine." Frowning, he asked, "How are things shaping up after that last bout of malfunctions?"

"Repairs are under way," the captain said. "Burnouts and overloads all over the station. Some sections are still without power as the priority repairs are addressed first, things like that. Nothing critical, but I hear some of the folks living in the apartment complexes aren't too happy." Rubbing his chin, he added, "As for the carrier wave, that idea you and Lieutenant Shepherd came up with seems to have worked. It stopped transmitting a little over eight hours after everything was shut down, just like the first time around."

Farber nodded. He had read Lieutenant T'Laen's report on the latest version of the signal, including her theory that whatever had transmitted it was performing the equivalent of a confirmation with regard to the first signal. As the station had not communicated anything resembling the reply, the originator of the carrier wave seemed to have lost interest.

For now, at any rate. It had been almost ten hours since full power had been restored to the station, and the mysterious transmission had not returned. There was no way to know if it ever would, or if it would be even more powerful—and damaging—than it had to this point. That, it seemed, would be a puzzle for Vanguard's crew to solve.

"Any word about casualties?" Farber asked.

Leaning against the booth's high seatback, Okagawa said, "Seems we got lucky this time. A few broken bones, some bruises and cuts like yours. Nothing that won't heal."

"A shame we can't say the same about Lieutenant Ballard, or Ensign Malhotra," Farber said, releasing a tired sigh as he reached for his mug and took a long pull of his beer. He grimaced as he swallowed the brew, which seemed suddenly to have lost its enticing flavor.

Okagawa said, "Everyone has done a fine job helping out the station's crew with their various troubles, Isaiah, but I have to say I'm particularly impressed with your work since we got here. I know it hasn't been easy with the . . . added difficulties."

"You mean my being a material witness in two murder investigations?" Farber asked. "It's been weighing on my mind a bit, sir, if that's what you're wondering."

"Well," Okagawa said, "you'll be happy to know there's some news on that front. The knives recovered from the cargo bay where you were attacked appear to be the same type of blade as that used to kill the ensign. That's the report from the station's CMO, at any rate."

His brow furrowing, Farber said, "So, whoever attacked us likely killed Malhotra, and was probably at least involved in planting those transmitters."

"Not a certainty, but it's definitely a working theory," Okagawa replied. "Search parties found four more of those transmitters, but they're being left in place for now until a way can be figured out to circumvent the self-destruct mechanism." Sighing, he added, "As for the transmissions themselves, so far all Commander T'Prynn has been able to determine is that they were routed from different points on the station to various ships that either were embarked at the station or passing in close proximity, including that Orion ship that's still docked."

His eyes widening in surprise, Farber said, "I can't believe Commodore Reyes hasn't torn that ship apart yet."

Okagawa shook his head. "Not that simple, I'm afraid. Given the open nature of that gaming facility and other . . . unsavory activities taking place aboard that tub at any hour of the day, anyone could have been on the other end of the communication. There's no hard proof linking it to the owner of the ship, which is pretty much par for the course when it comes to Orions."

"That's an understatement, sir." Though Farber himself had never had cause to cross paths with any members of the Orion Syndicate, he had heard stories of the sorts of activities for which they were known—slave trading, black marketeering, arms dealing, and so on. One of their infamous hallmarks was their ability to maintain deniability of their involvement in various illicit enterprises, particularly if it involved operating beneath the notice of the various sovereign governments within and bordering Federation space. Though the Orions claimed to be a neutral body when it came to the ever-changing political landscape, they had a habit of turning up wherever it seemed to be to their advantage.

If the captain of the Orion vessel docked at Vanguard indeed was involved in the string of thefts, infiltration of the station's communications system, and the deaths of Ballard and Malhotra, it meant that he was an especially cunning sort, but also bold almost to the arrogant extreme to carry out such acts and schemes right under the collective noses of more than a thousand Starfleet personnel.

Rising from his seat, Okagawa said, "Well, I don't wish to keep Commander zh'Rhun waiting. You know how she can be when she doesn't eat." He smiled at his own joke, though Farber watched it fade as the captain caught sight of something outside the window. "Speaking of Orions, there's something you don't see every day." He nodded in that direction, and Farber turned to see what had captured his attention.

It was an Orion man, standing near the entrance to another bar next to an Arcturian male. They appeared to be engaged in conversation, though each of them also was dividing his attention to the comings and goings of various passersby—paying particular attention to the female variety. Tall and slender, the Orion was dressed in a long tan robe that all but concealed everything below his neck. He gestured and pointed with his left hand, his movements slow and subtle, and everything about his body language suggested to Farber that he was doing his level best to remain inconspicuous, all while failing rather badly at the attempt.

"I recognize him," Okagawa said. "From a picture, anyway. Commander T'Prynn told us about him after zh'Rhun's little altercation aboard the Orion ship. His name's Jaeq. Hired muscle, supposedly."

As Farber watched the Orion and his associate continuing their conversation, the door to the bar abruptly swung outward, pushed open by a staggering, obviously inebriated Tellarite dressed in the dark coveralls of a merchant freighter crew member. The door did not swing with any great degree of force or speed, and when it struck Jaeq in the right arm it did so only lightly.

Despite that, he flinched, and Farber felt the small hairs rise on the back of his neck. With narrowing eyes, the engineer watched as the Orion grimaced in obvious pain as he reached for his shoulder, his right arm hanging limp at his side.

"Call security," Farber said as he bolted from his seat and navigated his way out of the bar, ignoring Okagawa's confused reaction to the sudden request. Without trying to appear too anxious, the engineer made his way across the thoroughfare between buildings in this part of Stars Landing's entertainment district.

He had almost crossed the concourse when Jaeq noticed him, his eyes narrowing in suspicion. Though Jaeq managed to school his features, Farber was sure he caught a hint of recognition on the Orion's face.

I'll be damned.

"Excuse me," the engineer said as he stepped closer, smiling. "Do you have the time?"

Confusion crossed the Orion's face, just enough for Farber to close the remaining distance. In one quick motion, he reached out and gripped the other man's right shoulder, and another expression of pain lanced across Jaeq's features.

"Still tender?" Farber hissed through gritted teeth. There was no mistaking the look of concern and growing panic on the Orion's face. "I thought we'd finish what we started down in the cargo bay."

His lips peeling back in a snarl that revealed stark white teeth, Jaeq pushed away and lashed out with his other arm, his fist aiming for Farber's head. Though the engineer ducked to one side and avoided all but a glancing blow, it was enough to make him move aside and give the Orion an opening. Jaeq kicked with his left leg, catching Farber in the stomach and sending him tumbling to the floor.

People around him scattered as they became aware of the altercation developing in their midst even as Farber pulled himself to his feet. Looking up, he was in time to see the Orion plunging into the throng of people milling about on the concourse.

"Stop him!" Farber shouted even as he set off in pursuit, his eyes tracking the bobbing and weaving of Jaeq's green head as he ran through the crowd. The lieutenant was only dimly aware of Okagawa's voice behind him, shouting that security was on the way. There might have been something about not chasing after the Orion, but he ignored it.

He ran as fast as his legs would push him, trying to close the gap Jaeq had opened up between them. The Orion was grabbing at people as he passed them, pushing past them and sometimes tugging them to the deck. Farber tried to dodge the living obstacles, but one misstep sent him stumbling to avoid a fallen Rigelian woman. As he regained his balance and renewed the chase, he was in time to see Jaeq disappear around a corner of the building at the end of the faux street comprising this section of the district.

Setting off again, Farber dashed down the concourse until he made it to the end of the lane. He rounded the bend and found himself looking at what essentially was a portion of Stars Landing's support facilities: warehouse doors and back entrances to the buildings comprising the restaurants, clubs, and other venues for this area of the esplanade. He counted thirteen doors of varying sizes, some open, some not. A few people were standing around, some of them sporting perplexed expressions while others appeared to be oblivious to what might have just happened.

And no sign of Jaeq.

Instead, Farber's eyes came to rest on the rumpled tan robe lying on the ground ten meters ahead of him.

Stealth suit.

"Damn it!"

Remembering the conversation with al-Khaled and Lieutenant Jackson in the cargo bay after the earlier altercation with Jaeq, Farber slammed a fist against the façade of the building. If the Orion had still been wearing the black garment underneath his robe, he likely had all he required to avoid being tracked by the internal sensors in this part of the station.

So intense was his mounting anger that Farber did not hear his communicator until it signaled a second time for attention. Retrieving the unit from his waistband, he flipped it open and pressed the activation control.

"Farber here," he said, pushing the words out between rapid breaths.

"Where the hell are you?" the voice of Okagawa yelled from the communicator's speaker grille.

"It was him, Captain," Farber replied. "The one who attacked me and al-Khaled. He killed Ballard and probably Malhotra, too. He got away."

Okagawa said, *"Security's alerted, Isaiah. Don't worry, he won't get far. In fact, there's really only one place he can go."*

CHAPTER
10

Ganz, Okagawa decided, was one gigantic son of a bitch.

The Orion seemed to fill the hatchway leading from the docking platform to his ship, the *Omari-Ekon*. Standing just inside the hatch's threshold, dressed in blue silken trousers and a matching shirt left open to expose his well-developed chest complete with an array of gold and silver piercings, Ganz was all but cloaked in shadow due to the reduced illumination inside the ship's airlock. The gloom lent a subdued gray pallor to his jade skin, and did much to enhance the expression of barely contained disdain clouding his face as he looked down at Reyes, who stood less than two meters in front of him.

"I want Jaeq," the commodore said. Though not a small man, Reyes still was dwarfed by Ganz's oversized physique and was forced to look up to meet the merchant prince's gaze. Still, it seemed not to bother the commodore as he stood before the Orion, his chin thrust forward, his body language communicating with no uncertainty that he was in charge.

Ganz's sole reply was to flex a pair of pectoral muscles that made Isaiah Farber's seem prepubescent in comparison. Otherwise, he remained silent, an arched eyebrow the only other indication that he had even heard Reyes's demand.

"I have proof he murdered two of my people," Reyes continued, "and almost killed another Starfleet officer. If you're harboring him aboard that tub of yours, then you're an accessory to the crimes." Stepping forward, the commodore placed his hands on his hips. "It'd break my heart to bust your ass, Ganz, but I'd get over it."

The Orion continued to regard Reyes a moment before his head tilted the slightest bit to one side. "Mr. Jaeq no longer works for me, Commodore. No one has seen him since this morning, and I'm certain he won't be returning." He paused, a small, knowing smile teasing the corners of his mouth. "It's as though he vanished into thin air."

I'll bet, Okagawa mused. Given what he knew of life within the Orion Syndicate, the most powerful weapon in a crime lord's arsenal was deniability. Jaeq's actions no doubt had endangered Ganz's vast array of illegal or even merely questionable activities. At the very least, they had brought the Orion unwanted attention from Starfleet. The easiest and fastest way to disassociate him from anything Jaeq had done would be to sever any and all ties to his troublesome employee.

In the Orion Syndicate, that usually meant only one thing.

Okagawa had no doubt Reyes understood the situation, as well. Nodding in amused understanding, the commodore said, "That's right, I heard scuttlebutt about some personnel issues you were dealing with. I guess what they say about being able to hire good people is true after all." He pursed his lips and made a cynical *tsk-tsk* sound. "Must really be annoying when we're talking about your right-hand man."

Ganz cast a glance to the trim Nalori standing just behind his left shoulder, whom Okagawa recognized as Zett Nilric, thanks to T'Prynn's hurried briefing prior to his and Reyes's coming down to the docking bay. "Mr. Nilric here is my business manager now," he said. "If you have need of my services, he'll be your point of contact."

As if to accentuate the statement, Nilric nodded once before reaching up to brush away a piece of lint from the lapel of his well-tailored charcoal suit. His expression was cold and calculating, no doubt in keeping with his reputed occupation as a professional assassin. Okagawa was certain the Nalori could kill both him and Reyes before either man might raise a hand in a futile attempt at defense.

According to what Okagawa remembered from T'Prynn's remarkably detailed dossier on him, Zett Nilric had been a lower-level employee within Ganz's organization, though doubtless looking for any avenue to advance his own standing. Judging from outward appearances, Nilric's ambition coupled with Jaeq's apparent series of hazardous missteps seemed to have provided just such an opportunity.

Bum luck, Jaeq.

Okagawa said, "My people discovered some alarming things about your former employee and a rash of thefts. Several odd communications between someone aboard the station and Mr. Jaeq, particularly with regard to assorted supplies and equipment located in different storage bays that would fetch impressive prices on the black market."

Reyes looked to Nilric before returning his gaze to Ganz. "Don't suppose either of you know anything about that, of course."

"Of course," Ganz echoed, though Okagawa caught the subtle, fleeting look of worry in the Orion's eyes.

The captain shook his head. "Damn shame about that. See, if Jaeq were here, I'd be able to tell him that we found his little network of hidden communications emitters that were used to sneak past the station's comm and sensor protocols."

"I haven't found his cohort yet," Reyes said, "but you can bet I will." He held his hands out in a gesture of questioning. "Wonder what he'll say when I get him in a small, locked room and ask him about his various business relationships?" Looking to Okagawa, he asked, "Better yet, put him in there with T'Prynn. She'd get some juicy details out of him. What do you think, Captain?"

"I think you're absolutely right, Commodore," Okagawa replied, struggling to keep from smiling.

To his credit, Ganz almost was successful in concealing any discomfort he might be experiencing as he listened to the commodore, who appeared to be enjoying catching the merchant prince off guard. Okagawa suspected Reyes had for some time been searching for some means of gaining the upper hand with the Orion.

"What does any of this have to do with me?" Ganz asked, his expression for the first time betraying mild strain as he clasped his massive hands before him.

"Depends," Reyes replied. "If all of the property that's gone missing from my station was to suddenly reappear from where it was taken, I might be inclined to ease up on my immediate efforts to find Jaeq's partner in crime. For a little while, anyway."

That caught Okagawa by surprise. Was the commodore actually offering Ganz, in addition to an opportunity for returning whatever stolen Starfleet property currently was in his possession, a chance for one of his people—Zett Nilric, perhaps—to find Jaeq's accomplice and resolve the issue "internally"? If so, it revealed a side to Reyes that the captain had not expected to see—a willingness to bend or even break rules, not for personal gain but as a means of bringing about resolution to tough problems.

He's commanding a station in the back end of nowhere, Okagawa reminded himself. *The rulebook's not always going to apply, is it?*

Ganz seemed to consider Reyes's proposal for a moment before nodding, once. "I'll look into the matter, though I can't promise any immediate results."

"The offer expires at 2300 hours, station time, tonight," Reyes said, any trace of cordiality now gone from his voice. "After that, I start turning over every rock I can find. Understood?"

Drawing a deep breath through his nose, Ganz replied through tight lips, "Yes."

"Fabulous," Reyes said, the word dripping with sarcasm. "Now, a few new rules for you: First, your vessel is still welcome to dock here just like any other civilian ship. You're still free to partake of the facilities at Stars Landing and to conduct legal business with any of the civilian merchants. What you're no longer allowed to do is initiate business contact with any Starfleet personnel, in any capacity. While I won't officially place your ship off-limits, you're to discourage anybody in a Starfleet uniform who might venture to your ship during shore leave from sticking around too long."

For the first time, Ganz frowned. "My competitors will notice that, I'd think."

Reyes shrugged. "Spin it any way you like. Whatever makes you look good, I don't care. Also, it should go without saying that I expect Jaeq's misadventures to be the last time I have to worry about Starfleet goods being stolen, either from my station or a ship making port. Anything goes missing, I'm coming to see you. Also, God help you if another one of my people gets so much as food poisoning from one of your buffets."

"What if I'm not responsible?" Ganz asked.

"Again," Reyes replied, "I don't care. Tell all your friends that there's a new sheriff in town, and that I like my life quiet and boring. Screw with the *mugato*, you're getting the horn. Are we clear?"

The Orion nodded. "As transparent aluminum."

There was no mistaking the ire rising to a boil beneath Ganz's façade of calm and control, Okagawa decided. It was easy to see that the Orion was not accustomed to being addressed in such a frank manner by anyone. Only a fool would believe that one stern lecture would be enough to ensure Ganz's compliance with the restrictions Reyes was placing upon him.

Of course, the captain knew also that Reyes certainly was no fool.

"Since we're being totally honest with one another," Ganz offered after a moment, "you might consider that while you're king of what I admit is a rather large hill, it's a hill sitting in the middle of a vast plain over which I hold much influence."

"That's the only reason your sizable ass isn't being stuffed into my brig right this second," Reyes snapped, and Okagawa saw the merchant prince bristling at the clear threat.

"On the other hand," the commodore continued, "that would be a waste of that influence you're so proud of. Instead, it occurs to me that if I could somehow avoid drop-kicking you into a jail cell, you might be predisposed toward helping me out on occasion—for example, should I need information on certain illicit ships or people passing through the region. Might go a long way toward making your life easier in these parts, wouldn't you say?"

Though Ganz said nothing for several seconds, Okagawa could see the Orion mulling over the proposal. He was no fool, either. While he no doubt saw the obvious upside to accepting a "business venture" with Reyes, Ganz was by definition not a lackey—to anyone. He would examine the situation from every conceivable angle, not only looking to see how he might benefit from the unorthodox arrangement but also attempting to see where the commodore might be laying traps.

A crafty bastard, Okagawa thought. *Dangerous one, too.*

Finally, Ganz bowed his head to Reyes. "An interesting offer. I'll take it into careful consideration."

"You do that," Reyes said, stepping away from the Orion. "We'll talk later."

Okagawa followed after the commodore as he turned and strode down the gangway toward the main corridor linking all of the ports along the station's main docking ring. Though he did not look back to confirm his suspicions, he was sure that the hot ache he felt between his shoulder blades had to be coming from Ganz's intense stare as the Orion watched them depart.

If looks could kill, and so on.

Waiting until they were well away from the airlock leading to the *Omari-Ekon,* Okagawa turned to Reyes. "Should I even ask what a *mugato* is?" When the commodore scowled at him by way of reply, he decided to change topics. Nodding toward the docking bay, he said, "Seems to me you two will be butting heads in the future."

"A gift for understatement," Reyes replied, releasing a tired sigh. "I don't suppose you'd believe me if I told you this was supposed to be a nice, quiet tour of duty for me? A twilight assignment before I retired?"

Recalling their earlier conversations in the commodore's office, Okagawa shook his head. "Not a chance. In fact, if I were a betting man, I'd say that Ganz is likely to be the least of your problems."

"No bet," Reyes replied, chuckling as he offered a knowing smile. Excusing himself, he turned and headed for the nearby bank of turbolifts, leaving Okagawa to contemplate the possible nuances layering the commodore's cryptic answer.

"I've got a funny feeling," the captain said, to no one in particular given that he stood alone in the corridor, "that this place is going to be anything but boring."

CHAPTER
11

"*Captain, my compliments to you and your crew. I don't know what we would have done without you, and if you think I won't catch hell for admitting that, you're sadly mistaken.*"

Standing at the engineering station near the rear of the *Lovell's* bridge and watching Diego Reyes on the main viewer, al-Khaled was surprised to see the commodore smile. Until this moment, the engineer was certain such a feat was impossible, despite unconfirmed rumors to the contrary.

"So, who owes who dinner?" whispered Jessica Diamond from where she stood next to him, her question inaudible over the hum and buzz of workstations and status reports coming over various intercom grids scattered around the bridge. The wager had been a friendly one, offered on the spot by Diamond as word of the commodore's hail was reported by Ensign Pzial, the *Lovell's* communications officer currently on duty. Al-Khaled had not even had time to accept or decline the bet before Reyes's gruff countenance appeared on the bridge's main viewscreen.

"Anyone who didn't get shore leave should be exempt," he mumbled from the side of his mouth, a comment that caught both the attention of and a raised eyebrow from Commander zh'Rhun, who stood in the turbolift alcove next to Diamond. Glancing over at the weapons officer, al-Khaled noted a mischievous glint in her eyes, the only fault in her otherwise deadpan expression as she, like everyone else on the bridge, turned her attention to the conversation between Reyes and the captain.

At least someone got to enjoy themselves a bit while we were here.

"Our pleasure, Commodore," Okagawa replied from where he stood before his command chair at the center of the bridge. "However, I do believe there's one last item to address before we depart." Looking to his right, he asked, "Isn't that right, Mr. Farber?"

Stepping down into the command well, the burly lieutenant nodded with a small grin. "I suppose so, sir. Thank you for approving my transfer." As he and the captain shook hands, Farber turned to the viewer. "And to you as well, Commodore. I'm very excited about joining Vanguard's team." He paused a moment before adding, "Lieutenant Ballard will be a hard act to follow, but I promise it won't be for lack of trying, sir."

Farber's request was not all that unexpected, al-Khaled decided. The younger man's enthusiasm while working with the state-of-the-art systems comprising the immense space station had been all but contagious. With the tragic loss of Curtis Ballard, Reyes was in need of a first-rate chief engineer, and Isaiah Farber was as qualified a candidate as the commodore was likely to find. Vanguard's gain was the *Lovell's* loss, of course, but al-Khaled could not fault his friend for wanting to take on a new challenge. The demands of being chief engineer of a starbase on the outer edge of Federation territory would fit that bill rather nicely.

On the screen, Reyes nodded. *"Don't thank me, Lieutenant. From what I saw, I'm getting a hell of an engineer."* Looking past Farber, he added, *"One of many, at least. Lieutenant al-Khaled, if you ever get tired of hurtling through space in that deathtrap, you give me a call. I'd be happy to have you, or any member of your team, for that matter."*

Offering a respectful nod, al-Khaled replied, "Many thanks, Commodore. I'll certainly keep that offer in mind."

"With all due respect," Okagawa said, the grin stretching his round face belying the mock irritation behind his words, "may we dispense with the poaching of my crew?"

Reyes smiled again. *"For now. Mr. Farber, I trust your personal effects were transferred without incident?"*

The young engineer nodded. "Yes, Commodore. All that's left is my duffel bag in the transporter room."

"Then I suggest you have yourself beamed aboard in the next two minutes," Reyes replied, *"before your old ship leaves you floating outside the docking bay. I don't like loiterers around my station, Lieutenant."*

"I guess that's my cue," Farber said. After shaking hands with Okagawa once more, the lieutenant moved to the upper bridge deck and made his final farewells. The real send-off had already been handled during the previous evening, with al-Khaled and Ensign Ghrex seeing to an impromptu going-away party after word of the sudden transfer made its rounds throughout the ship.

"It's been a pleasure, Isaiah," al-Khaled said as Farber shook his hand. "Good luck with your new assignment."

His fellow engineer nodded. "Thanks, Mahmud," he said before looking around at the rest of the bridge crew. "I've learned a great deal from all of you, and I'm proud to call you all friends. Hopefully, our paths will cross again one of these days." With a final nod and wave to the assembled bridge crew, Farber disappeared into the turbolift.

Al-Khaled sensed the momentary pause as everyone watched their shipmate leave, and for the first time since hearing of his friend's transfer request the engineer felt the void Farber had suddenly left behind. While he knew that moving from ship to ship and assignment to assignment was part and parcel of a career in Starfleet, al-Khaled always felt a momentary pang of regret when such an event occurred. Not just a gifted engineer, Farber also was a trusted friend. There was no doubt he would be missed by the entire *Lovell* crew.

Such is life in our line of work.

Al-Khaled's attention was caught by Ensign Pzial reporting that departure clearance from the station had been granted, followed by Okagawa giving instructions to zh'Rhun to get under way. Moving to stand in front of the helm and navigation consoles, the captain turned his attention back to the image of Reyes still displayed on the main viewer.

"Commodore," he said, "We've got our clearance from the dockmaster. Is there anything else we can do before we go?"

On the screen, Reyes shook his head. *"Thanks to you, we've got just about everything under control. There are still some outstanding repairs, a list of new or replacement components to install, along with the settling-in adjustments we were supposed to be dealing with now, anyway."* Shrugging, he added, *"Still, I expect we'll be fully operational within the month, ahead of our original schedule. After that, well, we'll certainly have our hands full. You can count on that."*

The statement was straightforward by design, al-Khaled knew. Though he and his team had worked with Starbase 47's engineers to identify the odd carrier wave as the source of the station's ills, that discovery had itself uncovered a host of new questions. Judging from the still-unexplained transmission's effects, there was no denying that its creators were or had been the keepers of wondrous, sophisticated technology. What other knowledge did they harbor? How did it compare to the Federation and its contemporaries?

From what Okagawa had shared with him—based on the very limited and vague information imparted by Reyes—these and many other questions doubtless would be pursued with vigor by the commodore and his people in the coming weeks. That much was obvious from the directive Reyes had issued—for all information pertaining to the carrier wave to be purged from the *Lovell's* databanks, and for any member of the crew with direct knowledge of the anomaly to be ordered to secrecy. It all pointed to the commodore's possessing far more information on the subject than he was able or willing to share, and the purpose for Vanguard's presence in the Taurus Reach extending far beyond simple support of exploration and colonization initiatives.

In front of Okagawa, the alpha-shift helm officer, Lieutenant Sasha Rodriguez, was intent on her console as she oversaw what essentially was the automated process of the station's tractor beams maneuvering the *Lovell* out of its docking bay. Behind her, Okagawa offered an informal salute toward the viewscreen.

"Best of luck to you, Commodore," he said. "If you ever have need of my people's particular talents, I hope you'll give me a call."

"I'll be sure to do that. Smooth sailing, Captain. Reyes out."

An instant later the image on the screen shifted from that of the commodore to a view of the docking bay's outer doors as the *Lovell* continued its exit maneuver.

"Transporter room reports that Mr. Farber made it over safe and sound," zh'Rhun reported as she stepped down to stand next to the captain.

Nodding at the report, Okagawa settled into the center seat. "Excellent," he said as he looked over his shoulder. "Well, Mahmud, what's our next assignment?"

Al-Khaled stepped toward the red railing that encircled the command well. "Computer systems upgrades at the Tantalus V penal colony, sir."

"A vacation hot spot if ever there was one," Diamond said, stone-faced.

Ignoring the weapons officer, al-Khaled continued, "T'Laen has already begun the initial diagnostics. She should be ready to begin the modifications upon our arrival."

"Outstanding," the captain replied. "Commander zh'Rhun, see to getting us on our way, would you please?"

As the bridge crew returned to their normal duties, Okagawa indicated the viewscreen with a wave of his hand. It depicted a receding view of the mammoth space station as the *Lovell* moved away at impulse power. "There's something I've been meaning to ask about that station since we got here. You think they could have built something bigger?"

A chorus of laughter echoed across the bridge and even as he joined in, al-Khaled could not help but consider the road not taken. If what he had encountered during their brief visit here was any indication, he suspected that Isaiah Farber, like Starbase 47, would soon face a host of intriguing, perhaps even astounding challenges. The chance to work on the impressive space station—positioned so far beyond the Federation's borders and on the doorstep of some vast unknown that seemed to be all but begging for attention—was a tempting notion, he admitted, but not one he was ready to accept just yet.

Though the *Lovell*, like the Corps of Engineers itself, might not be the darling of the fleet, it was a vessel with a heart, and a mission that—while perhaps mundane and even boring by description—brought its own multitude of intriguing possibilities.

They have their mission, whatever it might be, and we have ours.

That thought, and the lure of the path he had chosen not to follow, lingered as al-Khaled's gaze fixed on the now rapidly shrinking image of Vanguard station—a lone sentinel among the stars, and a beacon of light amid the darkness of mystery surrounding the Taurus Reach.

10 IS BETTER THAN 01

Heather Jarman

ACKNOWLEDGMENTS

Thanks to Keith DeCandido, a talented editor and a great guy who always inspires my best work.

"Stop." The request came out as a mixture of grunt and plea. Henry Winter could barely find his voice, what with the cramp in his side and his lungs smothering from the thick, acidic humidity down here in the tunnels. The master computer, he'd been told, required these atmospheric conditions. Though how the Bynars survived long enough to build and reboot a second master computer down here without suffocating was anyone's guess. Especially since it had taken them ten years. "I can't take—" A cough. "—another step."

The Bynar pair paused mid-scurry, their heads swiveling back to look at him in unnerving unison. Henry had yet to determine whether 110 was the shorter one or 111. And what minimal empathic abilities he had did him little good with figuring out who was who since the emotional makeup of Bynars tended to resemble a series of branching either/or questions.

"You had said, Commander, that—"

"—time was of the essence."

"She may elude us if—"

"—we wait. There is danger—"

Henry held up a hand to silence them. "Let's not assume facts not in evidence—" Another coughing spasm overtook him; he spat a clot of phlegm onto the ground. "Besides—I appear to be having difficulty breathing."

"We will stop—"

"—since you cannot—"

"—walk unless you breathe."

"We suppose that we can—"

"—slow down for a time."

Bracing his hands against his thighs, Henry nodded, grateful he wouldn't have to waste any more breath persuading them. Bynar pragmatism served them well in crisis situations, such as the present one. He leaned back against the smooth gunmetal-gray plating with a dull *thwap*. "We'll go soon. I'll be fine." He took a deep, wheezy, breath followed by a quick exhalation. Flecks of light orbited before his eyes; lightheadeness swamped him. His middle-aged body wasn't cut out for this pace. "Let's take five."

The Bynar pair exchanged looks.

Before they could ask, he answered. "Five minutes. A break. I need to get my blood sugar up." He unfastened his pack and began rooting around for a ration bar. The bars tasted like sawdust glued together with *weloo* tree sap, but he couldn't afford to be picky this far underground. He ripped open the wrapper and took the first, pleasure-free bite. The Bynars watched him intently. He might not like this particular meal, but he wasn't going to let them rush him. Henry gulped the gritty, saliva-softened glob, then took his next bite.

The Bynars, he figured, would keep track of time; they'd let him know the millisecond his five minutes expired. Of the thirty-five kilometers they needed to cover to search for their missing person, they'd covered twenty, at a brisk pace to Henry's mind. While he'd been prepared to turn around and send someone else to complete the job after every kilometer, his Bynar associates never wavered from their mission. The Bynars' uncanny ability to stay on task both impressed and irritated him. When they removed tricorders from their utility belts, ostensibly to collect data from their surroundings, Henry sighed with relief. Obviously they felt they had enough time to investigate their surroundings more carefully. Time equaled rest, and Henry could certainly use more rest.

At his annual physical last month, the doc had warned him that Marietta's homemade *lupa-lupa* pies might taste like a slice of heaven going down, but the increasing width of his middle placed strain on the natural arteries grafted onto his *second* synthetic heart. Henry wasn't faithful enough with his meds to make a difference in his health. If the arteries blew where he didn't have access to a top flight medical team (like down here in the bowels of Bynaus), he'd bleed out before he hit the ground. A natural optimist, Henry brushed the doc's concerns aside like so much white noise; those pies brought back sweet memories of his childhood on Betazed, and he wasn't about to give them up. Besides, in Starfleet JAG, one rarely found the need to maintain his fitness level at a three-point-five-minute-per-kilometer pace. Doctors worried too much. Forty years in Starfleet had earned him the right to eat for pleasure, not merely well-being.

Besides, this trip to Bynaus was supposed to be a routine criminal defense. He was to meet his client, figure out the nature of the misbehavior, and make sure the rights of a Federation citizen were protected. How was he to know he'd be called on to pursue his runaway client through the innards of the planet Bynaus! Talk about feeling like he'd fallen into a second-rate, late-nineteenth-century Earth pulp novel—*Digging to the Core of Earth* was it? What kind of computer was so important and delicate that they didn't allow transporter beams within its underground access tunnels anyway?

The Bynars took a few steps in his direction, using hand motions to wave him up off the floor. Excited chatter passed back and forth between them before one of the Bynars tried to press the tricorder into his hand.

His five minutes couldn't be up, he thought grumpily. Henry pushed himself off the floor with a grunt, brushed some *schmutz* off his uniform, and took the proffered tricorder. His eyes widened. "So this means—?"

"The missing person has been—"

"—in the vicinity sometime in the last—"

"—two hours. We are—"

"—on the right track," Henry said, getting the hang of this Bynar speak. He was pleased. The Bynars' efficient use of time and resources definitely had an upside. The three of them might have wandered through kilometer after kilometer of tunnels for days if they'd hadn't caught this break. At least now they knew that his client had passed this way and they stood a chance of finding her. Maybe he could convince a pack of the Bynars to emigrate offworld and become JAG investigators.

"It is blood—"

"—however. There could be—"

"—injuries."

Damn. Henry closed his eyes, squeezing out the image of his client dying slowly so far away from home. A new resolve filled him. "Let's get going, shall we?" Reenergized, Henry increased the length of his stride until he outpaced the Bynars; with his longer legs, he should have been leading the way from the start. Thanks to this latest lead, he might be home on Starbase 620 for Marietta's home cooking within a day or so if he could get this case wrapped up. Assuming the case was straightforward. He sighed. Too bad it was murder. And murder was rarely simple.

Before . . .

You'll never guess where I am. I even have an attaché—
Ensign Alban—assigned to help me, a newly promoted
junior-grade lieutenant. I can hardly believe what's happened myself, considering what it took to get me here.

But wait. I'll start from the beginning. I haven't talked
about this for a while because there didn't seem to be a
point. The more I thought about the situation, the more
irrational it seemed that the higher-ups in my organization seemed unwilling to see what was right in front of
their faces! Over the last four months, the stress drove me
to gnaw my fingernails down to their nubs. When they
started bleeding, I decided to shove my frustration to the
back of my mind where it wouldn't irritate me so much.

I'm an Academy grad. I know how to handle competi-
tion and difficult circumstances. I know this is my first
posting, but it's not like I've been a civilian desk jockey
for the last ten years and don't have a clue about life outside my cubicle. There's a war on, and dammit, I want
to be useful. I've been bucking for a chance to do some
planet-based recruiting—anything that will get help for
my friends out there flying around the stars. Nothing like

an in-person, face-to-face appeal, I always say, to light a
fire under people. We need to be more assertive, get in
their faces a bit, appeal to their patriotism. If you don't
give them a reason, no one in their right mind is going to
sign up willingly to face the Dominion.

Too bad it took the destruction of the *DiNovia* to finally
wake this organization up and solve my problem for me.
Not my problem—Starfleet's problem. You'd think that
having personnel stretched from one end of the quadrant
to the other trying to keep our fleet glued together with
spit and good intentions would have been enough to justify stepping up recruiting efforts. But no. Tragedy finally
won out over common sense. Too bad that's what it took
to wake up the big brass.

It's not like I'm not pragmatic. In every war there are
accidents and mistakes. Every time I see a list of friendly
fire incidents, it's all I can do to keep from crawling under
my desk and crying until I collapse. Those are my friends
out there. The calculations and stats we've spent decades
perfecting figure in "loss of life" due to error, especially
during a war. What I can't get past is when those errors
are preventable.

The military side, though, covering artillery and weapons—that's not my job. I help staff science and engineering departments. Whether my people (I think of them
as "my people" since I'm the one that aided in assigning them) survive a sneak attack is often dependent on
what kind of fancy flying the conn officer can pull off
and how accurate the operations and security officers are
with their targeting. I feel protective toward my people—I
want to do whatever I can to make sure they can do their
jobs.

When I put off my counselor training to join the office of personnel, I assumed the biggest problem I'd have
would be convincing the top guys at Daystrom to give up
lucrative research positions to join Starfleet's deep-space

recon programs. That assumption was wrong. We've finally reached a point in the Dominion War when I've had to add variables to my personnel equations to account for having too few people doing too much work. The most common complaint I hear these days is exhaustion. Who isn't tired during a war? But when my people get tired, big consequences can follow.

Which brings me back to the destruction of the *DiNovia*. Captain Met'gi added an additional S.C.E. team to Starbase 511 when it became obvious the existing staff couldn't handle the nonstop repairs coming in from the front. This poor S.C.E. team was pulled from the frontlines in the Bajoran sector and put straight to work repairing starships whose insides looked like bowls of tangled pasta. After working five straight shifts, the S.C.E. core specialist miscalculated the calibrations for the *DiNovia*'s coolant fuel ratios by 0.2 percent. The cascading warp core failure happened so quickly, the ship's chief engineer didn't have time to react. We lost a hundred and twenty good people in the explosion. Not because of the damnable Dominion, but because we have too few people to handle too much work.

My superiors finally took me up on my suggestion to look for new places to recruit personnel. Though a few individuals expressed reluctance (paranoia still lurks even ten years after the incident with the *Enterprise*), the board was persuaded by the *DiNovia* problem that they needed to exhaust more possibilities. Bynaus was an obvious example of an underutilized population.

Of course Bynars have served in Starfleet since the "appropriation" of the *Enterprise* from Starbase 74, but we haven't aggressively sought them out. If a pair wanted to join or serve as civilian advisors, assuming they passed the requirements and were willing to live by the rules, we accepted them the way we'd accept any Federation citizen. The Bynars' efficiency and skill in working on

computers is unparalleled in the Federation. A Bynar pair
can diagnose, repair, and upgrade a malfunctioning computer system in a fourth of the time that it takes engineers of other species. That being said, the Bynars aren't
well-known or understood in the Federation because they
keep to themselves. Only a small number of them leave
Bynaus at any given time, so most Federation citizens
can go a lifetime without ever meeting a Bynar pair. No
one I know will ever say, aloud, that they think the Bynars
are conspiring against the government, or that they present a danger to any of its citizens. But the old–timers
around the office, if you get them to talk "unofficially,"
will confess that it scares them how easy it was for the
Bynars to take the mighty *Enterprise*, without resistance,
right under the noses of the starbase and the *Enterprise*
crew. They deceived Commander Data and Commander
La Forge, for Pete's sake—no small accomplishment! For
that reason, there's always a bit of wariness when dealing
with the Bynars. These days, though, circumstances don't
allow us to be so cautious.

With the number of damaged ships Starfleet faces
these days, time is of the essence. Even the shipyards are
stretched to beyond their limits. The recruiting board is
finally willing to move past their previous misgivings and
actively search for Bynars who could help ease the work-
load of our stressed and strained S.C.E.

Which brings me to my current location: da-da—I'm
on the *Watson* on my way to Bynaus. I've never traveled
for work before, so I have to confess a bit of a thrill at
being able to see more of the Alpha Quadrant. Sure, I've
done the Mars caverns and made the occasional jaunt to
the standard recreation spots around my home colony on
Centauri. But this—going on official Starfleet business,
with an *attaché* even, to a place that almost no one goes.
It's so exotic!

I know, in my gut, that bringing the Bynars into S.C.E.

has the potential to shift the momentum in our favor. No one questions their ability to repair computers. My personal belief is that their capacity to build or design new computers could tip the balance of the conflict in the Federation's favor. I don't have any hard proof—just a feeling that we need these folks to help us out.

Or maybe the truth is that I have to believe that the Bynars can make a difference, because if they don't, I'm out of ideas. And I can't give up yet. I just can't. We can't afford to lose this war. Nothing I know of the Dominion leads me to believe that they would be benevolent occupiers. Who we are, our way of life—our very existence—is at stake here. The personal cost begins to rise too. So many of my friends from the Academy have gone into the grinder of the war machine and have never come out again. The loss of their lives has to have meaning. If we lose because of stupid mistakes, I'll never forgive myself for not doing my part to prevent those mistakes.

Captain Quinteros, the Starfleet liaison on Bynaus, transmitted to me some orientation materials that he requested I study before I arrive. *"Read it,"* he said during our conversation, stroking his salt-and-pepper beard thoughtfully. *"And then we'll talk when you get here."*

Even across the millions of kilometers that separated us, the tone in his voice and his body language told me that he doubted my proposal. I'm used to senior officers, particularly those who have been in Starfleet for longer than I've been alive, giving me those kinds of looks. The "she's a sweet young thing who will know better soon enough" look.

Quinteros is wrong. I know it. He has to be.

From *On Bynaus: A Starfleet Orientation Guide* by Captain Orfil Quinteros

To understand the Bynars, a familiarity with their origins is critical. Unlike many species who attribute their existence to a higher being or those who can trace their evolution through millions of years, the Bynars were the creations of an AI civilization based on the world we now know as Bynaus. Approximately a million years ago, these AIs (whose name has long since vanished from history) conquered the original inhabitants of the planet. Whether the AIs were created by the planet's inhabitants or came as invaders is unknown.

As the AI civilization grew and prospered, they discovered the need for organic slaves to perform functions that they didn't want to or that were better suited to creatures of flesh. The forebears of what became the modern-day Bynars were created. Thousands of millennia passed. The organics became more sophisticated, evolving to meet the needs of their environment. The AIs became complacent—some even began to see the organics as having worth beyond their servile functions. A small group of AIs believed the organics deserved rights and campaigned for those rights. The nucleus of a revolution was born. What started off peacefully became violent. The organics and AIs struggled for dominance. Ultimately, the organics prevailed. But the organics inherited a technologically sophisticated world from their AI masters. Gaining independence was only the first obstacle facing the organics.

The AIs had artificially engineered the planet's environment, from maintaining the gas ratios in the atmosphere and the gravity and providing nutrition to shielding planet-based technology from Beta Magellan's more damaging radiation. While the organics could learn the technology, they lacked the time to gain a comprehensive understanding of how to maintain and operate the systems before the systems began breaking down. The organics organized teams to study and master the technology so as to assure survival. Over time, as they gained control over the planetary infrastructure, they gradually reduced their group size from as many as a dozen to a pair. This model provided the template for the modern-day Bynar civilization.

The organics were not "designed" to function in pairs by their AI creators, but the modern-day Bynars continue to do so as it is a long-standing societal norm that exists as a survival mechanism for the species. The belief is that, should catastrophe strike, the demands of keeping Bynaus functioning are better met by groups. This social structure is enforced by powerful cultural taboos that promise the noncompliant will be cut off from Bynar society and banned from returning to Bynaus. In my time on Bynaus, and knowing Bynars, I have never known a Bynar who has chosen to remain a singleton.

THE BYNARS TODAY

Contrary to the perceptions of outsiders, the Bynars are neither genetically engineered to interact with computers nor biologically codependent on their mates. Almost immediately after a Bynar emerges from the birthing chamber, it is placed with another Bynar who has complementary biology. Each pair is made up of a Bynar who has the identity/function "one" and one who has the identity/function "zero"; there are no genders. Binary language defines their identity, their thought processes, and their interactions with each other and with technology. Each pair can work independently with virtually any technology. Should a massive loss of life occur, Bynar pairs can maintain their assigned technological functions, as well as take on the functions of others, with minimal outside assistance. Their facile abilities with computers are why Bynars can thoroughly learn virtually any technology at a pace that appears to defy natural organic abilities. The Bynars devised a mechanical data buffer that is worn on an individual's hip. It enables rapid communication and comes close to approximating the rate of data transfer within computer circuits.

For an obvious example of their skills, one need only look at the astonishing pace at which two Bynar pairs stationed on Starbase 74 transferred Bynaus's master computer database into the *Enterprise*'s computer systems. Naturally, the more working pairs, the more efficiency and speed that can be expected.

The Starbase 74 incident exposed vulnerability in the Bynar methodology: too much interdependence between the organic Bynars and the homeworld's master computer. The threatened demise of the main computer endangered every living Bynar. Such a weakness could not be allowed to continue unexamined.

Over the decade since the Starbase 74 incident, much of Bynar civilization has focused on the question of how much the Bynars can separate their existence from their world's technology. While survival in ancient times may have hinged on the uncontested embrace of technology, the modern-day necessity of maintaining this rigidly defined paradigm is being studied and debated among the Bynars. The discussion proceeds at a slow pace, however, because of how Bynar society makes changes.

Bynaus has one of the few pure democracies in the Federation. The absolute nature of the Bynar psyche allows them to examine problems objectively. One might conclude that linear, logic-based minds might reach the same conclusions.

Surprisingly, the results of their political and procedural discussions are hardly monolithic. Diversity of thought exists on Bynaus, though it is often subtle and appears incrementally. The great Vulcan sociologist Tuparak, who was the first nonnative scientist to study the Bynars after they had joined the Federation, compared the shifts in Bynar society to the changes wrought by wind erosion. "The process is so gradual, so subtle," Tuparak said, "that it can barely be noticed in a lifetime. But when one has the perspective of time, one can see how monumental change has been."

Individual Bynars reach different conclusions based on their knowledge and experience, gained from both work and their relationships with their mates. There is so little ambiguity in their thought processes that a simple up or down vote is possible on virtually every subject. The idea of each citizen having a vote or a say in their planet's global issues is not unreasonable. Every day at the same time, the Bynars participate in a virtual planetary meeting where referenda are voted on and announcements are made. To outsiders, it may appear that every citizen is required to be bogged down in minutiae, but the Bynars see the ability to choose as the ultimate expression of the liberty they fought to claim from their AI creators. No one is compelled to decide in a certain way. There is no "campaigning" or persuasion based on emotion. Bynars are utilitarian and pragmatic in the extreme. Logic and desired outcome have been key motivators—until the present day.

The subtle undercurrents of doubt brought on by the collective near-death experience previously referred to may slowly erode the Bynars' unquestioning acceptance of majority will. Citizen Services, the organization that oversees functions relating to Bynars' citizenry, reports a gradual trend toward more issues dealing with individual rights. For example, before five years ago, it was unheard of for a member of a Bynar pair to call into question a mate's behavior. Now, while it is rare, and Citizen Services will not comment publicly on such instances, unsubstantiated reports indicate that it does happen in present times. Such a trend may indicate a shift in Bynar society that calls into doubt whether a system of pure democratic government will continue. The concept of individuality runs contrary to all of Bynar civilization's social and cultural norms. Such a notion, to refer back to Tuparak, exists now only as the wind does: as an unseen force that has the potential to remake the face of this society.

Citizen Services Employee Report
Agent Unit 110/111
Assignment: Starfleet Recruiting Visit on Behalf of
   Starfleet Corps of Engineers

As requested by Captain Quinteros, Citizen Services will oversee the interaction of Starfleet representatives Lieutenant Temperance Brewster (female, junior-grade lieutenant, human, Centauri colonist, thirty Earth years, five months, two days) and Ensign Alban Topar (male, ensign, Bajoran, twenty-five years, three months, eight days). 110/111 accept this assignment from 10110/10100 and will facilitate any communications between Bynaus's citizens and the visitors. This unit will apply all rules and regulations governing interaction between Bynaus citizens and offworld visitors pursuant to section 5920 paragraph 7 of the Bynaus Policy Statement on Federation Membership, with reference to the special circumstance proscribed by Starfleet-Bynaus protocols. Official request for announcement to be made on the median planetary meeting regarding Starfleet Business has been submitted. Awaiting announcement details from Lieutenant Brewster. Captain Quinteros indicated that announcement will invite Bynars to volunteer for service in the Starfleet Corps of Engineers. Will update before 23:15:00.

Personal Log, Lieutenant Temperance Brewster

If a planet-sized machine made of organic, living material could be constructed, I imagine it would look and feel a lot like Bynaus. It isn't that this world isn't beautiful—it is. Sort of. In the way that the symmetry and precision of geometric figures are beautiful. The kind of minds that can conceive of and create such exquisite, meticulous designs are nothing short of astonishing, but I can't help but feel unnerved by the cold, calculating process behind it all. As if there is no tolerance for deviation from what is expected. I'm not sure how comfortable I am in an environment where everywhere I look, I feel like I'm living in the heart of a sterile machine. I never thought I'd appreciate litter on the streets or dust on the window ledges!

As I stepped off the transporter pad into the central transportation center, my first thought was that the inside of their buildings didn't look a lot different from any other Federation building I'd been in: metal paneling, transparent aluminum windows, chairs with stiff cushions in bland neutral colors. But then, when I reached down to pick up my satchel, I caught a glimpse outside.

My first impression of Bynaus dragged me back to my engineering classes at the Academy. This reaction surprised me: every fact I stuffed into my brain for the required engineering units promptly fell out as soon as I passed the exams. I still couldn't tell a converter coil from a plasma modulator. I'm still amazed—and yes, a little intimidated—by those who glory in the architecture of circuitry or the thrill of a machine that's efficient within point zero two. To me, the insides of a console look like hieroglyphics must have appeared to Napoleon's soldiers hundreds of years ago. It was all so much metallurgy, chemistry, electronics . . . streams of lights flashing and writhing like worms through coils. *Why* a person would want to become an engineer and design technology was more interesting to me than the technology itself. But when I glanced out at the surrounding city, I caught a glimpse, for the first time, of how one might perceive poetry in technology. I didn't greet the Starfleet liaison who had met us nor did I look to see what Alban's reaction was. Instead, I took several unthinking steps toward the windows where I could get a more complete view. Resting my hands on the cold gray metal ledge, I stared at the hum of activity outside.

In the two-dimensional perspective from above, looking down from a shuttle or an orbital platform, the Bynar complexes must have looked like intricate, thousand-year-old Moorish mosaics with their domes, conduits, cables, and flashing lights. Up close, these structures formed seamless, planar tessellations—dodecahedral spheres and pyramids. I swear I might have seen a trio of interlocking loop tunnels that formed Borromean rings, even though theoretically I didn't believe such a structure was possible. Even the buildings that had a seemingly organic design, when examined more closely, appeared to be fractals.

Metal, clear polymer, soothing colored lights, and patches of muted primary colors defined the city's aesthetics; even the splashes of color that appeared at regular intervals created a powerful sense of visual balance. Strips of shimmering metals running parallel to each other or lights outlined the edges of buildings. If I stared out the window long enough, the lines, lights and colors blurred into a figure resembling a highly complex game of Vulcan *kal–toh*. The Bynars appeared to live and work in a methodically plotted out design governed by theoretical mathematics.

Only the gray-violet-skinned Bynars in their silver and black uniforms, sticking out in stark relief against the pebbled surfaces of the buildings' exteriors, provided a random component. Their oversized, smooth skulls aren't attractive by most humanoid standards, particularly the pink, scarred suture in the back of their heads. I learned from Captain Quinteros's writing that the "scar" on the skull is where the Bynars are attached to their birthing chambers. Their movements lacked the rhythmic uniformity one might expect from androids, but there was such obvious purpose in their movements—like bundles of information zinging through a computer from one place to another—to exclude any sense of spontaneity. Even the living elements in the open spaces followed a grid pattern: rows of impeccably pruned trees surrounded by what appeared to be garden boxes, though I couldn't discern any details from such a distance. Wherever I looked, no Bynars lingered in what I thought of as the park, nor did I see the Bynars stopping to talk with other Bynars or even pause to study their surroundings. I shivered involuntarily, discomfited by the utilitarian nature of it all, feeling like I had stepped into a world of relentless efficiency—like the Borg but without the compulsion. Perhaps on some subconscious level, I wondered if I would be assimilated into the sea of sameness, fit like a spare part into the machine of this world.

Captain Quinteros, who had met us at the transporter pad, stepped up behind me. "I find the rhythms and patterns very soothing. Like the rattle of rain against my roof, which puts me right to sleep. The stability, the constancy, makes this place feel dependable. I know what to expect and it puts my mind at ease. The Bynars have little tolerance for chaos and confusion, and that suits me just fine."

I flushed, embarrassed to be caught. "I don't—I mean—I believe this to be—um—"

"At ease, Lieutenant," Quinteros said kindly. "Most visitors to Bynaus react the way you do. There's a reason why it's not on the Alpha Quadrant's list of favorite travel destinations."

I managed to muster a comment on how unexpectedly beautiful Bynaus was.

"Most visitors don't expect it," he said. "They assume a species that has a symbiotic relationship with machines lacks a sense of aesthetics. They expect the place to look like the inside of a Borg cube."

Warmth again spread through my cheeks at Quinteros's uncanny ability to speak my private thoughts aloud.

"All they need to disabuse themselves of that false notion is to take in the view from this transporter room," he concluded, opening his arms expansively.

"What's this place called?" I asked, stepping away from the window and toward the turbolift.

"Bynars don't name their cities—or any geographical location, for that matter," Quinteros explained as we walked. "For planning purposes, the surface is mapped on a grid capable of defining each spot of land on this planet down to the meter." He reached for a thin, rectangular object about the size of a tricorder hanging from his belt and handed it to me. "A planetary positioning guide. Voice activated. You tell it where you want to go, the guide finds the coordinates and provides you with directions. If you like, it will store instructions to places you want to go later. You can also back up data from any place onto its memory nodules."

"This has more in common with navigating a starship

than visiting a planet," I said, hoping my puzzlement over all things technical wasn't obvious.

"In a way," Quinteros said, "you're right. But the Bynars have engineered this device to be friendly to any species, regardless of their level of technological literacy."

"Does my discomfort with the mechanical show?" I asked, wondering if Quinteros had been a counselor in a previous assignment. One of the tenets of being a Starfleet recruiter is maintaining a pleasant, nonjudgmental persona; years of training should have smoothed over my old Academy hang-up.

"A little, though I doubt most people would notice. Living on Bynaus, I'm probably more attuned to the reactions of offworlders to this highly unusual place. I have to admit," he chuckled, "that I'm surprised to see a technophobe as a recruiter for S.C.E."

Quinteros wasn't the first person to make that observation—my senior officer was, when he'd interviewed me for the position. I'd often wondered why I enjoyed my job as much as I did. "My job is to identify and evaluate potential candidates for Starfleet. I assess their intellectual abilities, their emotional health, physical stamina—whatever Starfleet requires in a candidate to fill a position."

"You're plugging people into vacant slots? How different is your process from the Bynars who run their society similarly by assessing who best can do a job and assigning them to do so?" he said, offering a bemused smile.

I chose to ignore Quinteros's gentle poke at my hypocrisy. "There are many factors to consider. But in the case of staffing engineers, I think because I have so little aptitude for the discipline, it makes me that much more curious about why these people gravitate to what they do."

"Opposites attract?"

"I suppose."

Quinteros and I continued our genial conversation into

the turbolift. Upon arrival in the lobby, I discovered that a Bynar pair was waiting for us.

"Lieutenant Brewster, these are the representatives from Citizen Services who will advise you during your time here. They will help you navigate the process of sharing your mission with the Bynars." Quinteros turned and greeted the pair, then introduced them as 110 and 111.

I blinked, wondered if I should extend my hand, but settled on a polite shoulder bow instead. I loathed feeling like a typical greenhorn, but here I was, blundering around like I'd just gotten out of the Academy last week. Maybe taking this on as my first travel assignment was a mistake. I should have gone someplace easier—like Cardassia!

As I rose back up to my full height, I looked at them once again, trying to remember if Quinteros had indicated which one was 110 and which one was 111. I didn't have a clue. I hate it when people say they can't tell two or more individuals apart—it sounds lazy. As if they don't care enough to pay attention to the details that make a difference, such as vocal intonation, eye expressions, and other subtle variances. I know the Bynars aren't clones—they're not genetically engineered any more than humans are these days. Scientists may tweak for genetic diseases or congenital defects, but otherwise they allow nature to take its course. The Bynars conceive their offspring in labs; they are gestated in birthing chambers. I knew this intellectually. Logic struggled to overcome my eyes' insistence that the Bynars were identical.

"Hello," I said hesitantly. "110, 111. Thank you for your assistance."

"We have—"

I focused on the Bynar I believed to be 110.

"—arranged for a slot—"

Shifted my attention to the other—

"—on the planetary network."

—and back again.

"Is your statement—"

"—prepared?"

It took me a moment to realize that the dual-channel audio had stopped and that the pair now stood as still as robots. "Yes. I've prepared my stump speech," I said, offering them a friendly smile. "I'm hoping to convince some of the Bynars that it is their patriotic duty to join Starfleet."

"Stump—"

"—speech?"

"Patriotic—"

"—duty?"

I'd forgotten—the literal-minded Bynars had difficulty translating idioms. "My recruitment statement that I hope will persuade your fellow Bynars that they have a vested interest in helping Starfleet prevail in the current conflict."

"The Dominion—"

"—War." 110 and 111 cocked their heads in opposite directions, apparently satisfied by my explanation, and indicated that I should follow them.

As we walked out into the open, I attempted to follow 110 and 111's rapid-fire explanation of the day's schedule, rules, and procedure. In an effort to be polite, I looked from side to side each time the conversation switched speakers, but I lost track of what was being said. I gave up trying to know who they were individually and kept my eyes focused on the pathway through the city, consciously ignoring the sea of seemingly identical faces scurrying around me. My mission gave me purpose. I couldn't allow myself to be sidetracked by the white noise of the Bynar world.

Citizen Services Employee Report
Agent Unit 110/111
Assignment: Starfleet Recruiting Visit on Behalf of
   Starfleet Corps of Engineers

Lieutenant Brewster's statement was delivered over the interplanetary communications network at 22:46:07. Potential recruits will meet in Building C81 Quadrant 4 at 34:05:29. Citizen Services will tally responses and provide them to Lieutenant Brewster. CS agents will be in attendance at recruiting meeting to advise Starfleet on Bynaus protocols. Response over the network indicates that the message was received by those eligible to participate. This unit can conclude that the requirements set out by the Equality Protocol have been met.

Personal Log, Lieutenant Temperance Brewster

I can't talk about it now. I can't. I think I may have to throw up. Or scream.

Citizen Services Employee Report
Agent Unit 110/111
Assignment: Starfleet Recruiting Visit on Behalf of
  Starfleet Corps of Engineers

We ended the meeting after one hour elapsed and those in attendance received the information they had come for. This unit had some discussion with Lieutenant Brewster regarding appropriate social protocols within Bynar society. We sensed she did not fully understand our statements because she wanted to go through them multiple times. We are uncertain whether she is satisfied with our explanations. We will review them with her in the morning after we have had a chance to check the suitability of our statements against the information in the human database. This unit believes it can aid Lieutenant Brewster in attaining rational understanding on this issue.

Personal Log, Lieutenant Temperance Brewster

Three pairs showed up. Three pairs. On a planet of millions, only six people think that Starfleet is worth their time. As it turns out, after one of the pairs consulted with 110 and 111, they weren't eligible to join Starfleet because they hadn't acquired some skill certification or what-have-you that they needed to be eligible for offworld assignments. The pair had known this, but they had never seen an offworlder before and they were "curious."

"Curious." I travel across the quadrant asking those who enjoy safety and freedom from tyranny if they will stand up and offer assistance to those who put their *lives* on the line every day so that they can continue to enjoy said freedom and safety. And what am I met with? Curiosity. I'm a sideshow, not a representative of the organization that assures their ongoing existence. They continue on, oblivious to the plight of the rest of the Federation family, pressing their buttons, chattering away in their high-pitched fast-forward whirs and chirps, pondering little of significance beyond whether the entryway should be situated five centimeters further to the left or whether it's fine where it is. How can Quinteros stand it?! I've come all this distance for what? Does anything I do or say matter? I didn't even bother to call up my message account or check out the news nets. I don't want to see the

latest casualty list or know how many setbacks the fleet
has had because no matter what I do, I am incapable of
making a difference.

So this is how the non-meeting meeting went. Maybe if
I talk through it I'll settle down and realize I've done my
best.

Maybe not. But it's worth a try.

Alban and I are sitting there in a conference room with
a stack of padds loaded up with all the best of Starfleet's
recruiting literature sitting on the table. 110 and 111
take a spot near the back of the room, presumably to
keep track of who shows up and who doesn't. I have my
multimedia presentation ready to go. And this one's special—showing a 3D virtual representation of the inside
of a starship's main engineering, prominently displaying
computer banks with enough power to run a major met-
ropolitan area, even one on Bynaus. I'm confident that if I
can have their undivided attention for even half an hour, I
can persuade them or at least seduce them with promises
of the coolest tech toys they've ever seen.

Twenty or so seconds before the hour, the room is
empty save the four of us. Less than a minute later, there
are six Bynars seated at the table. I tell 110/111 to give
us a few more minutes to allow time for latecomers to
arrive. The Citizen Services agents look at me as if I'm
speaking in some obscure Pelapusian tongue and not
Federation Standard. It's not possible, their expressions
say, for Bynars to be late. But my brain refuses to accept
that I've come this far just to face a room of empty chairs.
110/111 don't start looking tense until a few more minutes have elapsed. They hand me a padd containing the
attendees' personnel records, stating again that these are
all the records that have been transmitted so I shouldn't
expect any late arrivals. I thank them politely but continue to wait.

When 110/111's chatter becomes high–pitched and fast

enough to make my head hurt, I start the meeting. I know that I'm talking too fast—that I may be skipping over the majority of periods and commas in my speech, but hey, the Bynars are used to fast-paced patter. The multimedia presentation begins and ends. I clasp my hands together and ask for questions.

A room of blank, barely blinking faces gaze at me.

So I start running through the list of the usual questions—once I join, what kind of training will I have, can I choose my assignment, and so on.

And still, the blank faces remain.

After the longest two or three minutes of silence that I can recall in a lifetime, I let the group know that I'm finished and that I'm available to answer personal questions.

A pair of Bynars hurries up to the front of the conference room to chatter with 110/111. I later find out that this is the pair that wanted to ogle me like a zoo animal.

I stand by myself, tapping my foot a little too compulsively, telling myself to calm down and that this disaster of a meeting was a fluke. Tomorrow will be better—I cling to that mantra. When the fog of anger lifts a bit, I realize that another Bynar pair remains at the table, engaged in a focused—dare I say—heated conversation. I move in closer, blatantly eavesdropping, catching a word here and there that leads me to believe they're talking about Starfleet. A pause in their discussions allows me to insert myself. Having nothing left to lose, I say it straight out: "You interested in Starfleet?" Two pairs of eyes turn on me.

I may have little to no experience dealing with Bynars, but I sense—something in the face, an expectancy—that one of them is interested. I direct my words to this Bynar. Body language is a funny thing. With very few exceptions (intelligence operatives and Vulcans, to name two) most species are incapable of repressing their involuntary physiological reactions to external stimuli. And this Bynar I'm talking to—this Bynar is listening to what I have to say. I believe I have a chance to set up, at the very least, a second meeting. A fast back-and-forth round of talk begins between the mates.

At one point, the less interested Bynar asks me about the phaser I have strapped to my thigh. This strikes me as an odd question but not completely unexpected. I've found that quite a few species—especially those on worlds who eschew any form of personal, self-defense weaponry for whatever reason—are fascinated by the idea of phasers. I unsheathe the weapon, hold it out in front of me (using proper Academy firing range stance), and offer it to the interested Bynar.

Before the phaser leaves my hands, 110/111 appear at my shoulder and inform me that the meeting is over. The CS agents dismiss the remaining pair. Whatever cue 110/111 have given is taken and run with. The Bynars practically flee the room.

If I were a violent person, I would have been sorely tempted to turn that phaser and point it at those meddlesome Bynar agents. Use a little firepower as a way of telling them to back down. But I don't. I've never hurt anyone, even in training.

Hands on hips, I challenge my Bynar handlers, who respond with the explanation that all the parties who want information, have information. The time has come to end the meeting, they say (of course in dual-channel sound). I don't believe it, and I don't think they believe it either. What I think is that this Bynar I've been talking with is interested in Starfleet but the mate isn't, so 110/111 are shutting me down. I did manage to get the Bynar pair's designations before they left—1010 is the one I'm going to follow up with. The mate is 0101. I announce my intention to follow up with 1010.

"Not—"

"—possible. We work—"

"—in pairs. All else—"

"—is unacceptable among—"

"—our people."

I still hear their words ringing in my head.

Of course, at the moment, I didn't accept their statement. "Fine then," I said. "Set up appointments for me at work sites, with supervisors who might point me to those with an aptitude or interest in Starfleet."

"As you requested we—"

"—set up the meeting. Those—"

"—who are interested attended. All—"

"—Bynars had a chance to come."

"Your efforts are now—"

"—terminated."

"You will not—"

"—recruit independently—"

"—at any other venue."

Their words flew at me so fast that I barely had a chance to process them. So I lit into them both. Told them that they'd hardly assisted me in helping me tailor my message to the Bynar population and that I held them—at least partially—responsible for the dismal failure that had been the result.

"We did—"

"—as we were—"

"—instructed."

"All citizens had a choice and—"

"—they rejected what you offered."

"You must—"

"—accept this."

What a cop-out.

What became clear is that these Bynar babysitters had no intention of letting me do my job.

I vented to Alban the whole way back to my quarters. Poor guy. Probably wishes he'd drawn another assignment.

There has to be a way around that. I will not return to headquarters having failed the fleet so spectacularly. I know the rules about respecting the cultures of every species in the Federation, but I cannot in good conscience allow this world to remain in isolation without at least trying to make them see the truth of what is out there.

Sitting here in my visitor's quarters, staring at my bed with its sheet creases running at perfect parallel lines along the top, inhaling air that is so sterile and dry that it sticks in my throat like spun cotton. I hate this place.

A soundless night has fallen outside. I stare out into the purple-gray darkness at the flashing lights, at the Bynars going to and from their work and their quarters, their focus so narrowly on the path before them that they fail to see the galaxy under siege beyond their small lives. The more I'm lost in the scene outside my window, the more my mind succumbs to the rigid, hypnotic rhythms that define this environment, lulling me into a sense of confinement. I shiver, irrationally imagining that the surrounding walls will squeeze me into a narrow box. I will scream for release only to have my terrified protests muffled by the relentless, regular pulse of this world. No one will hear me over the drone of progress. Once upon a time the Bynars were slaves to an AI race. Their isolationism will guide them surely into bondage again.

Wadding up the sheets in my hands, I destroyed any evidence of the perfect creases, of the smooth surface, and exuberantly I ripped the cloth from my bed and threw it on the floor. And this brought me such satisfaction that I started in on the nightstand and then the dresser, until every surface in the room was wiped clean and the room was strewn with clutter. Anger spent, I sprawled on the bed and stared at the ceiling.

Now I'm lying here talking to my personal log, hoping that maybe by talking this through out loud, it will make more sense. Unfortunately, that doesn't appear to be the case. Out of desperation, I disregarded 110/111's orders and sent a private message to the pair I met at the meeting. Can't hurt, can it? My dad always told me that quitting was a sign of a weak will. No way I'm going to go back to headquarters and have to explain that I failed to bring any Bynars into S.C.E. because I was too much of a coward to follow through.

Sleep is far away, so I pick up the padd that has the personnel files on it. I skip over the ineligible unit and move straight to the one who seemed interested. I peruse their stats, medical history, interpersonal evaluations once, then again. I've spent enough years evaluating seemingly impersonal data that I've learned to look beyond the dry facts. The more I read, the more curious I become. Definitely some irregularities in here that warrant further exploration. And they say Bynars are only about yes and no.

The comlink beeps. Can't think of who would want to talk to me at this hour. Not Alban, who could barely keep his eyes open due to travel lag. Funny, I'm not expecting anyone. It's not a visual or an audio message—just text. Odd. What's it say—I CAN HELP YOU.

So who sent it? . . . Hmmm . . . Now that's interesting. And there's a quadrant designation for the sender so I can actually track the sender down and see them in person. Where are my shoes—and that damn planetary locator too? Maybe I should copy that personnel data. Didn't Quinteros say I could back it up on the planetary locator? I'm going for a walk.

Citizen Services Employee Report
Agent Unit 110/111
Assignment: Starfleet Recruiting Visit on Behalf of
   Starfleet Corps of Engineers

We returned to our quarters after the meeting requested by Lieutenant Brewster of Starfleet. Lieutenant Brewster's unwillingness to accept the outcome of the meeting may require further involvement by CS. We recommend that the matter be referred to Captain Quinteros for discussion and clarification. We believe that repeated announcements on the planetary news nets will not yield different results. We could not advise Lieutenant Brewster as to why so few Bynars attended her meeting. Further study and analysis of this issue may be recommended, as Brewster's assertion that Bynaus could make a larger contribution to the war effort is legitimate and is, as yet, unsettled. A planetary study of the matter may be an effective use of resources. All citizens should have a say on the matter, so we will refer it. We will go offline until start of shift tomorrow.

**Interfleet communication, Captain Orfil Quinteros
to Commander Leland T. Lynch**

Contact me immediately upon receipt. There's a problem with your recruiting team.

Citizen Services Employee Report
Agent Unit 110/111
Assignment: Starfleet Recruiting Visit on Behalf of
  Starfleet Corps of Engineers

Our offline period was disrupted at 29:53:22 by a page
from Citizen Services Emergency Division. We were ordered
to Quadrant 925, Building 381, where a security detail would
await us. 925/381 is a facility known as population management that stores and updates Bynaus citizen status. All current
statistical data, including assignments, health, and geographical location, is accessible at 925/381. CSED denied request to
explain why we were ordered to visit 925/381 during the cus-
tomary offline period. We have concluded that an individual
or individuals must have been searching for information on
behalf of Lieutenant Brewster. She had been adamant during
our previous discussion that potential recruits be identified
and approached directly. We informed her that such a request
ran contrary to Bynar procedure. It is possible that she chose
to act without regard to our instructions. We will report further after we have visited 925/381.

UPDATE

Upon arrival at 925/381, a security team (made up of three
units) took us into the central access room. Another unit stood

guard at the door. We knew at this point that this was an unusual situation. We saw a Bynar on the floor, being examined by a medical unit. There was no sign of the other part of the unit, the mate to the Bynar who was being examined.

We were told that the Bynar being examined had terminated. This terminated Bynar had been part of a unit assigned to work in the records facility at 925/381. This Bynar had attempted to access information that was beyond its authorization level. This Bynar had ignored security advisories and proceeded to seek unauthorized access to the database. A warning to cease entry into the information nodule was not heeded, nor was a second warning. The Bynar proceeded into the forbidden zone. The processes of overriding protocols without the other partner in the unit prevented the Bynar from turning off the warning currents discharged as part of the security system. This caused a physiological breakdown that terminated the Bynar's existence. A closer study of the situation revealed the identity of the terminated Bynar: 1010, one member of a unit that had attended the Starfleet recruitment meeting. A review of the security record reveals that 1010 was given multiple opportunities to stop the intrusion on the database but elected not to. 1010 attempted to use both sets of security codes assigned to its unit. Further investigation will take place, but preliminary evidence indicates that there was no malfunction that caused the premature termination of 1010. 1010 appeared to have made a choice without the knowledge of 0101. Review of data collected by visual and audio sensors will affirm or negate this conclusion.

0101 is not on-site. 0101's offline period was interrupted for the notification of 1010's termination. 0101 has been admitted for medical treatment. Citizen Services has started identifying potential mates for 0101 who will emerge from birthing chambers in the coming shifts.

A security unit told us that Lieutenant Brewster was in custody in the adjoining room. Evidence suggests that Lieutenant Brewster is somehow tied to 1010's termination. Captain Quinteros has been contacted. Starfleet authorities will provide representation for Lieutenant Brewster. Representation will arrive during third shift tomorrow.

We exited the central access room. As part of her confinement by the security unit, Lieutenant Brewster's hands had been manacled, as is procedure. We observed that Lieutenant Brewster had unusually pale skin and appeared to be perspiring. Her uniform was not arranged as per Starfleet standards. Upon our entering the room, Lieutenant Brewster moved in her chair, the better to see us. We feel that we must transcribe her statements precisely so that her words can represent her position.

"I didn't do it." Lieutenant Brewster made this statement before we addressed her.

We informed her that a hearing would be held to determine whether she was responsible in the death of 1010.

"And what if you say I am?" she said.

We stated that if there was a defect in her processing that prevented her from understanding the instructions/orders we had given her, we would seek to repair the defect.

"And if there isn't a defect?"

Lieutenant Brewster said the word "defect" as if she didn't understand its meaning. We must discuss this with Captain Quinteros so that he can communicate the meaning of the word to her. We shared the following information with Lieutenant Brewster. We repeat it here so our superiors in CS can evaluate our actions accurately. In assessing Bynar behavior that deviates outside normal limits, a determination is made about whether a defect in thinking or physiological processing exists. In Bynar protocols, defects are often correctable by reprogramming the thinking or functioning processes. We went no further into our explanation because Lieutenant Brewster appeared to be in a physically compromised state that increased incrementally as we spoke. We felt she needed assistance from the medical unit, but the lieutenant refused our recommendation.

"What happens if a defect can't be fixed?" she asked.

Her voice sounded small and thin. We believe Lieutenant

Brewster must have been experiencing inhibition of her processing functions. We informed her that if a unit cannot be corrected and can no longer perform its function in society, it has already agreed, at the time of emergence from the chamber, to voluntarily terminate its existence.

Lieutenant Brewster's eyes rolled back into her head and she fell out of her chair onto the floor. We took this as indicative that perhaps there is a defect in her physiological processing that causes cognitive overload. We requested that the medical unit examine her to assure her ongoing health until a judiciary unit can assess her status and determine her fate.

Sensor Recording
Building 891/45
Holding Facility, Room 117

I'm sitting in the corner talking to myself. Whispering, actually. I know the sensors will record this and I don't care. Days or weeks from now, when my rotting corpse is being transported back to Centauri for my funeral, this recording will be my final words to my friends and family. They deserve to know the truth.

Besides, I need to think. My adrenaline has scrambled my thoughts and it's all I can do to repress my fight-or-flight reaction, so thinking aloud is proving helpful. I might look crazier than they think I am already, but I'm okay with that.

Yes, there's a cozy bed and I should be sleeping if I expect to have the clarity I'll need tomorrow when I face the proverbial "firing squad." As prisons go, the Bynars have a nice setup. I have plenty of nutritional supplements and water available to me. The bed is comfortable and the environmental controls are set to optimal human levels. I'm free to walk around, so this feels more like a hospital than a cell—they even removed the shackles from my wrists. From this vantage point on the floor, I can see outside my room to the guard station. There's maybe two pairs out there—tops—and they seem to come and go from their post pretty regularly.

I want out. No way I'm going to sit around here, expecting

Starfleet to rescue me, only to have my brain reprogrammed or worse—termination. I didn't think they allowed capital punishment in the Federation, but I honestly don't think the Bynars see it as capital punishment.

The more I think about it, the Bynars treat a malfunctioning individual the way they'd deal with a programming error: if the code can't be fixed, the whole trunk of commands needs to be eliminated. And the Bynars don't have any moral or metaphysical issues with ending life because they value life only insofar as a life can contribute to society. Good equals productive, fulfilling one's assignment, furthering the progress of the planet. There is no god, no codified commandments on ethics or behavior beyond the on and off branches created in binary language. A computer does what it is programmed to do—nothing more. The Bynars see themselves as organic extensions of computer processes. Crime occurs only rarely on Bynaus because crime requires irrationality, and computers aren't irrational.

So what does that make me? A malfunction to be fixed or eliminated? Yeah, I know a JAG is on the way, but I don't know whether the Bynars will wait or try to repair me before I have legal representation. I have to get out of here.

I have to prove it, but I think I know what happened and why I'm here.

It's not what anyone suspects.

Yesterday

Commander Henry Winter yawned, not wanting to give in to the impulse to curl up in the closest chair and sleep for another few hours. Interstellar warp travel always did a number on his internal clock. Never mind that he'd been successfully criss-crossing the quadrant for four decades—his body refused to adjust quickly. If asked, he'd blame his mongrel parentage. The genes of his half-Betazoid, half-Trill mother warred with the DNA of his human father. His body's remedy to the conflict was to give up—and Henry was fine with it. He liked sleep. Almost as much as he liked eating. But right now, in this moment on Bynaus, Henry knew he wasn't going to get off so easily.

"Lieutenant Brewster has—"

"—left her holding room and—"

"—we have no idea—"

"—where she has gone. The—"

"—sensors were disabled—"

"—temporarily. We are attempting—"

"—to locate her now."

Taking a deep breath, Winter studied the Bynar unit standing before him and thought through their words before responding. This inclination to think before he spoke made him a good lawyer, or so he'd been told. "So what you two are telling me is that my client has escaped your custody?"

The Bynar unit nodded affirmatively.

"That complicates things." A defendant who ran away, in Winter's experience, was guilty, terrified, or both. He'd read the preliminary data during his flight. Brewster, a relatively inexperienced field recruiter, hadn't had a lot of success in convincing the Bynars to join Starfleet. She'd had a disagreement with her Bynar advisers over how to proceed and retired to her quarters without resolving it. What happened next was unclear.

The Bynar Citizen Services unit assigned to the case stated their theory that Brewster made an arrangement, perhaps even a coercive one, to meet the Bynar unit 1010/0101 at the unit's assigned workplace, the archive of Bynaus's population records. She had sent a private message to them shortly after the meeting had ended. It had been a generic missive: "Nice meeting you. Can we talk soon?" But maybe there was more to it—a signal of some sort—that Winter couldn't see yet. The investigation asserted that Brewster wanted 1010/0101 to help her identify more units as potential recruiting targets.

At this point, the story became primarily conjecture, so Winter wasn't willing to take it as gospel. The data retrieval didn't go as planned—if it had, Winter wouldn't be on Bynaus. Brewster allegedly forced 1010 to ignore the warnings and push into forbidden areas. The security protocols put in place to protect the database led to the loss of 1010's life. Since 0101 had been under heavy sedation since 1010's termination, 0101 had yet to provide any testimony. (Henry hated that word, termination. It felt like a euphemism for death that actually sounded worse than the word *death*.) Brewster refused to make a statement without counsel, save to say that she had nothing to do with 1010's death. Her protests aside, what Winter had examined so far didn't do much to exonerate her. What little, sketchy evidence he'd seen had come from sensors. Those records placed her near the scene of the murder close to the time of the murder.

Still, the synchronization of data from various servers and storage centers hadn't been completed yet, so Winter refused to draw conclusions. Initially, Winter couldn't fathom why the data-gathering process was so laborious; usually he had what he asked for immediately. He then realized that one of the downsides of having a society so completely integrated with technology was that there were even more variables and systems than on a typical Federation world. Finding a way through the maze of systems and bureaucracy, especially in a pure democracy, took time. Consequently, he wasn't going to initiate a plea, consider court-martial, or seek deportation until he had more information.

"While you all are looking for Brewster, I'll want to review new evidence as it arrives as well as interview the units who have worked with Lieutenant Brewster," Henry said. "Don't forget to gather up her personal effects from her quarters— and while we're at it, I'd like the reports from the officers who interacted with her on the transport to Bynaus—see if she showed any signs of meltdown before she landed." He balled his hands into fists, rested them on his hips, and searched the crowd of Bynars gathered around him for whoever might be in charge. *Not a rank insignia among them and hardly any hint as to how to tell them apart,* Henry thought with a flash of annoyance. "I'd like a meeting with my counterpart that's heading up the criminal investigation. Can I see a raised hand letting me know who you are?"

The eight Bynars standing before him stopped chattering among themselves and gave him a curious look. A long moment elapsed as the blank stares continued.

"The police. The magistrate . . . A crime was committed. Someone broke the law," Henry said, feeling all the world like he was dealing with a group of first-year cadets in his Basics of Starfleet Law class. "Whoever deals with crime is who I need to talk to."

One of the black and silver clad pairs erupted in a burst of rapid back-and-forth chirps and trills before slowing down enough to involve him in their conversation. "Crime. You refer to Lieutenant Brewster—"

"—breaking protocols. Bynar code recognizes—"

"—the aberration in behavior but fails to—"

"—recognize the definition of crime."

"You have a dead body that isn't supposed to be dead. Someone did it. That's a crime. Any questions?"

The Bynars chattered among themselves, then turned to Winter and responded with a chorus of "No."

"Excellent. Whoever caused the death needs to be found and held accountable, whether that is Lieutenant Brewster or someone we haven't found yet. Let's go to work," Henry said.

Interview Transcript
Lieutenant Brewster
Submitted by Unit 110/111

UNIT 110/111: After you left your quarters, you went to
925/381.

BREWSTER: Yes.

UNIT 110/111: You had arranged to meet the unit 1010/0101
there?

BREWSTER: No. I made no arrangements to meet. I contacted
them, yes. Later, a message showed up. I noticed where
it came from and I went there. When I got there, I found
1010 on the ground. I didn't realize that 1010 was dead—I
mean terminated. Soon after, the security people showed up.
That's it.

UNIT 110/111: You wanted information from 1010/0101.

BREWSTER: I wanted my mission to succeed.

UNIT 110/111: To your way of thinking, your assignment justi-
fied the termination of 1010 if it meant you received access
to the information you wanted.

BREWSTER: I didn't kill anyone. I'm being set up. [*buries head
in hands*] You have to believe me. I didn't do it. I'm not saying anything else until my lawyer gets here.

Yesterday

Winter switched off the viewscreen and sat back in his chair, studying the terminal, holding his hands over his mouth and thinking. Something was missing. During his tenure in JAG, he'd known plenty of guilty defendants who claimed they were innocent. Oh, they'd put on quite a song and dance of tears and hysterics, even when a pile of indisputably damning evidence sat right in front of their faces. But Winter knew better, so those liars rarely escaped their punishments. His colleagues called it his "Betazoid edge." He didn't have the heart to tell them that his empathic abilities amounted to little more than a finely honed intuitive sense about people that rarely failed him. Whether it was genetics or acute observational skills didn't matter that much.

But something about this case nagged at him. Nothing in Brewster's Starfleet record indicated that she had any tendencies that would lead her to resort to violence to get her way. As an almost-counselor in training, Brewster might talk someone to death before she'd do physical harm. Rather, Brewster was a rah-rah true believer type who lacked the life experience that might have tarnished her fervent evangelism on behalf of Starfleet ideals. Winter would go as far as to call her naïve. She was passionate about doing the right thing, but not at any cost. The running away part . . . that he couldn't get around.

At first he assumed she'd resorted to extreme measures

to escape punishment, but then the Bynar units explained that she'd merely been committed to an observational ward, not a holding cell or a brig. The room's entrances and exits had nothing more than low-level locks that a child could bypass. All Brewster required to escape custody was an opportune moment to slip by her guards—none of the usual ruses, weapons, or assault tactics that usually accompanied a prison break. Apparently Bynars didn't have any sort of crime problem. When a "malfunction" (what Winter would call an illegal behavior) appeared in a Bynar, the "defective" individual willingly entered custody and remained there until the nature of the problem had been diagnosed and fixed. The Bynar focus on the collective good pervaded the psyche so completely that the notion of self-preservation was smothered by deference to the welfare of the masses. If a Bynar's presence endangered others, the Bynar would err on the side of complete submission to the authorities. The CS agents assigned to the Brewster case had assumed that Brewster would behave as reasonably as her Bynar counterparts would in the same situation, in hindsight a rather obvious error in judgment. The more time Winter spent on this case, the more he believed a massive cross-cultural misunderstanding had complicated matters dramatically. For this reason, Winter wasn't willing to assume his default position on runaways. A chime on his combadge indicated that Ensign Alban had arrived. Winter invited Alban into his makeshift office and asked the young Bajoran to take a seat.

Alban shifted in his chair, clenching and unclenching his hands, occasionally pausing to run his fingers through his unruly brown hair or fiddle with his ear where his earring would be, were it not for Starfleet dress codes.

Watching him made Winter feel antsy. "Is there a problem, Ensign?"

"No, sir," Alban said, straightening up and folding his hands in his lap. In spite of his immaculate uniform, he had a rumpled, just-got-out-of-bed air about him.

"Tell me about Lieutenant Brewster," Winter said, sliding the stylus out of its holder on the side of the padd. The conversation would be recorded by sensors, but he liked being able to note observations while he was interviewing a potential witness. "How long you've known her, what's she like as a commanding officer, how she's seen around headquarters . . ."

Alban's eyes dropped to the floor, then shifted up to Winter's face before settling on a spot just to the right of Winter's nose. "I've only been assigned to personnel for five months—since graduation. I've seen Lieutenant Brewster around. Been in a few meetings with her. I'm hardly an expert. You should talk to someone at Headquarters."

Winter raised his gaze from the padd and studied Alban. "I don't expect expertise. I want your thoughts and observations."

The ensign colored crimson, took a deep breath, and began again. "The lieutenant got her promotion about the same time I joined the group. She's never been a screamer—always polite about issuing orders, though—"

Winter leaned forward. "Yes?"

"She's always showing up to check on her direct reports without warning. Looking over their shoulders, watching everything they do, correcting them in public. She uses this sweet, soft voice, but she makes people nervous."

"Is she resented?"

"Not so much resented. When Lieutenant Brewster wants something done and she doesn't think she's being taken seriously enough, she will invade every moment of your life until she's satisfied." Alban shrugged. "Maybe . . ."

"Yes?"

"Maybe she's overcompensating. Trying to prove she deserved her promotion so she's always pushing too hard, putting too much pressure on herself and others."

"Is that why she wanted to be sent to Bynaus?" Winter had yet to identify why a young, attractive officer with a relatively cushy career for wartime was so bent on visiting a planet that most of the Federation forgot was a member. "To accomplish what no one else had done by bringing more Bynars into Starfleet?"

"That was the rumor," Alban said. "But Lieutenant Brewster is passionate about her work. She absolutely believes in what we're doing in Starfleet and she'll do whatever it takes to make sure Starfleet's interests are protected. Fond of the phrase *patriotic duty*."

Leaning back into his chair, Winter jotted down his impression of Alban's statement: idealistic, determined, inexperienced. *Certainly seems to be a formula for a major judgment error. So she didn't plan on killing anyone—these tendencies could lead to unintended consequences.* "You want to guess what my next question is, Ensign?"

Alban swallowed hard. "You want to know if, based on what I knew of her, I think she was capable of murder, especially last night since I was one of the last people to see her before she went into custody."

"Good call."

"I don't want to make her sound guilty," Alban said, his shoulders noticeably slumping. "But the lieutenant was angry last night after we left the recruiting meeting."

Winter took no pleasure in Alban's misery, but the ensign's obvious reluctance to provide specifics sent up all kinds of red flags. "Angry 'I hate it when I spill coffee on my uniform' angry or 'someone is going to pay if this doesn't get fixed' angry?"

Alban exhaled loudly. "The latter. I've never seen her so . . . unhinged. She could be snippy if you disagreed with her or you failed an assignment. But this was near stratospheric outrage. I couldn't reason with her because I was afraid she'd report me for insubordination. If she hadn't calmed down by morning, I was going to contact headquarters and ask for advice."

"Was her outrage directed at anything or anyone specifically?"

"Lieutenant Brewster had a finally honed sense of justice and fairness. She felt that Starfleet's efforts weren't given a chance to be successful and that the Bynars assigned to help us out were obstructing us."

Winter asked for clarification and Alban provided it, going into detail about what had happened during and after the recruiting meeting. A less experienced investigator might have found little of significance in the series of events. To Winter, a sense of unease refused to abate—all was not as it appeared to be. Subtext abounded, but whose subtext and why he had yet to ascertain.

After he dismissed Alban, he signaled the CS agents assigned to the case, 110 and 111, and asked them to see him at their earliest convenience. Winter wanted to rehear their version of events in light of what Alban had told him. He also checked with Security Services and discovered they had yet to figure out where Lieutenant Brewster had vanished to. Until his client could tell her side, he would do what he could to reconstruct her point of view. So if she couldn't speak for herself, what she left behind would have to speak for her.

What little evidence he had was strewn over his desk where he could pick up and contemplate each item or report. Winter, a visual thinker, believed the evidence functioned like an incomplete puzzle: if he could see how the pieces related to one another, logic might help him fill in the gaps. Unfastening a lid to a polymer container, he emptied the contents— Brewster's personal effects from her guest quarters—where he could see them. Most of what he saw was marked with an official Starfleet insignia; he surmised that she must have brought the things with her from Headquarters. A generic padd drew his attention; he reached for it, activated it, and discovered that it contained information on the Bynars who attended the recruiting meeting.

Nothing about the information struck him as out of the ordinary at first glance except . . . the last record activated on this padd belonged to the unit 1010/0101, one of whom was now dead. Last night Brewster had held this in her hands, studied the record, and left her quarters. She had also felt that whatever this padd said was important enough that she backed up the 1010/0101's files to another device. Brewster remained the de facto suspect because no one else appeared to have a motive, yet there was something about the murder that didn't work in Winter's mind. Perhaps it was the straightforward logic of the theory of the crime. The Bynars could barely grasp the notion of crime, in part because of its illogical nature, so naturally, their version of what might have happened would be rational. *But it doesn't account for an irrational human's behavior. If Lieutenant Brewster was as angry as Alban said she was, could she have behaved in such a cold-blooded, reasonable fashion?* He examined the timeline:

> Brewster enters quarters; sends message (Sensor log record 83042-1)
> Brewster receives message (Sensor log record 93201-56)
> Brewster leaves quarters (Sensor log record 389925-20)
> Brewster arrives at Building 925/381 (Sensor log record 57120-92)
> Security team arrives and discovers Brewster by the body

The message. Winter scrolled through an evidence list, located a screen capture of the message and called it up.

I CAN HELP YOU.

The sender had been 1010/0101. Had the message been an answer to a request Brewster had made at the meeting? Or had 1010/0101 initiated the meeting?

Wait a minute. A moment of clarity cut through the muddle in his mind. He focused on the message: the pronoun *I* was used. I referred to an individual. Bynars didn't function as individuals, they functioned in pairs. If 1010/0101 had asked her to meet, wouldn't they have used the pronoun *we*? For the first time since he'd been assigned the case, Henry believed he had proof that Brewster's protestations of innocence may not been the burble of a guilty conscience afraid of consequences.

★ ★ ★

When the Citizen Services agents arrived less than an hour later, he asked them once again to review their interactions with Lieutenant Brewster after the meeting. He'd get to his questions about the message later; he wanted to establish motive—other than guilt—for her to escape custody.

The CS unit offered to provide Winter with a security feed recording that would allow him to view, for himself, all of the postarrest interactions Lieutenant Brewster had had with Bynar units, including her escape. Security Services needed a little more time, 110/111 explained, to gather and sort the relevant data before they would provide Winter with a comprehensive collection of all the audiovisual evidence that could be located. They expected that Winter wouldn't have much longer to wait. The data was being reviewed by the sensor team supervisors for its final release as they spoke.

This revelation prompted a sigh of relief from Winters; he would be spared having to interview and reinterview the same parties in hopes of having new tidbits of information emerge. He did have one more question for the Bynar unit as he attempted to finalize his personal timeline. "So that's the only time you talked with her after 1010 was found—your on-the-record interrogation that I've already seen."

The unit paused, then said, "We talked to her—"

"—after we arrived. She said—"

"—she was innocent. She asked—"

"—about the consequences if—"

"—she was found—"

"—defective and we provided—"

"—that information."

"I think I managed to miss any record of this particular exchange," Winter said, looking over the reports listed on the padd before him. "This is the first I've heard of this conversation, so why don't you explain it to me?"

The agent unit protested that all the footage would be available soon, but Winter cut them off and asked them to explain the conversation.

He listened attentively as 110/111 provided him with the rudimentary outline of Bynar jurisprudence that they had shared with Lieutenant Brewster. When they got to the part where they told Brewster that either the defect that caused the misbehavior was fixed or termination occurred, Winter jumped out of his chair and asked the Bynar unit to repeat what they'd just said.

"If a unit cannot be fixed—"

"—and is no longer useful—"

"—it must be terminated."

"And you said this to Lieutenant Brewster?"

"Yes—"

"—we did."

Winter groaned aloud. "Brewster took off because she thought there was a chance you would execute her."

"Execute—"

"—her?"

"*Terminate* her. She was afraid for her life. Damn it all, we have to find that woman and bring her back." The Bynars, as sophisticated as they might have been technologically, saw the universe in such absolute, black-and-white terms that they failed to understand the subtleties of communication with other species. Simply put, they didn't understand that everyone didn't see things the way they did. In this respect, the Bynars had much in common with unsophisticated children.

"We wouldn't have—"

"—terminated her."

"She didn't understand it that way," Winter said, loading his padds into his satchel. "Based on what you've told me, I'm inclined to believe that Lieutenant Brewster may have been telling the truth when she claimed she didn't murder 1010."

"If that is correct—"

"—then who did?"

"I'm coming to that. I have one more question for you both. Examine this message that 1010 and 0101 sent Lieutenant

Brewster and tell me what you make of it." He shoved the padd across the desk toward the CS unit.

A flurry of high-pitched gibberish erupted between them.

Winter sat back in his chair, palms together, fingers flexing, and watched, not entirely surprised by their reaction.

"Not possible."

"Bynars do not—"

"—communicate in—"

"—this way."

"Contact the Medical Center where 0101 is resting," Henry said, gathering up the evidence padds and stacking them in his satchel. "Let them know that they need to bring her back to consciousness. We have to ask her whether her mate was dead before or after contacting Lieutenant Brewster." He'd hardly begun his request before 110/111 started issuing unintelligible orders into their comm units. When he rediscovered the padd holding the personnel records, he paused, cradling it in his palm before placing it in the satchel alongside the others. The document he'd been reading remained on the screen; he scanned the contents from a new perspective. An involuntary grin split his face. *We may have our answers . . .*

The search for Lieutenant Brewster continues. Visual sensor records indicate that the lieutenant left her holding room, rendered a Bynar security unit unconscious, and proceeded to look for a planetary locating device. Since we have ascertained that the device was taken, sensors and security units are studying the planetary grid to find the planetary locating device. No sign of the device has appeared. It is possible that in her efforts to hide, Lieutenant Brewster has gone to the only place on Bynaus that is not linked to the locating system: the tunnels and chambers far below the surface that are associated with the master computer preservation and maintenance. The grid analysis is only seventy-five percent complete, however. We will not go into the tunnels until all other possibilities have been ruled out. Commander Winter has indicated that he will be part of any search party.

The evidence logs regarding the death of 1010 are complete and have been placed in the custody of Commander Winter. While we are waiting for 0101 to be brought back to consciousness, we have discussed the inconsistencies we have discovered. Of most concern to Citizen Services is the apparent use of a singular pronoun in communication. Such a usage may exist but only in the intimate interaction between mates, never in public forums or with individuals of other species. This unit found this discovery to be uncomfortable as Bynars and as CS agents. We are searching for data that may support such a violation.

We have examined the personnel file given to Lieutenant Brewster and have discovered that 1010/0101 had recently received counseling after problems at a work assignment. The unit in question had been in their current positions only six time sectors. This assignment was the third in eight time sectors, a highly unusual circumstance. Not only did 1010/0101 move work locations, the unit moved residential areas as well. The diagnostician believed that 1010 may have been on the verge of malfunction and so required a complete change of circumstances. The irregularities in 1010's behavior patterns showed increasing discontent and inefficiency in the work environment. Examination of 0101 indicated a growing agitation and antagonism in the unit relationship. 0101 had been a model worker in previous work situations and had repeatedly stated how much satisfaction the work situation brought to the unit. The work transfer instigated to address concerns posed by 1010's behavior and work performance was not encouraged by 0101, though 0101 failed to file an official protest. In private sessions, not available to Commander Winter but open to CS agents because of 1010's termination, we have learned that 0101 expressed confusion regarding 1010's behavior but supported the transfer in the hope that 1010 would improve and that the previous assignment could be resumed. Within the past ten planetary rotations, 0101 learned that the unit 1010/0101 would no longer be eligible to return to their former duties due to instability in 1010's reasoning processes. We conclude that the recent denial may have provided the 1010/0101 unit with a motivation to attend the Starfleet recruiting meeting. We believe 0101 will affirm our conclusions. 0101 should be ready to interview by 18:56:432.

Starfleet JAG Report, Commander Henry Winter

After several delays, the relevant evidence came into my custody and I've had a chance to review it. Most of it affirms what is already known in terms of timeline. What came as a surprise was the video surveillance from Building 925/381 that showed Lieutenant Brewster aiming her phaser at 1010. The building entry records indicate that 0101 was on the premises, but was apparently not in the room at the time Brewster drew her weapon. This is different from the original report because security reported that they awoke 0101 in quarters. Additionally, this puzzles me because it is my understanding that the Bynars work together, not separately, so it doesn't make sense that 1010 would be accessing the records alone. Still, the message that Brewster received said, "I can help you," not "We can help you." Could 1010 have acted independently of 0101? Or did 0101 refuse to go along with 1010's plan and by so doing, sat mutely by, allowing 1010 to die? 0101's story will be critical to assembling the full picture of what happened.

The only audio we have has Brewster stating, "I'll do whatever it takes to help Starfleet win this war." The assumption is that Brewster held 1010 at gunpoint to force 1010 to access the forbidden personnel files. As much as I'm inclined to believe that Brewster feared for her life and took off to protect it, this evidence casts aspersions on the self-preservation motive. Brewster had a meeting with 1010, a reason to force

1010 to access the record, and we can place her at the crime scene.

I still need to review the recordings of Brewster's recruiting meeting as well as get an emergency warrant to subpoena her personal logs. All Headquarters can confirm for me now is that Brewster has accessed her logs since arriving on Bynaus and has recorded several entries. I expect to receive authorization sometime after I interview 0101.

Interview Transcript
CS Agent Unit 110/111 and Commander Henry Winter
with 0101

WINTER: State for the record your designation.

0101: We—[*pause, pained expression*] 0101 is my designation.

WINTER: Two cycles ago, your unit, 1010/0101, attended a Starfleet recruiting meeting. Who made the decision to attend?

0101: We did.

WINTER: You decided together, or were either you or 1010 more interested in the prospect of joining Starfleet?

0101 [*stumbling over words*]: Our unit was not satisfied [*long pause*] with our current work assignment. It was not a good fit. [*covers face with hands*] Citizen Services Work Task Force agents said we would be unable to change assignments again. 1010 could not be trusted. Diagnostics indicated that 1010 may have been—[*pauses again—tremors overtake 0101's body; medical units rush over, take a tricorder readout, administer medication; 0101 relaxes, indicates a willingness to continue questioning*]

WINTER: 1010 may have been what, 0101?

0101: [*relaxes, breathes slowly*] Malfunctioning.

WINTER: Had 1010 been referred to diagnostics for reprogramming or repair?

0101: Not officially. Our unit had been put on notice that

such—such—[*deep breath*] a possibility existed. Joining Starfleet may have allowed our unit to avoid 1010's being committed to reprogramming.

WINTER: What would have happened to your unit if 1010 had been sent for reprogramming?

0101: Our unit would have gone for evaluation.

WINTER: Not just 1010, but you as well?

0101: Yes.

WINTER: So 1010 would have been assessed for deficiencies and you would have been assessed, even though you were not malfunctioning. After the assessment, diagnostics would determine which of your physiological or mental processes needed repairing so your unit could continue to contribute to Bynar society.

0101: Yes.

WINTER: How did the CS determination make you feel—the notion that you needed to be fixed even though the problem was clearly with 1010?

0101 [*puzzled*]: The question. It is confusing. Feel?

110/111: [*unintelligible chatter back and forth with 0101*]

0101: Understood. The work our unit had performed before now was satisfactory to both of us. The new work was not for both parts of the unit. 1010 could not adapt or modify to work environments. All outcomes were determined by 1010. What was good for the whole unit was not relevant to CS. [*lapses into Bynar-speak*]

110/111: [*unintelligible chatter continues between the three Bynars; 0101 is obviously agitated*]

WINTER [*holding up a hand*]: Let me clarify, since obviously use of the singular and individual possessive pronouns is difficult for you. Basically, your contribution to work or to the unit was not figured into the analysis of the situation. 1010's malfunctions or problems determined what happened to the unit.

0101 [*quietly*]: Yes.

WINTER: Did you resent 1010? Let me rephrase—did 1010's

apparent inability to function in a work assignment that satisfied you make it more difficult for your unit—and you—to function within Bynar society?

0101: [*nods*]

WINTER: Are you in any way responsible for 1010's death?

0101: [*wails, collapses back onto bed and curls into fetal position; begins jabbering in computer-speak*]

WINTER: I'll take that as a yes.

[*more computer-speak between the Bynars*]

110/111: You are correct in your assumption, Commander.

WINTER: So what does this mean for Lieutenant Brewster? That an innocent woman has been terrified into running for her life? I'd recommend we use all our resources to find my client. If necessary, I'll ask Captain Quinteros to call in a Starfleet security detail to speed up the process.

(end recording)

Personal Log, Lieutenant Temperance Brewster

I've almost reached the access portal. A few more kilometers and I'm out of the tunnels, even if I have to crawl on my hands and knees, which is about where I'm at. I have no idea what I'll find when I open the door back into the Bynar world—or if I'll even manage to make it out before . . . before it becomes impossible to go on . . .

I knew they wouldn't be able to track me down here, but that strategy has proven risky. They probably won't be able to find me either. Even though it has taken me I don't know how long—I've lost track of time down here in the half-dark where there is no night or day or chronometer. Probably days. I'm so tired. I think I might stop and sleep. Besides, my feet feel like they have spikes driving through my arches—though that's the least of my problems. I suspect I'll collapse if I don't take a break. Half my water supply disappeared when I took that tumble during the venting. The rations I stole from the security station are nearly gone. My energy plummets with each passing hour. I don't know how this will end.

The CS agents might have figured out where I am by now and have a squad of armed Bynars waiting to take me into custody. Maybe I should rush into their waiting arms and take my chances with the Bynar penal system. If I'm lucky—and I don't seem to be—my JAG lawyer might have shown up.

At the very least, I want those I leave behind to know why I died: there's more to 1010's death than what anyone suspects. If I don't expose the truth, a tragic situation will go undiscovered, becoming a mere annotation to a file somewhere. It might be, as fate may have it, that I won't make it back to the surface where I can reveal the truth myself. But my hope is that, should I die, someone will ask questions: Why did 1010 make the choices it did? What was so important that 1010 was willing to risk death? And those questions will lead them to retrace my steps—the answers will show up eventually. Surely the fact that I took the time to transfer the data should be a big red flag shouting, "Look here!" Without understanding, more lives may be lost. I came to Bynaus believing I was on a crusade to help Starfleet fight the Dominion. Now I wonder if the outcome of my mission may help insure the ongoing survival of a world.

Maybe . . . maybe . . . maybe I can make a . . . difference . . .

(recording stopped due to inactivity)

Citizen Services Employee Report
Agent Unit 110/111
Assignment: Starfleet Recruiting Visit on Behalf of
    Starfleet Corps of Engineers

0101 has been determined to be medically stable and has
been sentenced to solitary holding until a punishment can be
meted out. The Citizen Services Judiciary Committee has suggested banishment to solitary duty in the master computer
maintenance facility. It is believed that such an assignment
will eventually lead to 0101's termination. There are no known
records of an individual Bynar surviving long-term assignment
to solo duty. There are no known records of individual Bynars
surviving banishment from participation in a unit. We have
presented the Judiciary Committee's assessment to 0101. This
information was received by 0101 with no visible reaction.
0101 appears resigned to the punishment. This unit found
0101's reaction to punishment to be unexpected. In this unit's
previous experience, for a malfunctioning unit or Bynar with
the difficulties ascribed to 0101, a degree of discontent or protest is the normal response. 0101's behavior does not fit within
usual parameters. Further investigation will be undertaken.
This unit has requested authorization to visit 1010/0101's quarters here as well as the unit's previous residence.

Starfleet JAG Report, Commander Henry Winter

I've spent the last four hours going through the recordings, and what I've seen troubles me. 0101 had to know that the crime was going to be discovered. First of all, it appears that 0101 sent the message that Lieutenant Brewster acted on. I've begun to believe that 0101 brought 1010 to Building 925/381 under false pretenses and that once they arrived, 0101 set in motion the events that led to 1010's death.

Even more damning: I just watched datafeed that showed Lieutenant Brewster showing her weapon to 1010/0101 after the meeting. The identical perspective and view of Brewster appears in the security feed that showed 1010's death. It is as if the shots of Brewster after the recruiting meeting were lifted out of one feed and strategically placed in the security feed to implicate her in 1010's death. So how much more of this data has been doctored? As far as I'm concerned, this creates enough reasonable doubt that Lieutenant Brewster is off the hook. I've transmitted all of the data to the nearest starbase for our security data experts to analyze. I suspect that much of what we've been given as "proof" has been fabricated.

Though 0101 has as much as admitted to being an accessory to murder, my gut tells me that there's more to her story than what we presently know. It was odd . . . I don't often have powerful empathic impressions. Being of mixed parentage assures that. But today in the medical facility as I was interviewing 0101 for the record, I sensed a powerful feeling of grief and regret—not guilt. Unless the murderer is a sociopath or has some other serious mental illness, there are usually undertones of violence or resentment at being caught wedded to a palpable sense of guilt. Whatever the case was for the unit 1010/0101, 0101 loved (do Bynars love?) 1010.

I keep coming back to the personnel records that Brewster had access to. The answer has to be in the file somewhere because we've learned, among other things, that Brewster beamed the contents of this padd into another device at some point before she disappeared. Something in these files was important enough that she made a copy. I have to figure out what that something is. I haven't had time to go through every minute detail in the record. Once I do, I'm not sure if I'll see it. Brewster is trained in personnel management. She's learned to read between the lines of bureaucratese to see what's left unsaid. I suspect she saw the unwritten meaning of 1010/0101's behavior and it prompted her to take off in an effort to both exonerate herself and confirm her hunch.

Speaking of Brewster, it appears that she went down into the tunnels. Security traced an unauthorized planetary grid analysis to a terminal near the holding area where Brewster escaped. She called up the map of the underground tunnels that the Bynars use to gain access to the master computer bank. Her destination was not the master computer, but apparently she wanted to be invisible to the above-ground world as she traveled from one location to another, so she took the tunnels. Brewster has yet to appear on the planetary grid—there is no sign of her planetary locator anywhere, leading Security to believe she remains belowground. Once 110/111 finish their investigation into 0101, I will join them in a search party to find Lieutenant Brewster.

Citizen Services Employee Report
Agent Unit 110/111
Assignment: Starfleet Recruiting Visit on Behalf of
    Starfleet Corps of Engineers

We received authorization to investigate the day-to-day
activities of unit 1010/0101. Using the personnel file as a template, we received the unit's schedule, including all comings
and goings for the last two planetary rotations. It is rare that
a Judiciary Committee authorizes a release of planetary locator device records, but murder is equally rare, so we received
permission to access the locator master files to ascertain
where the unit was and see if there were any irregularities. A
pattern became apparent. Cross-referencing 1010/0101's visits
to the diagnosticians with geographical locales, it appears
that the diagnostician visits coincided with visits to a location
within the unit's old residential facility. According to the grid,
the location is not a residential apartment, but an unused
maintenance area. We find this to be worthy of investigation.
Further, when we analyzed Lieutenant Brewster's last known
location before she descended into the tunnels, it appears
she was placing herself in a location that would allow her to
access the old residential building directly by traversing approximately thirty-five kilometers of tunnels. This hypothesis
is reinforced by the last request Lieutenant Brewster made of
her planetary locator device before she went off the grid. The

lieutenant asked the locator to plot and store the route from the tunnel access port to the residential building.

Of some concern to us is the conclusion that Lieutenant Brewster has had ample time to travel thirty-five kilometers and emerge back onto the surface grid. Though diagnostic protocols have been run and rerun, there has been no visual sighting or sensor reading that indicates Lieutenant Brewster has emerged from below. We have narrowed the possibilities and believe that Lieutenant Brewster is injured or has terminated. Commander Winter will join the search party.

The present . . .

Henry Winter chased after the Bynars as best he could. The good news was that the tunnels had a relatively smooth metal surface, roughed up enough to provide grip for their boots. The bad news was that the relentless sameness of kilometer after kilometer of eerie blue-gray lit tunnels had a hypnotic effect on Henry; staying engaged required increasing amounts of concentrated focus.

That the Bynars had found blood worried Henry. The discovery affirmed his suspicion that Brewster had been injured and was trapped down here, unable to get help. While the master computer access tunnels were regularly patrolled, the security and repair teams had tens of thousands of kilometers to cover in a given period of time. Steps might be retraced once every two or three standard weeks. Assuming that Brewster's injuries weren't life threatening, she'd probably die from dehydration long before a patrol found her.

At one point, the Bynars stopped at an information portal and accessed the tunnel monitoring system for any indicators of where Brewster might be or what had happened to her. They discovered that an environmental systems overload had happened nearby. This overload had caused a series of conduits to vent scalding hot, acidic toxins into the tunnels. Henry couldn't guess what would happen to a human who came in contact with the toxins, but he supposed it couldn't be good.

Ten minutes after the first break, 110/111's tricorder beeped a second time, then a third, and soon the beeps came so often that Henry lost count. Each time, Henry requested an update and each time the Bynars told him that more blood traces had been identified. Evidence of Brewster's injuries came more frequently the farther they went, implying that either her blood loss was accelerating or her injuries were forcing her to stop more frequently. Neither reassured Winter. Muttering curses under his breath at his own inability to move faster, he vowed he'd take his physical fitness more seriously from now on. He pushed forward at a pace that surprised even him.

Time passed—or perhaps it didn't. Henry knew only the steady up and down of his footfalls; he might have been running in place. The cramped stitch in his side from inadequate oxygen intake, the twinge in his knees, and the clammy perspiration on his face told him that yes, he did move. Whether he was headed anywhere was a different matter entirely. The tunnels blurred into gray sameness, a landscape in a long nightmare in which Henry ran in place, never escaping the demons behind him, never reaching sanctuary before him. The Bynars' rhythmic scurry (after his initial energy burst, they were perpetually five or six paces ahead of him) began to echo the thump-*thump*-thump-*thump* of his synthetic heart. Numbed by the relentlessness of their collective pace, Henry almost missed the slight deviation from the constant pattern of swaths of light followed by shadow puddles that had covered the length of their trek. A slight elongation of a shadow, a half-moon curve, went unnoticed until the Bynars came within steps of Temperance Brewster's crumpled form.

"Quick! Commander—"

"—come quickly—"

"—she is—"

"—unwell!"

Henry stumbled the last few steps before dropping to his knees and checking Brewster's pulse. The Bynars already had their tricorders out and were taking readings, but Henry needed to know, with his own senses, that she still lived.

Though faint and shallow, her heartbeat was steady. Her parched lips and pale, dry skin indicated dehydration. The real culprit, though, troubled him more: second- and, in a few small charred patches, third-degree chemical burns on her calves and parts of her thighs.

"She was caught—"

"—in the venting. The—"

"—hot chemicals burned—"

"—her and melted her—"

"—uniform fabric—"

"—into her skin."

Blood and clear ooze crusted around the edges of her wounds. She hadn't lost a lot of blood—just enough to make her dizzy. The burn trauma had done far more damage. None of her injuries were irreparable; the question remained whether they had enough time to get her to a medical center for grafts and skin restoration. His mind raced. Naturally he had Starfleet emergency first-aid training, but he couldn't recall the last time he'd had to do more than treat a hangnail. His thoughts bounced around like quarks in a particle accelerator.

Blessedly, the Bynars assumed control of the situation.

Without pausing to consult with Henry, 110/111 removed their medical kit from a travelpack and began attending to her wounds. Gratitude for their fast thinking and efficiency filled him. He was an old man with more than his share of shortcomings; at least this young lady wouldn't die because of them. He looked on approvingly as 110/111 administered two hypos, a rehydration agent and a pain-anti-infective medication. Though the burns couldn't be entirely healed without the accoutrements of a full facility, the Bynars did have the instruments to mend open, bleeding tissues and prevent any further damage from occurring. Henry sat back and watched the results of their labors on his own tricorder. Gradually, Brewster's vitals improved to a level he considered stable. The dreaded communiqué to the family wouldn't have to be sent this time.

He used this momentary downtime to allow his heart rate

to return to normal, his labored breathing to become more relaxed. After a moment's observation, he realized that Brewster had a portable recording padd in her hand. Carefully, he pried open her fingers and removed it. Examining the displayed menu for contents, he discovered that she had left a personal log on the device. The padd also contained a copy of 1010/0101's personnel file and a locator map to the same location 110/111 had identified in their research. Winter didn't know whether to credit great minds thinking similarly or dumb luck for the realization that both Brewster and he had reached similar conclusions regarding 1010/0101.

When 110/111 completed their work, Winter said, "Thank you. On behalf of Starfleet and Lieutenant Brewster's family."

110 and 111 chattered rapidly between themselves, and then turned to Henry, their faces wearing the nonplussed expressions of guileless children.

"We did what—"

"—needed to be—"

"—done."

Commander Henry Winter wished for all the worlds that he could have several platoons of officers he could trust to be as wise in their judgment as these Bynars.

Citizen Services Employee Report
Agent Unit 110/111
Assignment: Starfleet Recruiting Visit on Behalf of
  Starfleet Corps of Engineers

We delivered Lieutenant Brewster to the Medical Center at grid 834/29 at approximately 19:56:21. The medical unit on duty performed triage and indicated that Lieutenant Brewster would make a full recovery from her injuries.

While we have not officially removed Lieutenant Brewster from the list of possible culpable parties in the premature termination of 1010, enough evidence exists to indicate that it is highly unlikely that Lieutenant Brewster caused 1010's termination.

We are proceeding to 1010/0101's former residence now. Records indicate that 1010/0101 made regular visits to this location over the past several cycles. These visits continued even though all two hundred Bynar units assigned to this residence had been vacated a full two cycles ago. This facility, which is more than fifty rotations old, was also condemned by the Building and Architecture Committee so that an improved residence facility could be built. The visits increased recently; 1010/0101 would transport to this location after every completed shift at population management. A security unit evaluated the building's access records and discovered that 1010/0101's visits were not authorized and that existing security protocols were overridden to allow the visits. We have reached our location. The building is abandoned; CS access codes will allow us to pass through secured entry points. We will report shortly.

UPDATE

We are uncertain as to how to explain what we have seen. We will relate what happened, but we are not satisfied with our understanding of the situation.

With Commander Winter, we proceeded up several levels to 1010/0101's former quarters. The environmental controls have been programmed to nonoccupancy standards, so the facility is uncomfortably warm. The air is stagnant and polluted with minute particulate matter that accumulates when ventilation is turned off. The interior is of antiquated design and is not aesthetically suited to current Bynar standards to assure optimal offline and private unit interaction. When we reached the assigned area, we entered the interior. No apparent abnormalities were visible. The standard-issue furniture, though deteriorating and dirty from particulate accumulation, remains inside. There is no evidence that the rest chambers have been accessed or the nutritional services center was being used. We conclude that 1010/0101 visited here but did not reside here.

We proceeded out of the public room into the unit's private space. Nothing unusual was discovered in this room either. The space appears abandoned and unused. After our analysis of the room, Commander Winter reexamined all the furnishings in the room, dropped down onto his hands and knees, and crawled along the floor. This action puzzled us because everything on the floor was visible. We asked what had caught his attention, and he indicated that he noticed (we are conveying his exact words, though we are uncertain of their precise meaning) "that some of the dust on the chairs had been disturbed or lay in thinner layers than in other parts of the quarters—as if the furniture had been moved around or rearranged." He reached a corner of a sitting vessel and said, "Ah ha." We believe "ah ha" to be colloquial and we do not have a translation. Winter pushed the furniture off the floor mat and we saw what he had noticed: the sitting vessel, based on the indentations on the floor mat, had been moved repeatedly and not returned to the same location. Beneath the furniture, we discovered a large ventilation access grating that had not been replaced correctly, indicating that it had previously been removed. These oversized ventilation access points were standard in antiquated residential designs. New residential facilities use permeable membranes for air filtration and circulation.

Commander Winter removed the ventilation grating and descended feetfirst into the duct work. We followed after him. The fit was tight for Commander Winter horizontally. He made a comment about "pie" that this unit did not understand, but he managed to crawl through in spite of the difficulty. This unit determined that this section of the vent system had been accessed before our investigation. The scrapes, dents, and scratches on the interior vent surfaces indicated that objects or individuals had used this as a passageway on other occasions.

About six meters into the vent system, we arrived at another ventilation access portal that opened into an unknown room. Commander Winter pried the vent out of the floor of the passageway. Like the vent in 1010/0101's quarters, this vent was easily removed and showed indications that it had been used as an access point previously. Commander Winter jumped into the room below. This unit followed behind him.

To describe what we observed requires that we explain that in the entirety of our existence on Bynaus, we have never seen a room like this before. The grid map indicates that this was an unused maintenance storage area. What it had been transformed into was not a storage area. All the walls and the ceiling had been doused with color. These colors are not the muted, vetted hues that the Building and Architechtural Committee has designated as being psychologically and physiologically suited to Bynar existence. These are bright, vibrant, stimulating, but unnatural shades of green, purple, pink, yellow, and red. There is no discernible pattern to the color. Some of the color appears to have once been liquid that was thrown against the walls. Initially, this unit was uncertain how to process this visual stimulation, but after we had acclimated, we realized that figures had been painted on the color blots. We have seen exhibits of Bynar aesthetics on many occasions, but there was nothing in this space that complied with any known rule of artistic expression.

Commander Winter asked this unit to come take a closer look at the walls. We approached his location. He pointed out that countless rows of 1's and 0's covered the walls and ceilings. He requested that we analyze the code to see if there was any discernible order to the numbers. We scanned the data, discussed it between ourselves, and used our storage devices to enhance our ability to examine so many surfaces simultaneously. We discovered that a message had been left in the code, a record written by 1010. Commander Winter calls it a diary.

This unit is having difficulty explaining what the diary says. Though we have had extensive training in the norms and problems that the Bynar citizenry faces, we have never encountered a situation like this. The information is disturbing. We had a difficult time overcoming a strong visceral reaction to what we saw. We did not believe it was possible for a Bynar to believe as 1010 did or to experiment as that Bynar did. 1010's record evidences a disturbed and deteriorating mental state. A disorganized mind fragmenting into illogical branches with no possible outcome. We have no proof that 0101 is or was aware of this refurbished maintenance room. Logs indicate that 0101 did transport here with 1010 each time the maintenance room was accessed. We will return to 0101 to discuss this discovery and ascertain if 0101 can provide any additional information.

What is now the question, for this unit, is to what degree 0101 was responsible in 1010's death. 0101 had motive to terminate 1010; this is not doubted. This unit knows that 0101 had reason to believe that the unit 1010/0101 would ultimately be severed and 0101 designated to bond with a new mate. 1010's processing breakdown made such an outcome inevitable. An exceptionally disturbed entity, 1010 may have behaved in such a way to hasten termination, mitigating the circumstances of what has been deemed a crime. We assert that a crime may not have been committed. Only 0101 can answer whether that is the case.

Personal Log, Commander Henry Winter

Wow. As a lawyer, I'm fluent in polysyllabic communication. I'm finding, however, that my vocabulary fails me. "Wow" will have to suffice.

Working with 110/111, we retraced 1010/0101's travel patterns of recent months. This led us to 1010/0101's old apartment halfway across Bynaus. Apparently the pair had been returning to visit a maintenance-room-turned-art-grotto that they'd been accessing via the ventilation system. Or at least 1010 had been returning, because 1010's journal was written all over the walls. 110/111 wouldn't give me a verbatim translation—I believe what they read bothered them a good deal—but from what they did tell me, it sounds like it was a manifesto of sorts, a paean to individuality that would qualify as blasphemy on this world. 110/111 refused to give me details, but it sounded like 1010/0101 had pushed the boundaries of their interpersonal relationship to engage in behaviors that would be seen an abnormal by other Bynars. To an ultrarational asexual species that reproduces in a lab, I'm confident that most romantic/sexual expressions would be seen as freakish, since reason and logic rarely figure into love. My CS agent counterparts informed me only that 1010/0101 had what would have been a passionate, tempestuous relationship for Bynars. Whether that means that they screamed at each other or kissed for hours on end, I can't imagine—just that 1010's death may have more in common with a crime of passion than I'd originally thought.

And what a loss 1010 is. This is a Bynar that could have made a major impact on the Federation art community. I haven't seen art and color like that since the neo-Impressionist movement originated on Trexus V. 1010, no question, was an artistic visionary.

I haven't spent long on Bynaus, but I've been here long enough to get a sense of the Bynar aesthetic. In short, art doesn't exist here—at least not the way most planets in the Federation define it. Unless an object can serve a pragmatic purpose, it isn't valued. Architecture on Bynaus is extraordinarily complex and ornate in a mathematical, technological fashion. 110/111 explained to me that colors are used for their psychological benefits, each tint or shade calibrated to address the Bynars' visual intake. Use of color that disturbs or disquiets the viewer isn't known here. Even landscape has a utilitarian purpose: the exchange of gases in the environment and a healthy planetary ecosystem. All trees, plants, flowers, and vegetation are engineered to meet carefully calculated formulas that maintain environmental stability. The precision and care that is applied to every aspect of Bynar life is admirable in the sense that they maintain a peaceful, stable, functioning democracy where crime, disease, and conflict are essentially unknown. And yet . . . when I witness what happens when a fanatically protected system breaks down, as clearly it did with 1010, I don't see catastrophe, I see genius.

Preliminary Hearing/Pt. II Interview with Bynar 0101
Present: Commander Winters, Captain Quinteros, CS
Agents 110/111, Judicial Units 0110/1001, 1100/0011

Summary of Part I (90 minutes): Commander Winter
presented evidence, including travel reports and pictures
of the modified maintenance room, to 0101. Commander
Winter asked 0101 to identify and explain each item to
the interviewers. A short recess was taken. Interview
resumed at 21:47:03.

WINTER: Explain the maintenance room to this group. What
it was, why you went there.

0101: There is no longer any usefulness for such a place. It will
be destroyed when the construction committee begins work
on the new structure. It is irrelevant.

WINTER: I disagree, and I think all the others in this room believe it is highly relevant. The CS unit 110/111 has recorded
the binary code on the walls of the room and rendered a
linguistic translation. Perhaps they should start reading it to
you to refresh your recollections—

0101 [*shuddering*]: Not. Necessary. The room served as a retreat. A private place. 1010 failed to perform well at work assignments. 1010 required a place to work through the issues
that prevented success. The maintenance room served as that
place.

WINTER: So why the colors? The often illogical ramblings written all over the floor, the walls—even the ceilings?

0101: 1010 is terminated. To diagnose the malfunction now that 1010 is gone fails to serve the Bynar community.

110/111: We disagree. Citizen Services needs to examine what went wrong so that such deterioration will be prevented from reoccurring. Should such defects be determined to exist in others from 1010's batch, aggressive examination of other units will be required.

0101: [*grunts, pales noticeably; medical unit checks vital signs and determines nothing is wrong*]

WINTER: Based on our interview and the evidence, the Judiciary has indicated that a further examination of 1010's apparent breakdown is warranted. A full public inquiry into the failure of the system to prevent further damage—

0101: No! No! You can't! 1010 was not defective! How can such a thing be said and tolerated! [*shakes head back and forth violently*] 1010 was glorious and brilliant. Other mates would be lucky to have one with such an ability to see the worlds in such a fashion! [*pauses; winces*] I—I will not allow this to happen. 1010 must be protected.

WINTER: Is that what you were doing when you framed Lieutenant Brewster? Protecting 1010?

0101: [*nods*]

WINTER: Tell us about 1010.

0101: 1010 was unusual from the beginning. But after the Great Death—

[*Winters looks to the others in the room for clarification.*]

QUINTEROS: The Great Death—the incident with the *Enterprise* when the Bynars nearly became extinct.

0101: The Great Death disturbed 1010. 1010's productivity decreased. When we were at work, instead of working, 1010 would look at the way the light would come through the windows or talk about how the colors on the workstation made 1010 feel. Feel. 1010 talked about feeling. 1010 did not know what to do with feelings. Our unit went to the diagnostician for counseling but found that only fully reprogramming 1010 would fix the situation. Being reprogrammed would change 1010. What made 1010 unique would be lost. Our unit worked together to find a way for 1010 to survive. The maintenance room became the space where 1010 could release all the thoughts and feelings that could not be expressed elsewhere. Those thoughts and feelings were not dangerous.

110/111: Why did the unit take measures to hide these expressions if they were not dangerous?

0101: Most units could not understand or would not admit to understanding what 1010 expressed. We knew that if 1010 admitted or expressed thoughts that disturbed others, we would be told that 1010 needed to be fixed.

WINTER: Which brings us to the recruiting meeting. What was happening in your unit at this point?

0101: We had been working at population management for long enough for our unit to understand it was not working. The supervising unit informed our unit that a transfer was not possible, that our unit had exceeded the number of transfers we were eligible for and that if it became necessary to transfer our unit again, we would be sent to the diagnostician for evaluation and reprogramming. Our unit knew that 1010 was gradually losing the ability to function. Our unit did not want to exist with other mates. The only logical conclusion was that our unit might face termination. We believed that our unit might survive if we could leave Bynaus. Starfleet presented us with an option.

QUINTEROS: So why didn't you take that option and join up?

0101: 1010 did not believe that our unit's problems would be solved. We believed that we might expose Bynaus to the Federation in a way that would damage the homeworld.

110/111: Such a choice demonstrates rational thinking. Was that the motivation for terminating 1010?

0101: I—I—

WINTER: [leans forward] You didn't terminate 1010. 1010 committed suicide—1010 terminated 1010.

[*High-pitched, rapid discussion breaks out among the Bynar units in the room.*]

0110/1001: If a Bynar terminates by choice, an inquest and tribunal is held. This is a disturbing situation that will require more investigation.

0101 [*shouting*]: I—I loved 1010. 1010 did not deserve to be examined the way we examine broken equipment! [*rocks back and forth*] What must be said is that I was supposed to terminate with 0101. We were a unit. A unit must not separate. 1010 had courage and kept the promise. I—I could not. We had promised before we went to the meeting. I—I proposed we go so that I could avoid the promise.

WINTER: *That's* why you brought Lieutenant Brewster into the mix—because 1010 terminated first and when you couldn't bring yourself to follow, you needed to protect 0101. 1010 was already dead when you contacted Lieutenant Brewster.

0101: From working in population management, the procedures that would apply to this situation were known to me. The data I needed to change to make Lieutenant Brewster look responsible was available and accessible. Lieutenant Brewster would be deported, never allowed to return to Bynaus. The evidence was not enough to require that she be reprogrammed. 1010's death would go away and be forgotten. Better the lieutenant than—

110/111: Requiring your unit to be scrutinized and reprogrammed.

0101: [*nods*]

WINTER: Why didn't you go through with your self-termination?

0101: 1010 accessed the terminal, knowing that the security system would send current into the body if the violation of the database continued. 1010 went first. [*long pause*] I watched. I thought I would not want to become part of another unit. Termination would be better. When 1010 terminated, fear filled this body. I could not do it. [*very softly*] Even if it meant living—*alone*—I wanted to live.

Citizen Services Employee Report
Agent Unit 110/111
Assignment: Starfleet Recruiting Visit on Behalf of
   Starfleet Corps of Engineers

This unit is prepared to close this assignment. Lieutenant Brewster departs Bynaus tomorrow. No Bynars accepted the offer to consult for or join Starfleet. The matter regarding 1010's termination has been referred to the Judiciary for further consideration and analysis. 0101 has been assigned to master computer maintenance and will live as an individual. The diagnostician unit stated that there is no indication that living as an individual will result in 0101's termination as has been in the case in the majority of banishment designations. This analysis does not strike this unit as unreasonable.

There are several issues this unit would like to comment on before submitting this report for final approval. First, the question of 0101's individuality coming in conflict with the Bynar way of life is of concern to Citizen Services. It is our observation that a public inquest may create unrest in the population. This unit has never encountered a situation like what happened with 1010/0101, but the statement by 0101 that the Great Death may have instigated this sequence of events raises the possibility that there may be more in the situation of 1010.

Further, 0101's apparent satisfaction with this punishment has raised questions with this unit about whether the assumptions society makes about individuality do in fact create optimal functioning for all Bynars. Whether the taboos that have existed since the liberation of our Illustrious Forebears continue to serve Bynaus should be discussed by Citizen Services Regulatory Committees. Revisiting the Archives of the Ancients to learn the reasoning that was relied upon to devise our contemporary codified laws may illuminate why we live as we do—and if there is cause to question it. This unit has many questions. We are attempting to organize these questions in such a way that they will be useful to Citizen Services. It is possible however, that there are no answers on Bynaus.

SUBMITTED AT 11:23:54

Personal Log, Lieutenant Temperance Brewster

My intent in coming here was not to create an existential crisis on this lovely, peaceful world. Though Citizen Services has hushed up 1010/0101's situation, I have been told that rumors abound and that opinions may not be what the CS guys expect. The Great Death was a transformative point for Bynaus. I don't think they've started to understand what it means to their world.

I'm still not the biggest fan of this place—too much micromanagement, and change moves at an exhaustively slow pace. There are plenty of aspects of Bynaus that would make me an uncomfortable resident. I don't know how Quinteros does it. That being said, I have learned that indeed, there are some universals: love and the fierce desire to protect and shield those we love exist among all species. My love, my concern for those in my Starfleet family brought me here and led me, in some respects, to behave irrationally. I have no defense for my poor judgment except to say that I thought I was doing what was right. I return to Headquarters a wiser student of humanoid nature. I've discussed my concerns with my lawyer, Commander Winter. He's assured me repeatedly that though all charges have been dismissed, he suspects I still have some questions, not just about the legal issues, but what happened while I was on the run. We'll discuss those on the way back to Headquarters. After 0101 was interviewed, Winter told everyone he needed a long nap and a big supper, so as soon as our ride back to Earth showed up, he said his good-byes and transported off the surface.

Clearly, I'm a long way from being the counselor I one day hope to be. But not all was sobering life lessons. I believe some good came out of this trip. Take for example a last-minute development. As I approached the transporter pad that would beam me up to the *Brasilla*, I heard footsteps behind me: 110/111. My initial thought was that they had come to say good-bye. Bynars didn't strike me as sentimental types, but maybe this case had changed this pair's point of view.

I was wrong.

The pair looked at each other, talked back and forth in their high-pitched incomprehensible dialect, then looked at me.

"This unit would—"

"—like to come with—"

"—you."

My eyebrows disappeared somewhere in my hairline. "Why?" I asked.

"We seek—"

"—answers that—"

"—we believe we—"

"—may find elsewhere."

"Would there be—"

"—a place for us—"

"—as civilian advisers—"

"—in S.C.E.?"

The idiotic smile that split my face probably was incomprehensible to the Bynars who seemed to have little understanding of nonverbal communication. I didn't wait for them to have second thoughts. "Welcome to Starfleet, 110/111. The Corps of Engineers is grateful for your service."

MANY
SPLENDORS

Keith R.A. DeCandido

*To Dean, Christie, Dayton, Kevin D., David, Aaron,
Dave, Greg, Scott, Dan, Jeff, Ian, Mike, Robert G.,
Glenn H., J. Steven, Christina, Heather, Christopher,
Michael M., Andy, Loren, Randall, Allyn,
Kevin K., Paul, John D., Glenn G., Terri, Ilsa, John O.,
Cory, William, Phaedra, Robert J.,
Steve, Michael S., and Richard*

*What a long, strange trip it's been—you guys
have been the best, and I look forward
to more voyages on the* da Vinci
with you and everyone.

HISTORIAN'S NOTE

Chapter 1 of this story commences at the same time as the second-season *Star Trek: The Next Generation* episode "The Measure of a Man" (2365). Chapters 2–9 proceed through the second, third, fourth, and early fifth seasons of the show, with Chapter 10 shortly after the fifth-season episode "Disaster" (2368). The Epilogue jumps ahead eight years to early 2376, taking place a few months prior to *The Belly of the Beast*, the first *S.C.E.* story, shortly after the Dominion War ended in the final episode of *Star Trek: Deep Space Nine*.

CHAPTER

1

Captain's log, Stardate 42523.7.
We are en route to the newly established Starbase 173 for port call. Crew rotation is scheduled, and we will be off-loading experiment modules.

Ensign Sonya Gomez had been practicing The Speech for days.

Originally it was just a speech, one she would give upon meeting her new commanding officer, saying what an honor it was to be serving on her new ship. When she got the word that her request had been approved and she was to be assigned to the *Enterprise*, it suddenly became The Speech. This wasn't just some old assignment; this was the flagship! She'd be reporting to Lieutenant Geordi La Forge, about whom she'd heard so much from her friend, Lian T'su, who'd graduated a year ahead of her (and would be her roommate on the ship).

Along with another Academy classmate, Ensign Dennis Russell, Sonya had reported to the *Enterprise* at Starbase 173, and then gone straight to main engineering to meet their new CO, The Speech running through her head the entire time she walked through the corridor. She tried to figure out what to do with her hands. Next to her, Denny looked maddeningly calm.

La Forge took only a few minutes to introduce himself,

show them around, and give them duty assignments. Neither ensign got the chance to say anything. "Sorry to cut this short, but I've got a senior staff meeting in a few minutes. Welcome aboard." Despite the hurried nature of the introduction, and the terse tone La Forge had had throughout, he said the last two words with a genuinely warm smile. With the VISOR the lieutenant wore covering his eyes, it wasn't easy to judge his mood, but that smile put Sonya at ease.

But she hadn't had the chance to give The Speech. Worse, she'd studied the engine specs, expecting to be quizzed on them, but La Forge did no such thing. Sonya was assigned to gamma shift at first, serving under Ensign Esmeralda Clancy. This would give her plenty of chances to show off her knowledge of the *Galaxy*-class vessel, and get to do it in the lower-key atmosphere of the night shift.

The tour ended at the upper core on deck thirty-one. She and Denny walked down the corridors of the deck toward the turbolift. "You didn't get to give your speech," Denny said with a cheeky grin.

"I know. The opportunity never really presented itself." Sonya stifled a yawn. "I need to get some sleep."

"What'd you do last night—or were you up rehearsing The Speech?"

Sheepishly, Sonya said, "That and studying the ship's specs. I was up all night."

Smirking, Denny shook his head. "Figures."

"Denny, I don't want to be—"

"I know, Sonya, I know, I was there for your meltdown before finals, remember? Look, it'll be fine."

Sonya was already tired of hearing that. "Anyhow," she said after realizing that glaring at Denny was doing no good, "since my shift doesn't start for eight hours, and I was already off-kilter from the starbase's different cycle, I'm gonna catch up on my sleep, make sure I'm in good shape for gamma."

Nodding, Denny said, "Sounds vaguely planlike. Me, I'm gonna see when the holodeck's available. From what I hear, these *Galaxy*-class ships have state-of-the-art holography, and I've got a great program I want to try out."

Remembering Denny's proclivities from the Academy, Sonya said, "Another murder mystery?"

Rolling his eyes, Denny said, "*Yes,* another murder mystery. This one's from New York City in the late nineteenth century."

"What, you're gonna solve Jack the Ripper again?"

"That was London. And I already did that."

Sonya chuckled. She remembered that Denny had reprogrammed one of his endless murder mystery holodeck scenarios so that the person who solved the Jack the Ripper case was able to reveal that the killer in question was possessed by an interstellar energy creature, as had been revealed by a Starfleet vessel a century earlier. He had said that getting the reactions of nineteenth-century humans accurate had proven challenging.

"Uh, excuse me," said a voice, and Sonya looked up to see a fellow officer—a junior-grade lieutenant, in fact, wearing the gold of operations and security—coming toward them. He had unkempt brown hair, wide brown eyes, and smile lines around his mouth. "I'm, uh, running late for a staff meeting."

Sonya and Denny stepped aside to let the officer pass. As he did so, he turned, and gave Sonya a long look before turning and jogging down the corridor.

"Who was that?"

Denny shrugged at Sonya's question. "Probably one of the senior staff La Forge was having a meeting with."

"Is it my imagination, or was he looking at me funny?"

"Maybe, but I wouldn't put too much stock in it—most people look at you funny."

Punching Denny lightly on the shoulder, she smiled and they continued to the turbolift.

Sonya took in her new quarters. They were *huge.*

She had spent most of the last year memorizing everything there was to know about the *Enterprise,* and had found her quarters without a tour guide, or asking the computer. Sonya's sense of direction had become legendary at the Academy— by the middle of her first year, the fourth-years were asking *her* for shortcuts around campus—and she was now confident that, just from her intensive study of the ship's specs and diagrams, she could walk from here to the cargo bay with her eyes closed.

Even so, even knowing from those specs just how large the quarters she would share with a fellow ensign would be, she wasn't prepared for the massiveness of the space.

An advantage of the constant annihilation of matter and antimatter that powered a Starfleet vessel was that it provided energy to spare. One of her Academy professors, upon learning of Sonya's assignment to this ship, had laughed, nodded her head, and said, "Ah, the *Galaxy*-class—a monument to waste." Having specialized in the study of antimatter, Sonya knew as well as anyone how true that was, but she'd never really thought of it in terms of giving even lowly ensigns on a ship that was a thousand strong so much *room*.

The quarters included a main room containing two desks, a round table, several chairs and a couch, and a replicator. On either side were two smaller rooms. She approached the first, and found it filled with an impressive array of Bolian artifacts. Assuming that this belonged to Lian—who'd had a passion for Bolian art for as long as Sonya had known her—Sonya walked over to the other room, which was undecorated, and furnished with a bunk, another desk, and another replicator, as well as a door that she assumed went to the commode.

As she had indicated to Denny, ship's time was off a bit from the starbase; she checked the computer station on the desk and saw that alpha shift had ended a few minutes earlier. Lian was, like Sonya, on gamma, serving at ops on the bridge during the night shift, so her roommate's lack of presence here was a bit of a surprise.

Lian and Sonya had shared a plasma physics class a year earlier. Though the former was a year ahead of the latter, they'd become fast friends, and Lian had continued to write to Sonya from her posting to the *Enterprise*. Reading of Lian's adventures and her descriptions of the amazing new *Galaxy*-class ship, Sonya realized that this ship was where she simply *had* to be assigned. She'd been driven from the moment she'd first applied to the Academy, but the letters from Lian made her realize that this was the only place she could possibly go.

She realized that catching up on sleep wasn't really an option. While she'd made a thorough study of the ship's specs, she still needed to compare that to how the engines were now with the specs it had at Utopia Planitia a year and a half ago.

The doors parted with a swish, and Lian entered. She was rubbing her round face with her hands, her dark curls poorly held in by an attempt at a ponytail.

"Lian!"

Taking her hands away from her face to reveal her large, expressive eyes, Lian T'su burst into a grin. "Sonya! You're here!"

The two friends ran to each other and embraced in a tight hug. Though they'd stayed in touch, they hadn't seen each other since Lian's graduation a year earlier. "It's so great to see you," Sonya said to Lian's shoulder. "I'm *so* glad we got assigned together."

"We were lucky," Lian said. "Phylo was just promoted to junior-grade lieutenant, and she transferred to the starbase. She couldn't handle the pace here all that well. So I had the space, and quartermaster was kind enough to say yes."

They broke the embrace. Lian reached behind her head and yanked the hair-tie out, letting her curls spill loose about her shoulders. "*Much* better. Sorry, I was doing a double shift, and on alpha, I try to keep my hair up." She smirked. "Something about the captain being around makes you want to remain tidy."

"I bet. Why were you doing a double?"

"Commander Data *resigned*. I couldn't believe it when I heard." Lian walked over to the replicator. "Green tea, hot." The replicator hummed, and a ceramic mug with steam rising from its mouth coalesced into being. She took a quick sip of it, and a transformation came over her: her eyes brightened, her other features softened, and she seemed to slouch a bit. "Much better."

"Why did Commander Data resign? Isn't he the android?"

"Well, even if he hadn't, I still would've pulled a double." Lian slowly walked over to the couch. Sonya did likewise. "He was being transferred to the starbase so they can experiment on him."

Sonya frowned. "Experiment? Can they *do* that to an officer?"

Shrugging, Lian said, "Apparently. Anyhow, Commander Riker didn't have a chance to redo the shift rotation, so he asked me to stay on for alpha, and I did. We're just orbiting the starbase, so it didn't require a lot of concentration." She took another sip of the tea, then set it down on the table. "But enough about me, how're *you?*"

"Excited." Sonya leaned forward on the couch. "I haven't met Ensign Clancy yet—Lieutenant La Forge said I'd be working for her—and I just can't *wait* to get started when gamma starts."

"Good." Lian stood up. "I can take you to Ten-Forward, then."

"That's the lounge, isn't it?" Sonya asked.

Lian nodded.

"I can't. I've got *way* too much to do."

"Sonya—"

Also standing, Sonya said, "No, I've got to unpack and get ready for the first shift."

"There's nothing to get ready *for,* Sonya."

"I have to make a good impression with Clancy. I don't want her to think I'm just some dumb ensign right out of the Academy. I want to show her what I can do."

Lian shook her head. "Sonya, you don't have to prove yourself."

"Yes, I do. You just said your last roommate couldn't handle it. I *have* to."

"Look, La Forge is going to be very easy to work for. He's a good officer, and a great supervisor. Engineering was a disaster area before he got his hands on it."

"Wasn't he the one in command when you got battle bridge duty that time?"

"Yes. He was excellent under pressure, kept us all focused." She smirked. "Well, me and Solis. I think Worf was born focused."

"Worf is the Klingon?"

Lian nodded. "He's been in charge of security since Yar died. It's too bad—she was a good officer. Worf's a little too tightly wound for security."

"I thought security people *had* to be tightly wound."

"Maybe." Lian shrugged. "Anyhow, you should come to Ten-Forward."

Shaking her head quickly, Sonya said, "I have to study the ship's engine tonight. You remember what Dr. Ra-Havreii said?" She stood straight and put on the Efrosian's gentle, deep voice. " 'A ship ceases to resemble its blueprints—' "

Lian joined in, doing her even better impersonation of their former Academy professor. " '—within the first month of it being in space.' Sonya, you'll have plenty of time to study it while you work on it."

"I can't do that—I need to be ready to do this job *right now*."

Letting out a long sigh, Lian said, "You haven't changed a bit, Sonya." She chuckled. "No, I take it back—you've gotten *worse*. Sonya, you're already *here*." Before Sonya could say anything else, Lian held up a hand. "All right, if you don't want to come, I can't force you, but I need to relax, so I'm going. If you want to join me—"

"—just take the turbolift up one deck, go right, keep on down that corridor until I get to section 2B, make a left, then make an immediate right, go straight until I hit Ten-Forward."

Laughing, Lian said, "I suppose I shouldn't be surprised that you already know your way around. We'll talk later, okay?"

"Count on it."

After Lian left, Sonya went into her room, stared at her duffel for a moment, then sat at the computer desk and called up the up-to-the-minute specs on the *Enterprise*'s warp core. Lian had said that engineering had been a mess, which tracked with the letters Sonya had been getting. The *Enterprise* had gone through an unprecedented four chief engineers in its first year. With that, the fact that the ship was the first off the line of a new class of vessel, and the types of things the flagship dealt with on what seemed to be a weekly basis, the engines had probably gone through a lot. She needed to know what the engines were like.

She also wondered who that guy was on deck thirty-one.

CHAPTER
2

Captain's log, supplemental.
As happened with our sister ship, the *Enterprise* is beginning to experience a series of system failures. So far they are random, but I fear they could be early symptoms of what happened to the *Yamato*.

"Need some help?"

Sonya looked up with bleary eyes to see a vaguely familiar officer, wearing a junior-grade lieutenant's pips on a gold uniform. "I'm sorry?"

"I asked if you needed some help."

It took Sonya a minute to remember where she was. "God, I must've drifted off. I'm sorry, I—" She inhaled through her nose, exhaled through her mouth—a stress-reduction technique her sister, Belinda, had taught her when they were kids, and one that occasionally worked. This was not one of those occasions.

She'd worked two straight shifts, having come on early during beta shift, and worked all the way through gamma. Ever since downloading the log from their sister ship, the *U.S.S. Yamato*—which had subsequently exploded, killing all aboard—the *Enterprise* had been suffering from massive systems failures.

La Forge had put her and Clancy in charge of making sure

nothing untoward happened with the warp core. It was a catastrophic collapse of the *Yamato*'s warp core that had led to its
destruction. Clancy was currently in the upper core, testing the
diagnostic systems.

Finally, she placed the face of the lieutenant in front of her
as the one from deck thirty-one her first day on board.

"I'm sorry," he said, holding out his hand. "Kieran Duffy. I
just came on, and Lieutenant La Forge thought you could use
a hand. You're Clancy?"

"No, Sonya Gomez," she said, returning the handshake.

"Ah, okay. Sorry, I've been on alpha and beta, so I never got
to know you gamma folks. Never much of a night owl, myself."
He grinned. "Not that it matters, since it's always night out
here. So, uh—do you?"

Sonya blinked. "I'm sorry?"

"Need help?"

"Oh." Sonya picked up her padd, as she found she had no
recollection of what she'd just done or what she had to do
next. "I just ran a diagnostic on the antimatter control systems.
They're fine, amazingly enough. Now I have to reset all the
control functions on the warp drive, since right now they're
reading that the core's been ejected."

"You sure it hasn't been?" Duffy made a show of looking
over at the warp core. "No, wait, there it is. Guess we'd better
reset it, then."

Sonya rolled her eyes. "Honestly, Lieutenant, I don't."

Now it was his turn to blink. "Don't what?"

"Need help. I'm perfectly capable of doing this myself."

"Maybe, but the ship's falling apart at the seams, and you've
been working for two straight shifts. I just got out of bed,
so I'm a lot more bright-eyed and bushy-tailed than you." He
looked at the top of her head. "Okay, with that hair, maybe
you're more bushy-tailed, but you get the idea."

"Lieutenant—"

"Look, Lieutenant La Forge ordered me to help you out,
and he sorta kinda outranks both of us. For that matter, I

technically outrank you. So let's just assume that whole 'need help?' thing was rhetorical. What's after the reset on that little list of yours?"

Sonya stared angrily at Duffy for a second, then finally looked back down at the display on her padd. "Make sure the flow regulators are still functioning."

"Fine, I'll do that."

Where did La Forge find this idiot? "No, you can't, because you need the computer for that, and I'll be resetting it."

Duffy frowned. "No, I won't. I can just—"

Her voice rising, Sonya said, "Lieutenant, you can't check the flow regulator systems if the computer's being reset!"

"Uh, Ensign?" Duffy was staring at her with a concerned look.

"What?" she snapped.

"You didn't say flow regulator systems, you said flow regulators, which I can check by opening up the antimatter housing and taking a gander."

"The regulator's completely okay," Sonya said, "I just checked it—" She looked down at the padd again. "—half an hour ago. It's the systems."

"You didn't say the systems."

"Yes, I did."

He walked closer to her. He was a lot taller than she, and he was now staring down at her. "Ensign, the word 'systems' never escaped your lips."

"Fine, if you say so," Sonya said, though she was sure, absolutely *sure*, that she had said "flow regulator systems." "After that is a diagnostic on the containment unit."

Sounding almost triumphant, Duffy said, "Which is a separate system, and which I can do while you reset the computer."

Letting out a long breath, Sonya said, "Whatever you say, Lieutenant." She walked over to the computer and started up the reset sequence. "It *can't* be the flow regulators, anyhow. This is a computer problem, not a mechanical one."

Duffy was now standing over at one of the wall consoles and

calling up the diagnostic for the containment unit. "Or it's a design flaw."

Looking up sharply, Sonya said, "It's *not* a design flaw."

"How do you know? The *Galaxy*-class has only been out for a little over a year. Sure, they ran every test possible in Utopia Planitia, and the shakedown went okay, but a ship this size has about a thousand things that can go wrong."

"This *isn't* a design flaw. I've studied this ship from stem to stern, Lieutenant," Sonya said angrily, "and there's no way this is due to a design problem. For one thing, like I said, it's the *computer* that's having a malfunction. It could be an invasive program—a tribblecom."

"Oh, come on." Duffy turned away from the containment unit diagnostic to look at her with amusement. "The *Enterprise* is protected against that kind of thing. Besides, tribblecoms don't do *this* kind of damage. I think you're letting your imagination run away with you, Ensign."

Sonya couldn't believe she was listening to this. "I don't have an imagination, Lieutenant," she said before she realized what words were actually escaping her mouth.

Duffy burst out laughing. At her aggrieved look, he got control of himself. "I'm sorry, Ensign, that was just too good."

"I miss something funny?"

Mortified, Sonya whirled around to see Clancy standing behind her. Bad enough this idiot was intruding on her work, now he was making fun of her. "Uh, sorry, Ensign Clancy, I—"

"Ah, *you're* Clancy," Duffy said, stepping around Sonya with his hand out. "I'm Lieutenant—"

"—Duffy, right," Clancy finished, grasping the lieutenant's hand. "Geordi said you'd be helping out. Thanks."

"No problem. I'm doing the diagnostic on the containment unit while Ensign Gomez finishes resetting the warp drive controls and checks the flow regulator systems."

"Good," Clancy said.

Duffy smiled and turned back to the containment unit.

Hoping her cheeks weren't turning as red as she feared,

Sonya looked down at the display and finished the start-up sequence for the reset.

Just as she realized what had gone wrong and had lifted her hand to fix it, Clancy said, "Uh, Sonya, are you sure it's a good idea to—"

"I know, Ella," Sonya said quickly. She and Clancy had gotten on a first-name basis fairly quickly, especially since it was often just the two of them working together. Sonya had set the entire engineering system to reset, not just the warp core controls. If she'd done that, they'd also lose impulse. At present, they were heading toward some planet or other at sublight, and losing impulse control would be disastrous, especially with everything else going wrong. As she input new commands, she said, "It was a mistake, I'm sorry."

"Actually, it was my fault," Duffy said from behind her. "I was distracting the ensign with the joke about the monk, the clone, and the Ferengi. That's, uh, why I was laughing—I was trying to get *her* to laugh, you see."

With an amused glance at Sonya, Clancy said, "Doesn't appear to have worked."

"No, sir," Sonya said. Then she found herself unable to resist smiling. "I'm afraid I don't find Mr. Duffy at all humorous."

"Well, it isn't really that good a joke. Anyhow," Duffy said, "it's all my fault for distracting her. Won't happen again."

Clancy nodded. Sonya found herself relaxing for the first time since the *Yamato* blew up. When Clancy turned her back, she gave Duffy a grateful look for taking the heat. He just gave her a goofy grin in response, and got to work on the containment unit.

Halfway through alpha shift, La Forge had insisted that Clancy and Gomez go off duty. Both women had tried to convince him that they were fine, but when Ella referred to their CO as "Fa Lorge," and Sonya found herself incapable of remembering the term "warp core," they both agreed that they needed rest.

Sonya paused only long enough to do a personal log, during which she found herself saying how cute she thought Kieran Duffy was once she got past his goofball exterior, and then she crashed.

Lian woke her up ten hours later, at which point it was all over.

Sonya walked over to the replicator. "Hot chocolate, please." She turned to Lian while the replicator hummed with her order. Her roommate was seated on the couch with a green tea cupped in her hands. "What happened?" The hot chocolate materialized, and she said, "Thank you," then walked over to join Lian on the couch.

"It turned out that there was an Iconian computer program in the *Yamato*'s log. It was overwriting our computer sys—"

"I *knew* it!" Sonya said as she sat down. "I *told* him it had to be a tribblecom of some kind."

"This wasn't just a tribblecom, and who's 'him'?"

"Duffy—a lieutenant from alpha shift. La Forge asked him to help me and Ella out. He insisted it was a design flaw, and when I told him it was a tribblecom, he *laughed* at me. Okay, there was something else, when I misspoke, but still, he was *laughing*, the big jerk. And what do you mean it wasn't just a tribblecom?"

"If it was, it was a tribble the size of the moon. This program was rewriting the entire computer system. They finally fixed it by purging the memory and restoring it from the protected archives."

Sonya nodded. "Makes sense. It means they lost everything from after we downloaded the *Yamato* log, but—" Her eyes widened. "Oh, no!"

Lian tilted her head. "What's wrong?"

She bounded up from the couch and went over to the terminal, only to see that her personal log wasn't there. In fact, everything after stardate 42609.1 was gone: her last two personal logs and the log of all the repairs she did on two and a half shifts. "Now I've got to write all that all over again."

"So's everyone else, I wouldn't worry about it."

Thinking back over what she wrote in the more recent personal log, she decided it was best. *What was I thinking, talking about how someone's cute in a personal log? What if somebody reads that?*

Shaking it off, she sat back down while Lian told the rest of the story, about the Romulan ship, the Iconian base they found, and the away team peculiarly led by Captain Picard himself, and how Data was almost killed by the same program that invaded the *Enterprise*. Sonya was relieved at that. While she had yet to be formally introduced to the android, she'd seen him in engineering a few times, and had of course heard about the captain's defending him on Starbase 173, helping establish the android's sentience, which Sonya had actually thought was a given, though Lian hadn't. She was glad he was okay, and that nobody was seriously hurt.

"But that's not the *really* good part," Lian said with a smile. "I've got a date!"

Sonya blinked. "Huh?"

"You know Soon-Tek Han in security?"

"No." Sonya didn't even know who any of the other engineers besides Clancy, Duffy, Russell, and La Forge were. She had far too much work to do to pay attention to security people.

"He's very nice, and he's invited me to have dinner with him in Ten-Forward tomorrow. Isn't that *wonderful?*"

"I guess," Sonya said hesitantly. She couldn't imagine the notion of having *time* to go on a date. She had her duties, and then she spent her off-duty time going over everything, to make sure she hadn't missed something, or catching up on the technical journals so she wouldn't lose track of what was going on while she was out here, or sleeping. Plus, there was always extra work. Geordi La Forge ran an efficient engine room. He had been working with some noncommissioned kid—Lian had said he was the son of the former chief medical officer, and was an "acting ensign," whatever that meant, due to his great genius—to adjust the deuterium control conduit, even though it was well within specified norms, and if he was going to nit-pick the engines *that* much, Sonya had to stay on her toes. The notion of a social life seemed utterly alien to her.

"Well, I hope you two have fun," she said gamely, wishing the best for her roommate.

"Thanks. He said he was going to pick the cuisine. Can't wait to see what it is."

Sonya smiled, then checked the chronometer and frowned. "Ugh, I'm back on shift in twenty minutes." She looked down at herself. "I gotta shower and change."

Both women rose and moved to their respective bedrooms.

"I need sleep," Lian said. "Talk to you later, Sonya!"

Sonya started removing her uniform as she entered her bedroom. Heading toward the commode, she ordered the computer to read her the table of contents from the *Journal of Applied Warp Mechanics*. The latest issue of *JAWM* had been released the day before, but in the hustle and bustle of the Iconian mess, she hadn't gotten to it. As she showered, she instructed the computer on which articles to flag.

She was *not* going to be caught out without knowing *everything*.

CHAPTER

3

Captain's log, stardate 42737.3.
It has been six weeks since our entrance into the Selcundi
Drema sector. Each system has revealed the same disturbing
geological upheavals on every planet.

Sonya was reading an article on her padd while exiting her
bedroom and trying not to scream. "I don't *believe* this!"

Lian was eating breakfast at the large table. Swallowing her
steaming oatmeal, she asked, "Don't believe what?"

"This idiot is writing an article on subspace accelerators."

Frowning, Lian asked, "Didn't you write a paper on that?"
before scooping more oatmeal into her mouth.

"Yes, and this Doctor—" She touched a control to get the article header, with the author's name. "—Xe'r'b'w'r's'o is talking
through her fur. The magnetic containment unit she has will
break down after the first time it's used, and her alignments
are all completely off-kilter. Anybody builds an SA to these
specs is just asking for trouble—it's more likely than anything
to just fall *apart*. I *proved* that in my paper, but she doesn't even
cite it!"

Lian shrugged. "So write to the journal and complain."

Walking over to the replicator, Sonya shuddered and said,
"Oh, I can't do that." To the replicator, she added, "Hot chocolate, please."

"Why can't you?"

"I'm just a Starfleet ensign—when I wrote the paper I just was a third-year cadet. Dr. Xe'r'b'w'r's'o is the leading authority on subspace at Thelian University—I couldn't just write in and say she's an idiot. I mean, sure, in our cabin, that's one thing, but I can't write a *letter*." She looked at Lian. "Can I?"

Shaking her head, Lian said, "I don't understand you, Sonya. You're one of the brightest people I've ever met, and you push yourself to be better than the best—but you refuse to realize it."

Sonya almost shrunk in her chair. "I'm not anything special."

"Yes, you are." She held up a hand. "Forget it, I'm tired of beating my head against that particular wall. I have to go. Soon-Tek and I are having breakfast."

Staring at Lian's now-empty bowl of oatmeal, Sonya asked, "So why did you just eat oatmeal?"

"Because he wants to have a Vulcan breakfast. Vulcan food makes me gag, but he likes it, so I agreed, and stocked up on oatmeal first." She smiled. "Hey, listen, what're you doing after your shift?"

"I've got to finish this journal, and then there's the paper I promised to *JAWM* that I really need to finish. And I may wind up pulling a double, if the wunderkind's team asks for another sensor recalibration."

"Oh God, another one?" Lian rose from the table and laughed. "How many different ways can they scan these planets?"

"I'm starting to think it's infinite." The young "acting ensign"—Wesley Crusher—had been put in charge of a team of *Enterprise* science officers to determine why all the planets in the Selcundi Drema sector suffered from horrendous geological instability. The team hadn't made much progress, but it wasn't for lack of finding new and more interesting ways of scanning a planet's surface over the past several weeks.

"In any event," Lian said, "me and some others have been

getting together in Ten-Forward to chat and gossip and such. It's myself, Costa, Van Mayter, and Allenby."

Sonya vaguely recognized the other names—the first two were engineers, and Allenby was a shuttle pilot, maybe—but said only, "I don't have time, Lian, honest. There's just so much to *do*."

Lian walked over to the replicator to recycle the oatmeal bowl. Shaking her head, she said, "Sonya, one of these days you need to relax. Maybe go on a date yourself. What about that Duffy guy?"

Sonya blinked. She'd hardly thought about Duffy since the Iconian mess, and hadn't seen him except to pass in the corridor once or twice. "I don't know."

"Well, you should still come to Ten-Forward. For one thing," she said with a feral grin, "I've gotten some *really* good gossip. Do you know that Data's been talking to some girl on one of the Dreman planets?"

Sonya looked askance at Lian. "That's crazy. Isn't that a Prime Directive violation? Data isn't capable of that, is he?"

Lian shrugged. "He's sentient, remember? To my mind, that makes him capable of anything."

Now it was Sonya's turn to grin. "Weren't you the one saying he was just an android?"

"Maybe I was wrong." Lian went to the door. "I've got to get to breakfast. If you change your mind, we'll be in Ten-Forward, at the corner table, at 1930." With that, she left.

Sighing, Sonya finished reading the doctor's article. When she was done, she thought on Lian's words. Perhaps she should write the letter; perhaps she did need to slow down; and perhaps she should see how Kieran Duffy spent his off-duty time.

The computer startled her out of her reverie. *"Ensign Gomez, you have received a communiqué from Belinda Gomez on Earth."*

Getting up and stretching, Sonya said, "Put it on the screen." She turned to face the wall with the viewscreen, which lit to life with the Federation logo, followed by the round face of Sonya's older sister.

"Hey, Ess, it's me. Just wanted to check in with you on your big old starship. I got your last letter, and I'm not sure what scares me more. First you say that your captain was duplicated and that three of your crewmates were trapped in a re-creation of a bad novel. Then you talk about those inspectors from the starbase checking over your work. The part that scares me is that you didn't think the first part was a big deal, but you wouldn't stop complaining about the second part. You're weird, Ess, you know that?

"Anyhow, all's well on the home front. Looks like we're going to the Federation Cup again this year. We've just got one more game to go, but I'm pretty sure we'll be able to nail it down. We just have to beat the Stars tomorrow night, but their goalie's a pushover.

"I had dinner with Mami *and* Papi *last night—they're doing well.* Papi *says you don't write enough, but that just means you only write once a day. Anyhow, I gotta go. Talk to you later, Ess!"*

Sonya shook her head. Belinda's soccer team was going to the Federation Cup. Again. The last time they played the Stars, Belinda scored all three goals in a 3–0 victory.

And she got to see their parents more often, being on Earth.

All thoughts of acceding to Lian's requests left her mind. She couldn't afford to take the time for letters to journals or gossiping in Ten-Forward or going on a date—not when she had her sister the famous soccer player to live up to.

When Sonya arrived in engineering for her shift, Clancy was waiting for her. "I've got some news, Sonya. When we're done in Selcundi Drema, there'll be some changes."

Sonya didn't like the sound of that at all.

"Don't worry," Clancy said quickly, "they're good changes. There'll be some crew rotation, is all. Ensign Gibson's transferring off, and I'm taking over beta shift at conn."

Sonya's eyes widened. "You're getting bridge duty? Ella, that's great!"

Clancy smiled. She'd been bucking for bridge duty since before Sonya came on board. "And you're getting bumped up, too. La Forge wants you on alpha."

Her stomach dropping, Sonya said, "Alpha shift?"

"It's a great opportunity," Clancy said, as if Sonya didn't know that.

"Oh, definitely. Absolutely. This'll be great." Sonya let out a breath as Clancy smiled at her and headed over to another part of engineering.

This is going to be a disaster, Sonya thought, crestfallen. *Working right under La Forge's nose? I'll never be able to live up to that standard.*

"Excuse me, are you Ensign Clancy?"

Sonya looked up from the console to see the wunderkind himself. "No, I'm Ensign Gomez."

"Oh, sorry—Wesley Crusher." The young man offered his hand, and Sonya took it. He had a firm grip. "I'm heading up the team looking into the—"

"—geologic instability, I know," Sonya said with a smile. "What do you guys need *this* time?"

"An icospectrogram. The problem is, stellar cartography's using the starboard sensor array for their mapping, and if they stop what they're doing to give us the sensor nodes we need, they'll have to start over."

Sonya chuckled. It sounded like the young man had been rehearsing that speech before coming in here. "Can you use the port array?"

"The problem is I need five—"

"—contiguous arrays to make it work, so I need to reassign nodes four, seven, and eight in order to give you guys enough to work with, right?"

The kid grinned. She couldn't help but grin back—the kid's enthusiasm was infectious. "That's right. Thanks a *lot*, Ensign, I *really* appreciate it."

"It's not a problem, and call me Sonya." She felt ridiculous being called "Ensign" by this kid for some reason. "Give me a few minutes to finish up what I'm doing here, and then I'm all yours."

As Sonya completed the diagnostic she was in the midst of, she couldn't help but ask, "Why are you running an icogram, anyhow? You think there's dilithium on these planets?"

"There might be, yeah. Ensign Davies found indications of tracher deposits."

Sonya nodded. "And where there's tracher, there's dilithium. Makes sense. You definitely want to be as thorough as possible."

"Exactly what I said!" Wesley got a wide-eyed look that Sonya had seen all too often in the mirror. "Davies thought it might be a fool's echo, but Commander Riker put me in charge of finding out what's happening, and we've got to cover all our bases."

"Yeah, but"—Sonya took one last look at the diagnostic, saw it was compiling normally, then turned to face Wesley—"dilithium wouldn't explain this instability. I mean, you'd need more dilithium than there's ever been in one place, and not even Archer IX has *that* much dilithium."

"Maybe." Wesley seemed a bit deflated. "It might be a dead end, but we've got to be sure. Besides, it can't hurt to find out if there's another source of dilithium."

"True." Sonya smiled. "All right, then, let's go redistribute the sensors."

CHAPTER
4

**Memo from Ensign Esmeralda Clancy
to Lieutenant Geordi La Forge, stardate 42760.9.**
I believe that Ensign Sonya Gomez bears watching. She has
one of the finest engineering minds I've ever seen, but she's
in danger of burning herself out. She has tremendous drive,
but to the exclusion of all else. I've never seen her in Ten-
Forward, she's never booked leisure time on the holodeck,
she's constantly working extra shifts, and I've never seen
her socializing with anyone beyond her roommate. It's my
recommendation that she be given more guidance than I've
been able to provide.

Alpha shift hadn't been as bad as Sonya had feared. Although Geordi La Forge was a perfectionist, he wasn't an unreasonable one, and he never asked his people to do anything
they couldn't. He was very hands-on, to the point where Sonya
wondered why he bothered even having a staff, but he could
delegate when it was called for.

She also saw a lot more of Wesley Crusher. Although nomi-
nally assigned to the bridge as the alpha-shift conn officer,
Wesley—partly in preparation for his Academy studies, partly
due to the kid's sheer brilliance—also did quite a bit of work
in engineering. The icogram he'd requested had been the
right call, as had Sonya's caveat. It would indeed take more

dilithium than had ever been recorded to have it be the reason for the geologic stresses wracking Selcundi Drema, but that's just what the icogram found on Drema IV. The *Enterprise* was also able to prevent that world from being destroyed, thus saving its native civilization. Sonya had heard a lot more rumors like the one Lian told her about Data talking to a girl on the surface, and several people had said they saw Data walking the corridors with an alien child nobody recognized, but again, Sonya didn't put much stock in the rumors.

She did, however, put stock in Wesley. The kid was the genuine article. They'd spoken a few times since she switched to alpha, regularly interrupting each other and throwing ideas back and forth.

When she had her first break on her third day on alpha, she walked over to the replicator near the corridor entrance and requested a hot chocolate.

Laughter from her left caused her to look up to see La Forge chuckling and walking over to her. "We, uh—we don't ordinarily say 'please' to food dispensers around here."

Sonya smiled. Lian had said much the same thing when she ended her first dinner request with a "please," and she gave La Forge the same answer she had given Lian then: "Well, since it's listed as intelligent circuitry, why not?" However, with Lian, she'd stopped there. Now, she went on. "After all, working with so much artificial intelligence can be dehumanizing, right? So why not combat that tendency with a little simple courtesy?" Turning to the replicator, she reached for the hot chocolate and said, "Ah, thank you."

"For someone who just arrived, you certainly aren't shy with your opinions." As La Forge spoke, he walked into main engineering.

Sonya absently followed him, gripping the hot chocolate with both hands, and realizing she should've cut herself off. Lian was used to her babbling, as was Ella, and Wesley had been babbling right back. But with La Forge . . . "Have I been talking too much?"

"No." La Forge said the word emphatically, but Sonya wasn't having any of it.

"Oh, I do have a tendency to have a bit of a motor-mouth, especially when I'm excited." *Or awake.* "And you don't know how exciting it is to have gotten this assignment." And then, suddenly, before her brain could tell her mouth to shut the hell up, her mouth barreled forward with The Speech. "Everyone in class, I mean *everyone*, wants the *Enterprise.*" *Wanted, you idiot, you're not a cadet anymore!* "I mean, it would've been all right to spend some time on Rana VI, do phase work with anti-matter—that's my specialty."

"I know," La Forge said, "that's why you got this assignment."

Sonya's stomach started doing cartwheels. *He knows my specialty!* Then she mentally berated herself. *Of course he knows my specialty, he's the chief engineer. He doesn't just take people sight unseen.* Shaking her head, she said, "I did it again. It's just that—"

La Forge's voice was soothing. "I know—you're excited. Look, Sonya—"

Eager to receive whatever wisdom the chief engineer was going to provide, she said, "Yes?"

"I don't think you want to be around these control stations with that hot chocolate, do you?"

She looked down at the hot chocolate, as if seeing it for the first time. "Oh, I'm sorry. I shouldn't even *have* this in engineering. It's just, we were talking, I forgot I had it in my hand." She started to back away from La Forge with almost the same speed with which she was digging herself into a hole verbally. *Just shut up and walk away.* "I'm gonna go finish it over here."

Realizing as she walked that that probably wasn't the best way to end the conversation, she stopped, turned, and faced her CO. "Lieutenant La Forge?"

He nodded.

"This is *not* gonna happen again."

Again, he nodded. Satisfied that she hadn't embarrassed herself *too* terribly much, and at the very least pulled it out at the end, as it were, she nodded back and turned around, intending to take the hot chocolate to the corridor.

As she turned, she crashed right into someone wearing a red uniform.

Great, that's all I need. Someone on the command track getting hot chocolate all over their uniform wasn't exactly going to help Sonya do better with La Forge.

Then she looked up and saw the bald head, hawk nose, and stern expression of Captain Jean-Luc Picard.

Sonya had, of course, seen the captain before. He'd come down to engineering once or twice—not as often as Commander Riker or Lieutenant Commander Data—and she'd passed him in the corridor. On the latter occasions he had given her a nod and a curt, "Ensign," obviously not knowing who she was personally, but able to discern the single pip on her uniform denoting her rank.

This was, however, their first face-to-face encounter.

And she spilled hot chocolate on him.

She spilled a lot more on herself, but that somehow seemed not to matter so much.

"Oh, *no*! Oh, I'm sorry, oh, Captain—"

"Uh, actually, it's my fault, sir." That was La Forge, coming to her rescue. *Great, first Duffy, now La Forge. Is everybody on this ship going to have to cover for me every time I do something stupid?*

"Indeed?" said the captain, sounding dubious.

Of course he sounds dubious, you idiot. Sonya started wiping at the captain's uniform with her hands. "Oh, I wasn't looking—it's all *over* you."

"Yes, Ensign, it's all over me," Picard said in a voice that could've frozen the hot chocolate, which, somehow, he was now holding in his right hand.

"At least let me, sir," she said, still wiping at his uniform shirt.

The captain grabbed her wrist with his left hand to arrest her futile attempts at drying him off. "Ensign, uh—Ensign—?"

Realizing he was making a request, Sonya straightened. "Oh! Ensign Sonya Gomez."

La Forge added, "Ensign Gomez is a recent Academy graduate, Captain. She just transferred over at Starbase 173."

"Is that so?" the captain said to La Forge. Then he looked at Sonya with an expression that wasn't as harsh as Sonya feared it would be. "Well, Ensign Sonya Gomez, I think it would be simpler if I simply changed my uniform."

"Captain," La Forge said emphatically, "I must accept full responsibility for this."

"Yes, Chief Engineer, I think I understand." Picard looked at La Forge, then at Sonya.

And then it happened again. Sonya's mouth took off at a full run before her brain knew what was happening, and the rest of The Speech—which had been cut off by La Forge telling her he knew her background—came pouring out.

"I just want to say, sir, that I'm very excited about this assignment, and I promise to serve you, and my ship—your ship—*this* ship—to the best of my ability."

"Yes, Ensign, I'm sure that you will." The captain didn't sound in the least bit sure, and Sonya couldn't really bring herself to blame him. *You don't call it "my ship" to the captain!*

Turning to depart, Picard said, "Carry on." Then he stopped, looked down at his right hand, and then offered the hot chocolate cup back to Sonya. Meekly, she took it, and the captain exited.

Never in her life had Sonya Gomez more wanted the earth to swallow her up. Except, of course, they were on a starship, so she'd have to settle for something else—a warp core breach, maybe?

"Oh, my—" She looked at La Forge, whose VISOR made it difficult to read his expression, which came to Sonya as something of a relief. "First impressions, right? Isn't that what they say, first impressions are the most important?"

"I'll give you this—it's a meeting the captain won't soon forget."

La Forge walked off. Sonya stood there for several seconds. *My career's over.*

In the time it took Sonya to return to her quarters and change into a fresh uniform, the entire engine room was alive with gossip. Several people referred to her as the hot-chocolate demon, everyone cringed when she walked near the replicator, and she overheard Cliff Meyers describing the spilling of hot chocolate as "the Picard Maneuver." By the time the lunch break rolled around, Sonya was about ready to crawl *into* the warp core.

It was La Forge who again came to her rescue. "Sonya, how'd you like to get some lunch?"

From behind him, Duffy said, "Don't let her order a hot chocolate, Geordi!" Next to him was Denny, who snickered.

"I'd like that very much, Lieutenant," Sonya said meekly.

As they walked down the corridor toward the turbolift, Sonya said, "I can't begin to tell you how sorry I am, sir. If you want to transfer me off—"

"Now why would I do that?" La Forge chuckled. "If I transferred everyone who did something embarrassing, the engine room'd be empty in a week. All I care about is the work, and your work is excellent. I read your graduating thesis—now I wouldn't have requested you if you weren't the best."

Again, Sonya's stomach started doing cartwheels. She had no idea that La Forge had *requested* her, much less read her thesis. Looking down and smiling, she asked, "Where are we going?"

"Ten-Forward. We're gonna forget about work. We are gonna sit, talk, relax, look at the stars." He pointed a vaguely accusatory finger at her. "*You* need to learn how to slow down."

It was the same thing Lian had said to her on her first night, and she believed it even less now than she had then. "Oh, no no no no, I can't do that."

La Forge stopped walking; so did she. "You know, you're awfully *young* to be so driven."

This was hardly the first time she'd heard those words, and she gave the lieutenant the same answer she always gave: "Yes,

I am. I had to be. I had to be the best, because only the best get to be here. Geordi—" She cut herself off, realizing she'd just committed the latest in a series of faux pas. "Lieutenant," she amended, lowering her head.

"It's okay," La Forge said. And indeed, most of the people in the engine room referred to the lieutenant by his first name. But most of the people in the engine room hadn't spilled hot chocolate all over the captain, so she wasn't sure where her boundaries lay. "Go on."

"Whatever is out here, we're going to be the first humans to see it—and I wanna be a part of that. I want to understand it."

"Sonya, relax." La Forge started walking again, and Sonya kept pace. "You're here. You've made it. But you won't last long bangin' into walls. It'll be there for you, believe me."

"Okay," she said in a small voice.

"Look, I promise I won't let anything exciting slip past without letting you know, okay?"

"Okay," she said with more authority.

"Okay." La Forge smiled as they entered the turbolift. "Deck ten."

The lunch had been one of the most pleasant experiences of Sonya's career to date. One of the many reasons why Sonya had turned down Lian's offers of eating here or in the mess with other people was that she had some bad memories of family dinners. It all depended, of course, on how *Mami* and Belinda were getting along that week. When they were in one of their bad phases, Sonya felt as bad sitting at the dinner table as she had in engineering the entire morning. Those memories were hard to ignore.

But La Forge was an easy conversationalist. He had Wesley's intelligence, but the ensign's youthful enthusiasm was replaced in La Forge with a casual happiness. The lieutenant was doing what he loved doing and what he was particularly good at.

When they returned to engineering, it was back to duty, especially since both the captain and a shuttle had gone missing.

"Obviously," Duffy said in a stage whisper to Kornblum, "that hot chocolate that Gomez ordered was actually a gateway to another dimension and it sucked the captain in before he could change his uniform."

Before Sonya could say anything, Denny walked up. "Hey, c'mon, leave her alone, Duff."

"C'mon, it's just a joke. She understands, right?"

Smiling, Sonya looked at Duffy. "Actually, the hot chocolate was really a special acidic compound that only attacks people of the rank of lieutenant or higher. So watch it, or I'll spill it on you, too."

Everyone laughed at that. Sonya felt like someone lifted the world off her shoulders, as she realized they were laughing with her rather than at her.

"Honestly," Kornblum said, "that wouldn't be the weirdest thing that happened on this ship. Remember when the captain got sucked into that energy cloud that killed Singh?"

"Or when that duplicate captain from the future showed up?" Duffy added.

"Or when that Ferengi controlled his mind and trapped him on the *Stargazer*?" Kornblum said.

"Or Q."

"What's a Q?" Denny asked.

"All right, that's enough." That was La Forge, walking over from the main engineering console. "We just heard from the bridge. The captain's back."

Sonya frowned. "What do you mean, back?"

La Forge shrugged. "All I can say is, the shuttlecraft's back in the bay, and the captain's in Ten-Forward."

Sonya shook her head in confusion. "Does this count as something exciting?"

Chuckling, La Forge said, "If it is, it slipped by me, too."

The engineers all went back to work. Sonya saw that the antimatter containment unit needed a bit of an adjustment.

She worked on that for a little while, until the warp core activated.

"What the hell?" The readouts said that the helm was inactive, and that they were moving at quarter impulse, as they had been since the search for the captain had ceased. Yet the warp core was pounding away as if the ship were at warp nine.

La Forge was by her side in an instant. "What's happening?"

"I . . . I don't know."

From behind her, Kornblum said, "Sir, according to the velocity meter, we're traveling at warp twenty-two."

"That's impossible," Sonya said.

"Yeah, well, so's the captain disappearing and reappearing," La Forge muttered, "but they both fit the MO of somebody I *really* didn't wanna see again."

The next few hours would, Sonya knew, live in her nightmares for the rest of her life.

The somebody La Forge didn't want to see was Q. Though Denny didn't recognize the entity, Sonya did, from her studying of the *Enterprise*'s missions while at the Academy. He—if the masculine pronoun even truly applied—was a fantastically powerful creature who'd toyed with the ship twice before, including on her maiden voyage. Now he'd sent the *Enterprise* to the Delta Quadrant, several thousand light-years from the Federation, right in the path of a species known as the Borg.

Sonya had said she wanted to be here seeing things no human had seen before, and she got a hard lesson in the cliché about being careful what you wish for. The Borg ship had attacked the *Enterprise,* carving out portions of three decks, costing the ship eighteen people. During the frantic repair cycle in engineering, La Forge had had to keep her on track, as she found herself unable to wrap her mind around the fact that eighteen people, some of whom she probably knew, were dead. The *Yamato* had been bad enough, but she didn't know anybody there. *What if one of the casualties is Lian? Or Ella? Or—*

La Forge, bless him, had kept her in line. "We'll have time to grieve later. Right now, let's get those shields up."

Sonya had hoped that "later" would be in her quarters. Eventually Q had taken pity on them and sent them back home to the Alpha Quadrant before the Borg could destroy them. La Forge had let alpha shift—who had all stayed on well into beta—go. Sonya had gone to her cabin only to find Lian crying.

One of the eighteen people lost to the Borg ship was Soon-Tek Han.

Finding herself unable to say anything comforting to Lian, and respecting her desire to be left alone, Sonya instead went to the one place where she had felt comfortable since coming on board the *Enterprise*.

While sitting in Ten-Forward, watching the stars go by as they flew toward Starbase 83 for repairs, Sonya heard a voice. "Surprised to see you here."

She looked up to see Kieran Duffy, but said nothing.

Looking down at her drink, Duffy smirked and asked, "That's not hot chocolate, is it?"

The clear glass had an equally clear liquid in it, so Sonya knew the lieutenant was simply teasing. "Tequila, actually. My *papi* always kept a bottle of Petròn Annejo for special occasions, which usually meant he only took it out when somebody died. I couldn't think of anything better to order."

"Yeah." Duffy himself was cradling what looked like a beer or ale or somesuch. Both were, of course, syntheholic. *Enterprise* policy was that its crew was expected to stick with synthehol where at all possible. Besides, Sonya really didn't want to get drunk; she tended to lose control with alcohol, and she had enough control problems as it was.

Realizing how uncomfortable it was having Duffy hover over her, Sonya said, "Have a seat, Lieutenant—unless you're scared I'll spill the tequila on you."

Duffy chuckled. "Thanks. And I'm not worried about that, unless you meant what you said before about the acid."

"No." Sonya threw back some tequila. While the synthehol version didn't get her drunk, it didn't have the same burning sensation as it went down the throat, either, which Sonya found herself missing.

"You okay?" he asked.

"Not really." Sonya let out a long breath and shook her head. "I just can't get it right in my head, you know? Eighteen people just—just *gone*."

After taking a sip of his ale, Duffy asked, "You ever have Commander Schönhertz at the Academy?"

"Well, it's *Captain* Schönhertz, but yeah."

"She got promoted? Good for her." Duffy started turning his ale glass in place. "Well, remember what she used to say?"

Sonya wondered how old Duffy was, if his Academy days were long enough ago that Schönhertz was still a commander. *And he's still a j.g.?* That didn't speak well for his career prospects.

Aloud, she said, " 'Space is mean.' "

"Yup. Except that's not really it. Space isn't mean, because mean implies malice. What space is is uncaring. It's a brutal environment, but it's not a nasty one, because it's not trying to kill you. It just is the way it is. All we can do is work with it best we can." He smiled. "That's why I like to fly."

"You're a pilot?"

"No, I mean *fly*. My uncle got me a pair of gravity boots for my birthday when I was a teenager. I *loved* those things—didn't stop using 'em until I hurt myself."

Sonya winced. "What happened?"

Shrugging, Duffy said, "Zigged when I shoulda zagged." He got a faraway look in his eyes. "I should dig them out, try 'em on the holodeck."

"What's the holodeck like, Lieutenant?"

"Hey, c'mon, we're off duty, *Ensign*. It's Kieran."

"Sonya."

"Good. And you haven't been on the holodeck yet?"

She looked down at her drink. "Haven't had the time."

"That's crazy. Last time I checked, humans only needed eight hours of sleep, and each shift is only eight hours. That leaves eight hours to do whatever you want, and you haven't been on the holodeck?"

Sonya looked up. "It's not that simple. I have to keep up with the journals and work extra shifts sometimes, and—"

Duffy got a confused look on his face. "La Forge isn't making you do this, is he? That isn't his style."

She looked back down at the drink. "Not really."

"Trust me, Sonya, you don't need to beat yourself to a pulp. La Forge is a good guy, and he's obviously taken an interest in you. That's a good sign, really. The lieutenant has pretty high standards—which makes you wonder what he sees in me, to be honest."

"I'm sure that's not true," Sonya said meekly, though she had to admit to have been thinking the same thing.

"Ah, he's kinda stuck with me. I was part of the original shakedown crew, I served under MacDougal, Argyle, Logan, and Lynch before La Forge got the promotion, and I don't really want to go anywhere else. This is a *great* ship."

"That's true."

They kept talking for a while after that—through another drink each—and Sonya found herself unable to recall the specifics of the conversation, but she did feel a lot better when it was over.

When he tossed back the last of his second ale, Duffy got up. "I gotta go—people to do, things to see. It was nice talking to you, Sonya."

"Same here," Sonya said with a smile. "Thanks, Kieran."

"You're welcome."

CHAPTER
5

Captain's log, stardate 42923.4.
Despite misgivings, I have agreed to Starfleet's request that the *Enterprise* divert to the Braslota system to take part in a war-game exercise. Joining us as observer and mediator is the Zakdorn master strategist Sirna Kolrami.

"Hey there, HC."

Sonya gritted her teeth at Kornblum's greeting as she entered main engineering. For months, the nickname had modulated from "Ensign Hot Chocolate" to "Ensign HC" and now to simply "HC." Never mind the fact that she hadn't touched the stuff since her now-infamous encounter with Captain Picard. Never mind the fact that she'd been responsible for implementing Commander Riker's plan to save La Forge from the Pakleds who'd kidnapped him, thus saving her CO's life and earning herself a commendation. Never mind the fact that she'd taken up Earl Grey tea, the captain's favorite drink, as penance. The nickname remained.

Even in Ten-Forward, people greeted her thusly. The only exceptions were the fellow members of the "corner office," as it had come to be named. Trying to take the advice given her by Lian, Geordi, and Kieran to heart, Sonya had finally taken her roommate up on her offer to join the group of friends in Ten-Forward for drinks. The rest of the group included Tess

Allenby, who served as a shuttle pilot and the backup conn officer for both beta and gamma shifts; Gar Costa and Helga Van Mayter, both fellow alpha-shift engineers; and later, at Sonya's own urging, Denny Russell. They took up the port-side corner table. Guinan, Ten-Forward's enigmatic host, often had their drinks ready before they arrived—for Sonya it was Earl Grey—and other people generally knew not to sit there.

"You hear the scuttlebutt, HC?" Kornblum asked her now in engineering.

Sighing, Sonya said, "If you mean about Lieutenant Worf and that Klingon emissary on the holodeck, yes, I did hear." And she wished she hadn't. Klingon sex was one of those things about which she felt it was better to live in blissful ignorance.

"Nah, that's old news—I mean about the *Hathaway*. I hear La Forge'll be taking some people over there for the war game."

"Really?" Sonya now noticed Riker was in engineering talking to La Forge about something. "Isn't Commander Riker commanding the ship for the exercise?"

Kornblum nodded. "Wouldn't that be great?"

"I don't see why. It's an eighty-year-old ship. What possible use could there be in crawling around an old wreck like that?"

"Oh, I dunno, sounds like an engineer's dream."

Sonya shuddered. "More like a nightmare. I studied some of those old matter/antimatter systems at the Academy. It's embarrassingly primitive. Plus, they couldn't recrystalize their dilithium back then. It was a mess."

"Well, I hope you like cleaning up messes, then, Ensign."

Whirling around, Sonya saw that La Forge had come up behind her without her noticing. "Sir?"

"Commander Riker's asked me to come along on the *Hathaway*, and asked me to pick the engineers. You were at the top of my list."

"Oh. Uh, thank you, sir." Her first thought was that this was *not* what she had in mind when she signed on. She wanted to seek out *new* life, not seek out something that was abandoned eighty years ago with good reason. But she'd trained her mouth over the last few months to not put her first thoughts to words. Sometimes it even worked.

"There'll be a mission briefing here in two hours."

"I'll be there, sir."

After La Forge walked off, Kornblum winced. "I'm sorry, Sonya, I jinxed it for you, didn't I?"

Thinking back to an embarrassed captain saying, *"Yes, Ensign, it's all over me,"* Sonya sighed and said, "It's not your fault, Bernie. I've been jinxed since I walked onto this ship."

Sonya had been staring at the console innards for a full minute.

Forty-one *Enterprise* crew had beamed over to the eighty-year-old *Constellation*-class *Hathaway*, led by Commander Riker—or, rather, Captain Riker. For the duration of this mission, he was in command of the *Hathaway*, and so was properly referred to as "Captain." The mission specs called for a complement of forty, but Riker had asked for Wesley Crusher to come along for educational study.

Staring at the underside of this console, where La Forge had sent her once he got the lights working in engineering, Sonya was grateful for Wes's presence, as they were going to need all the help they could get. She was sitting cross-legged on the floor, staring at the unfamiliar duotronic components and wondering how the *hell* they flew through space in the twenty-third century with this garbage.

In a shipwide announcement, Riker had said that they wouldn't be getting much sleep, and Sonya could see why. Even if nobody slept and worked double time, she doubted they could get this wreck going in the two days they had.

To make matters worse, Sonya felt like a fifth wheel. La Forge had presumably taken her along for her expertise in antimatter, but the *Hathaway* was warp-inactive, with no antimatter on board to power a warp drive. Even if they had antimatter, there was no dilithium, either, just some chips of crystals that were of the less-refined variety one got in the twenty-third century when recrystallization wasn't possible.

"Something wrong, Sonya?"

Sonya looked up to see Helga Van Mayter standing over her. The brunette was holding a tool Sonya didn't recognize at first. "Is that a magnospanner?" She hadn't seen one of those since she was a plebe.

Helga nodded. "Yeah, I need it for the manifolds. What's the matter here? Can't you get the plasma flow going?"

"You kidding? I'm afraid to *touch* it!"

"Why?"

She waved her arms. "*Look* at it! I can't even find the Shange shunt."

Helga laughed. "There isn't one."

Sonya's eyes went wide. "How can there not be a Shange shunt?"

"Mostly by virtue of Shange not inventing the thing until sixty-five years ago. Besides, all the shunt does is speed up the reaction time and make it easier to diagnose flaws. It's not like you really *need* it to run the ship."

That went counter to everything Sonya had been taught. In fact, she remembered Professor Naharodny going on at some length about how if you lost your Shange shunt, you might as well blow the ship up.

"Look," Helga said, "I need to tune up the manifolds. When I'm done, I can walk you through this, if you want."

"No, no, that's okay," Sonya said quickly. Helga had her own duties to perform, and Sonya was tired of people covering for her. "I'll figure this out."

"You sure?"

Sighing, Sonya said, "Not really, but I'm gonna do it anyhow."

Helga smiled. "Good. 'Cause the manifold's gonna take at least three hours." She walked off.

Letting out another sigh, Sonya went back to peering at the inside of the console.

★ ★ ★

Four hours later, Sonya was grinning ear to ear. Helga, it turned out, had been right—all the shunt did was streamline the impulse drive. She'd doped out the entire system and figured out what needed repairing, what needed replacing, and what couldn't be repaired or replaced but still worked around.

La Forge came up to her at almost a dead run. "Sonya, just the person I'm looking for."

Clambering to her feet, Sonya brushed several locks of hair out of her face and wiped sweat from her brow with her sleeve. Holding up the padd she'd been taking notes on, she said, "I've done it, Geordi, we'll have full impulse as soon as—"

"That's great, Sonya, but we need you for something else."

Sonya blinked. "But if the impulse drive—"

"Did you do up a schedule like I asked?"

She stared down at the padd. The haphazard notes she'd doodled could, she supposed, be translated into something resembling a schedule. "Sort of."

"Give it to Costa and Sherman, I need you at the core."

Again, Sonya blinked. "Geordi, the warp core's inactive, what do you—"

"Just—come with me, Sonya, okay?"

Sonya shook her head. "O-okay. I'll be right there." She looked around, saw Gar Costa, handed him the padd, and then walked off.

"Criminy, HC, is this even in English?" Gar asked, but Sonya ignored him, walking over to where La Forge and Wesley were working with some kind of widget that was hooked up to where the antimatter injectors would be were there any antimatter.

When Wesley moved out of the way, Sonya saw the widget more clearly, and realized it was a module designed to channel high-energy plasma reactions with antimatter. She also realized that she'd seen it before, and not on the *Hathaway*. "Isn't that your plasma physics homework, Wes?"

Smiling sheepishly, Wesley said, "It was."

"Now it's our best shot at warp drive," La Forge said as if it were the most natural thing in the world. "I need you to calculate the best thermal curve to give us a controlled reaction."

"And then what?" Sonya asked. She'd been thinking purely in terms of impulse engines for several hours, so it took her a second to reboot her brain, as it were. She ran over the specs of the module from what Wesley had told her. (She also wondered how the hell he smuggled it over here, since they weren't *supposed* to bring things over from the *Enterprise*. If they could have, Sonya would've brought a Shange shunt and saved three and a half hours of her life.) "That thing doesn't have more than a few micrograms of antimatter, right?" she asked Wesley.

He nodded.

"You think the chips we have will be enough to channel the reaction?"

La Forge shrugged. "If it doesn't, we're stuck at impulse, which is where we were in the first place. But the *Enterprise* won't be expecting it."

"They won't be expecting us to blow up, either." Sonya grinned. "But it should work, yeah. I'll get right on it."

"Good."

She went off to a computer terminal to start working up the equations. Then she stopped. "Uh, Captain Riker *did* okay this, right?"

Both La Forge and Wesley said "Right" a little too quickly.

"O-o-o-okay." This once, she was more than willing to let someone else take the heat.

By the time they were two hours out of the simulation, Sonya was ready to cry.

The impulse engines were up and running as expected. Gar said that "once we translated your notes," the schedule was spot-on. The problem was that the control systems they had available to them were limited, especially since they had to adapt components from the impulse drive in order to accommodate Wesley's module, which meant that the impulse and warp drive components were doing double duty instead of being separated as usual.

"It's only a simulation," La Forge said, "and it's only for a couple of hours. Even the duotronic circuits can probably handle double duty."

"That's not the problem," Wesley said. He had that open-mouthed expression of his that Sonya had learned meant he was scared he was going to get yelled at.

La Forge folded his arms. "So what *is* the problem?"

Sonya picked it up. "We're still not a hundred percent sure the warp drive will work right. We've only got enough antimatter for a short warp-one jump, and a lot of these components are old and worn out. They haven't been used or maintained in eighty years, and they're not as adaptive as our tech is now."

"The worry," Wesley said, "is that we're going to overload the control systems, at which point the impulse *and* warp drive will both shut down."

La Forge sighed. "Great."

"Sir," Wesley said with a pained look at Sonya, "I know you signed off on this because if it didn't work we'd still have impulse power. So if you want to—"

"Wes, we can't give up now. We've already hooked everything up." He sighed. "All right, the captain'll be down in an hour for a status report. I want to quintuple-check *everything*. Wes, you look over the crystals and the reaction chamber. Sonya, you do the injectors. I'll handle the control circuits. Let's move it, people."

Sonya went to check the injectors. She ran every diagnostic she could think of, then realized that the standard diagnostics she was used to didn't take everything into account—*like*, she thought with a dark smile, *the lack of a Shange shunt*. She found herself rewriting the diagnostics, which was wise, as she found four programming flaws and one bad hookup she would have missed otherwise.

As she knelt behind the warp core realigning the injector

after fixing the bad hookup, she heard Riker's voice booming out over engineering. "The simulation begins in one hour."

"You'll have warp drive, Captain," La Forge said, "though it may not be what you expected."

That's the understatement of the decade, Sonya thought.

"I think that deserves some kind of explanation."

"We'll have warp one for—"

Wesley cut in. "Just under two seconds."

Sonya thought that was generous. One-point-four was her best guess, but Wesley seemed to think he minimized the excess flow of the antimatter.

"That's not long enough for an escape," Riker said thoughtfully, "but used as a surprise, it may give a strategic advantage."

"Sir," La Forge said, "*all* of this is theoretical."

"And if your theory fails to pay off?"

Here it comes, Sonya thought as she fit the injector back in.

"Have you ever driven a Grenthamen waterhopper?"

"Sure."

"Ever pop the clutch?"

Sonya barked out a laugh and almost dropped her tools. One of the things she loved about La Forge was his way of explaining things. Given half a chance, Sonya would babble for half an hour in jargon before even getting to the interesting part. With two questions, La Forge had conveyed the appropriate information to Riker without getting overly technical.

"You're saying we're gonna stall the *Hathaway?*"

With remarkable calm, Wesley put in, "And the *Enterprise* will waltz right over and pulverize us."

Sonya walked out from behind the warp core with a nod to La Forge. Riker smiled at her. "Ensign Gomez."

"Captain Riker."

"It's going well, I hope."

"I think so. And . . . and I've learned a lot, sir. These old ships have a lot of fascinating technology. It's impressive, really, they have no Shange shunts, duotronic circuitry, dilithium crystals that break down, no EPS conduits, no isolinear chips, and I'm babbling again, aren't I?" That last was added when Riker broke into what could only be described as an indulgent smile.

"That's all right, Ensign. As long as you keep the hot chocolate out of the engine room, we should be fine. Carry on."

Sonya let out a long breath through her teeth.

An hour later, Sonya sat in engineering, working up a new diagnostic program while keeping an eye on the engines. The war-game scenario had gone rather badly. Lieutenant Worf had hacked into the *Enterprise* security computer and tricked them into thinking a Romulan warbird was attacking. In the confusion, the *Hathaway* got several dozen simulated hits on the *Enterprise*. Then, just when La Forge had run into engineering to tell Sonya to help him and Wesley implement the warp jump, a Ferengi warship, the *Kreechta*, showed up and attacked the *Enterprise*. The latter vessel was unshielded, since its tactical systems were in simulation mode for the war game, and so was especially vulnerable. Transporter and weapons were down.

The daiMon in charge had given the *Enterprise* ten minutes to give up the *Hathaway*, which they had erroneously concluded to be a prize of value to the *Enterprise* in order for the *Galaxy*-class ship to be firing on it.

La Forge and Wesley had gone back to the bridge to talk to the *Enterprise*. La Forge had left Sonya in charge of engineering, telling her in no uncertain terms to make sure the warp drive worked, as it was now likely their only means of escape from the *Kreechta*.

Now she was monitoring the conversation between the two ships. Data was speaking at the moment. *"Premise: The Ferengi wish to capture the* Hathaway, *believing it to be of value. Therefore, we must remove the ship from their field of interest."*

Kolrami, the Zakdorn observer and moderator, spoke up. *"And they will soon relocate it after a two-second warp jump."*

"One-point-four," Sonya muttered. She still didn't think Wesley's module had enough antimatter for two whole seconds.

"*There is a way,*" Picard said. "*Number One, can you hear this?*"

"*Yes, sir,*" Riker said, "*we're all here—waiting for you to pull another rabbit out of your hat.*"

"Gar," she said to Costa, "check over the inertial dampeners. With this warp drive, the last thing we want is to lose that or gravity."

"Right—wouldn't want to escape the Ferengi just to go splat on the bulkheads." Gar ran off to check that.

"*Mr. Data?*" Picard prompted.

The android said, "*On the captain's command, we will fire four photon torpedoes directly at the* Hathaway."

They actually have torpedoes. That's something, Sonya thought as she finished off the diagnostic program.

Data went on: "*One millisecond after its detonation, the computer will trigger your warp jump.*"

Sonya started running the program, and then immediately opened up a new program file on the terminal in front of her. *If this is going to work, we'll need to get this cranky old computer to do it.*

La Forge said, "*I think I hate this plan. Data, we're not even sure our warp jump will work.*"

"*If the warp engines fail to function,*" Data said, "*the result could be—unfortunate.*"

"*Very unfortunate—we will be dead.*" That was Worf, as ever the voice of bluntness.

Sonya, however, was pretty sure she could do it. She'd spent two days navigating these silly old duotronics, and she was fairly confident that she could make them tap-dance if she had to. Tying the warp drive-execution into the detection of a torpedo explosion was something she *should* be able to do.

"*Captain Riker, I cannot order you to do this,*" Picard said, which struck Sonya as remarkably generous. Were she in

Picard's place, she wasn't sure she'd stop short of giving that order.

"*What the hell.*" Riker sounded rather morbid. "*Nobody said life was safe.*"

Sonya looked around, saw that Chao-Anh Aleakala was sitting nervously. "Chao-Anh, I need a fresh set of eyes on this."

Looking almost relieved, Chao-Anh came over and eyeballed Sonya's padd.

Picard's voice sounded over the speakers. "*The advantage is that it will appear from the* Kreechta's *perspective as though—as though you were destroyed in the explosion.*"

As she read over the program, Chao-Anh muttered, "Unless of course we *are* destroyed in the explosion."

"We'll be okay," Sonya said. To her own surprise, she believed it.

"I hope you're right, Sonya." Chao-Anh, for her part, didn't sound like she did.

Worf said, "*That will deceive them only for a few minutes. Their sensors will soon locate us.*"

"*We'll only need a few minutes, Mr. Worf,*" Riker said, "*because you're going to prepare another surprise for them.*"

That confused Sonya. She knew that Worf could get into the *Enterprise* computer by virtue of being the ship's chief of security. *I guess he has an equal facility for Ferengi computers.* Chuckling to herself, she thought, *They probably get their security protocols on the cheap anyhow.*

Chao-Anh said, "I'm not sure about the timing. I'd go for one-and-a-half milliseconds to play it safe."

"We can't fine-tune it that much," Sonya said. "Besides, Data's the one who said one millisecond. You're gonna doubt him?"

"*Then we're agreed,*" Picard said on the speaker. "*On my mark—four minutes.*"

Data added, "*Remember, Geordi, if the implementation is off by one millisecond, the* Hathaway *will not survive.*"

Sonya gave Chao-Anh a "see?" look. The other engineer simply shrugged.

Sounding more worried than Sonya had ever heard him, even during the Borg attack, La Forge said, *"Data, that's the one part of this plan we're all absolutely sure about."*

One minute later, La Forge and Wesley entered engineering. Both Sonya and Denny Russell walked up to them with padds in hand.

La Forge looked right at Sonya. "Tell me the warp drive's okay."

Handing him the padd, she said, "Okay, and already programmed to go off when the *Enterprise* tries to blow us up, per Mr. Data's plan."

Briefly, La Forge smiled. "Bless you, Sonya. What've you got, Russell?"

Denny held up his padd display. "I've plotted a course that minimizes risk of gravitational fluctuations from either Braslota or the planet when we go to warp. With your permission, I'll send this to Ensign McKnight on the bridge."

"Do it." He walked over to the core. "Let's get this party started."

Wesley went over to the injector control systems, Sonya right next to him. The kid looked nervous as hell. "I hope this works."

"If it does, we owe it to you, Wes," Sonya said. "If you hadn't smuggled that thing over, we'd be stuck."

"And if it doesn't work, the *Enterprise* will blow us up."

Sonya shrugged. "Like the captain said, nobody said life was safe."

"Yeah, but with these old control systems and the duotronic circuits, and—"

"Hey, don't count the *Hathaway* out. There's some life in these old circuits."

Wes smiled. "Weren't you the one who was afraid to touch anything two days ago, HC?"

Pointing an accusatory finger, Sonya said, "Don't *you* start with the 'HC.' And . . . well, let's just say I've been converted."

Sonya had only been half-listening to the monitored

communications between the *Enterprise* and the *Kreechta,* but then she heard Picard say, *"You believe the* Hathaway *has value? We deny you your prize. Fire!"*

"Here it comes." Sonya held her breath.

The ship rocked for a second—*Dammit, Gar,* Sonya thought, *you were supposed to* fix *the intertial dampeners if they weren't working!*—but then steadied.

Then the walls seemed to stretch for a second. Looking down, Sonya saw that her hands were doing the same thing. It looked similar to the visual distortion of the stars one saw at warp speeds, but of the *ship,* not what was outside it.

Looking over at Wesley, she saw that his face was also distorted, like it was in a fun-house mirror. But oddly, Sonya didn't feel any pain.

Then everything snapped back to normal. This time there was no jerking of the ship. *Good work, Gar.*

She checked the display. "Warp speed operational for one-point-nine seconds." She looked over at Wes. "You were right."

Now Wesley was grinning ear to ear. "Looks like I was, yeah."

When they arrived in Ten-Forward, the "corner office" already had an Earl Grey tea, a green tea, a synthehol Scotch, a birch beer, a synthehol bitters, and a *raktajino* sitting in front of each place.

Lian raised her green tea as they all took a seat and said, "To Ensigns Gomez, Costa, Van Mayter, and Russell for earning commendations on the *Hathaway!*"

"Here, here," Tess Allenby said, hoisting her Scotch. She and Lian were the only ones from the corner office who hadn't been assigned to Captain Riker, though they had been sent to the battle bridge after the Ferengi attacked, in case the *Enterprise* needed to do an emergency saucer separation.

They all sipped from their drinks and cheered. "You all did amazing work," Lian said. "Everybody's talking about it."

Denny shrugged as he swallowed his birch beer. "Just another day at the office."

"C'mon," Tess said, "doing what you did with an eighty-year-old ship? I'm amazed the thing didn't fall apart when you blew on it."

"Don't be so sure," Helga said. "Those old systems'll surprise you—right, Sonya?"

Grinning at her Earl Grey, Sonya said, "Yeah, okay, so I took a little while to get the hang of it."

"More than a little while," Helga said conspiratorially.

"All right, all right, more than a little while. But we did it, didn't we? We made a warp drive and we beat the Ferengi."

Gar held his *raktajino* near his face, as if ready to sip it at a moment's notice. "We made a warp drive with spit and baling wire."

"And the Crusher kid's experiment," Helga added.

Tess made a face. "Not that little twerp again."

Sonya was surprised by the vehemence of her reaction. "Tess?"

"Look, Sonya, I know he's your friend, but . . . I mean, c'mon, he's a *kid*. He hasn't taken one class at the Academy, and Picard's got him doing alpha-shift conn duties. I'm *never* gonna get on the bridge during alpha as long as he's on the ship, especially if he keeps pulling miracles like this."

"Tess, I . . ." Sonya hesitated. She'd really grown to like Wes over the past few months, but she hadn't realized that the "acting ensign's" position might have had a deleterious effect on the not-so-acting ensigns.

"Look, it's okay."

"You should say something to Riker," Helga said. "He's a good guy."

"Please—*he's* the one in charge of the kid's 'education.' Who do you think put him in charge of that mineral survey in Drema? The worst thing I can do is complain to Riker about his precious boy genius."

An uncomfortable silence descended over the corner office

for a second before Gar said, "Hey, I hear La Forge is doing rotations again. He's putting Kieran on warp diagnostics." He waggled his eyebrows at Sonya. "So now you two can flirt all shift."

Sonya almost spit her tea. "What?"

Lian gave Sonya an accusatory look. "Flirting? With Lieutenant Duffy? Sonya, you didn't *tell* me."

"We are *not* flirting."

"Coulda fooled me," Denny muttered.

"Don't *you* start," she said with a glower at her classmate.

"Hey, *I* wasn't the one giggling during the maintenance cycle."

Tess shot her a look. "Giggling?"

"He—" Sonya sighed. "He told a funny joke. The law of averages was bound to catch up to him eventually, and he'd say something funny. I was just being polite."

"During a maintenance cycle," Denny deadpanned.

"Look—"

"And then there was that time during the Mariposa mission," Gar said.

"And when you two were on the damage-control team when that old Klingon ship attacked," Helga added.

"And when—"

"All right!" Sonya said, interrupting Denny. "Maybe we are flirting . . . a little."

"For very large values of 'little,'" Denny muttered.

"But that's all it is. I'm *not* interested in Kieran Duffy. He's not nearly as funny as he thinks he is—in fact, *nobody's* as funny as *he* thinks he is—and besides, he's *still* a j.g. He's been in Starfleet for *years*, and that's as far as he's gotten. That's a classic case of career dead-endedness."

"So?" Lian asked.

Sonya hesitated. She stared at Lian for a second. All her reasons were true, of course, but that wasn't the overriding factor. She had, over the past months, taken it easy, and allowed herself to have a social life.

But she hadn't taken the next step with Kieran Duffy for one simple reason: she didn't want to go through what Lian went through when the Borg attack took Soon-Tek from her.

Tess used Sonya's mention of career dead-endedness to rant about Wesley again, which in turn led to Denny speculating about his parents, which led to Lian and Helga telling Sonya, Denny, and Tess about Beverly Crusher, which led to a discussion of Dr. Pulaski and her transporter phobia, and soon nobody was talking about Tess's bitterness or Sonya's love life, which suited Sonya just fine.

CHAPTER
6

Captain's log, stardate 43198.7.

The *Enterprise* remains in standard orbit while we investigate the tragedy which has struck the away team. Lieutenant Marla Aster, ship's archaeologist, has been killed in what should have been a routine mission. Whatever the explanation, it will not bring back a valued and trusted officer.

"Hey, Sonya, wait up!"

Sonya paused to let Kieran catch up with her in the deck ten corridor. She was heading to the turbolift, and thence to engineering. Both were on beta shift now—they'd been assigned there for the past few weeks, ever since their encounter with the Shelliak—which started in a few minutes. She'd been grabbing a bite to eat in Ten-Forward and reading a fascinating article in the latest *JAWM* about soliton waves. "What's up, Kieran?"

"You've been holding out on me, Ensign."

Frowning, Sonya said, "I don't know what you mean." Then she added with a smile, *"Lieutenant."*

He grinned back at her. "I mean you never told me Belinda Gomez was your sister."

"It's not like it's a secret or anything." Sonya tried not to sound defensive. The fact of the matter was, she *had* kept it a secret. She had enough of dealing with being in the shadow of

Her Sister the Soccer Star for most of her teen years, through to her time at the Academy. "You never asked."

"Oh, okay. I'll remember that from now on when I meet people. 'Say, you don't happen to have any famous siblings or other relatives?' I mean, c'mon, Sonya, it's not like most people would keep that a secret. She's a great player."

"I know, I just—" She sighed. "I spent a lot of time being in her shadow, that's all. You know she saved my life when we were kids? I fell into the Gulf of Mexico when we were out on a rowboat, and she dived in and kept me from drowning." Sonya shook her head. "That was just the start. After that, it was always, 'why can't you be like your sister?'"

"You should invite her on the ship, then. You'll eclipse her in a nanosecond."

Sonya gave Kieran a dubious look. "C'mon. I'm just an engineer."

"'Just' an engineer? Kiddo, you've been Geordi's golden girl for months. Besides, who else would have the *chutzpah* to spill hot chocolate on a god?"

At that, Sonya couldn't help but laugh. Just recently, the natives of Mintaka III had mistaken the captain for a deity. It had taken a certain amount of work—and a near-fatal injury to Picard—to convince the Mintakans that the *Enterprise* captain was not divine.

"It's not that big a deal," she said as they approached the turbolift. "She's just my sister."

"Hah. There's no such thing as 'just' a sister. I've got one, too, y'know—Amy. Devoted her life to making mine a living hell. Why do you think I signed up for Starfleet? Gets me far away from her and her practical jokes."

They stood and waited for a turbolift. "Since when do *you* have a problem with practical jokes?" Sonya in particular was recalling an incident involving Ensigns McKnight and Prixis that required a molecular debonder to be applied in sickbay to their hair. The joke around the ship was that it was that incident in particular that led to Dr. Pulaski transferring off the *Enterprise*.

"I have no problem with *my* practical jokes. It's *hers* that are the issue. There was this one time—"

The doors opened to reveal La Forge. Right around the time Pulaski left—to be replaced by the woman *she* replaced, Beverly Crusher, Wesley's mother—La Forge had been promoted to lieutenant commander. According to what both Kieran and Denny had heard, La Forge had had several of his personnel requests denied because the people he wanted were full lieutenants, and Starfleet wasn't comfortable with a chief engineer not being the senior-ranked person in the engine room. La Forge expressed his frustration to Riker, Riker expressed it to Picard, and the captain gave La Forge a field promotion to lieutenant commander after only a year as a full lieutenant.

"Duffy, just the man I want to see. You need to come with me to the transporter."

"What's happening?" Sonya asked.

"The away team got into a scrape—a bomb went off."

Sonya's stomach fell. "Is everyone okay?" She knew that Worf was leading the team, which also included one civilian scientist who was on loan to Starfleet, and two archeaologists, Marla Aster and Leo Antonidas.

La Forge shook his head. "Lieutenant Aster didn't make it."

Kieran's eyes went wide. "Oh my God."

"Commander Riker wants us to go down there, figure out what happened. Ensign Gomez, report to engineering—you're in charge till I get back."

That surprised Sonya. She guessed that all the junior-grade lieutenants on beta shift were going on the team. "Yes, sir."

"Duffy?" They proceeded to the forward turbolift that would take them to the transporter.

Sonya shivered as she stepped onto the lift. She didn't really know Marla Aster that well, but she did know that she was a single mother, and had a son on board the ship. *What'll happen to him?*

★ ★ ★

Beta shift had been tense and unpleasant. It was one thing when people died in battle, as they did against the Borg, but stupid accidents like this didn't sit right with anyone. Sonya found herself reminded of the conversation she'd had with Kieran about Captain Schönhertz and space being mean and/ or indifferent.

After the shift ended, she went to Ten-Forward, and found Kieran nursing an ale. She asked Guinan for a tequila, and then went over to Kieran's table. "That's not hot chocolate, is it?"

Seemingly despite himself, Kieran laughed. "No, it's ale."

"Mind if I join you?"

"Never." Kieran said the word rather emphatically.

Sonya took a seat. Guinan brought the tequila over. She held it up and gave the toast that they had told her at the Academy was traditional when comrades were lost in battle. "Absent friends."

"Yeah."

They both drank.

"You knew her, didn't you?" Sonya asked.

Kieran nodded. "We met right after she came on board about eighteen months ago. She was having some kind of problem with the replicator in her cabin—wouldn't give her kid his favorite drink, which was this vile fruit concoction. So I fixed it, and we got to talking—even went on a date or two. Nothing really materialized, though. I don't think she was entirely over her husband, y'know?"

Sonya nodded, though she, in fact, didn't know. She'd never lost anyone closer to her than three grandparents she barely knew.

"Still, she was a great lady. And Jeremy's a really good kid. God, I don't know *what's* gonna happen to him."

"What was she like?"

Kieran spent the next half hour or so telling Sonya various and sundry facts about Lieutenant Marla Aster, from her proclivity for pink clothing while off duty to her ability to talk for several hours at a time on the subject of the amazing discoveries on Jureosa to her courtship with her husband when they were both studying at Endurance University on Mars.

The recollections were interrupted by La Forge's voice on the intercom. *"Lieutenant Duffy, Ensign Gomez, report to main engineering."*

They exchanged quick glances, gulped down the rest of their drinks, and headed out. "Wonder what's up," Kieran said. "And hey, Sonya—thanks."

As they approached the turbolift, Sonya smiled up at him. "No problem, Kieran. You were there for me when *I* was moping in Ten-Forward after the Borg. Seemed only fair to return the favor."

"Yeah."

CHAPTER
7

Captain's log, stardate 43489.2.
We have arrived at Angosia III, a planet that has expressed a strong desire for membership in the Federation. Prime Minister Nayrok has taken Commander Riker and me on a tour of the capital city.

"Garfield Costa, step forward."

Next to Sonya, Gar took a single step forward. They were in formation in engineering, along with Ensigns Kornblum, Russell, Sherman, and Van Mayter, facing Geordi La Forge and Data. Behind the chief engineer and the second officer were the rest of the engineering staff, most with big smiles on their faces. Several of them had already been promoted as well; Geordi had gone in reverse order of rank, ending with the ensigns who were making j.g.

Data handed Geordi a box, which he opened to reveal a hollow pip. He stepped forward and affixed it to Gar's collar. "I hereby promote you to the rank of junior-grade lieutenant, with all the duties and privileges that entails."

Gar nodded, beaming. "Thank you, sir."

He stepped back, and Geordi said, "Sonya Gomez, step forward."

Until he said those words, Sonya hadn't been able to bring herself to believe that she was really being promoted. Indeed, ever since the infamous hot-chocolate incident, she'd been convinced that her collar would go without any more pips until she finally took the hint and resigned her commission and went into a line of work where she could do less damage.

But after the *Enterprise*'s mission to the Romulan Neutral Zone ended, the promotion list came out, and Sonya was thrilled to see her name on it. Among other things, it meant she got a cabin to herself. Not that she had anything against Lian, but she hadn't had a room to herself since she was seventeen.

Besides, Lian's name had also been on the promotion list, so she was getting a cabin of her own, too, where she said she intended to celebrate along with another new promotion, Lieutenant Tanaka, one of the medical technicians, whom she'd been seeing for a few weeks now.

Ella Clancy had also been promoted; sadly, Tess Allenby wasn't, which Sonya feared would simply make her friend even more bitter toward Wes. In fact, Tess was the only member of the corner office who remained an ensign.

Kieran hadn't been on the list, either, which meant that he and Sonya were now of the same rank. Sonya wasn't sure how she felt about that.

Sonya stood proudly as Geordi affixed the hollow pip to her collar. *I can't believe this is happening.*

"I hereby promote you to the rank of junior-grade lieutenant, with all the duties and privileges—"

Feeling like she was going to explode, Sonya said, *"Thank you, sir."* Then she realized what she'd done.

Geordi, however, just shook his head and chuckled. "—that entails," he finished. Everyone else laughed as well.

To her amazement, Sonya didn't feel embarrassed. She was too happy.

Data and Geordi went down the line to the other engineering ensigns in alphabetical order, ending with Helga.

Afterward, everyone in engineering cheered. Even Data, after a fashion.

Turning to Lieutenant Della Guardia, Geordi said, "We've got to get to the bridge—you're in charge, Alfredo."

"Yes, sir," the newly promoted full lieutenant said.

Data and Geordi departed. Sonya knew that Picard and Riker were going to be given a tour of the Angosian capital, so Data was in command of the ship, and Geordi liked to put in time on the bridge, she knew. She suspected that was a hold-over from his time as the alpha-shift conn officer before he was given the chief job. If there was one thing she'd learned about Geordi in a year on the *Enterprise,* it was that he liked to be in the thick of things.

Kieran walked up to her. "Congrats, Sonya. See, I told you. Watch it, inside a few years, you'll be running this place, while I'll just be an ordinary j.g."

"Don't be so sure of that," Alfredo Della Guardia said. "You got yourself a mighty fine performance review, there, Duff."

"I did?" Kieran sounded surprised.

"He did?" Sonya sounded the same.

"Hey!" Now Kieran was mock-outraged.

Alfredo shrugged. "His work's picked up. Maybe you're a good influence on him."

With that, Alfredo walked away.

Sonya wasn't sure what to make of that.

The festivities concluded, it was time to go back to work. With the promotion, Gomez was put in charge of the warp core, which had been Della Guardia's responsibility. La Forge generally preferred to rotate folks, so they were experienced in all aspects of engineering, not just their individual specialty, but he said Sonya's antimatter expertise would prove handy, especially since the *Enterprise*'s warp drive had gotten a lot more and varied use in the past couple of years than expected. The *Galaxy*-class was still a relatively new design, after all—though the Borg threat had sent Utopia Planitia into overdrive with new ship concepts—and could, Geordi said, use some hand-holding.

As she ran a diagnostic on the warp core, she thought about

Alfredo's words. She hadn't really seen herself as influencing Kieran in any way. True, they'd been spending more time together lately. She found she was enjoying his company more and more, in part because he seemed to be taking life more seriously.

Or maybe it was that she was taking life less seriously. The promotion to j.g. had validated what Geordi, not to mention Ella, Lian, Kieran, Wes, and pretty much everyone else on board, had been saying for a year now: she deserved to be here. And she'd learned quite a bit—probably more in one year on this vessel than she had in four years at the Academy. She'd hot-wired an eighty-year-old impulse drive, helped outwit some alien kidnappers, done damage control against foes ranging from Borg to out-of-date Klingons to unknown aliens to a ten-thousand-year-old booby trap, and learned so much about different approaches to ship engineering.

More important though, she had learned what Geordi had instructed her to learn: to relax.

"General quarters. All off-duty and civilian personnel report to quarters immediately."

Sonya looked up sharply as she entered main engineering to report for her second day of duty as a lieutenant. The computer's instruction didn't apply to her, as she had just come on duty, but she wondered what had prompted it. Yesterday, the *Enterprise* had taken on an Angosian prisoner named Roga Danar, and this morning was transferring him back to a penal colony on one of Angosia's moons. Sonya's initial thought— *What could possibly have gone wrong?*—was immediately suppressed. A year on the *U.S.S. Enterprise* had wrested out of her the notion that nothing could go wrong almost as fast as the notion that there were things that didn't have a solution.

From transporter control, Cliff Meyers said, "I don't believe this—Danar *broke out* of the transporter field!"

"That's not possible," Kieran said.

Geordi ran over to stand behind Cliff. "I've seen this guy in action, Duffy, don't be so sure of that."

From behind Sonya at the main console, Ensign Koji Oliver said, "Turbolifts are down, security fields going up on the lower decks." Then he frowned. "Turbolifts are back up."

"Who ordered that?" Sonya asked.

"The bridge." Gar sounded as confused as Sonya.

Geordi went over to the main console next to Koji. "Probably a trick—everyone on the ship knows the turbolifts should be down, but Danar may not. If he sees the lifts are working, he might take one and then we'd get him."

"Sir," Kieran said, "I'm not tracking Danar at all. Are we sure he's loose?"

"He's invisible to sensor scans," Geordi said.

"Oh. Sorry, sir."

Sonya sighed. Kieran should have known that.

"Phaser on overload! Seal this deck!" That was Worf's voice on the speaker. Before Sonya could even register the words, Geordi had pounced on the console and sealed off section twelve of deck thirty-six.

Sonya held her breath as the seconds ticked by.

Then: *"Captain, the overload has been averted."*

Everyone in engineering exhaled. Geordi lowered the force fields in that section, but kept the security fields up. Sonya went back to the warp core to see that her diagnostic was done, and the warp core was functioning normally.

"It'll be okay," Kieran said. "I'm sure Worf'll take care of the guy."

"Hang on, something's wrong," Koji said. "One of the force fields on this deck just went down. The bridge didn't—"

Koji's words were cut off, and Sonya heard something fall. She whirled around to see Koji being flipped over someone's back and onto the console by a fast-moving figure who backhanded Geordi hard enough to knock his VISOR off. Both Kieran and Cliff moved to stop him, but they were taken down, too.

Sonya was about to cry out Kieran's name as he crumpled, broken, to the deck, but before she could, she felt a blow to the side of her head, and the universe went dark.

The next thing Sonya knew, she was lying on a biobed in sickbay, a throbbing, nauseating pain in her head, and Nurse Temple standing over her. "Wha—what happen'?"

"You're fine, Lieutenant, just a bump on the head. You'll be okay in a little while."

"Kieran . . . Geordi . . . engineer—" She tried to sit up. This proved a rather big mistake, as the room started jumping around, bouncing back and forth, and generally behaving in a very silly manner.

She quickly lay back down.

The nurse smiled and said, "Notice I didn't say you'd be okay *now*. Rest, all right? The doctor will be by to see you in a second."

Temple walked off. Sonya looked around, saw Cliff and Gar, as well as Dershowitz from security on three other biobeds, and Koji sitting in the central biobed, holding his right arm gingerly while Dr. Crusher applied a bone-knitter to it.

What happened to Kieran?

Sonya realized that that was the foremost thing on her mind. The last thing she saw before being rendered insensate was Kieran falling to the floor. She didn't know if he was alive or dead, and the fact that he might be dead scared her, even more than the notion that Geordi or anyone else might be.

She figured that everything was fine—that Worf caught Danar or, at the very least, that Danar was no longer a threat, since everyone in sickbay seemed fairly calm.

But that left her with her own thoughts, which were primarily of Kieran. *I've been an idiot,* she realized. Not that this was a huge revelation—she'd been an idiot in some manner or other for most of the last year—but that didn't make it any less so. She'd been making excuses for not pursuing a relationship with Kieran, all of which sounded very reasonable when she'd spelled them out at the corner office, and which sounded completely ridiculous in light of what just happened. *What if the Borg come to the Alpha Quadrant? What if the next time we're in the Romulan Neutral Zone, the captain doesn't have two Klingon ships up his sleeve? What if one of those weird anomalies we come across blows us to bits? What if the next computer virus sends us the way of the* Yamato?

Dr. Crusher finished with Koji and walked over to check on Sonya. A smile on her pretty pale face, she went over Sonya with her scanner. "You're looking more awake, Lieutenant. How do you feel?"

"Nauseous, and my head hurts."

"Perfectly normal." She pulled a hypo out of her blue lab coat pocket and applied it to Sonya's neck. Almost immediately, her head cleared and her stomach felt like a stomach again instead of a whirligig. "That'll mask the symptoms until the concussion subsides. I wouldn't recommend returning to duty until your next shift starts—which, according to the duty roster, isn't for another twenty hours."

Sonya blinked in surprise. It had only been four hours since she'd gone on duty and GQ was sounded. "Thank you, Doctor. Uh, Doctor?"

"Yes?"

"What happened?"

Crusher chuckled. "Sorry, I guess you couldn't have known. Danar managed to escape. Nobody was killed, thankfully. Worf got a few bruises, Lieutenants Meyers and Costa also got concussions, Ensign Oliver broke his arm, and Lieutenant Duffy cracked a rib. Everyone else was just stunned a bit."

Sonya felt a profound sense of relief at the fact that Kieran was okay.

"Now get some rest—doctor's orders."

Smiling, Sonya lazily raised her right arm in salute. "Yes, sir."

She let herself drift off to sleep thinking that she needed to talk to Keiko Ishikawa.

★ ★ ★

The pleasant scent of wild roses from Earth, *toyar* from Betazed, and fire flowers from Berengaria wafted in the carefully circulated air of the *Enterprise*'s arboretum on deck seventeen. Sonya stood in the middle of the tree nursery—the flowers in question were in the main part of the arboretum—knowing that what she was doing was crazy.

She had talked with Keiko, who had assured her that she would keep the tree nursery clear from 1900 onward. Keiko had a twinkle in her eye, adding, "It's about time you two got your act together." But then, Keiko had recently started seeing Chief O'Brien, so she had such things on her mind anyhow. In fact, Keiko's recent romantic bent had been one of the deciding factors in her choosing the arboretum as the site for her and Kieran's rendezvous.

"Rendezvous," listen to me. Bad enough I lied to Kieran to get him here, telling him there was a symposium. I guess I just wanted to hedge in case he said no, or wasn't interested. Sonya hadn't been on a date since she was a young teenager; she'd been too busy pushing herself to the next level, whether it was school, the Academy, or the *Enterprise.* By deceiving Kieran, it gave him an easy out, in case she'd totally made a *targ*'s ear out of the whole thing.

She was dressed in civilian clothes—a loose brown blouse and equally loose pants of the same color over black boots. It was, as far as she could remember, the first time she'd worn anything other than her uniform when not in her cabin. Lian had joked that she needn't have bothered packing clothes when she'd come on board. But it wasn't right to show up for a date in uniform.

At a little after 1900—being on time had never been Kieran's strong suit—she went out to stand near the aft door. A few minutes later, Kieran walked up to her. He was wearing a dark blue short-sleeved shirt with a yellow jacket over it, his pants the same color as the jacket. At first she winced, until she realized that the color perfectly matched the *toyar,* which were in full bloom, and which Keiko had made the centerpiece of the arboretum. That didn't make the outfit any more palatable, but Sonya resolved to live with it for as long as the clothes remained on.

She found herself hoping that wouldn't be too terribly long.

He offered her his arm, which she took with a smile, and they both entered the aft door.

"I guess we're the first ones here," he said as the door closed behind them with a soft swish.

The smile growing, Sonya reached up and gently turned and lowered Kieran's chin toward her. His brown eyes were filled with surprise, anticipation, and confusion, all at the same time. She whispered, "Kieran, there's no symposium."

Her hand moved up to his cheek and she craned her neck to kiss him full on the lips. To her great relief, he returned the kiss, though it took him until after she'd grabbed the back of his head to pull him closer that he thought to put his arms around her.

CHAPTER
8

Captain's log, stardate 43992.6.
Admiral Hanson and Lieutenant Commander Shelby of
Starfleet Tactical have arrived to review the disappearance
of the New Providence colony. No sign remains of the nine
hundred inhabitants.

They were the best months of Sonya's life.

Geordi wasted very little time in putting them on separate
shifts. He had no problem with fraternization in theory, but
he also wanted his people focused on their work, not on each
other. So Sonya was put in charge of gamma shift, which was
a promotion of sorts, since she was responsible for the entire
engineering section during the "night" hours. Kieran, mean-
while, worked alpha with Geordi.

The relationship seemed to do them both good. Kieran
received more commendations, and he said he was taking
the initiative more. As for Sonya, gamma shift seemed to respond well to her leadership skills, which amazed her, as she
hadn't been aware she *had* any leadership skills. In fact, Commander Kurn, of all people—a Klingon who'd temporarily
taken over as first officer as part of an exchange program—
had given her a satisfactory rating for her work on gamma
shift, notable for it being the only satisfactory rating he gave
to anyone.

Working on alpha, Kieran tended to have the best stories, from him and Chief O'Brien unwittingly contaminating the ship with invidium—which led to Kieran being teased almost as much as Sonya had been after the hot-chocolate incident— to preparing a meeting room for the Legaran negotiation.

Not that it was all fun. Bernie Kornblum had been killed, shot by an Ansata terrorist who was attempting to blow up the ship, and everyone had believed Data to be dead as well, though that turned out to be a ruse. Several people had also been injured in an attack by a Romulan vessel during the en- counter with "Tin Man."

Still, things were going very well. The *Enterprise* did a lengthy survey of the Zeta Gellis Cluster, which included a rather bizarre first contact. Geordi started dating Christy Hen- shaw, which benefited the entire engineering staff, as it meant their boss was in a perpetual good mood. Kieran had joined the corner office, replacing Lian, who'd been transferred to the *Hood*, where she'd be the beta-shift ops officer under Riker's former CO, Captain DeSoto. Wes had been given a commission to ensign, complete with red uniform and pip, an action that pleased everyone except Tess Allenby.

All was well on the *Starship Enterprise*.

And then the Borg returned.

It started with the New Providence colony on Juret IV, which had been destroyed in a manner similar to that of the planets the *Enterprise* scanned in system J25 in the Delta Quadrant. A Borg expert named Elizabeth Shelby had been detached to the *Enterprise* to verify the likelihood that the Borg were respon- sible, which she did in short order.

Sonya hadn't been able to sleep the night before. Kieran, of course, slept like a rock. He'd been on board when they'd last encountered the Borg, but for him, it was just one more mission.

For Sonya, it had been a lot more.

When she came on for gamma shift, Geordi, Wes, Data, Marguerite Sherman, and Bigay Ampalayon were all standing around the main console, along with a blonde wearing a red lieutenant commander's uniform. Sonya assumed this to be the infamous Shelby.

"Look at Commander Borg go," Helga Van Mayter muttered when Sonya walked past her.

"Commander Borg?" Sonya said with a smile.

"Well, she's supposed to be the expert. Never mind that we're the only ones who actually *saw* the damn things, but hey, *she's* the expert. You know, she beamed down early with Data? I heard Riker chewed her aft shields after *that* one—especially after she cleaned him out in poker."

"She cleaned out *Riker*?"

Helga nodded.

Several hours into gamma, Riker came by asking for a report. "Everybody's up late tonight," Helga muttered.

"Can you blame them?" Sonya asked.

"Not really. God, I hope they're wrong."

"Yeah."

"Commander, I think we should call it a night." Riker's voice carried across engineering. Sonya looked over to see that Riker, who had been sitting on the console's edge in front of Bigay and Marguerite, was now standing. "That's an order. We'll reconvene at 0500."

Four whole hours of sleep, Sonya thought, then realized she was being unfair. Besides, Geordi and Wes were the types to keep gnawing at a problem until they'd completely chewed it, and Data never slept anyhow.

Shelby then said, "Sir, if I may be allowed to continue with Mr. Data, who does not require rest—"

"*You* need rest, Commander," Riker said.

For anybody else that would've been it. In fact, if Shelby had really gotten the reaming Helga had described, she shouldn't have even gone that far.

Instead, she went further: "If we have a confrontation with the Borg without improving our defense systems—"

"If we have a confrontation," Riker said firmly, "I don't want a crew fighting the Borg at the same time they're fighting their own fatigue. Dismissed."

With that, Shelby left, quickly followed by the others. Geordi gave Sonya a nod, which she returned.

Hours later, at 0415, Geordi came running into engineering. His uniform was rumpled, as if he'd slept in it, and hadn't bothered to change into a new one. All things considered, Sonya figured that to be precisely the case.

"Geordi?" Sonya said quizzically.

"I got an idea while I was sleeping. Something I read about shield nutation modification."

Sonya frowned. "You mean the talk T'Dar gave at the FES?"

Snapping his fingers, Geordi said, "Yes! That's the one. If we modify the shield nutation, we might be able to hold off the Borg attack."

Sonya thought over what the Vulcan scientist said at the Federation Engineering Symposium. "T'Dar's hypothesis was that the emitters would have to be realigned." She shook her head. "Geordi, that'd take days."

"We probably don't have days." Geordi let out a long breath. "Okay, start on it, at least. At this point, every little bit'll hel—"

Suddenly, without being entirely sure why, Sonya said, "The Klingons!"

Geordi gave her what might have been a penetrating gaze if his eyes were actually visible. "I'm sorry?"

Then it all came back to her, leaping forward from her subconscious, which had made her utter the phrase in the first place. "I just read a monograph last week by a Klingon engineer named Kurak—something about altering shield configuration. *JAWM* translated it and ran it. Computer, call up monograph from the most recent *Journal of Applied Warp Mechanics* by Kurak, daughter of Haleka."

The screen in front of Sonya and Geordi lit up with the text from the journal. She started scanning it. "There we go." She highlighted a paragraph and enlarged it.

Geordi read it over, seeing that it was a program for remodulating shields that would not require realigning the emitters. The intent was to be able to modify shields in battle. "This'll work—we're not reconfiguring, we're remodulating, but the theory should still apply." Grinning, Geordi gave Sonya a pat on the arm. "Nice work, Sonya."

Beaming, Sonya said, "Thank you, sir."

"You and Van Mayter get on this right away. And then, when gamma's over, you all go to bed."

Sonya hesitated. "But if we're not finished—"

"Give it to Duffy and Barclay. What Commander Riker said to Shelby applies to you, too." Sonya was about to object, pointing out that she hadn't been able to sleep in any case, when Geordi said, "Trust me, we'll come across the Borg soon enough, and when we do, I'm gonna be asking two hundred percent from everyone. Until then, though, I want you all rested. That's an order, Lieutenant."

Those last four words were said in as formal a tone as Geordi La Forge ever used. Straightening, Sonya said, "Yes, sir, Commander."

Geordi relaxed again. "All right. I'm gonna see what we can do about phasers. Higher EM frequencies might mess up their subspace fie—"

"*Commander La Forge, report to observation lounge.*" That was Riker.

Tapping his combadge, Geordi said, "On my way, Commander." He looked at Sonya. "Get to work, then get some sleep."

Sonya nodded.

"*Sealing doors to core chamber. Warning: inner hull failure. Decompression danger, deck thirty-six, section four. Sealing main engineering.*"

The computer's announcement sent Sonya rocketing awake from a fitful sleep.

Kieran!

She leapt out of bed, still in full uniform, having feared that this very thing might happen while she slept, and not wanting to waste any time getting on duty where she was needed.

As she entered the turbolift, her combadge chirped. *"La Forge to all off-shift engineering personnel, report to Lieutenant Duffy on deck thirty-six. I'll be on the bridge."*

Relief washed over Sonya at the news that Kieran was okay. Maybe they were lucky and they were able to evacuate before engineering was sealed off.

Kieran was waiting when she arrived at the main engineering console. The core chamber was behind a blast door. Also present were about a dozen engineers, plus some people from security. Sonya tried not to think about who she *didn't* see: Alfredo Della Guardia, Denny Russell, Bigay Ampalayon, Beth Bracken, Cliff Meyers . . .

When everyone arrived, Kieran—sounding more grave than Sonya'd ever heard him speak—said, "The Borg cut into the deck, causing a hull breach. Nineteen people were unable to get out of the area, of which we've scanned eleven outside the hull."

"Lieu—lieutenant?" That was Reg Barclay, who was standing over the navigation display. "We're—we're moving. According to—to this readout, we're headed for the Paulsen Nebula."

"Captain's probably hoping to lose 'em in there," one of the security guards said.

"All right," Kieran said, "let's get to work. We need to seal the breach and get this damn blast door back up."

They were the worst days of Sonya Gomez's life.

The loss of Denny Russell had hit her the hardest. They'd been classmates at the Academy, after all. His deadpan calm had always been a welcome contrast to Sonya's nervous enthusiasm.

But all of them were devastating losses to the *Enterprise*. The eight whose bodies hadn't been scanned were found wedged into odd parts of engineering after they sealed the breach. It hadn't been easy—working in a nebula with the Borg searching for you made for difficult and tense work—but they did it.

Nine of the nineteen were the security guards assigned to engineering when the ship was at red alert, who would not have left until all the engineers were out. The ten engineers' names were imprinted on Sonya's brain from seeing it on a display: AMPAYON, BRACKEN, BRUNER, DELLA GUARDIA, EL'SRYK, FRIEDEL, MEYERS, RUSSELL, T'LOTA, ZELENETSKY.

As soon as engineering was back online, Geordi came back along with Data and Wes, and shared with the others the plan to modify the deflector dish to emit a high-EM phaser blast big enough to take out the Borg cube. What was left of all three shifts of engineering was tasked with this, and some people from security were brought in to assist.

Still, the names flashed in Sonya's vision, but she refused to let it get to her, not when they were forced to leave the nebula, not when the Borg subsequently attacked them, not when the Borg kidnapped the captain, and not when the Borg cube broke off and made a beeline for Earth.

We'll have time to grieve later.

Shelby had taken a team over to the Borg cube to get it out of warp drive, and possibly rescue Picard. Once they were at impulse, the ship's warp power had to be transferred to the deflector so they could use the weapon. Sonya was standing at the warp core, her hand hovering over the control that would execute the program she and Reg Barclay had hastily written to perform the transfer. For now, they were pounding away at warp nine-point-six just to keep up. In less than an hour, they'd have to shut down the warp engines anyhow, just to keep the structural integrity field from failing. As it was, Kieran was standing over the SIF readout with the same nervous tension that Sonya hovered over her console, keeping an eye on it to make sure it didn't break down sooner.

Then the Borg ship went out of warp. Wes took the ship to impulse, and as soon as the warp engines stopped, Sonya ran the program. "Power being diverted to the deflector."

Kieran smiled grimly. "SIF reading nominal."

From the tactical systems station, Marguerite Sherman said, "Deflector at seventy percent power and rising."

A feed was coming in from the bridge. Sonya had been barely paying attention to it until the away team reported back. What caught her ear were Worf's words, in reference to the captain, whom they did not rescue: *"He is a Borg."*

Oh my God.

Reg shot a nervous look at Sonya. "He—he *is* a Borg? What does—what does that *mean*?"

Sonya shook her head. "I wish I knew." She shuddered. "No, I take it back, I *don't* wish I knew. Not even a little."

Riker was arguing with Shelby and Crusher about getting the captain back versus firing the weapon—with Riker on the side of firing the weapon—when the Borg hailed the ship.

The voice technically belonged to that of Jean-Luc Picard. It was the voice that Sonya still heard in bad dreams about hot chocolate saying, *"Yes, Ensign, it's all over me."* But now, the voice that had distressed her a year and a half ago was a dull, mechanized montone.

"I am Locutus of Borg. Resistance is futile. Your life as it has been is over. From this time forward, you will service us."

Riker's voice followed. *"Mr. Worf—fire."*

Marguerite said, "Power's building. Energy discharge in six seconds."

Everyone in engineering moved to stand behind Marguerite to see the weapon that would devastate the Borg.

The energy beam hit the Borg cube.

And had no effect.

"No," Sonya muttered.

From the bridge, Worf confirmed: *"The Borg ship is undamaged."*

"It can't be." That sounded like Shelby.

"We're losing the coolant!" Reg said.

That was followed by the computer's confirmation, which was scarier in its matter-of-factness than Reg's hysterical ranting. *"Warning: Warp reactor core primary coolant failure. Warning: Exceeding reactor chamber thermal limits."*

Marguerite said, "Warp engines shutting down—weapon powering down," which matched what they were saying on the bridge.

"They couldn't have adapted that quickly," Riker said.

"The knowledge and experience of the human Picard is part of us now. It has prepared us for all possible courses of action. Your resistance is hopeless, Number One."

Hearing Locutus's dry, mechanical tones speak with Picard's voice chilled Sonya to her toes. *We're dead.*

Kieran said quietly, "The Borg ship's leaving."

Or not. Sonya wasn't sure why the Borg didn't finish them off, but gift horses had bad breath, as her sister always said. "All right, we need to get warp drive, deflectors, and shields back online. Let's move it, people."

Later on, when she would tell people about it, they would say it was anticlimactic. Sonya thought that was insane, and said so. They chased the Borg—who plowed through a Starfleet armada at Wolf 359—to Earth, managing to bring Picard back home along the way. Or, rather, Locutus, as the captain was still a Borg drone. But Data was able to use Locutus—with some subconscious help from Picard himself—to put the Borg to sleep. The cube exploded over Earth shortly after that.

The first person to give the anticlimactic declaration was Belinda, whose face on the comm screen looked disappointed. *"That's the best you guys could do."*

"I'm not about to argue with the results, Bee."

"Well, I'm glad you're home, at least, mija. *You gonna come down and see us?"*

Evasively, Sonya said, "I don't know . . . depends on the repair schedule." Belinda's soccer career had come to an end due to a knee injury, and she was back living with *Mami* and *Papi*—which, unfortunately, was tense for everyone, as *Mami* was not pleased that her eldest daughter had come home. Sonya really didn't want to face the familial strife after barely surviving the Borg.

"How's that boyfriend of yours?"

She broke into a huge smile. "He's wonderful. It's been great—we just get along so well. We can talk about *anything*, really."

"But you just talk about engines, right?"

Sonya was about to tartly answer in the negative, until she thought about it, and realized that she and Kieran did talk about work a lot. Then she remembered their last date before the Borg mess. "No, that's not all we talk about. I loaned him my Brautigan book."

Belinda's eyes went wide. *"The one* Papi *gave you? Wow, this must be true love."*

When she turned fifteen, Sonya's father had given her a twenty-first-century leather-bound edition of *The Complete Works of Richard Brautigan,* which had become her favorite book. She had told Kieran about it, and he asked to borrow it, see what all the fuss was about, especially since he'd never heard of Brautigan.

"So how's he like the book?"

"Don't know, he hasn't read it yet. Anyhow, things are going great with Kieran."

"Glad to hear it, Ess. Looks like you're doing well on that luxury liner."

"It's *not* a luxury liner!" Sonya said defensively, and proceeded to give a lecture to a laughing Belinda about the state-of-the-art nature of the *Galaxy*-class vessel.

Eventually, they finished, and Sonya signed off, giving another evasive answer about whether she'd be able to get down to Vieques to visit the family. Then she went down to engineering, since her shift was about to start.

She came across Kieran in the corridor. "I can't win," he said without preamble.

"What is it?"

"I'm finally back on Earth for the first time in years, so I figure, great, I can drop in on Mom and Amy, see how they're doing. There's only one problem."

Smiling impishly, Sonya said, "They're on vacation on Betazed?"

"They're on vacation on Betazed. I completely forgot about that."

Kieran had told her about the vacation his mother and sister were taking two months ago. Somehow, Sonya couldn't bring herself to be surprised that she remembered that and Kieran didn't.

"So now I've got nowhere to go, unless you have a better offer?" Kieran waggled his eyebrows.

"Honestly, I don't," Sonya said quickly, trying to ignore the pit that opened in her stomach just then. "Belinda and *Mami* are at battle stations, and—"

Kieran held up a hand. "Say no more." He'd heard her stories about the on-again-off-again war between Guadalupe Gomez and her oldest daughter, and therefore knew that when it was on again, it was best to be elsewhere. "Tell you what. I suggest that we suck up mercilessly to Geordi and volunteer to stay on board during the repair cycle."

Sonya grinned. "Suits me fine."

Turning around, Kieran joined her in walking back to engineering, where they found Geordi talking to someone on a comm screen. They waited patiently until he was done, and when he turned around, Sonya saw a look he hadn't had on his face since their trip to Starbase Montgomery a year and a half ago, which was also the last time engineers who didn't report to Geordi got their hands on his engines.

Seeing the two of them, Geordi quickly put on a happier face. "What can I do for the two of you?"

"Sir," Sonya said, "we'd like to volunteer to stay on board during the repairs—help you keep an eye on McKinley's people."

Kieran grinned. "Make sure they don't turn the warp core upside down or anything."

All the tension seemed to leave Geordi's body. "You don't know how glad I am to hear you two say that. I didn't wanna ask anyone else to stay behind, but if you're volunteering—"

"Absolutely, sir," Kieran said.

"Thank you. I won't forget this."

"Just name your firstborn after us, sir," Kieran deadpanned.

Geordi chuckled, and walked over to the warp core.

Sonya stared up at him incredulously. "Are you nuts? Sonya Kieran La Forge would make a *terrible* name."

They laughed together, kissed quickly, and then Kieran headed off to his quarters while Sonya went on duty for the last formal shift before the repair cycle began.

CHAPTER
9

Captain's log, stardate 45130.1.
We have turned Dr. Kila Marr over to the authorities on Starbase 413, following her unauthorized destruction of the crystalline entity. We are now proceeding to Mudor V.

"Sonya, good, I need you to—"

Before Geordi, who had just arrived from the bridge, could finish his sentence, Sonya said, "I've realigned the warp coils and run a level-two on the deuterium injectors. They looked a little spotty."

Geordi stopped in his tracks and shook his head. "I was just going to mention the warp coils. What was wrong with the injectors?"

Sonya shrugged. "Nothing major, just a point-one reduction in the flow. I figured it was best to check. The diagnostic'll be finished in half an hour."

"Great." Geordi grinned. "You're gonna work me out of a job, Lieutenant."

Again, she shrugged. "Just doing my job, Commander." *Not that it's much of a challenge.* She wasn't so impolitic as to say that out loud, of course. *"Of course," right. Two and a half years ago, I would've blurted that out, along with fifteen other stupid things.*

But that was when she had reported on board. She had

slowed down, and she'd learned not to babble—at least not so much.

More to the point, though, she had learned the *Enterprise*—inside and out. She knew every trick of the warp drive, she knew every plasma conduit, every injector, every ODN conduit, every isolinear chip in the engine room, if not the entire vessel.

There's nothing left to learn.

That wasn't entirely fair. The ship had its share of surprises, from the faulty replacement piece from McKinley that caused a warp-core breach—and, indirectly, a witch-hunt on the *Enterprise*, before Picard put a stop to it—to Wesley's experiment that trapped his mother in a warp bubble.

Wesley was gone now, finally having enrolled in the Academy, which had disappointed Sonya, but had thrilled Tess Allenby, who had taken over at conn on alpha shift, only to transfer to the *Lexington* shortly thereafter, along with Gar Costa. The corner office had been reduced to herself, Kieran, and Helga, and had left the latter feeling like a third wheel.

And then Helga had died rather brutally during the *Enterprise*'s encounter with some odd dark matter that had been phasing parts of the ship out of existence for brief seconds. The floor under Helga Van Mayter had done that, and rematerialized while she was in the middle of falling through it. It was one of the most grisly deaths Sonya had ever encountered, and it still gave her nightmares, which usually ended with her screaming and Kieran comforting her.

With Tess, Lian, Wesley, and Gar gone, and Helga and Denny dead, Sonya found that she didn't really have anyone left on board to talk to except for Geordi and Kieran. There were lots of new faces, including Martin Kopf and Robin Lefler, both recent Academy graduates who were thrilled to be assigned to the flagship. Sonya recognized their excitement from a distance, as she realized with a start that she no longer felt it. Indeed, she'd found herself avoiding Kopf and Lefler because they reminded her too much of how she used to be.

The shift went uneventfully—a welcome respite after the

tumult of their disastrous mission to the Melona IV colony and subsequent pursuit of the crystalline entity responsible for the planet's destruction—and Sonya went back to her cabin, asking the computer for messages. She barely registered the usual litany of journals, personal messages from *Mami* and *Papi*, and various duty-related queries, but was shocked to hear the computer conclude the list with: "*A communiqué from Captain Schönhertz of the* U.S.S. Oberth."

Sonya blinked. *I didn't know the captain got the* Oberth. Her old professor had always sworn she'd never take starship duty again, and Sonya wondered what had changed her mind.

"Computer, play comm from Captain Schönhertz."

The round face and thick, curly blond hair of Katrine Schönhertz appeared on the small comm screen on her desk. "*Hello, Sonya. I hope this message finds you well. I've been hearing good things about the work you've been doing on* Enterprise. *You're probably wondering why I'm calling from a ship, since I said I'd never take starship duty again if my life depended on it. Well, my life* doesn't *depend on it, but I got an offer I really couldn't refuse. It's a one-year project that will be studying some new ways of dealing with antimatter. We've got one slot left on the team, and I brought up your name. I've appended the missions specs to this message. This position is for a full-grade lieutenant who knows her way around an antimatter injector, so you fit the bill nicely—or, rather, you will shortly.*" Schönhertz's eyes suddenly went wide, and she said, "*Okay, I wasn't supposed to tell you about your impending promotion, but your CO'll probably be giving you the good news in a day or two.*"

She barely listened to the rest of the message. *I'm getting promoted!* She was thrilled to see that her hard work had paid off and that she'd be advancing—

—to another position on the *Enterprise* that wasn't likely to be qualitatively different from the one she had now.

Worse, even the vessel's missions had become mundane. *No, that's not fair—nothing that happens on this ship can possibly qualify as mundane.* But her complaint to Geordi that she wanted to be there when the *Enterprise* came across what was out there was now three years old, and after two Borg attacks, getting involved in a Klingon civil war, playing host to everyone from primitive colonists to Vulcan diplomats to transcendent aliens to Acamarian thugs to Counselor Troi's insane mother, encounters with Shelliak, Romulans, Ansata terrorists, Gomtuu, Talarians, two-dimensional creatures, and more spatial anomalies than she could shake a stick at, not to mention regular visits from Q, Sonya began to grow weary of it. Too many of those missions had body counts attached to them.

Besides, she had her career to think of. Where could she go from here? Geordi wasn't going anywhere anytime soon, and that pretty much cut off her only real avenue of advancement. If she was going to be a chief engineer, which was something she truly wanted, it wasn't going to happen here unless something happened to Geordi, and that didn't bear thinking about.

And then there's Kieran. With a shock she realized that she hadn't even thought about him until now, which was horribly unfair, as Kieran had become very important to her. Indeed, he was pretty much the only thing tying her to the *Enterprise* right now.

That's not enough. It was a thought that left her sad. But she had worked too hard to become the best Starfleet officer she could. For three years, that meant learning the ropes on the flagship. Now, though, the best thing she could do for her career was move on.

Schönhertz had said there was only one position, so Kieran couldn't come with her. Besides which, Kieran had already made it clear on numerous occasions that he had very little ambition within Starfleet, which jibed with his slow promotion track. He'd be lucky to make lieutenant commander by the time he was forty. And he'd also said numerous times that he had no interest in leaving the *Enterprise.*

Of course, that was before we started dating.

Taking the transfer would mean breaking up with Kieran. Or at least separating from him.

No, breaking up. She could barely keep up with duty and a

relationship with somebody she served with. Subspace relationships were never, in Sonya's experience, successful. The only ones she'd seen work were people who were already married or otherwise committed before the separation, and she and Kieran weren't anywhere near that level yet.

I have to tell him, she thought, and only then realized that she had already mentally packed her bags for the *Oberth*.

CHAPTER

10

Captain's log, stardate 45156.1.
Our mission to Mudor V has been completed, and since our
next assignment will not begin for several days, we're enjoying
a welcome respite from our duties.

You've got to tell him.

Sonya had been saying this to herself for days, ever since
she and Kieran both got their formal promotions to full-grade
lieutenant at the beginning of the Mudor V mission. They were
now holding station for a few days, and Geordi had given both
his new full lieutenants "a few days off before I drop your new
duties on you." At present they were in civilian clothes, headed
for the arboretum. Keiko was nine months pregnant with her
and Chief O'Brien's child, and several officers had volunteered
to do some occasional gardening duty to take a load off the
botanist.

The vagueness of Geordi's phrasing regarding new duties
had been at Sonya's request. She wanted to be the one to break
the news to Kieran that she was transferring to the *Oberth*.

"So I'm assuming we're gonna have to weed the *famtils*
again," Kieran said cheerfully.

"Probably," Sonya muttered.

"Sonnie, is something wrong?"

"Hm? Oh, nothing."

Kieran stood up straight and said in stentorian tones, "The sound you have just heard is a lie." Back to his normal voice: "C'mon, what's bothering you?"

Before Sonya could even come up with an evasive answer—all the while admonishing herself for not giving him the straight answer he deserved—the ship started shaking. Lights flickered on and off, and the ship continued to buck and weave. "What the *hell*—?" Kieran said before he was knocked to the floor. Sonya was gripping the door frame of one of the labs they were passing en route to the arboretum.

Finally, the shaking stopped, though the red alert siren was still blaring, and emergency lights were all that illuminated the corridor.

Kieran looked up at Sonya from his prone position on the deck. "I ask again, what the *hell*?"

"Dunno," Sonya said. "We must have hit something *very* hard." She tapped her combadge. It was the start of beta shift, and Geordi had left a skeleton crew in engineering, with Lieutenant Aleakala in charge of the five people on shift. "Gomez to engineering. Chao-Anh, what's—"

"*I can't talk, Sonya. Come on, everyone, get out now!*" Behind Chao-Anh, Sonya could hear the four-note chime that meant a bulkhead was dropping. There must have been a core breach or a hull breach.

"*All decks, brace for impact!*" That was Lieutenant Monroe, who was in charge of the bridge during this light shift.

Kieran had gotten to his feet. "What, *another* one?"

The words had barely escaped his mouth when the ship rocked again, sending them both to the deck. Sonya's ears were then assaulted by an explosion, as the door to one of the labs down the hall exploded. She recalled that Lieutenant T'Proll was supervising an experiment with quaratum. Several containers of the stuff were in the cargo bay right now, more than they needed for their current allotment of thrusters, for T'Proll's project.

Sonya had a bad feeling that it was the quaratum that

exploded, and the only way for that to happen was if there were lethal radiation levels in the lab, which, thanks to the blown door, would be in the corridor in a minute.

As one, Sonya and Kieran moved to drop the emergency bulkhead. Kieran got there a moment sooner, and gave her a goofy grin as he pulled the lever that lowered the duranium door from the ceiling.

While Kieran did that, Sonya tapped her combadge again. "Gomez to engineering." Her combadge gave a low trill indicating that it wasn't functioning. Walking over to the bulkhead, she touched the computer screen, but it didn't respond. "Great, comm's down, and power's down." She looked at Kieran. "I don't suppose you're hiding a tricorder in your pants?"

"If I said I was just glad to see you, would you hit me?"

"I'd certainly consider it."

"Then I'll just say, no, I don't."

Sonya glanced down the corridor away from the emergency bulkhead they'd just dropped. "Come on, we need to get to engineering, see if Chao-Anh needs help."

Kieran nodded and followed her, only to find that another emergency bulkhead had been dropped. Looking up and down the bulkhead, as if it would provide answers, Kieran finally said, "You know, I don't think I *want* to know why that thing was dropped. I just hope it wasn't because of something on *this* side of it."

"Yeah." Sonya looked up. "Maybe we can use the crawlways."

"For what, exactly?"

"To get to engineering."

"Sonnie, we don't know how bad the radiation is up there. And we don't know—"

"We don't know *anything*," Sonya snapped. The she sighed. "Sorry, but we can't just *stand* here and hope somebody rescues us. The ship is obviously in big trouble, and we have to help. We're closer to engineering than the bridge anyhow, so let's get down there and see if there's anything we can do."

After considering the point, Kieran nodded. "Yeah, you're right. I just hate crawling around in there, y'know?"

Sonya couldn't help but smile. "Mr. Gravity Boots can't handle confinement?"

"I'm a creature of the air. That's why I like to stay in the nice, big, spacious engine room."

Sonya and Kieran crawled for the better part of an hour, and only made about ten meters' worth of real progress. They were constantly doubling back, going around, and avoiding various obstacles in their path, most of which were due to yet another catastrophic malfunction. While it was possible for a ship like the *Enterprise* to have one or two malfunctions like this, it was almost impossible for so many systems to completely fall apart at once.

"We must have hit a quantum filament," Sonya said when they took a brief rest at one junction, sitting across from each other in what passed for a wide space in the crawlways.

"That's crazy. The bridge would've seen it coming."

"Only if they were looking for it, and why would they be? You know how wide those things aren't," she said with a grin.

"Nah, I'm thinking Romulan attack. Or maybe a new Borg weapon."

Sonya shook her head. "The damage was too catastrophic, too across-the-board. Weapons fire wouldn't do that—or if it did, it'd be enough to crack the ship in half, and we'd have felt it if that happened."

"I don't know, Sonnie—"

"Kieran, remember when we first met?"

Cutting himself off, Kieran blinked. "Yeah, but I don't see—"

"You told me that it was a design flaw, I said it was a tribble-com. Who was right?"

"Oh, *that* first meeting."

It was Sonya's turn to blink. "What other first meeting was there?"

"Okay, I was thinking of the day you came on board and I

passed you and Denny in the corridor on the way to a staff meeting."

"We didn't really meet, though," Sonya said with a smile.

"We exchanged words. I said I was running late for a staff meeting."

Sonya honestly didn't remember the conversation that clearly—that day was a haze of nervousness and anticipation and her inability to give The Speech to Geordi—but decided not to let him know that.

He's going to be disappointed enough when I tell him what I have to tell him.

Slapping his knees, Kieran made as if to rise. "Shall we boogie?"

"Kieran, I'm leaving the *Enterprise.*"

"What?"

"I'm leaving the *Enterprise.* There's a position on the *Oberth* open—a one-year mission dealing with new ways to harness antimatter, under Captain Schönhertz. I'm taking it."

Sitting all the way back down, Kieran said, "Oh."

"I'm sorry, I wanted to tell you sooner, but I didn't know how."

"Did okay just then," he muttered.

"It's a great opportunity, and—"

"Yeah, it is, and you'd be stupid not to take it."

Her mouth hanging open for a moment, Sonya finally said, "Really?"

"Of course. Geez, Sonnie, I don't expect you to be a slug like me for the rest of your career. I mean, yeah, you're on the *Enterprise* now, but you're one of dozens. That's fine if you're me and don't want to stand out in a crowd, but on the *Oberth*? You'll be sitting pretty. I bet you'll be running the place inside a year."

She smiled, relieved more than she could adequately express that Kieran understood. "I hope so, since it's only a one-year project."

Kieran laughed. Sonya had never been so glad to hear that wonderful sound as she was now.

"Come on," he said, getting up for real this time. "We've got work to do."

They arrived at a crawlway just above engineering on deck thirty-two, after three hours of crawling around, a journey that should have only taken one hour at the most. Yes, the *Enterprise* was large, but they had started out fairly deep in the saucer section. Unfortunately, the damage from what Sonya was morally certain was a quantum filament had been extensive. Many of the crawlways were cut off for one reason or another.

"Genry, we've crossed the ice!" Kieran said when they arrived over the corridor outside engineering.

Sonya looked at him with confusion.

"Sorry," he said, "old book I read when I was a kid. *The Left Hand of Darkness* by Ursula Le Guin. There's this long journey, and at the end—"

Before Kieran could finish, he was interrupted by a tapping on the floor beneath them.

Kieran and Sonya exchanged glances, then shifted so they weren't kneeling on the hatch. Sonya tried to open it, and saw that it was jammed. "Somebody must be stuck down there."

"And me without my P-38—it's in the same pants as my tricorder."

Figuring she had nothing to lose, Sonya yelled. "Is somebody down there?"

A muffled voice said something, but she couldn't make it out.

"Lousy duranium—too soundproof," Kieran muttered.

Sonya started looking around the crawlway. "There's got to be some way to open the hatch."

Kieran reached into his pocket. "All I've got is this weedwhacker."

Looking at the long, cylindrical item that was used to remove weeds at the root without overly disturbing the ground, Sonya started turning over possibilities in her mind. "What we need is a sonic enhancer."

Frowning, Kieran said, "How would that—" Then he brightened. "Oh, right! Perfect! Except we don't have a sonic enhancer." Then he grinned. "But we do have the Elllix bafflers. They're running along the ceiling there."

Glancing up, Sonya grinned. Reaching up, she pried a panel loose, then looked at the components running through the wall. "Now that's ironic."

"What is?"

She grinned and looked at Kieran. "We need the weed-whacker to pry the baffler out before we can modify it so that it will turn the whacker into a P-38."

"Life's full of little ironies," Kieran said as he handed over the weed-whacker. "We make a good team."

Sonya found she had nothing to say to that.

Within two minutes, Sonya had gotten one of the bafflers out. Four minutes after that, they finished the modifications to the weed-whacker. Ten seconds after that, the hatch was open.

Six engineers stared up at Sonya and Kieran: Chao-Anh Aleakala, Robin Lefler, Martin Kopf, and the other three who were on duty with them, whose names Sonya was embarrassed to realize she didn't know.

It doesn't matter, she thought sadly. *I'm leaving.*

"I am so glad to see you two," Chao-Anh said. "We're running out of air down here, and I don't know *what's* happening in engineering. We heard someone raise the blast door, but we can't get in there, and we couldn't get the damn hatch open."

Kieran grinned. "Let's see what we can find out up here. Care to join us in Leg Cramp Central?"

A few hours later, it was over. Riker and Data—or, rather, Data's head, since his body had been electrocuted—got to engineering, and raised the blast door. The bridge had dumped power to a monitor down there so they could restore the anti-matter containment field. Sonya had been rather nonplussed to see how close they had all come to blowing up, especially since—had Riker and Data not arrived when they did—the field would have collapsed when she and Kieran were still crawling around in the drive section. Everybody had a story to tell of what they were doing when the filament hit, from Troi taking command of the bridge after Monroe's death, to the captain being stuck in a turbolift with three children, to Lieutenant Mahowiack riding herd on a group of teenagers who were suddenly trapped in a lightless, sealed-off holodeck. But the story on everyone's lips was the fact that Keiko gave birth to a baby girl—and Worf, of all people, was the midwife.

Soon enough, they were en route to Starbase 67. Geordi threw a partry in Sonya's honor, at which the only drink available was hot chocolate. Sonya groaned, and so did everyone else when Captain Picard showed up to wish her well. He even gamely took a sip of hot chocolate, and left without a drop on his uniform, to Sonya's relief and everyone else's disappointment.

Upon arrival at the starbase, Sonya and Kieran said their good-byes in his cabin. Kieran had been very supportive—until today. His usual flippancy was muted; he kept putting off letting her leave until she had to force herself to return to her quarters so she could clear them out. When she went to the airlock to disembark, her hastily packed duffel bag over her shoulder, he was waiting for her.

"This is it, then?" he said. It was the same thing he'd said six times in his quarters.

"Kieran, please, I need to go. The *Oberth* is waiting for me."

"I know. I didn't mean to hold you up, I just wanted to say good-bye."

Sonya was going to say that they'd done that, but one look at his face made her realize how cruel that was. Kieran wasn't very good at saying good-bye. She thought it was in part due to his father dying while he was away at the Academy, though she figured that might have just been her own amateur diagnosis. Either way, she couldn't begrudge him getting one last farewell.

And she was going to miss him.

Kissing him gently on the cheek, she said in a quiet voice, "Take care of yourself, Kieran."

With that, she walked past him, and went down the gangway, refusing to let herself turn around one last time. If she did, she wasn't sure she'd be able to resist his wide, pleading brown eyes.

EPILOGUE

Captain's log, stardate 53122.9.
Our new first officer, and the new head of the *da Vinci*'s
S.C.E. team, Commander Sonya Gomez, is reporting for
duty today—and about damn time, too. With the Dominion
War over, I'm looking forward to going back to less perilous
missions like the one that claimed Commander Salek at
Randall V. From everything I've heard, Salek's replacement
should live up to her predecessor's high standards.

The ships just keep getting smaller, Sonya couldn't help but
think.

Of course, when one's career begins on a *Galaxy*-class vessel,
almost everything is a come-down in terms of size, but each
subsequent vessel she'd served on, from the mid-size *Oberth* to
the compact *Sentinel*, had been smaller than the last, and the
Sabre-class *da Vinci* was the smallest of all of them.

She hadn't any intention of leaving the *Sentinel*, even with
the promotion to commander, but she was also specifically requested by Captain David Gold of the *da Vinci*, based on recommendations from Admiral Ross's office that apparently included
the kind words of the legendary Montgomery Scott. With that
much brass behind it, Sonya could hardly turn the assignment
down, especially since it meant supervising, not just an engine
room, but a mobile Starfleet Corps of Engineers team that went
out solving the galaxy's problems. It was a great opportunity.

Gold had no engineering background of which Sonya was

aware. However, he'd been in charge of the *da Vinci* for several years now, ever since its assignment to the S.C.E., after a well-regarded tour commanding the *Progress*. Besides, Sonya had spent all of her adult life among engineers, and that led her to the conclusion that the best people to supervise them *weren't* engineers.

The only fly in the ointment was when she looked at the crew roster and saw who her second in command would be, which was why she was thinking about the size of the ship and the history of her captain right now, as it was easier than thinking about her second officer.

Kieran.

When the gangway door at Starbase 96 slid open, there he was, standing in the *da Vinci* corridor. She hadn't lain eyes on him in eight years. He had gained some weight, and while his unkempt brown hair still covered his entire head, it had thinned a bit.

His amused brown eyes and easy smile hadn't changed. The latter widened when he saw her.

"Sonnie!" And without warning, he grabbed her into a massive bear hug.

Until this very second, Sonya had no idea how she was going to react to seeing Kieran again. To her relief, it was joy, and she returned the hug with almost as much enthusiasm. That big smile had been missing from her life, and she was so happy to have it back. "Kieran, it's so good to see you."

"Same here, Sonnie, same here."

They finally broke the embrace and stared at each other. Sonya found her eyes going to the gold collar under his black-and-gray uniform jacket. "Figures. You've only gone up one grade rank. You should have *my* job."

Kieran shuddered. "No chance. Don't want it. I prefer to have power *without* responsibility. Salek was great at that administrative stuff, and so're you. After all, you ran an engine room, and did a damn fine job, too. I heard about that trick you pulled with the warp field on the *Sentinel*."

Sonya found herself blushing. Altering the *Sentinel*'s warp field to make it seem like a Cardassian ship while they were stuck behind enemy lines was a trick and a half, especially coming after a prolonged fight with some Jem'Hadar ships, but it had gotten her a commendation. Captain Amalfitano had said it was at the top of the very long list of reasons why she got the promotion to commander.

"Anyway," he said as he led her down the corridor toward the turbolift, "you're gonna love it here. We've got a tac systems specialist who served on DS9 with O'Brien, so we can trade chief stories. Oh, and we have two Bynar civilians to do the computer work."

That surprised Sonya, as she hadn't remembered seeing that on the crew roster. But if they were civilians, they wouldn't necessarily have been on that roster.

Kieran continued to babble on the way to the bridge. When the doors parted, Sonya found herself in a space that was smaller than the quarters she and Lian T'su shared on the *Enterprise* eleven years ago. A thin strip of deck ringed the bridge, lined with consoles, with a command well a step down that included conn, ops, and the command chair.

A white-haired, blue-eyed, pleasant-faced elderly human stepped up from the latter as Kieran spoke. "Captain David Gold, this is your new first officer, and the new head of the S.C.E. team, Commander Sonya Gomez."

Sonya smiled and said, "Permission to come aboard, sir."

"Granted." Gold returned the smile. "Welcome aboard. I understand you and Duffy served together under Jean-Luc Picard on the *Enterprise*."

"Uh, yes, sir," Sonya said. *Of course he knows. Kieran probably told him.*

"Good. I've known Picard since his Academy days, and he doesn't turn out bad officers. It'll be a pleasure to have you two working together."

"I'm sure it will, sir."

And Sonya found that she meant it. She wasn't sure where her relationship with Kieran would go from here, or even if it would, given their positions in this ship's hierarchy. *Not to mention on a ship of this size.* The population of the *da Vinci* was four percent of that of the *Enterprise*—that would mean their lives were in a fishbowl. *A relationship might not be the wisest move.*

But that was for tomorrow. Today, she was on a new ship, looking forward to a wonderful new assignment, and she already knew that she could count on at least one member of her team.

I can't wait to see what happens next.

ACKNOWLEDGMENTS

As should be obvious, *Many Splendors* weaves in and out of several episodes of *Star Trek: The Next Generation* during its second, third, fourth, and early fifth seasons. I would therefore like to first of all acknowledge the works of the following writers, whose dialogue was ruthlessly poached: Robin Bernheim ("The Hunted"), Maurice Hurley ("Q Who"), David Kemper ("Peak Performance"), David Mack (*S.C.E.* #24: *Wildfire* Book 2), Ronald D. Moore ("Disaster"), and Michael Piller ("The Best of Both Worlds, Parts I–II").

In addition to the above-listed, the works of several screen-writers and eBook authors informed my writing: Hilary J. Bader ("The Loss"), Dennis Putman Bailey & David Bischoff ("Tin Man"), Peter S. Beagle ("Sarek"), Rick Berman ("Brothers"), Sally Caves ("Hollow Pursuits"), Lawrence V. Conley & Jeri Taylor ("Silicon Avatar"), Drew Deighan ("Sins of the Father"), Steve Gerber & Beth Woods ("Contagion"), Shari Goodhartz ("The Most Toys"), Maurice Hurley ("The Arsenal of Freedom"), Brian Alan Lane ("Elementary, Dear Data"), Philip LaZebnik ("Darmok"), William Leisner (*S.C.E.* #57: *Out of the Cocoon*), Robert Lewin ("The Arsenal of Freedom"), David Mack (*S.C.E.* #24: *Wildfire* Book 1), Richard Manning & Hans Beimler ("The Emissary"), Joe Menosky ("In Theory," "Darmok"), Steve Mollmann & Michael Schuster (*S.C.E.* #62: *The Future Begins*), Ronald D. Moore ("The Bonding," "Sins of the Father," "Family," "In Theory"), W. Reed Moran ("Sins of the Father"), Aaron Rosenberg (*S.C.E.* #33: *Collective Hindsight* Book 1), Hannah Louise Shearer ("Pen Pals"), Dean Wesley Smith (*S.C.E.* #1: *The Belly of the Beast*), Melinda M. Snodgrass ("The Measure of a Man," "Pen Pals," "The High Ground"), and

Dayton Ward & Kevin Dilmore (*S.C.E.* #4–5: *Interphase* Books 1–2). I also made use of my own past *S.C.E.* work (#2: *Fatal Error*, #10: *Here There Be Monsters*, #21: *War Stories* Book 1, and #28: *Breakdowns* in particular).

Finally major thanks to CGAG and The Mom, who made it all better.

ABOUT THE AUTHORS

TERRI OSBORNE made her professional fiction writing debut in 2003 with the critically acclaimed "Three Sides to Every Story," the Jake Sisko and Tora Ziyal story in the *Star Trek: Deep Space Nine* tenth-anniversary anthology, *Prophecy and Change*. Her other fiction work includes " 'Q'uandary," the Selar story in the *Star Trek: New Frontier* anthology *No Limits; Star Trek: S.C.E.: Malefictorum*, the landmark fiftieth installment in the series; and "Eighteen Minutes" in the tenth-anniversary anthology *Star Trek: Voyager: Distant Shores*. Beyond that, she is hard at work at more fiction, both in and out of the *Star Trek* universe, including an original dark fantasy novel set in Dublin, Ireland, in 1940. Find out more about Terri at her Web site: www.terriosborne.com.

STEVE MOLLMANN is studying for a Ph.D. in English at an unknown university at an unknown location in the United States. He is not being coy; at the time this was written, he simply had no idea where he would be by the time you read this. He obtained his M.A. in English at the University of Connecticut, and hopes to pursue a career as a scholar, specializing in British literature, especially its intersection with science and technology. Also in that gap of time, he will have gotten married to his then-fiancée, Hayley. He has met Michael Schuster on more than one occasion.

MICHAEL SCHUSTER lives in a picturesque Austrian mountain valley, with half a continent and one entire ocean between him and Steve Mollmann. A bank employee by day, he likes to come up with new (or at least relatively unused) ideas that can be turned into stories with loving care and the occasional nudge. With Steve, he is the co-author of two short stories in the anthology *Star Trek: The Next Generation: The Sky's the Limit*. Their first novel, *The Tears of Eridanus*, will be released as part of the collection *Star Trek: Myriad Universes: Shattered Light* this December. Currently, the two are hard at work building their own universe-sized sandbox to play in. More information about them (including annotations for *The Future Begins*) can be found at http://www.exploringtheuniverse.net/.

RICHARD C. WHITE is the author of *Gauntlet Dark Legacy: Paths of Evil*, which was iBook, Inc.'s best selling media tie-in novel in 2004. Additionally he has written three short stories: "Redshift" for *The Sky's the Limit*, a *Star Trek: The Next Generation* anthology by Pocket Books, "The Price of Conviction" for *The Quality of Leadership*, a Doctor Who: Short Trips anthology by Big Finish, LTD, and "Assault on Avengers Mansion" for the *Ultimate Hulk* anthology by Byron Preiss Multimedia/Marvel Comics. *Echoes of Coventry* was Rich's first foray into the *Star Trek* universe.

Additionally, Rich is active in the Science Fiction community as a member of the Writer Beware committee for the Science Fiction and Fantasy Writers of America. He is a member of SFWA and the International Association of Media Tie-In Writers

Rich spent over fifteen years in the U.S. Army, where he served as an analyst, a linguist, an instructor, and a cryptanalyst. He is currently employed by a defense contractor as a tech writer/editor. He lives in Central Maryland with his wife and daughter, and four cats who wonder why he spends all his time on the computer and not waiting on them.

DAYTON WARD. Author. Trekkie. Writing his goofy little stories and searching for a way to tap into the hidden nerdity that all humans have. Then, an accidental overdose of Mountain Dew altered his body chemistry. Now, when

Dayton Ward grows excited or just downright geeky, a startling metamorphosis occurs.

Driven by outlandish ideas and a pronounced lack of sleep, he is pursued by fans and editors as well as funny men in bright uniforms wielding tasers, straitjackets, and medication. In addition to the numerous credits he shares with friend and co-writer Kevin Dilmore, Dayton is the author of the *Star Trek* novels *In the Name of Honor* and *Open Secrets*, the science fiction novels *The Last World War, Counterstrike: The Last World War, Book II*, and *The Genesis Protocol*, as well as short stories which have appeared in the first three *Star Trek: Strange New Worlds* anthologies, the Yard Dog Press anthology *Houston, We've Got Bubbas, Kansas City Voices Magazine* and the *Star Trek: New Frontier* anthology *No Limits*. For Flying Pen Press, he was the editor of the science fiction anthology *Full-Throttle Space Tales #3: Space Grunts*.

Dayton is believed to be working on his next novel, and he must let the world think that he is working on it, until he can find a way to earn back the advance check he blew on strippers and booze. Though he currently lives in Kansas City with his wife and daughters, Dayton is a Florida native and maintains a torrid long-distance romance with his beloved Tampa Bay Buccaneers. Visit him on the web at http://www.daytonward.com.

KEVIN DILMORE has found ways to make a living from his geek side for quite a while now.

It all started in 1998 with his eight-year run as a contributing writer to *Star Trek Communicator*, for which he wrote news stories and personality profiles for the bimonthly publication of the Official *Star Trek* Fan Club. Since that time, he also has contributed to publications including *Amazing Stories, Hallmark*, and *Star Trek* magazines.

Then he teamed with writing partner and heterosexual life mate Dayton Ward on *Interphase*, their first installment of the *Star Trek: S.C.E.* series in 2001. Since then, the pair has put more than 1 million words into print together. Among their most recent shared publications are the novella *The First Peer* in the anthology *Star Trek: Seven Deadly Sins* (March 2010) and the short story "Ill Winds" in the *Star Trek: Shards and Shadows* anthology (January 2009).

By day, Kevin works as a senior writer for Hallmark Cards in Kansas City, Mo., doing about everything but writing greeting cards, including helping to design *Star Trek*–themed Keepsake Ornaments. His first children's book, *Superdad and His Daring Dadventures,* with illustrations by Tom Patrick, was published by Hallmark Gift Books in May 2009.

A graduate of the University of Kansas, Kevin lives in Overland Park, Kansas. Keep up with his shameful behavior and latest projects on Facebook and Twitter.

HEATHER JARMAN lives in Moscow, Russia, where she spends her time juggling the demands of mothering a high schooler, the transatlantic parenting of three daughters in university, playing amateur tour guide to visitors, trying to master French cooking using Russian ingredients, and studying European art and architectural history. She hopes to return to novel writing when her sojourn abroad wraps up in 2011.

KEITH R.A. DeCANDIDO is the co-developer of *Corps of Engineers,* and was the series editor for the bulk of its run. His other writerly contributions to the series can be found in the print volumes *Have Tech, Will Travel, Miracle Workers, Some Assembly Required, Wildfire, Breakdowns,* and *Wounds.* He has contributed a great deal to *Star Trek* fiction since 1999, including the *Next Generation* comic book *Perchance to Dream,* a short story in *The Sky's the Limit,* the eBook *Enterprises of Great Pitch and Moment,* and the novels *Diplomatic Implausibility, Q & A,* and *A Time for War, A Time for Peace;* the *Deep Space Nine* novels *Demons of Air and Darkness* and *Ferenginar: Satisfaction Is Not Guaranteed,* a novella in

Gateways: What Lay Beyond, and a short story in *Prophecy and Change*; the *Voyager* Mirror Universe novel *The Mirror-Scaled Serpent* and a short story in *Distant Shores*; the Klingon novels *A Good Day to Die, Honor Bound, Enemy Territory,* and *A Burning House*; the *Lost Era* novel *The Art of the Impossible*; the crossover duology *The Brave and the Bold*; the Myriad Universes novel *A Gutted World*; stories in the anthologies *Tales of the Dominion War, Tales from the Captain's Table, Mirror Universe: Shards and Shadows, New Frontier: No Limits,* and *Seven Deadly Sins*; and issues of the *Alien Spotlight* and *Captain's Log* comic books.

Keith—who was granted a Lifetime Achievement Award by the International Association of Media Tie-in Writers in 2009—has also written novels, short stories, comic books, and more in a variety of other media universes ranging from *Farscape* to *Doctor Who* to *StarCraft* to *Supernatural* and beyond. Find out more at his website at DeCandido.net or read his inane ramblings at kradical.livejournal.com.